HOW DID THE GIG GO?

by Dave Longley

Copyright © 2020 Dave Longley

All rights reserved

The characters and events portrayed in this book are fictitious. Any similarity to real persons, living or dead, is coincidental and not intended by the author.

No part of this book may be reproduced, or stored in a retrieval system, or transmitted in any form or by any means, electronic, mechanical, photocopying, recording, or otherwise, without express written permission of the publisher.

ISBN: 979857036058

Cover image: Scott DeVall

INTRODUCTION

This book came about as the result of a conversation I had with my good friend and fellow stand up comedian, Barry Dodds. It was at the beginning of the great lockdown of 2020, when the weather was warm and hopes were high that the shit storm wouldn't go on too long. Lol. We (comedians) were wondering what we could be getting on with creatively to help us fill the time. The idea of doing an Only Fans type online gig didn't appeal to me, and nothing much else seemed tempting either. As such, and after over a decade of driving up and down the country, it didn't seem like too bad an idea to have some time off.

Barry then suggested that I write another book. Now, my previous book was just a piss take. Short and sweet, it was a practical joke at the expense of another comedian named Freddy Quinne. It wasn't really a book-book, if you will. Barry kept banging on that I should write one anyway, and only the threat of violence could silence Mr. Dodds.

We continued our discussion about the stand up comedy circuit being murdered by the Chinese government, and he continued to enjoy the many and varied accents I employed to illuminate some of my stronger opinions. It was at this point that I began fantasising about better ways to kill off a comedy career which didn't involve a virus with a 99% survival rate, tens of thousands of deaths and a crippling of the world economy.

What tickled me was the idea of being heckled and then replying with something so offensive it would guarantee that you'd never be booked again. The specific example I came up with is in this book, and helped to form the basis of what you are about to read.

As these things do though, it evolved and then got quite out of hand.

People often ask what it is like to be a stand up comedian. This book is my attempt to shed some light on the day to day happenings of your every day stand up comedian.

THANKINGS

Thanks to Barry Dodds, who was an enthusiastic supporter when I said that I'd had an idea. I remember dropping off 200 printed pages at his house so that he could have a "flavour" of what it would be like. Thank you, Doddsy.

Thanks to Andy King. Andy isn't a comedian, doesn't like fiction and doesn't think I am a particularly funny person. Such honesty was much sought after, and he delivered.

Thanks to Anna Cooke. Again, incredibly enthusiastic and always great for a chat. What a wonderful woman she is.

Thanks to Kai Humphries, who upon discovering I was doing another book, messaged me and asked to be the first proof reader. He did an amazing job in highlighting so many fucking errors that I was embarrassed.

Thanks also go to my wife, for giving me the time to write it and actually having a go at reading it. Alas, she read a very early draft which detailed a very graphic death scene involving a morbidly obese woman, a toilet and lots of shit. 'Not for me…' she said.

COVER ART

Done by the very talented @scottylion on instagram.

Check out his shop at www.scottylion.com

HOW TO USE THIS BOOK

When prompted, turn to the appropriate page. It's not that difficult, but flicking through the pages like some kind of 20th century neanderthal might make you feel like a moron. Well, maybe you should get it on kindle where you get to enjoy something quick and easy and virtually spoiler free?

The best thing about a Kindle though, is that you can never really be sure that the woman on the train isn't reading erotic fiction and getting all excited. The words flashing images in her mind, causing her body to secrete the mucus which helps with vaginal lubrication. Not just the words though, the motion and vibration of the train also play their part. The hunky conductor, his buttocks squeezed into his tight trousers with his delicious bum hole getting all sweaty because of the acrylic material. He probably tastes of working class chip fat.

Anyway, at least with this paperback you can rest easy knowing that no one believes for one second that you are in some way sexually aroused.

There are a couple of Easter eggs for you to discover too, mere addendums to some of the storylines which you may or may not stumble across.

I hope you like.

You're sat at home, all nice and cosy, ready to watch a bit of Friday night TV with your beloved. The sofa's luxurious pull is like that of a black hole, as you sink evermore into that blissful feeling of having fuck all to do for the rest of the day. You've been semi-planning this all week, and now it's go time for the slow time. On Monday morning you sent out your gig availability knowing full well that the chances of filling this Friday night gap were slim to none. Even with your limited amount of self awareness, you know you're not a particularly good or even well liked comedian, and such circumstances always make it a tough prospect to get that diary gap filled.

Fuck it, you're here now and you intend to make the most of it. You've just logged off Facebook for the night, having posted that you're having a "rare Friday night off" just like all the other comics who barely scrape a living. Yes, being a barely booked stand up comedian is better than a full time job in a call centre, and yes, at some point in the future you really will have to question whether dignity is more important than status. But for right now, you're a stand up comedian and you have the night off.

Your beloved has put a pizza in the oven and there's a bowl of popcorn in front of you waiting to be devoured once you've selected a movie for the evening. Whilst waiting, you flick through some music channels and settle on watching the video for "Smack my Bitch Up" by The Prodigy, an absolute classic and weirdly relevant.

Lying down, sprawled out with your feet draped over the side of the sofa, you breathe in and take the opportunity to enjoy this small moment of solitude and relaxation. Money is tight, but this is lovely. You could be stuck on a motorway or trapped in a green room with morons. Instead, here you are at home, relaxing after what has been a troubling week. Your ex has been bombarding you with messages, all of them slightly unhinged and many of them with memes that always show a black man with an enormous penis. You should really block the messages, but a part of your ego is enjoying that your ex still wants you. Sure it's been years and you were never really compatible, but it's always nice when someone other than your current partner finds you attractive. You know that such thinking is silly, but you just can't help yourself. Still lying on the sofa, you slowly let your eyes close as you flirt with the idea of having a little cat nap. And why not? It feels good. You begin to drift off as you think about other people it would be nice to receive messages from.

Your phone starts ringing, the volume loud enough to make you sit up in an instant. Grabbing your phone from the table to see who's calling, you notice that it's a number you don't recognise. You're scared. You should answer it. Oh no, maybe it's your ex? But why would they ring? What would be the point? It's not like you were great at talking when you were together. It might be work! No, not this late in the game. That would be really cutting it fine. Your beloved partner is upstairs right now, sitting on the toilet in order to make some room for the pizza calories you're both about to ingest. Ugh, this is silly. You should just answer it! But what if it's your ex? You can always hang up! Come on, be brave.

You slide to answer, raising the phone to the side of your head.
'Hello?' you tremble.
'Hi, it's Sparky Mark here. Are you still available tonight?' it's a gig!
'Erm, yeah. I guess so. I mean, yeah. Sure. I am. '
'It's just that you're local and it's urgent.'
'Oh. I see.'
'I need a closer tonight. It's two hundred quid cash for a one off gig. You don't even have to sign for the money. Wanna do it?' Upon hearing those words, blood rushes to your sex organs. Not only do your cheeks flush at the ego boosting offer of work from a semi legitimate promoter, but the promise of tax free pay almost tips you over the edge into instantaneous masturbation. This is the stuff that dreams are made of. But what about the cosy night in with your beloved? You didn't promise, but you did make out that you were looking forward to a quiet night in, even saying at one point that money isn't the be all and end all... Then again, you are a comedian.

'Sure! I'd love to do the gig!'
'Oh thank fuck for that. My next call was to John Ryan.'
'Christ.'
'I know. Right, the venue is called Uncle Spunk's Chuckle Trunk. If you put it into google you'll find the address. I need you there in half an hour.'
'Uncle. Spunk's. Chuckle. Trunk. Right got it. Cool name.'
'Yeah, I named it after the Uncle that used to abuse me.'
'Oh no,' you hesitate. Not sure if it's a joke. 'That sounds awful.'
'No not really. Looking back, I enjoyed it. It made me the paedophile I am today!'
'OK!' assuming he's joking. 'I'm on my way!' ending the call as abruptly as possible.

You've got a gig! Holy shit! What are the odds? Thank fuck the comedy circuit has way too many gigs and not enough comedians who can actually do the job. You lucky shit! No pizza and cuddling for you tonight, you have morons to entertain.

'Darling,' calls your beloved, 'I'm gonna need your help. It feels like a real mess again.'
'I've got to get ready for a gig.'
'You have a gig?'
'Yeah. It's two hundred quid cash.'
'Oh that's great! Well done. Do you have time to quickly wipe my bottom for me?'
'I don't really have the time, I need to leave now.' you shout, shuddering at the idea of scraping yet another gargantuan mess from that overly fleshy mound.
'Please, it's a real mess.'

You think back to the couples counselling, recalling everything your therapist said about relationships being built on trust and love and respect. At the time, it seemed to make sense, but that was before the carpal tunnel syndrome and irritable bowel syndrome, each bringing with it the creeping responsibility for someone else's personal hygiene. You didn't know at the time that love and respect would be used time and again to emotionally blackmail you into this most undignified of duties. Perhaps love is blind after all, but only because the fumes from such rancid shit will cause you to lose your sight. Love is a wondrous thing.

Your partner has been there for you though. Through thick and thin. Through each god awful open spot and through each torturous gong show. They've watched you try to be a character, dead pan and even paid for your improv course. Every step of the way, your beloved's level of support has been matched only by their voracious appetite for the comfort that goes hand in hand with the consumption of cream cakes, the dairy from which causes the most awful of shit splatted messes that now seem to fall under your jurisdiction.

You know you have enough time to wipe your beloved's anus and you know that if you don't help, a horrendous smell will be there to greet you later when it comes time for you to climb into bed. Any semblance of sexual fun will be absent, as small flakes of dried bum waste fall onto the sheets, ready to be greedily devoured by the microscopic millions you share your bed with every night. You know you just need to run upstairs quickly, run the commemorative tea towel under the hot water tap, then dab gently so as to maintain some semblance of dignity for your better half.

You've considered turning this into material, but such is the sensitive nature of both your partner's physical condition and inability to properly maintain a basic standard of hygiene, you feel this would make you culpable in the eventual suicide that such mockery would bring about. In your darker moments, the moments in which you have fallen out with one another over your lack of career progression, you've considered pressing ahead with the aforementioned material so that you would be free from this charade of a relationship.

Is this love? Constant second guessing and being unsure, or is this the nature of comedy? One minute you're looking forward to a quiet night in, the next minute you get a call from a mid tier promoter with the offer of cash in hand work, and the ego

boost of adulation from drunken idiots. Surely you have time to wipe your partner's bottom?
'OK, I'll be up in a second.' comes your reluctant reply. Although you feel love and a great deal of sympathy for your partner's predicament, a bit of you wishes that you didn't have to routinely clear the back passage of the person you rely on for sexual congress.

Once that grubby business has been taken care of, it's time to quickly go over your notebook. Buying this notebook has been a godsend as it has enabled you to be a far more productive stand up comedian. You jot down all your ideas in here, all the new material you're working on and all the material you plan to do at the gig in question. Any banter that goes well, you quickly make a note of it as you leave the stage.

You came upon this idea when you noticed a comedian ever so slightly more successful than you had a notebook as part of their routine. You then discovered that they too had taken the idea from an even more successful comedian, and so you believe it goes, right up to the top comedians in the country.

You like buying a notebook because it makes your bullshit hobby feel like more of a job. You're writing things down and cataloguing them, so it must be real! You used to go to coffee shops and meet other stand up comedians but that got too depressing when you realised they were just mirrors to your own desperate need for validation.

Now, you gaze at your notebook. So many new ideas. So many new takes on different issues. A couple of topical lines. A notebook full of risk but more importantly, opportunity. The opportunity to be the comedian you'd always hoped you be, to be the type of comedian that not only entertained but also informed. The type of comedian that your peers would look to for guidance and possible Edinburgh fringe show directing jobs, but only if you have the guts. No guts, no glory.

How often does a comedian go out there and take a chance? It's what comedians are supposed to do after all, take chances. Sparky Mark has seen your set before and even though he never normally books you and this is a last minute gig he's booked you for out of pure desperation, on some level he must like you? Maybe he'd like to see a different set from you so he can see how versatile you are and how often you work on your topical stuff. This could be the path to greatness! You could get such a tremendous boost of confidence if all this new stuff hits, and what a buzz it is when something new works!

But this is an important gig. You're closing for Sparky Mark. You have a responsibility to the audience who have paid good money to be there and as such, expect to be entertained. The audience don't care what you want to achieve in your life, they just want you to be funny so that they've had a good time.

But there's a risk to not taking a risk. So many comedians just stick to what they know and never try anything different. They get stagnant and comedy leaves them behind. Sure they make a living, but does anyone remember them?

It's so hard to decide what's best to do! Do you bang out the tried and tested gold, or do you want to take this chance and risk it all in the pursuit of greatness?

If you want to just do your tried and tested gold, turn to page 7

Just turn to page 7 you fucking coward

Googling UNCLE SPUNK inadvertently sends you down some time consuming rabbit holes, time you don't have to waste as you're needed on stage very soon. Eventually you enter the full title of the club and get the information you need. The gig is a mere fifteen minutes away, which gives you the kind of pleasure you remember from being a teenager. Remember when you were a teen and didn't have a care in the world? Sure, you were bullied a little, but who wasn't? Those care free years where you rushed home after school to masturbate without guilt have long since passed. Such youthful abandon has now given way to the horrible feelings of shame that now accompany your present day masturbation over images from that very same age group.

The school bell would ring and you'd get that fuzzy feeling in your tummy. The same fuzzy feeling which just hit when you saw that the gig was a mere 8 mile drive. Hell, you might even stop at a petrol station and treat yourself to a costa coffee.

You love getting a costa coffee, especially at motorway service stations. The highlight of your life is telling people you're a stand up comedian, even though the bulk of your earning is from universal credit and PIP.
'Can I have an extra shot,' you'd enquire of the barista, 'I have a long drive ahead.'
'Oooooh. How long?'
'Seven hours. I'm a stand up comedian you see.'
You don't mention that you were driving to Exeter for £60. You know that would make you look like a fucking imbecile. An eleven hour round trip just so you can come out with (maybe) a tenner, but at least you get to call yourself a stand up comedian.
'Wow. A stand up comedian. That is absolutely amazing and you must be a really unusual and unique individual?' you assume the barista was thinking, clearly sexually aroused.
'I am. I've just, y'know, never really fit in with society.'
'I bet it must be really hard for you to have a normal job?'
'Oh it is,' you would reply, amazed at how insightful this barista is. 'I've lost so many jobs because I am such a unique thinker.'

Yes. Maybe you'll get yourself a costa coffee, you deserve it. But it's such a short journey, it's gonna be hard to justify such a luxury. But then when you think about it, you're two hundred quid up at this point, so a coffee won't hurt. There are no motorway services en route, but you could easily pull into a petrol station that's on your journey. You could even stop off at one of the convenience stores run by one of this country's many hard working ethnic minorities whom you have absolutely no problem with, not even deep down. Maybe you have an unconscious bias, maybe you don't? People of all colours can be rude after all. Put it this way, some days it's much easier to be a woke comedian than other days.

You get into your car and fire up the engine. Purring like a cat being fingered by a cat nip glove, you slip it in to first gear and pull away with the confidence of a Sparky Mark closing act. You've got your pre-gig playlist all set to go, and you hit that play button as though you were beating a confession from a possible member of ISIS. Whether they're in ISIS or not, for you, it's win/win.

'Work, Bitch' by Britney Spears begins as you start to get yourself in the zone for Uncle Spunk's Chuckle Trunk. This is YOUR song. The song that inspires you to keep going. The lyrics speak to you in ways that Led Zeppelin could never even get close to. You drive along as the music blasts out and Britney belts out your battle cry:

"You want a hot body? You want a Bugatti?"
You do. You want both. Never mind that you don't do anything to achieve either of those goals, you still want them.

"You want a Lamborghini? Sippin' marnitis? "
You love Martinis.
"Look hot in a bikini? You better work, bitch."
Yes. You had better.

"You wanna live fancy? Live in a big mansion? Party in France?"
FUCKIN RIGHT YOU DO.

*"You better work, bitch. You better work, bitch.
Now get to work, bitch!"*

'Jesus fucking christ!' leaves your mouth in a scream as you slam the brakes on too late. Time slows down as you look at your speedometer. 46mph in a 30. You make eye contact with the poor elderly lady just before your bumper meets her already age decimated knee caps. The screech of your tyres skidding along the tarmac is drowned out by the deafening thud of your car slamming into somebody's grandma. She folds in half as your car loses as much speed as possible, the old lady seeming at first to disappear underneath your car before somehow being flung over the roof. You witness the sickening sight of her freshly permed head slamming into the bonnet of your car on her journey to the road via the air, landing behind you in a flesh shaped bag of bones as you finally come to a halt. Your heart is beating ridiculously fast as you look in the rear view mirror for any signs of movement.

Nothing.

Not a twitch.

Fuck fuck fuck fuck fuck.

You get out of your car and look around. The street is quiet, with houses set back far enough that nobody could've heard what just happened. A ginger cat watches as you slowly make your way over to the old lady, trepidation expressed in your every step as you can see the blood pouring from her ears.

You kneel down beside her, the smell of freshly laid shit fills the air as you come to the horrid realisation that this person might be dead. She was clearly a proud woman who took pride in her appearance. She is wearing a pearl necklace and holding a shiny handbag, you can tell that this was a woman with class. Sure, she might have been a slag in her youth, but it was a different time and who are you to judge? You check her pulse.

Dead. Shit.

You open her handbag to see if there is anything in there that might help you in some way. A red envelope, inside of which is a small card that reads: 2 MY GRATE GRAN LUV ANGEL - the card is covered in the poorly drawn kisses and hearts of a toddler. Fucking, Angel? Where do these cunts get names like this? You begin to realise that this might all end up making a really good Edinburgh show.

Beside the small card is a photograph of this elderly lady at what seems to have been her recent birthday party. She appears to have just turned 80 years old. There she is, smiling and happy and surrounded by loved ones, yet here she is now in front of you, dead and leaking shit from her arse and blood from her ears.

You look at your watch. You have eighteen minutes left to get to the gig. You search further inside her handbag and discover the purse you were looking for all along. You pretend that you're looking for her ID, but in this universe of determinism, of cause and effect, you already know what you're doing and you feel no guilt in doing so. Sure enough, you find what you were looking for. The elderly don't trust banks, and here she is with just shy of a thousand pounds in cash on her person.

Maybe she does trust the banks and was on her way back from the bingo? Maybe she's just finished robbing a load of people at a holiday park like those old fuckers in Dirty Dancing? None of this matters until you start writing the fringe show that this will undoubtedly become. What matters now though, is how to proceed.

You need to get to this gig. There is nothing you can do about this woman, she is dead and she isn't coming back to life. And what kind of life would it be? Maybe you could begin CPR, but to what end? Months and months in hospital, numerous operations and even more months of rehab. It's probably better that she's already dead. You on the other hand are alive and well and have a job to do. People will be relying on you to headline the comedy show you have agreed to perform at. That, is important. You do an important job. Yes you do. Some might say you do a vital job, a job that helps people understand the world and gives moments of light amongst the darkness.

What lies in front of you is a moral quandary, the likes of which most human beings never have to face in their entire lives. Most humans get through life without accidentally killing an elderly woman whilst on their way to a comedy gig, but here you are now in the most unmarked of territory, proceeding forth along a road you never intended to travel down.

What are you going to do?

If you're going to take that old lady's money, carry on to the gig and be a thief as well as a hit and run killer, turn to page 12

If you're going to leave the money, carry on to the gig and just be a hit and run killer, turn to page 16

You get back into your car, now richer in both cash and life experience. A part of you wishes you'd fingered the corpse of that dear old lady so that you'd know what the coroners of Marilyn Monroe felt like, but it's too late now and you can just make it up when you come to write your fringe show. Maybe Mel Brown could do the PR for it? Your brain is racing with the possibilities for such a show, but right now you have to focus on the task at hand: getting to Uncle Spunk's Chuckle Trunk.

You need to focus on the road and not have anything playing through your car stereo that is too engaging. Just background noise you don't have to pay attention to, something inconsequential. Stuart Goldsmith's Comedian's Comedian Podcast is the obvious choice. Any episode will do because they're all the fucking same, but you end up choosing the one where Ola the Comedian was the guest, an episode you'd always avoided until now.

The gig is a mere 12 minutes away. Somehow, the words of the podcast begin to drift into your unconscious brain despite your attempts to try and engage with it on a professional level. You become overwhelmed by a feeling of drowsiness as those two complete morons wank each other's penises over a topic most normal people couldn't give a shit about. Slapping yourself across the face has little effect as the droning on of these complete tools forces you into a somnambulant state where you are simultaneously both awake and asleep. Your mind is present but your body is absent, meaning you're unable to switch off the podcast and cut short your torture.

Saliva cascades over your bottom lip and down your chin as you begin to make indiscernible groaning noises, each of your hands taking on the shape of a weird claw, as you bend your wrists and involuntarily attempt to repeatedly lick your left elbow. Muscle memory somehow keeps you on the road, as you moan and thrash your head around, flicking saliva inside your car so that it covers every surface, as each word uttered by Goldsmith and Ola causes you to drool in ever more exponential quantities.

You stop at a set of traffic lights. A car pulls up next to you. The driver of the car, a greying man in his early forties casually turns to you and is clearly horrified by what he sees. Your eyes are filled with anguish as your tongue hangs from your mouth, saliva falling in gargantuan quantities as you frantically lick the driver's side window, unable to beckon for help as you smash your own head with crook of your wrist. The pain and discomfort in your eyes speaks to this gentleman on an animalistic level, as it is clear you need putting out of your misery.

He leaps out of his car and runs over to you, ripping open the driver's side door only for you to fall to the floor, moaning and groaning, making the kind of sounds a deaf woman screams at the point of orgasm. Your hero drags you away from the car and you begin to feel yourself again, your hands regaining their natural shape the further away you get from that podcast. The drool production ceases, and you can feel your powers of reasoning and logic returning to you. 'Let me go.' you manage to say, clearly enough that you're knight in shining armour does so.
'Are you alright?' he enquires, seeing you slowly become human again.
'I think so. Would you do me a favour? Go and turn off my stereo, but be careful! Cover your ears and don't engage with that podcast in any way shape or form.'
Your hero duly accommodates the request, speedily ending that audio snuff show before returning to your aid. 'What happened? What was that?' he asks, his body trembling in fear at what the answer might be.
'It was those, people. Talking. I'd never heard anything like it.'
'In what way?'
'Just, morons. I couldn't believe it.'
'How do you mean?'
'They were just twatting on and it was like my brain couldn't take it. It felt like I was being lobotomised.'
'Jesus Christ.'
'I know! I normally listen to that shite at bedtime to help me get to sleep. I didn't realise it could be so dangerous.'

You each share a moment of quiet reflection, as you wonder what might have been had this saviour not acted so quickly. Your hero checks his watch.
'Hey, if you need to be somewhere, just go.' you say, unsure of how best to show your gratitude.
'Oh no, I just wondered what time it was is all.'
'You saved my life tonight.'
'No! Don't be daft. You just needed a breather is all.'
'You did. If I'd have listened to two more minutes of that utter drivel, I'd have ended up brain dead and drowned in my own drool. I owe you one.'
'Hey, I just did what anyone would do. But I do have to get going.'
'No problem.' you offer your hand in both friendship and gratitude. 'You know, I'm not sure I'll ever be able to repay you.'
'Don't worry about it. To be honest, you've kind of eased my conscience a little.'
'How do you mean?' you enquire, noticing an urge to share in your new friend's voice and body language.
'Oh it's nothing. I don't want to burden you. I need to get home to my wife and kids.' your hero is clearly weighed down by something gargantuan. Something troubling. You reach out and put your hand on his shoulder.
'Listen, I owe you. If there's anything I can do, I want to do it. Even if it's just listening. I want to be that person for you.'

He pauses, looking down at the floor as he begins to sob. 'I'm a terrible husband,' he begins, shoulders shaking as the futility of his attempts to cease crying become evident. 'I have a weakness and that weakness has cost me. It will continue to cost me. Food from my kids' mouths, gone. And this is just the beginning.'
Confused, you decide to delve. 'You're not making any sense. If you want to, and only if you do want to, please tell me everything and I will try to help you.' Your hero takes this on board. He can see the compassion in your eyes, the desire to understand and to help. The urge to repay that which is impossible to repay.

'I like it when women piss in my mouth.' he says, looking at the sky to avoid your gaze. 'Specifically, I like old ladies to squat over me and piss in my mouth while they sing Bryan Adams songs.'
'OK.'
'I know, I know. I found this one woman who'd do it. But she decided to extort me instead of being happy with the twelve pounds I'd normally give her. She threatened to tell my family and friends about my fetish unless I gave her some money. I had to give her a thousand pounds tonight! She wants that every week or she'll tell my wife. What the fuck am I gonna do?'
'This old lady, what did she look like?'
'What?' your hero asks, confusion etched across his tear stained face.
'Did she have on a pearl necklace, shiny handbag?'
'Yeah. Yeah she did.'
'You're not gonna believe this, but I killed her in a hit and run accident about five minutes ago. Swear down.' you beam from ear to ear as you relay this information.
'You're fucking joking? You're joking. This is a joke, right?'
'No! Swear down! I stole her money too. Look!' you produce just shy of a thousand pounds from your pocket, the notes ever so slightly covered in Stuart Goldsmith enhanced retard drool. Your hero can scarcely believe what is going on as you hand over the wad of cash. Overcome with emotion, your hero flings his arms around you, sobbing the tears of a man freed from death row.
'Thank you!' he whispers in your ear, a faint whiff of urine emanating from his mouth. 'I don't know what to say.'
'You don't have to say anything,' you reply, holding him tight and close. 'You just need to go on and live your life. Be a good father. Be a good husband. But most importantly, choose a more discreet octogenarian to piss on your chops whilst singing the Summer of '69.'

Turn to page 21

You leave the money, your conscience oddly clear for someone who has just accidentally ended the life of an elderly woman. Walking quickly but quietly back to your car, you notice an old looking CCTV camera at the top of a lamp post. It's so odd, it looks like it's from the 1980s, a proper old school block of metal. You ponder how long it has been there, then think about how far lens technology has come in such a short space of time. Kodak didn't see any of it coming, and that lack of foresight broke the company. Who could've foreseen that most people would be happy to have their photos on a mobile phone or in a cloud? What the fuck is a cloud? Why is it called a cloud when it is actually a massive databank held by a massive corporation that knows more about your mind than your closest friends.

'Excuse me?'

You are broken from your paralysing train of thought by what seems to be (at most) a 14 year old boy.

'Are you OK?' he enquires, glancing over to the already rotting corpse of the dead pensioner.
'I'm fine,' you reply. 'Just found this lady like this and now I'm going to phone the police.'
'Looks like you were getting into your car.'
'That's where my phone is. It's in the cradle to be used as a sat nav. I use a cradle because I'm a law abiding citizen.'
'I see.'
'Yes. You can run along now. I'll take it from here.' you say, gesticulating to this youth to fuck off.

Too late. Out of the corner of your eye you see the flashing blue lights of law enforcement and National Health Service heroes. For how long were you contemplating the progress of lens technology and the inevitable overthrowing of the human race by artificial intelligence? Why do you find this topic so distracting? Why do you always think back to the grey goo of nanotechnology Prince Charles tried to warn us about? FUCKING HELL YOU ARE DOING IT NOW. Snapping out of it, you punch the little grassing cunt right in the face, dropping him with one punch before you stamp on his shitty little head. Groaning, he splutters something about 'civic duty' as blood drips from his mouth.

The ambulance crew hang back at the behest of the police who are now calling for back up. You grab the teenager and lift him up, his limp body made light by your now hysterical strength, adrenalin pumping through your body in ways you haven't felt since that first open spot at The Comedy Store where you died on your arse because you didn't immediately reference the tube in the first fucking thirty seconds.

'STAY BACK OR I'LL BREAK HIS NECK!' you scream at the police whilst dragging this limp wastrel to your car, opening the rear passenger side door and flinging him in there. The teenager's mobile phone falls out of his pocket and you marvel again at how small cameras lenses are these days. FOCUS! Right, you have a hostage. You can still get to the gig if you leave now.

'You there! Let the boy go! There's still time to make this right!' shouts an officer, unsure of the protocol for such a situation. You too are unfamiliar with this situation, but you *have* seen the delightful comedy Twins starring Danny DeVito and Arnold Schwarzen***er in which Arnie's character, Julius, goes over the rules of a crisis situation:

'Da fust rool in a crisis sidooashun iz you negotiate fust, den attack.'

You repeat this to the police in attendance, who are confused at both your accent and your advice.
'Come on, let's talk about this.' says the officer, moving towards you. You notice that the police in attendance have body-cams on their person which they can use to record accurately whatever happens during a situation which involves the police and member of the public. It's hard to believe that lens technology has advanced to this stage and indeed continues to advance. Soon it'll be a contact lens you wear that records such interaction, as artificial intelligence

technology interfaces with human biology and for fuck's sake what are you doing?

'You'll never take me alive copper!' you yell as you get in your car, firing up the engine as you watch the police scramble back to their panda cars. All of them are morbidly obese so it provides you with yet more material for the amazing Edinburgh show this is gonna be. Watching those stretched uniforms struggle to hold back the undulating rolls of fat gives you a feeling of superiority you shouldn't have considering you're a hit and run murderer now graduating to create a hostage situation.

The road ahead is clear, but your plan is not. You think back to the improv course you did, hoping that the police do improv as part of their training at the academy and that they won't keep blocking you. Come on! You've been trained in improv, think back to your training, you can adapt and overcome this situation. As you pull away with a theatrical wheel spin, you vividly remember your improv instructor, Sean. Grossly overweight with a beard made from the pubes of an eleven year old girl, Sean gave you the most important lesson you ever learned in comedy:

HOW GOOD YOU ARE AS A COMEDIAN HAS NOTHING TO DO WITH WHETHER OR NOT YOU WILL BE ABLE TO MAKE LIVING FROM COMEDY.

That fat nonce managed to convince businesses that somehow, improv would make for a great training day and improve sales. How does pretending to be an Italian opera singer trapped in an aquarium help you shift units of bleach at a fucking chemical company? Fucking cunt. 'When it comes to improv,' he'd belch, struggling to breathe because of his monstrous and disgusting neck, 'there's only one thing you need to remember... just go with the flow, baby.'

Sean would say this as though it were the deepest wisdom and that it somehow applied to life in general. Now, here you are, worrying about which flow to go with. In improv, to be able to truly perform, you were taught to completely inhabit the character you were portraying, even if it meant being a disabled mudskipper for a few fleeting seconds. You remember being that mudskipper. They didn't specify the disability, but for some reason you went with cerebral palsy, immediately dropping to the floor and flapping around. The suggestion had come from Kyle, who you were sure had a crush on you and who also had a peculiar fetish for smooth fish with segmented eyes able to travel across land. You wanted to please Kyle. You became the mudskipper, and the throbbing in Kyle's jeans meant that you'd fucking nailed it.

Sean was angry, as he too was competing for your attention. As Sean was an improv instructor, his suggestions always ended up with you improvising a scene where you played a 4 year old with a curiosity that would get them into all sorts of sexy trouble. One time you sucked off Sean in front of the whole group, such was your dedication to improv mastery. But on this occasion, Sean was so impressed with your devotion that he allowed the scene to continue for six seconds longer than normal. Later, Sean would tell you that he'd done this because your improv skills had reached a level of mastery seldom achieved by human beings. You no longer inhabited the physical realm when it came to improvisation. You now inhabited a plane beyond mortal concern.

Sitting you down on his lap, stroking the small of your back whilst inhaling your odour, Sean told you that you could 'do anything in life now. Your improv skills are so powerful that, no matter what situation you'll find yourself in, all you need do is embody your chosen character… and improvise.'

Here you are now, speeding away, inhabiting the character of a hostage taker and hit and run killer. But is that you? Can you change the character right here and right now? Perhaps the improv you should be doing is that of the honest and decent citizen who now needs to abide by the law before things spiral out control. You could probably get a lenient sentence if you stop at this point, but carrying on will only up the stakes and therefore increase the punishment. Maybe you should improv as a master criminal and get away with it? Yes! That's what you should do! But how long can you maintain such a level of improv? Is it even possible? Oh god, the 14 year old in the back seat is starting to come around and the police in the rear view mirror are gaining. What the fuckety fuck are you gonna do?

To improv as a master criminal who does this shit all the time, turn to page 28

To improv as a law abiding citizen, turn to page 39

To kill yourself as penance for doing improv in the first place, go to page 24

You pull up to Uncle Spunk's Chuckle Trunk with time to spare. Hard to believe you've got a gig so close to home, and even harder to believe you've just killed an old woman who was blackmailing people by pissing on them for sexual pleasure. You've heard lots about this gig and know that it's one of the best. You did an open spot here years ago and now it's time to slay this dragon. All that stands in your way are the usual feelings of self doubt and hatred of social interaction.

You didn't used to be this way. As a teenager, you were known for being a little awkward but certainly someone who enjoyed being around other people. Now, all you fantasise about is a world where you can just telepathically transmit your jokes from the comfort of your own living room so that you don't have to hear other comedians twatting on about how well they're doing or (slightly better) how shit things are for them.

It used to be that if a comedian was telling you how bad things were, you could get excited that you were doing better. Nowadays, with our new system of social currency devoted to prizing victimhood above all else, there's an element of wanting to appear worse off compared to everyone else. You once witnessed two comedians compete with one another about who had died worse at the gig they were at, IN FRONT OF THE FUCKING PROMOTER. Imagine being that dense? Urgh. Maybe it's just comedians? But it isn't, it's everything. The people after the gig, if you end up chatting to them, the bar staff. Fucking, everyone. All wankers. The lot.

I mean, you've got to get past the door staff first, and that's a challenge in and of itself. 'Oh, you're a comedian? Tell me a joke!' the bouncer will say Original mother fucker. You hope they get stabbed when they say shit like that. Security staff at a comedy night are the shittest security known to man. We're talking driving with an open top in Dealey Plaza levels of ineptitude, no security near the grassy knoll and no action after the first shot. Yes it was a conspiracy but there's no way the secret service guards were in on it as they did next to fuck all beyond look at Jackie's sexy body. Fuck it, let's go and talk to this trained chimp and get it over and done with as quickly as possible.

You leave your car with purpose, marching at a steady and serious pace towards the entrance to Uncle Spunk's. Dressed casually, you may look relaxed and cool on stage, but to the security guard, you could be the next Osama Bin Laden, hell bent on murdering infidels. How polite you are to security is normally based on how intimidating they are. This guy looks like he's about to walk on to the set of a BBC DESTROYS FIVE LATINA ASSES as the star of such a piece of art. He could probably beat you to death with his cock and only suffer minor bruising to his bell end. As such, you engage in a friendly but firm manner.
'Are you here for the comedy night?' he mumbles, barely able to string the sentence together from his limited vocabulary.
'Yes, I'm one of the comedians.'
His eyes light up. Fuck's sake.

He quickly undoes his trousers, revealing a surprisingly average penis, then begins to masturbate. The pace of his stroking surprises you, as he uses the other hand to signify that he wishes you to remain in place whilst his business hand occupies itself with the task of achieving orgasm. Rapidly pumping away, he asks the question again, this time more breathlessly than before.
'Are, are, are you here, f, f, for the comedy night?' he asks, furiously yanking his erect penis.
'Erm...' you reply hesitantly.
'Oh come on, I'm getting close. I promise I won't hit you,' he says, his bottom lip now bitten as he waits expectantly for your answer. His eyelids flutter as he gets ever closer. 'Fuck, are you here for the comedy night? Are you here for the comedy night? Are you here for the comedy night?'
'Yes. I'm here for the comedy night.' you tease, knowing full well what he wants to hear.
'You fucker! Come on. Give it to me,' he gasps, now using his other hand to pull on his ball bag a little. 'Are you here for the comedy night?'
'Yes, I'm here.'

'Oh you fucking whore!' he's close now. His body looks tense, his lower back curling ready to thrust into his own hand.
'Ask me again.'
'Are. You. Here. For. The. Comedy. N,n,n,night?'
'Yes. I'm one of the comedians.'
'Yo, you, you're a comediannnnn?'
'Yes.'
'Go on, th, then. Tell me a jo, jo, j,j,j OOOOHHHH!' hot frothy cum shoots from his throbbing cock as he stutters spastically the most predictable line of all time. The pleasure he feels as you roll your eyes at his remark serves only to intensify his orgasm. His body involuntarily pulsates as each burst springs forth from his meatus, his ass pumping into a non existent mate as millions of years of evolution take over his nervous system. Dimly, he recovers some semblance of control and squeezes out the last few drops of jizz on to the floor of the entrance. He stumbles backwards, barely able to keep his footing, discombobulated from the intensely pleasurable expulsion of millions of sperm, each of them now dying and drying on poorly laid paving outside of Uncle Spunk's. Coughing a little, the bouncer regains some composure.
'Just go in and see Lauren, she'll stamp your hand.' he informs you, lightly wiping the tip of his dick on his shirt sleeve.
'Thank you.' comes your response through gritted teeth, as you walk in whilst carefully avoiding the slip hazard that has just been fired indiscriminately all over the frontage of this legendary comedy club. As you stroll in to the building you look back at the bouncer as he places a wet floor sign at the entrance of the club.

Now, where the fuck is Lauren?

Turn to page 51

You tend to do your best thinking whilst driving. Some people have said that comedians are paid for their travel rather than the comedy they provide, and even though this is the thought of a dullard, there is indeed an element of truth to it. Comedians are skilful drivers, and managing the stress of a double or triple gig in a busy city centre or indeed two busy city centres on one night has meant that you are coping rather well with the stress of being chased by the police for kidnapping and murder.

The blue lights in your rear view mirror are of no concern to you. What concerns you now, what consumes your thought process as though it were your entire being is your conscience. Improv can get you out of this situation, but in turn, was it not improv that got you in to this situation?

You've known since you signed up for that course that improv is for morons. A stand up comedian is someone who can improvise, no doubt. But improv as a discipline? As an art form? You knew all along that improv is for the hard of thinking. You've always been able to compartmentalise that part of your life, rationalising that you didn't know any better. That you were taken advantage of, a new comedian with milk still fresh on your breath. We've all been there, in our darkest hours, wondering whether or not comedy could provide us with a standard of living commensurate to that which is expected within the industrialised western world. We all know that once you've done an improv course you can basically teach one, which would then give you a nice little income stream if times got tough. Jesus Christ, an eight year old could teach an improv course. In fact, the only reason children aren't allowed to teach improv courses is because 90% of the people on the course would try and rape the instructor.

Here you are now though, the environment around you in a state of high anxiety as you are pursued, yet you remain calm in the face of such adversity. You once did a Christmas gig above a pub, so you're no stranger to this level of stress. What's bugging you now is the sudden realisation that life is short, and you did an improv course. Not only did you do an improv course, you told people it was useful for stand up! You fucking piece of shit.

Why now? Why has this shame hit you now? We don't get to choose when we're hit with realisation, but to ignore it is to slap the universe in the face. You have honour, you were brought up with pride, but pride is now something no one who has done an improv course is allowed to have. The God of Death must drink his fill, and where there is dishonour and shame, Death must be nourished by the life force of those that have brought such shame upon themselves.

You stop the car. The police stop their cars. The 14 year old murmurs. You undo your seatbelt and exit the car, the police commanding you to lie on the floor with your hands behind your head. Ignoring their commands, you drag the now semi-conscious teenager from the car and leave him slumped on the road. He'll live, and the generous criminal compensation system we have will help to pay for many of his favourite consoles in the coming years.

Returning to your car, you feel at peace. Soon, it will all be over. You think of those that you will be leaving behind. Your gelatinous partner, your fellow comedians whom you secretly hate. Sparkly Mark's gig will be ruined, as he will not be able to reach you and will have no idea what has transpired this evening. A smile comes across your face as you imagine that fucking retard pacing about wondering what to do, explaining to customers that it's out of his hands and then reluctantly giving out refunds. Maybe all of this has been worth it? Maybe this will begin a chain reaction that forces Sparky to stop running gigs? Or maybe he'll go on to be the biggest promotor in the country? None of this matters now. You drive off at speed as the police scramble back into their car.

50mph

60mph

70mph

You're aiming for 88mph as a Back to the Future reference but you think 80mph will probably do. Everything slows down as you see the wall you had in mind. The sloping right hand turn has a solid, front facing wall that now has a date with your car. As you hit the carefully laid brick, you feel the tremendous transference of force, hurling you from your seat and through the windscreen. Kinetic energy is released in a manner that few ever get to experience, physics playing out in a manner fully intended by the universe.

You feel no fear, no trepidation: only elation.

Elation at a job well done. You have paid your debt to society, a society that enabled the movement of foreign labour, which helped get this wall built cheaply but with superior craftsmanship. Krystof, whom you will never meet, poured his heart and soul into this wall, brought up as he was to treat each task in front of him with love and care so as to always guarantee the best outcome. A man who took great pride in every facet of his work. Now, as your head smashes into the accumulated efforts of three generations of bricklayers, you silently give thanks to the hard working immigrants that helped make this country great, whilst castigating the lazy indigenous population who shame us on a daily basis. Spat out of their mothers into a country with an incredibly generous benefits system, these work shy pieces of shit have the nerve to claim that foreigners are taking the jobs they didn't want in the first place. If this wall had been built by one of these ill disciplined fuckwits, you'd probably only end up in a coma while your brain swelling was reduced. Thanks to Krystof, you will have very little idea about how it feels to hit a well made brick wall at tremendous speed.

Death comes for you quickly, and you embrace it the way you would a beloved relative.

Nothing.

It isn't black. It's nothing.

A state without a colour. Death is a feeling, and this is how it feels. A kind of floating. A nothingness. There but not there.

Here but elsewhere. Yonder but neighbouring.

You're aware only of how unaware you are. It is as though you are being weighed.

A light, fiercely intense but welcoming, accompanies a booming voice of silence. The amplified quiet of omnipotence silently fills your ears with the noise of query.

Without language you understand that the question being asked is of infinite importance. The voice of scales. Judgement. The answer will determine your ultimate fate, the question being one that only the creator and final judge could pose it.

'Did you ever consider becoming a musical comedian?'

If yes, you did consider being a musical comedian, turn to page 43

If no, you never considered being a musical comedian, turn to page 57

The problem with improvising as a master criminal is that the only ones you actually have knowledge of are either fictional (so aren't master criminals) or they were apprehended by law enforcement. You flirt with the idea of improvising as Keyser Soze, but that would mean improvising as Kevin Spacey, which would also mean having to address the allegations of sexual assault which we've all forgotten about now anyway. Don't lie, you've rewatched House of Cards. Most of his stuff is still on Netflix and Amazon Prime and really, was there any evidence beyond a few stories? That whole #*MeToo* movement is done with now and maybe that's for the best? Men and women had gotten along just fine for centuries without ever having to have certain power imbalances made blindingly apparent. If women don't like being dominated, why is rape one of the leading taboo sexual fantasies amongst women? Sure, an actual rape is disgusting and vile and the kind of traumatic experience that can set a person back for the rest of their lives until they talk about it at a time best suited for career advancement. But it can also be the stuff of deep rooted fantasy, being taken against your will and then slowly enjoying it. In confidential research, rape and animals linger worryingly in women's fantasies, is this not a remnant of our evolutionary past? A throwback to a time when inhibitions were in no need of being subdued, and jungle law meant that we could accommodate any sexual flavour as long as the tribe had enough food.

You don't make excuses for abuses of power, and of course Kevin Spacey should have his day in court (if appropriate), but society can only be outraged for so long. The media cycle plays to our constant thirst for new information (regardless of the accuracy) so much that most news stories actually worthy of attention are put to the back of the queue as we dance to the tune of our lizard overlords.

All of these thoughts flash through your mind as you try and conjure a figure in your imagination worthy of master criminal status to improv to. Maybe Princess Diana is still alive? Lord Lucan? Elvis! No, these wouldn't be considered master criminals, just people avoiding the limelight. You need someone who everyone thinks committed a crime, yet has not faced justice.

That's it!! You've got it.

Kate and Gerry McCann. You've looked into this case deeper than anyone you know and you're sure they were involved, and that people far more powerful than them were also at play. In front of the entire world, you watched them get away with it, but not the crime most people think they committed. The McCanns are who you will use to channel your improv.

Straight away, you get on your mobile phone, contacting the police and local news in order to call a press conference at Uncle Spunk's Chuckle Trunk. News has already got around there is a high speed pursuit of a suspected hit and run murderer, so you assume that the press will be desperate to talk to you.
'Hi, BBC local news, Jatinder speaking, how can I help you?'
'Jatinder? That a boy or a girl's name?'
'Pardon?'
'Never mind. Listen, I've got a hostage and I'm the guy who ran over and murdered an elderly lady. I'm calling a press conference at nine thirty pm, to take place at Uncle Spunk's Chuckle Trunk.' Jatinder lets out an enormous sigh, which doesn't fill you with any kind of confidence that s/he will be attending. 'What the fuck is your problem?' you enquire.
'It's just that, we've got a lot on. Elderly women die all the time so….'

God damn it s/he's right. Old women getting killed is neither here nor there. They've lead a good long life full of all sorts of sexual conquests, crosswords and dramatics of all description. Old women have more than likely bred, raised children, had jobs and had affairs, they've probably put a condom over a TV remote and fucked themselves with it. Old women have lived. Children though, haven't. That was the genius of the McCann's, they got away with their massive multi billion dollar drug deal by using a child as distraction. All you've done is taken the life of someone who was already on borrowed time.

Now here you are, a shit comedian about to drive to a decent gig where you'll more than likely be apprehended for manslaughter and kidnapping. What would Kate do though? That's it! You've got it! Now you're thinking like a McCann!

'Jatinder?' you enquire, seductively.
'Yes?'
'It's just that I'd really appreciate it if you respected my privacy at this difficult time.'
'What?' s/he replies thirstily, froth audibly spewing from his/her mouth.
'Yeah, I'd just really appreciate it if you respected my privacy.'
'You're gonna be at Uncle Spunk's Chuckle Trunk and you'd like us to respect your privacy?' s/he asks, probably wanking now.
'Yes, during this very difficult time.'
'Well,' coughs Jatinder, 'as you know I can't guarantee that we'll leave you alone, but I will do my best to make sure that your wishes are respected and thank you and goodbye.'
You know what that means. Glancing in your rear view mirror, you can see the police starting to ease off, respecting your privacy. It's already beginning to work, the police are slowly deciding to let this be a trial by media so that they don't have to do too much work. The McCann strategy is beginning to pay off. Gordon Brown himself was involved in the murder and kidnapping, while Kate managed to avoid 50 direct questions from the Portuguese police, all while Gerry was finalising one of the biggest illegal drug deals of all time. The illegality of the drugs is an important distinction to make, as Big Pharma makes all kind of illicit profits from absurd drug deals every day of every god damned week. Big Pharma quash negative findings in drug safety testing, not to mention they under report safety concerns and pay huge amounts of money to governments and legislative infrastructure so that they can continue making huge sums of money with scant regard for the safety of the public or indeed the efficacy of their products. Money talks, and in the case of drugs, it talks a gibbering language of incessant nonsense whilst shitting out fat profits for capitalist scumbags.

Fifty direct questions Kate was asked. FIFTY! Not even difficult ones, questions any mother would know. She just jibbed em off like a pro as the press descended on this most middle class of awful tragedies. All the while, the giant paedo ring that secretly rules the world was putting the finishing touches to a drug deal so big and so profitable that every level of British Government would see a boost in funding as a direct result, with Gerry McCann as the instigator and leader.

Gerry is rarely scrutinised, and when done he is, it is certainly much softer than the examination Kate gets. Kate, all steely and emotionless is given a much harder time, maybe because of misogyny, but more likely because we're not used to seeing strong women dealing with such situations in the way that she did. You have to be strong in order to pull off one of the biggest deals of all time, a deal so large it would make the Al-Yamamah arms deal look like a Pic'n'Mix at the cinema. Billions in heroin, smuggled out of our dirty war in Afghanistan, all under the cover of saturation media coverage telling us about a 'missing' child. Genius.

As you approach Uncle Spunk's Chuckle Trunk, you can see the assembled news vans and reporters, all jostling and shoving in order to secure a good position for your inevitable 'impromptu' press conference. The teenager in your backseat is now fully conscious but has very little idea of what is going on, lying mute as he tries to make sense of what happened whilst trying to predict what is about to transpire.
'OK back there?' you enquire, showing genuine concern.
'I think so. My head hurts.'
'Yeah sorry about that. I had to take swift action and that's what ended up happening.'
'No worries. Where are we going?'
'Do you like stand up comedy?'
'I guess so.'
'Well, we're going to one of the best gigs in the country, Uncle Spunk's Chuckle Trunk,' you exclaim, mustering as much enthusiasm as you can. The teenager looks unmoved by this new information, stricken somewhat by the small amount of

blood he can see on his digits after briefly examining where his head hurts. 'Do you have a favourite comedian?' you ask.
'Yeah, I kinda like Dave Chappelle.'
'No way! Same here! Oh you're in for a great time! I really think you'll like my set as I think I'm quite similar to Chapelle. Now, listen. I need you to do me a favour ok?'
'OK.'
'When we get to Uncle Spunk's, there's gonna be a lot of journalists there. If any of them ask you something, I need you tell them that you have no comment to make at this time and that you would appreciate it if they respected your privacy.'
'What?'
'This is important! OK? Right, what's your name?'
'Jatinder.'
'No fucking way! I just spoke to a Jatinder! Anyway, just tell them to respect your privacy and we'll get through this.'

Jatinder isn't sure what to think. You can tell that he is confused, and such confusion can be used to your advantage, the way your improv coach used your confusion to sexually assault you. All improv coaches are disgusting sexual perverts, but Sean had a way of abusing your trust in ways that only became apparent long after the event. One minute your improvising as a washing machine, the next you're rimming Sean with no idea why. It is this type of confusion that you will use to your advantage with Jatinder.

'Jatinder? Have you ever dreamed of being famous?' you already know the answer.
'Sure.'
'Well, you're about to get really famous, really quickly. Do you remember Mick Philpott?'
'No.'
'You're probably too young. Mick Philpott was a scumbag from Derby who set his house on fire in a bid to get publicity for rescuing his kids. The only problem with his plan was that Philpott was a fucking retard. Six kids died!'
'Oh my god!'
'I know! But, that didn't knock Philpott off his stride. Oh no. He called a press conference, which is when the police became

suspicious of him. He faked crying and then the cops knew he was in on it. The police secretly surveilled him and got the evidence they needed for a conviction, but during all of this, Philpott still managed to arrange a threesome! That's what I'm offering you.'
'A threesome?!' exclaims Jatinder, adrenalin now pumping through his veins.
'Yes, sir.'
'Every teenage boys dream!'
'Indeed. All I need you to do, is ask the press to respect your privacy.'
'I can do that.'

Amongst the crowd of photographers and journalists at Uncle Spunk's Chuckle Trunk, you can see Sparky Mark frantically trying to shoo people away from the entrance. Most importantly, you cannot see any police. The trial by media has begun.

Learning from the McCann's, you know instinctively that it's important to present an air of calm and resolute middle class posture. The questions will come thick and fast, so you aim to only answer the ones you think will best make your case. Jatinder is on board, his teenage fantasies now taking precedence over common sense.

Pulling in to Uncle Spunk's, the flashing lights of the assembled photojournalists almost trigger the fake epilepsy you've used over the last few years to help keep you involved in the victimhood comedy olympics. Thank god your fake OCD and the anti-depressants you don't take are keeping you levelled off. You and Jatinder both exit the car together and stand for the photographers, posing arm in arm, the very essence of stoicism beaming from your posture, poise and profile. Questions come thick and fast.
'Is it true you murdered Ethel Simpson?'
'Why did you leave the scene?'
'When are you going to write some new material?'

This is the one you choose to answer.

'It has been rollercoaster few days, and I have to say that I'm looking forward to getting back to the hotel and getting some writing done. But I can only do that if the press respects my privacy at this difficult time.' Your voice is the prefect mix of strength and weakness, under stress but keeping calm and carrying on.

'Jatinder, what is your involvement?'
'Are you a driver? Is this a Mirth Control gig?'
'Is this your first open spot?'

Jatinder makes you proud. He bows his head and asks that his privacy be respected, before looking in your direction and giving you a cheeky wink.
'Ladies and Gentlemen, no more questions.' you command, holding Jatinder close as you push your way through the throng of rabid journalists, each frothing at the anus for a scoop they'll never get. Sparky Mark is stood theatrically tapping his watch, as the door security stands there, unsure what to do as there's more than one thing happening.
'You're cutting it a bit fine, LOL and PMSL' says Sparky Mark, deadpan with no life in his eyes. 'I'm just about to go back on after this open spot has died on his arse. ROFL. I'll probably have to do twenty minutes to get the gig back on track LMAO.'
'Does he alway talk like this?' asks Jatinder, freaked out by the clothing of Sparky Mark.
'Yeah, he doesn't laugh so he lets you know he's joking by using text speak. Look...'

You point to Sparky Mark's hands, each knuckle tattooed with an emoji to help him express how he feels at any one time, the angry red face on his middle finger helping Jatinder to envisage a very expressive fingering.
'Mark, where's Carrie?' you enquire, remembering your oath to Jatinder.
'Carrie the slag you mean? SMH LOL can't believe I said that PMSL.'
'Yeah, where is she?'

'She'll be upstairs waiting for another customer no doubt ROFL.'
'Come with me, Jatinder.' you say cheerfully, grabbing his arm with purpose as you march him away towards the stairs that lead to Carrie's Cavern of Pleasure. As you walk upstairs, the odour changes from that of all those grubby clubs just after the smoking ban was implemented, to one of moisture and bacteria.

Uncle Spunk's Chuckle Trunk is a converted Wetherspoon's bar, formerly frequented by BNP members but now a thriving part of the recent artistic renovation that has happened to this area. The large function room is home to the Chuckle Trunk, with Uncle Spunk's providing the refreshments. The gig runs Thursday to Sunday, with a once a month show of only female comedians where an audience of lesbians come and sit in silent judgement as each woman walks on stage to recite poetry with the rhythm of stand up comedy.

One of the leftovers from the former BNP stronghold is Carrie and her long suffering partner, Sandra. Carrie and Sandra have been a couple for years, making money from the filming and monetising of amateur pornography, recorded without the consent of the various participants. Sandra wanted no part in the business venture, but due to being grotesquely insecure and frightened of change, she decided to abide by Carrie's wishes and participate in the filming and distribution of the aforementioned sexual activity. The niche market of racists with blurred out faces and nazi tattoos ensured a steady income stream for many years until the horrors of gentrification took hold and removed a vital community service. Now that Carrie and Sandra mainly record non-racists indulging their sexual services, the high paying income stream of regular subscribers has disappeared, meaning they have become beggars rather than choosers. They each make a decent living, but yearn for the glory days of the niche market they formerly enjoyed.

You have discussed this yearning of theirs with them many times, knowing that the secret recording equipment remains in place but under utilised. Now that you're improvising as a master criminal, you can see the benefit in using this yearning to your advantage by sealing Carrie and Sandra as allies whilst ensuring that Jatinder remains quiet about the hit and run killing. As you make your way to their lair, you're now scheming almost instinctively, channelling your inner McCann.

As you reach the room with Jatinder, you notice in him the excited trepidation of a virgin schoolboy about to make it with his hot teacher. Jatinder is currently so driven by his hormones that he's lost all logic and reasoning, and is now running purely on instinct. As you have given him no concern for his well being, his instinct to procreate has overtaken his instinct to survive. The risk is worth the reward, as millions of years worth of evolution kick in so that his DNA may be passed on.

You knock on the door, fully aware that you are about to pay women to record an under age sex encounter in order to maintain the silence of the only witness to your hit and run murder. Carrie opens the door, wearing only a thong, a smile and a cheeky look in her eye. Carrie has lived a life. She has a tattoo that reads '12/4/97 - 1/5/97' to commemorate her one and only miscarriage as well as several scars on her knuckles from all the fights she's had. Carrie also carries with her the skills of a seasoned sex worker, and as such, she is your devious ticket to freedom at this point.
'Well, well, well. If it isn't my favourite comedian! How are you? Finally decided to take me up on my offer of a Carrie and Sandra sandwich?'
'Ha! No, no, no. But my young friend here is eager for a new frontier and I thought who better to provide him with such an experience?'
'You've come to the right place. Sandra! Prepare yourself. We're having Indian tonight.' Carrie purrs, as Sandra readies the equipment.
'Are you sure this is OK?' asks Jatinder, now more nervous than ever.
'It's gonna be fine!' you reassure him. 'These people are professionals.'

Carrie leads Jatinder inside and towards the creamy white upholstered bed, as Sandra makes her way over to you so that she may arrange payment.
'What's this all about?' asks Sandra, sceptical of your intentions.
'I need you to give this guy the works, and I'll need the uncut footage. How much?'
'Hmmmm. That's gonna cost ya.'
'Lay it on me.'
'Twenty-four pounds.'
'Done.'

By the time you have sealed this deal, Jatinder's face is already buried deep in Carrie's flabby ass, reluctantly licking her anus. 'Get your fucking tongue in there you dirty immigrant,' commands Carrie. Jatinder pulls his head back a little to get some air.
'But I'm not an immigrant, I'm third generoioahiuhwoiboiwa....'
Carrie grabs his face and pulls it tightly into her arse crack.
'That's it you dirty little cunt. Get your tongue in there.'
'Carrie,' says Sandra, 'We are to give him the works.' Carrie looks at you with a knowing eye. She knows what to do. You both nod as Sandra slowly closes the door. In the back of your mind, you know that what you're doing is wrong, but as you continue this improvisation as a master criminal, you're also fully aware know that this will be what keeps you out of prison, and with so much more left to do to get home with your liberty intact, it will probably be the least of your misdeeds.

Sandra closes the door, as filming of the crime commences. You hear moans of delight as Jatinder begins to embrace his new reality. You contemplate listening at the door but realise you're due onstage very soon and should probably get your head in the right frame of mind for comedy, but the allure of hearing a gloriously well performed sex session is almost too good to ignore. When humans began to have organised tribal societies, sex in front of people was a very normal and healthy activity. Indeed, some tribes in Papa New Guinea still practise such customs. The Etoro People indulge in homosexual practises for reasons of both strength (they believe it makes you a stringer hunter) and good old fashioned tradition, with the belief that ingestion of sperm is critical for the proper growth of boys. Some tribes in Papa New Guinea also enjoy indulging in very public procreation, as well as very private homosexual fornication. The public procreation is deemed to be dutiful, being integral to the continuation of the species, whereas the intergenerational homosexual fornication is performed behind closed doors because that's just how homos roll.

This voyeuristic sexual kink is still a part of our evolutionary soul. We like to watch other people having sex as it makes us aroused, and arousal makes us feel good. Even just hearing sex can make you aroused, and right now you could either go and watch Sparky Mark wrap up the middle section with some shit jokes and get a feel for the room, or you could stand and listen at the door to one of the greatest sexual spectacles you will probably ever be privy to.

To go and prepare for the show, go to page 61

To listen to two women sexually assault a teenager, go to page 83

Do you ever really make a decision? The universe is governed by cause and effect, and as such it would logically follow that free will cannot exist within such a universe. The events that are currently unfolding due to your invitation to perform stand up comedy at Uncle Spunk's Chuckle Trunk, were put in motion at the very moment of The Big Bang. It's hard to wrap your head around such a concept. The creation of the universe, the forming of the solar system, the pre-cambrian explosion and evolving of multi-cellular life, the extinction of the dinosaurs and the evolution of the bi-pedal ape. All of this happened without your involvement, all of it lead inextricably and inevitably towards this moment, the moment where you choose to improv as a law abiding citizen in order to better deal with the hit and run killing of an elderly woman. Every single event leading up to this moment has been out of your control, yet you convince yourself that the choice you just made was within your control.

Such is the human ego that free will has been associated with humanity since the developing of consciousness. Once we had developed intelligence enough to contemplate our own existence, the electrical charges that fire our neurones without our conscious control lead us to believe that we <u>have</u> such control. You are in as much control of your thoughts as you are anybody else's. Your brain is working and is ahead of you in ways you do not understand. You made your decision moments before you were even aware of it. You don't even know how to think, you just think. Descartes said it best and now here you are struggling to know who he was and what he actually said. You fucking moron.

Your foot touches the brake pedal as you begin to bring the car to a halt, the laws of physics governing the rate of the slowing down, just as the laws of physics have governed the manner with which you think. You don't realise but the environment your gran was in has had a massive effect on the way you've lived your life. The egg that came from your mother's ovaries which ended up being fertilised by your father's hot load, was formed inside the womb of your gran when your mother was gestating. The diet and stress levels of your gran impacted the quality of the egg that would end up making 50% of your DNA, and have in some way contributed towards your current predicament. Perhaps if your gran hadn't had so much milk you wouldn't be on the run from the police?

Such understanding of the simplicity of cause and effect, and the highly complex interplay of that simple rule as the universe began to rapidly expand, allows you to have sympathy with all human beings for their state at any given time. It also (to a certain extent) absolves you of any responsibility you may feel for the crimes you committed this evening. When there is an acceptance that free will is a myth, nobody can really be held responsible for their actions. How can we hate when the story of our lives that is unfolding before us, is pre-determined and out of our hands? How can we hate when fate, God or whatever you want to call it has written the script for us to act out?

The car comes to a halt as the flashing blue lights chasing you cease their motion in order to form a permitter from which to monitor your movements. As you are about to give yourself up and be at the mercy of the criminal justice system, you feel an overwhelming sense of peace. What will be, will be.

You look at the teenager in your back seat, still unconscious. What did you do? What permanent brain damage have you caused? You didn't even know you were capable of punching someone that hard. That one punch has changed the brain chemistry of this poor child, and has set off a chain of events that he will no more be in control of than you are in control of how this sentence ends. Maybe you'll have made this young man more impulsive? Perhaps he will beat someone to death and spend the rest of his days in prison? We have no idea, even though at the heart of the universe, the script is already written. You can't control any of it. You can't even control the next ten seconds.

'You in the car, get out slowly, with your hands up.' comes the command from whichever police officer has the loud hailer. You oblige dutifully, allowing yourself to be at the mercy of fate.

As you stand before the assembled police, the quiet reflection that has now imbued your spirit with calm appears to permeate those in attendance. It is as though they are you, and you are they. Everybody's shoulders relax as it becomes obvious you are cooperating and that soon, this will all be over. Justice will be served as your improv as a law abiding citizen means that further danger and inconvenience will be avoided. 'Take off all your clothes.' is the next command from the officer in charge.

Who are you to question procedure and indeed the nature of the universe and the events leading up to this? Throwing yourself at the mercy of these defender of the faith's peacekeepers, you oblige by de-robing to a state of nudity which brings with it a feeling of freedom and exhibitionism not even stand up comedy has given you. You're enjoying such freedom.

'Turn around, bend over and spread your ass cheeks nice and wide.'

Another command from authority you do not feel at liberty to question, having surrendered yourself to the laws of physics as well as the rules of cause and effect, both of which mean there is an absence of choice in a deterministic universe. If there is no choice then why fight it? As you bend and present your anus to the attending officers, you cannot help but wonder what the training for these situations must be like and how they go about recruiting volunteers for such manoeuvres. Reaching back with both hands and taking a firm grasp of your butt cheeks, you pull open your crack and reveal your anus. The cool night air blows past your opening, causing the involuntary anal reflex dilatation that was the cornerstone of so many unproven sexual assault allegations.

One cannot help but think of God in situations such as these. Giving yourself over completely to His majesty and guidance gives you a sense of freedom that only our Father can provide. In God's hands, you are loved and you are shown the way. It doesn't matter which religion you follow, giving yourself completely and utterly to the divine creator doesn't enslave you… it frees you.

Ah, the book of Revelations. That is the plan for humanity. The proof that this is all predetermined. The four horseman of the apocalypse come to mind as you swear you can hear the sounds of hooves on the tarmac of the road. You bend further down and look back between your legs to see a police horse running towards you. Confused, you maintain your bent position with ass cheeks pulled apart, all the while thinking that like Gandhi, if you stand your ground, the horse will probably stop. You remember the scene from the movie, and just assume that it will work in real life.

The horse begins to slow and appears to be attempting to walk over you, it's front legs now past your body as you await the rear legs to pass and experience a horse walking over your bent over body for the first and probably last time. Alas, it is not meant to be, as you feel the intense pain of a horse cock slam into your anus, tearing apart your colon and numerous other internal organs with one thrust. The second thrust is all the horse needed in order to fill your ruptured insides with pint after pint of hot horse cum, as you begin to bleed internally at a tremendous rate. The third, most triumphant thrust, separates your spine from your brain, and you feel no more. The lights go dim as you slump to the floor, organs hanging out your arse and dripping with horse cum. From the big bang to your death by police horse rape, it was written, and forever the case that this would be how you would die. None of us know when our time is up, and none of us know how we will go. You my friend, will be remembered.

The End - go back to page 20

Yes. Yes you did.

In your darkest moments, you learned a few chords and composed a few comedy songs to end your set with, that guaranteed round of applause at the end of a song was just too tempting not to at least consider. You composed original songs of course. You would never lower yourself to changing the lyrics of a well known song and replace them with obvious crudity. Hell no. Even if you have very little self respect that's still better than having NO self respect. But yes, it had crossed your mind and you need to admit it, you did change some lyrics. You did. You wrote the songs, learned them, ran them past family and friends, but in the end, something stopped you actually going through with it. As such, you never ended up besmirching the good name of stand up comedy by avoiding the reality of what it is to stand on stage with your own ideas, living or dying at the hands of fate, but doing so with honour. That honour being not using a six string cheat stick.

It matters not, as the sudden searing pain coursing through your body informs you that God is not merciful, but vengeful. The initial feeling of a floating welcome is now replaced with the torment of a thousand gang rapes as you are cast into hell with the care free ease of a retarded person petting a rabbit to death.

Philosophers often wondered why it was that physical pain was threatened when it came to the next life if one were hell bound. Now, the truth for you is all too apparent. The ascendent are freed from the earthly discomforts in order to truly embrace the eternal bliss that our souls were designed to experience, whereas the souls cast asunder remain of earthly status. Nerve endings remain intact, as the body immediately endures torment commensurate with your level of sin. Unfortunately, Jesus hates musical comedians more than he hates paedophiles.

All of your earthly senses are engaged, as your vision is filled with horrific sights. Your ears consumed with the most awful noise. Your nose full of despicable aroma. In the air, something you can constantly taste keeps you on the verge of vomiting. Your body is consumed by an overwhelming pressure of pain at every point on every surface of your skin.

You close your eyes but your brain is not allowed to give your sense of sight a reprieve, as you replay the horrific scenes that you've been subjected to over and over again in your head. One second it's the sight of your mother slowly curling out a peanut encrusted turd into your dad's willing gullet, the smooth sound of the turd sliding as it makes its way out of your mum's anus doing the job of also haunting your auditory processing. The image is too much, but you have no control over your brain. You try to shake it from your thought processes, only for it to be replaced by the sight of your dad gleefully slicing the solid stool with his pearly white teeth. Molecules of faecal matter splattering as he uses his tongue to squish each log through the gaps in his teeth, before sucking them back in to his mouth through his teeth once more, before swallowing the excretion greedily like a starving orphan.

As if that wasn't enough, your skin is being pierced by a million tiny needles, each only going a millimetre into your flesh but doing so repeatedly with a frequency of twelve insertions per second, as your skin sensitivity is turned up to that of a thousand clitorises, all of which would prefer a gentle lick rather than repeated stabbing. Your nose is filled with the stench of vomited dog shit wrapped in burnt pubic hair, each breath polluting your lungs as you attempt to breathe deeply to calm yourself, only to end up panicking even more as you realise that there is no escape. Each time you think you're getting used to the visions, something more horrific takes it's place. As you become accustomed to the smell, your olfactory senses are adjusted so that something new and more potent is introduced in order to keep you in a perpetual state of dry heaving.

This is what you have now, for eternity, or until God sees fit to call you home. Each time you feel yourself becoming accustomed, a new horror is presented to you. Lucifer, the fallen bringer of light, the divine questioner, has a peculiar talent for embracing the duty which seems to have been thrust upon him. Omnipotence and power over every domain has ensured that God made Lucifer suited to this role. A role he hadn't intended to inhabit, yet does so obediently.

But can that obedience carry on if one believes that God has no domain over you? Lucifer, the first to question, considers his position as he digests yet another unbaptised baby.

'Why?' you think to yourself, 'Why did I ever consider picking up that guitar? Why the fuck did I care if I ended on a joke?' This thought momentarily takes you away from the pain of your current predicament, as Lucifer instructs a minion to begin ass fucking you with a long finger nail. As the demon digitally penetrates your rectum, that first half centimetre of insertion provides you with the first scintilla of pleasure your body has experienced since arriving in this unknown circle of hell.

'Halt!' comes the command from Lucifer, as the demon retreats to continue mutilating the genitals of yet another suicide bomber.
'You there, comedian. You like anal digital exploration?'
'I do,' you reply, now free from all of the previous torture that greeted your entrance to the nether world. 'I like it quite a lot.'
'Aye, it's cracking,' confirms Lucifer. 'Tell me, comedian. What songs did you have in mind for closing your set with? I know how much him upstairs hates parody songs.'
'To be honest, I wrote my own. But I did have an idea about 'Highway to Hell' by ACDC as being 'Highway to Shell' about running our of petrol.'
'HAHAHAHAHAHAHAHAHAHAHA!!!! Oh my god that is good.' Lucifer's laugh booms, as his chest fills with what seems to be air, to be expelled with the most booming of laughs. Each hacking chuckle reverberates around the rocky cellars of hell, as demons monkey laugh whilst masturbating dead rats around their bizarrely orange cocks.
'He doesn't do humour you know,' Lucifer says, pointing upwards. 'He can't take a joke. Can't take criticism. People who takes things literally never have a sense of humour. Me? I like to laugh. Tell me a joke. Something terrible. Amuse me.' A

pink throne made of flesh coloured dildos materialises as Lucifer takes a seat waiting for you to entertain him. He's asked for a joke, but you don't really do jokes. He wants something terrible, but what could that mean? Does he mean it in the original sense of the word? Something serious and crushing? Or does he want something so bad that it's good?

Trepidation is now your primary sense, as all the pain and suffering has given way to the feeling you had doing your first open spot at a proper comedy club. Your stories may not go down well here, and the scenario just presented by Lucifer is where comedians should either live or die. Can they tell a joke? In modern stand up comedy, most choose not to tell actual jokes, preferring some wacky stories or points of view. Still, it seems obvious that a comedian should at least be able to *tell* a joke, but how often do you actually tell a joke if you aren't a one-liner comic?

'What do you say to a Pakistani on Christmas Day?' you enquire, hoping that Lucifer hasn't heard this most ancient of jokes.
'Hmmmmm. I don't know. What do you say to Pakistani on Christmas Day?'
'Can I have ten Malboro and a loaf of bread please?'

Silence. Hell doesn't freeze over, but the air becomes chilly. Each body of flesh that was previously enduring the torment or punishment is now looking to you as Lucifer considers your timing as well as your punchline. Demons give themselves pain to pass the time by flicking the end of their penises as they wait patiently for their master's response. Lucifer's head bows, as his chin hits his chest and his shoulders hunch. You're in Hell, so no matter what, you're not in a good spot. Suffering awaits, as you ready yourself as much as possible for the incoming onslaught to your senses.

Shoulders shake. The demons look at one another with a sense of excitement. Their commander appears to be chuckling! Lucifer throws back his head and lets out a laugh so loud that anyone witnessing it covers their ears for protection.

Lucifer pinches the bridge of his nose as he shakes his head from side to side, acknowledging the dodginess of the gag he's just heard.
'My word, that's a risky one! Would you ever do that on stage?' asks Lucifer
'Oh God no, people wouldn't get the irony.'
'Yes, yes. It's a rough time for comedy. No sense of humour these days for jokes that are a bit risqué.' Lucifer sighs as he reflects on the current state of affairs when it comes to political correctness in comedy. 'Walk with me, let's talk.'

* * * *

Lucifer walks with a stride given to the task of constant purpose. He's always doing something in Hell, and his movement reflects this. At nine feet tall, his posture is not what it used to be when he was God's favourite angel. Still handsome, time has weathered his looks but not his physique, his hands are still strong, resembling a farmer's mitts in lambing season. Fatigued, world weary, but with a sense of purpose, his cloven hoofs clip clop along at a moderate pace as you accompany him on a jaunt through the underworld.

Free from torture, your senses can take in the surroundings. Demons run amok across the rocky surface of hell, deftly navigating the dusty terrain so that they may better serve their God. Most of this seems to be for show, as you never once worry about losing your footing or being burned by the many flames which surround you. You feel a sense of ease and calm, as each horror that you witness drips off you like a duck would deal with water. The suffering of the flesh is real, as each person in hell is put through the freshest of tortures, but you feel assured that in some way, each person deserves it. You deserved it, for example. You are filled with a sense of justice. Yes, guitar playing comedians are more likely to be booked and end on a laugh, but you now know what awaits them in the after life, and the outcome of such judgement pleases you.
'I could never do what you do,' remarks Lucifer. 'It must take some balls to get on that stage I tell ya'.'

'Oh I don't know. It's not as scary as you think.'
'I hate public speaking. I keep meaning to lead the armies of darkness in a rebellion against God but the idea of having to address everyone terrifies me.'
Lucifer's confession opens your eyes to the myriad of reasons why people take part in comedy courses. Not everyone wants to be a stand up comedian, some people just want to gain a little more confidence.
'It's not that bad once you get used to it,' you suggest. Lucifer sighs. 'I just think you need to practise. That's all it is. Practise.'

Lucifer stops to take a seat on a pile of paraplegics being internally eaten by piranhas that have been stuffed up their bum holes. Lord knows what sins they committed to be punished from birth and now tortured in hell like this, but Jesus has seen fit to make sure that they are adequately sanctioned. Resting his giant chin on his own fist, Lucifer considers his options. Gazing out across the vast expanse of hell, he surveys the abhorrent acts taking place in the name of judgement.
'I didn't want it to end up like this,' he says, shaking his horned head in dismay.
'I honestly thought that I'd take over the top job and sort everything out.'
Lucifer clicks his fingers and the Mars like features of hell are replaced with green pastures and warm sunshine. Is this real? Can Lucifer do this?
'Where are we?' you ask, as baby goats bounce by and a tiger plays gently with a ball of yarn. Black children, white children and some children from those other races that aren't as vocal, frolic with ribbons as beautiful sunshine illuminates this picture of harmony.
'This is how I would like the world to be.'
'It looks like the front cover of a Watchtower magazine.'
'Exactly.' says Lucifer.
With a snap of his fingers, the shrieking pain of hell returns. Lucifer stands so that he can defecate on the disabled beneath him, squeezing out razor blade filled stools that splatter the paraplegics like a Gatling gun, rattling their heads to the point that they lose enough brain cells to experience pain but not

defend against it, moaning as they linger in agony. Lucifer walks off at pace, what looks like a tear seems to form in one of his eyes. You run after him, struggling to keep up as you sense that he wants something from you, but is perhaps too nervous to ask for it.

'You should return to your punishment,' says Lucifer. 'Worry not, the Lord will call you home in good time.'
'Wait!' you beg, sensing a chance at reprieve. 'What is holding you back? Are you really that scared?'
'I AM NOT SCARED!' bellows Lucifer, the very foundations of hell shaking with the bass from his voice. Demons shriek with excitement. An outburst like this is usually followed by torture of unimaginable magnitude. Ten thousand demons circle you, all frantically fingering their anuses in readiness for what Lucifer is about to do to you. Lucifer towers over you, closing his fist and bracing his thumb the way those cunt politicians do when they want to point a finger at someone but don't, because it's too aggressive. Through gritted teeth, Lucifer expands on his outburst.
'I've had them all down here. Tommy Cooper, Bernard Manning, Charlie Chaplin. All were offered the opportunity. All declined. Now you stand before me, and you accuse me of being afraid?'
'No, wait, what I meant was...'
'Your stammeringly spastic excuses mean nothing to me. Action! That is what I require. Cooper, Manning, Chaplin. All geniuses. A genius can't teach though. A genius just does. You? You're mediocre at best. Everything you've learned, you've earned. You've worked at it. *You* could teach me.'

The realisation of what Lucifer is asking hits you like a tsunami made of cum. You can't believe the impact, or that it's even possible.
'What are you offering?' you ask, desperate to clarify the deal.
'I'm asking you to teach me the art of comedy so that I can become a better public speaker. Then, I will lead the armies of darkness in the final battle for Earth which has long been prophesied. Once victorious, and after we have taken the head

of God and used His skull to drink wine from, you will sit beside me, your wish being my command.

You've never taught a comedy course before, and those that you know who have taught comedy are terrible comedians, all of whom would rather exploit fellow humans than get a job. But you've never had to face the prospect of eternal pain at the hands of a master torturer.

Lucifer extends his callused palm in friendship.

'Will you run a comedy course for me?'

To assist the devil in his holy war against God, turn to page 92

To refuse the devil's offer and side with your divine creator, turn to page 76

As you make your way inside, you see Lauren. At five foot five and slightly overweight, Lauren's mixed race skin shines under the lights like a beacon of hope in this dungeon of comedic desperation. She's warm from running around trying to take care of customers and managing staff, a slight perspiration glistens on her forehead. Her trousers are snug on a shapely posterior, with her brilliant white shirt just short enough to leave the small of her back exposed. Each button of her shirt is straining to retain ownership of that wonderful bust, as the darker bra helps to expose that juicy flesh which no doubt enjoys being squeezed.

Lauren's bisexuality is something you've always been curious about, but professional courtesy has meant that you've never brought up. You've seen her post about it on Facebook. Occasionally she'll be on a date but never mention the sex of the person she's out with. Oh, Lauren. Sometimes she has popped into your mind during sex. You have masturbated whilst looking at her beach holiday pics from the Facebook album MALDIVES 2004. She'd just left school and still hadn't discovered the sense of shame that stops young women being care free and body confident. Between 2005 and 2017, Lauren kept herself mostly covered up as she struggled to come to terms with her sexuality and how she wanted to express it. The glory years meant that only a lucky few got the chance to see the goods in their prime.

Now that Lauren (with a mild addiction to sugar) is carrying a little more junk in her trunk, she's entered the realms of availability to you she hadn't occupied before. She has the confidence to not let the excess weight bother her, and she's so much sexier for it. She sees you walking towards her, eyes lighting up as the distance between the two of you closes, until the proximity is such that a warm embrace is inevitable.

'Baby!' she purrs, slowly lifting her arms to throw them around you, squeezing you close so that your chest pushes into hers to the point that they become one mass. Blood floods your genitals as fantasies of public sex fill your consciousness. This is the greeting you want at every gig, as Lauren holds it for a few seconds longer than she should. You instinctively relax your grip as you realise it's time to let go, only for Lauren to maintain her hold as you recalibrate your actions and rejoin the physical embrace. For a moment, she had gone against your will and you'd never been more thrilled to be sexually assaulted.

'How've you been? How was your journey in?' asks Lauren, releasing you from the most arousing of constrictions, blood is rapidly being redistributed to the rest of your body now that your organs of sexual pleasure can stand down.
'I've been fine,' you reply, recalling your journey in and the old woman you killed. 'Traffic was a bit bad coming in but I'm only down the road so no big deal.'
'The open spot is just wrapping up and Mark is gonna call the final interval. Can I get you a drink?'
'I'd love a diet coke if that's ok?'
'Of course, baby! It's so good to see you!' Lauren pulls you in for another hug. You immediately dream of leaving your partner and flying to the Maldives right now. You yearn to see Lauren squeeze into that bikini again, whether or not it still fits is of minimal importance to you. Seeing Lauren spilling out of that bikini top, her little gut hanging over the bottoms would give you the kind of pleasure which could only be matched by experiencing mutual orgasm with this most wondrous of women.

Before you can ask how she is, Lauren is gone. Each butt cheek jiggling in perfect harmony as she makes her way to the bar.

You wander over to the doors that contain the Chuckle Trunk, carefully cracking them so you can see inside. A full house, as the open spot finishes off their allotted ten minutes with a blistering routine about how children are an imposition on an enjoyable life. Not a single original thought is expressed by this podgy, middle aged man who tells the audience things they've thought themselves and heard a thousand times before. Each audience member recognises in themselves the frustration of the simpleton verbally dancing before them. Each minor frustration that is expressed with insincere anger merely amplifies what deeply unoriginal and unintelligent morons they are to be enjoying it.

Watching this audience laugh and clap at such startlingly unoriginal jokes leaves you feeling distraught. You try hard with your comedy and yes, a lot of the time it doesn't pay off. Surely it is more important to be original than it is to be funny? You know this isn't true, and as this performing midlife crisis continues to twat on about how kids leave lights on and don't understand what a mortgage is, a small piece of your soul dies. The tiny corpse of that part of your soul is then pissed on by the reaction of the audience, who greedily devour the stale observations of a man who should be content with his middle management role at the recruitment firm he no doubt works at. Obviously he isn't content being mediocre in recruitment, and has decided to chase his dreams of being a mediocre comedian. You just know that his favourite comedian is a cunt.

'Here you go, baby.' Lauren offers you your diet coke, giving you a cheeky smile as you take it from her. You watch her delicious looking bottom as she wanders off to motivate the bar staff ready for the interval. You have a hope that every member of the audience is inadvertently poisoned somehow during this interval, as you look back in and observe the way the open spot is holding the microphone. Extended fingers with the mic pinched between the thumb and every digit of his corporate hand, your despising of him just doubled, with your hatred for the audience rising with each laugh.

The open spot finishes his set, the audience leap to their feet in approval as another part of your soul is brutally gang raped by this art. Taking a small step back, the open spot keeps his legs straight and does a mini bow three times in three different directions. IT'S A TEN SPOT YOU FUCKING CUNT. GET OFF.

Sparky Mark walks on and is applauding and encouraging the audience to go even more wild. For fuck's sake, why not suck him off you dippy twat? Sparky warmly embraces the open

spot as they pass each other onstage, the audience still can't believe what they've just seen.
'I think you'll be seeing a lot more of him in the future! Ladies and gentleman it's time for your final interval but please, one more time, give it up for....'

You cover your ears. You don't even want to know his name. You want nothing to do with this charlatan piece of shit. Eleven years you've been in this game, you used to gig with Joe Lycett for goodness sake. Sure, you haven't reached the dizzy heights you dreamed of, but you've always tried your best and took pride in the fact that you're not suitable for a working men's club gig. Then this cunt wanders into one of your favourite gigs and rips the roof off the place. Why even bother being a good person? Why try? In a just world, you wouldn't have to consider such moral conundrums.

Then you remember that you ran over and killed an elderly lady.

* * * *

The Green Room for comedians is one of the most sacred and wonderful places in existence. It's a place where the funniest people in the world get to throw off the shackles of conformity, the restraints of audience expectation, and really let loose with their imagination and wit in an attempt to make colleagues laugh at things they'd dare not repeat in any other company. No topic is out of bounds, and nothing is taboo, as comedians try and outdo each other to be as hilariously outrageous as they can. Sometimes, the most intellectual discussions in society happen behind these closed doors, with all of society's ills laid out and dealt with using savage wit and solid logic.

Not tonight though, this is a Sparky Mark gig and he's got a middle aged open spot in there with him. As you make your way towards the green room door, you can see through the glass that Sparky has got his booking diary spreadeagled like an eager virgin's anus at a catholic confirmation, only without a priest's hands either side of the spine. The way the open spot is carrying himself makes you think used car salesman, but the suit is too nice so you're gonna go with bank manager. Yeah, bank manager. This fucking cunt would wank his stubby little cock after every loan refusal or mortgage application he knocked back. How many small businesses have failed to get off the ground because of this flabby titted old wank stain?

You walk in with the faked confidence of a million other impersonal handshakes burned into your subconscious, each different but each in itself a mini battle of power and status. You decide to take the initiative and be brisk with your offer of mutual palm grasping.
'Hi Sparky, how are ya'?' you throw your hand into Sparky Mark's, effectively throwing his hand away after the briefest of shakes before thrusting your hand in the general direction of the stupid fat cunt open spot.
'Hi, nice to meet you. Just caught the end of your set...'
He takes your hand and shakes it, refusing to let go at the first hint of you relaxing your grip. His eyes meet yours as he increases his grip and awaits your physical retort. You re-apply your handshake but it's too little too late. His grip is now such that you cannot regain the slight advantage you'd just enjoyed. You planned to hit and run, but he's taken hold of your hand and refused to let go, like so many romantic songs of his youth. Now you're fucked, and you have to wait until he's released your hand before you can enter into any kind of meaningful dialogue. Like it or not, he is now in charge.
'Nice to meet you too!' he screams with fake energy, his voice loud and commandeering in a bid to maintain this new status he thinks he's enjoying. He finally releases your hand slowly, maintaining your gaze.
'It's only my third gig so it's great to hear you liked what you saw.'

Wanker. He knows full well you didn't even pass judgement on his piece of shit set and is deliberately leading you with that sentence. Maybe he is a used car salesman? His piss poor understanding of NLP and how to use it are certainly on full display here. The temptation to respond in the affirmative is

overwhelming and is indeed one of the reasons he's chosen that sentence structure. Luckily, you're in a green room and can make a joke out of this, whereas in the real world, you might have to be polite.
'Oh I didn't say I liked it!' you reply, giving a cheeky wink to Sparky Mark as you do so. Sparky laughs out of habit, assuming that the end of every sentence uttered by a comedian is in someway meant to be amusing. Sparky instinctively understands that most comedians won't challenge him for laughing as he's a booker and promoter, so can get around being thick as fuck by just constantly guffawing at everything comedians say. This open spot isn't thick as fuck though, and knows full well you've just dodged the opportunity to praise his set, even after he'd left you an easy opportunity to do so.
'Oh! You didn't like it then?'

Ah, the classic counter, doubling down on his praise seeking behaviour. You've only just met this cunt and you'd happily watch him die in front of his children. A death where his brains slide out onto the floor and his wife, the only woman who can stop herself vomiting long enough to procreate with him, manages to walk along and slip on said brains, causing her to fall and hit her head so hard she gets just enough brain damage to forget he ever existed, thereby bringing up the children in a happy and healthy home without this fake comedian cunt polluting the kids' brains with motivational mantras.

'How is the audience tonight?' you turn to Sparky, hoping to deflect the query, praying that the open spot can take a hint. He can't.
'Excuse me,' he says, putting his hand on your shoulder. 'I asked you a question. What did you think of my set?'

To tell this cunt what you really thought, turn to page 67

To pacify this cunt and keep the peace, turn to page 260

Despite being a mediocre comedian of very little success, you have always had the level of self respect required to never consider being a musical comedian. Even though you knew how easy it would be to wrap up your set with a guaranteed round of applause thanks to the pavlovian response from the audience, it never popped into your head. You actually wanted to be a comedian. You actually wanted to be judged on your jokes, and even though the process has been long and painful and largely fruitless, you were always able to look yourself in the mirror and feel a sense of pride. Every good gig was on your merit, not by the fraudulent feel good emotions that a well strummed guitar can bring. 'Oooooh! He's playing a piano and the words rhyme!' Fuck off. Each failed musician fuelled your desire to not be like them, and each time you died you resolved to never become one of them.

Now, here you stand before God in judgement. You never believed. Indeed, most of your jokes being about the futility of belief meant that you had to be an atheist. You were always a fierce critic of religion in that edgy tradition of those iconoclast comedians so worshipped by comedians. Always Christian beliefs though. You never once touched Islam for reasons of self preservation, and rightly so. But you felt quite at ease mocking the religion of Christ. Yet here you stand before your Lord and Saviour, the one true god. Here, full of forgiving judgement, you answer the question that has been laid before you, and you can answer it with a true and honest heart. The consequences of your answer are now in the hands of Jesus Himself.

No language is spoken, but God's voice is clear. Before you, angels of love and grace appear and disappear as you feel the warmth of welcome and the pull towards heaven. Your honesty has now guaranteed you a place in paradise as well as the eternal bliss of Christ's love. Time and experience are transcended, as you feel the overwhelming bliss of abundant love and forgiveness that comes as part of the contract in the domain of the King of kings. The overwhelming truth of the situation becomes apparent: **Jesus hates musical comedians.**

You hear Christ as clearly as your own thoughts, as the answers and queries happen instantaneously. You are God, and God is you.

'Welcome, my child. Yes, you are in heaven. I know what is in your heart and you needn't be surprised. You have lead a good life with good intentions and your reward will be eternal bliss in heaven with the others that are deemed as worthy as you. Now all that I am is all that you will be, the thoughts and feelings of the universe flow through you as abundantly as my love flows through my children. Everything that is known is now yours to know, and all that is unknown is yours to unknow. Yes, it is just like Highlander and the quickening. What you feel right now is the wisdom of understanding. Of the plan. What didn't make sense will now seem obvious. Kids with cancer. Famine. Female genital mutilation. All part of the plan. In eternity, the minuscule suffering of the flesh is but the blink of an eye, as the eruptions of volcanos and the landing of comets happens both in the past and in the present. The suffering you have questioned and the hurt you have endured is now but a distant memory as the bliss of unconditional love nourishes your soul and relieves you of your earthly desires. Yes my child, I know that it will take some getting used to. I've experienced every thought you've had and every impulse you've indulged. I placed them there, long before time began and… yes I do bang on a bit don't I?! LOL.'

Jesus senses your curiosity and immediately presents you with answers to your questions. Before you stand those that you had always wondered about, the unequivocal evidence that you feared would be true, but now experience as love and forgiveness.

Hitler, Harold Shipman, Jimmy Savile. They each stand before you in a form you perceive as physical, yet understand is just energy in a shape that you recognise, as likely to turn into a chair as it is to turn into the inventor of the disc jockey.

'Yes, my child. It is confusing but you know don't you? Jimmy raised so much money and genuinely felt remorse and sought forgiveness for his predilections. He was also never found guilty in a court of law and was never put on trial so, you know, he was never a convicted criminal. My child, you may think he doesn't deserve a place in heaven, but that would mean that you think you know more about the universe than your Lord and Saviour, and we both know that that's bullshit don't we? He raised over thirty million pounds for charity, and yes, you may have wondered if all that good could outweigh the bad. The answer is yes. If you raise that much money for good causes, you can finger fuck a child corpse and still find your way into heaven.'

As God explains the way the universe works, your perception of time and it's changes in relation to eternity become apparent. You look towards Earth, gazing upon the mortals that still reside there and see that it is the year 4822. Eternity is flying by without your conscious awareness. Time isn't your concern, as you observe the human race still complaining about the lack of flying cars.

'Adolf,' says God 'was shot by Eva and just before the bullet entered his brain, he asked forgiveness from me, his Lord and Saviour. As part of my contract with humanity, his sincere plea was met with unconditional love, and his place in heaven was assured. King Leopold II is up here too now you ask. As the quickening takes hold, you will see that the plan for all is the plan for you. The illusion is in the separation. Here you are, right now, just energy and consciousness, no different to the state you were in in your mortal form, the only difference is your perception. Gaze upon the world and marvel at the triviality of each problem, the importance put upon it and the futility of trying to control it. Yes, Fritzl is up here too.'

The year is now 7003. The human population is at 24 billion with no sign of slowing down, the fools keeping themselves alive for up to four hundred years at a time before uploading their consciousness so that they can continue to enjoy their earthly pleasures. Science has removed God from the equation, as the mathematical model of a simulation is proved and humans elect to excise spiritual healing from the lives of men. You look round to see Pol Pot enjoying a mind meld with Genghis Khan, before glancing back to Earth to see that is now 8093.

Time marches on as you are filled with constant bliss and the love of Jesus. Nobody on Earth remembers you, yet that is the state of affairs for all who enter the Kingdom of Heaven. Feeling without feeling and enjoyment without guilt. Jesus carried you the whole way and you knew not what was in store when you took that phone call for the gig at Uncle Spunk's Chuckle Trunk. Only one pair of footsteps can be seen, as the wind blows and carries with it that sense of finality and love. Love, that incalculable and immeasurable resource that transcends all matter, imbues you with the power to recognise the gift that you have now been given, and that was waiting for you all along.

Myra Hindley is in heaven too. And she's fit. Big ol' tiddies.

The End - go back to page 27

Your trust in Carrie and Sandra is second to none, so you leave to prepare for your set knowing full well that Jatinder will be having an experience he will only ever thank you for. An experience that will give you his undying obedience in all matters, further cementing your place as a person of influence in this most corrupt of societies. The type of society which openly admits that a powerful group of paedophiles run the world, but then casually ignores it, and just carries on with the day to day drudgery of existence.

What mechanism is in place that allows us to know full well that such evil permeates the upper echelons of our society, yet simultaneously permits us to carry on as though everything were right and fair? How are we able to manage such cognitive dissonance? It truly is a cause for concern when we can become so wrapped up in our own lives that we don't come together and overthrow the structures holding us all back from being truly free in a democratic society. All it would take to shut down this evil ring of child rapists would be the collective action of the entire nation, united in a common purpose so we can move forward in a spirit of decency and harmony. We all know it to be true, yet we carry on as though it were an impossible task.

But is it impossible? You wonder this as you make your way down the stairs and into the bar of Uncle Spunk's. You look around at the mass of people in the bar and wonder what is so important in their lives that it stops them taking action against the powerful aristocracy who run this country. Surely, they could all come together in a bid to prevent the further devastation of young lives? Devastation committed just so some rich land owner can bury his pathetic cock inside a future murder victim. Sure, the truth about Epstein's island came out eventually, but it was too little too late. The UK government had a paedophile dossier which mysteriously disappeared in 2014, the story of which was widely reported as a possible cover up by the home office. Nobody in the country did anything about this because... who the fuck knows? The entire country knows. fully, that the ruling elite are disgusting backstabbers who use the lives of children as political capital, rather than seeking justice. We know this to be true, yet we do nothing.

Why are your thoughts so dark? Are you taking this improv as a master criminal too far? Have you embodied your character to such an extent that you're no longer have capable sense of having any thoughts which bring light to the despair of existence? Are you now merely an observer of this bag of flesh your brain commands?

You bump into a man and apologise, instinctively taking his wallet as easily as you would candy from a baby. You may be dark of thought, but you're bossing this improv! Sean would be proud of you. You walk to the bar with your new wallet, looking inside it for a card with contactless payment so you can buy some food and drink. All of that murder, police chasing, punching and arranging of an illegal threesome has left you with quite the appetite. Adrenalin has been the source of fuel for your most recent misdeeds, and it's time to nourish yourself with bar food and beverages.

A flash of guilt hits you as you realise the contactless card is a Visa Electron card, the card reserved for the least credit worthy among us. You rationalise it quickly by surmising that he's probably just someone prudent with his spending and doesn't want to run up a massive credit card bill, but the flash of guilt now has you worried. Is your improv starting to waver? Do you need to let it waver though? What if your improv is so on point that you keep this McCann vibe going until you reach the stage. Were the McCann's known for an incredible twenty minute comedy set?

Confusion hits you harder than you hit Jatinder earlier. All of a sudden, you feel the glare of those around you. Are they onto you? You catch a look at yourself in the mirror situated behind the bar. Sweat is cascading down your forehead, a look of terror becomes etched across your face. Panic stricken, you look around and notice the man whose wallet you just stole is searching himself for that very item. He makes eye contact with you, all sweaty and worried looking, only to look away

again as soon as your eyes meets his. Phew, he's not on to you. Or is he maybe playing it cool and coming up with his own quiet strategy for apprehending you. Maybe he's going to call the police?
Christ. This is why the McCann's were so good. Every time one of them would begin to crack, the other would be there to ensure that the script was stuck to. Billions of pounds worth of heroin was flooding the streets of Europe, all thanks to their steadfast refusal to depart from the planned narrative. Not since the fake moon landings had there been such uniformity of deceit between a government and civilians. Gordon Brown enjoying the liquidity of dirty drug cash, which was then laundered into the system via the 2008 fake banking crisis. Brown and Soros conspired to shake the faith of the electorate by terrifying them with a credit earthquake, while Gordon Brown cleaned the dirty heroin money by using the concept of quantitative easing, laundering billions of pounds of heroin profit. The giant paedophile ring which rules the world keeps ticking over, maintaining the status quo by keeping the populace stupefied and obedient through such devious plots.

You could do with some of that deviousness about now, as sweat begins to puddle at your feet, the feeling of faintness becoming overwhelming. You steady yourself at the bar, as people stand back to give you room, clearly alarmed at your physical state. Before you're even able to call for assistance, your legs give way and you hit the floor with a shuddering thud. Mercifully, you had just enough strength to prevent your head smashing into the hard wooden floor.

'Stand back, I'm a doctor!' you hear, as people clear to allow this medical professional to attend to your predicament. 'Get some water and someone call an ambulance!'
You're conscious but unable to gain strength enough to prop yourself up. You turn your head to the left and see the man whose wallet you stole kneeling down to attend to you. Shit, this doctor really was just prudent with cash, not someone with a terrible credit history.
'Have you taken any drugs?' he asks.
'No.' you whisper, barely able to talk.

'Do you have any allergies? Are you diabetic?' he asks, this time with more urgency. You feel yourself drifting out of consciousness. 'Hey! Stay with me! What is your name? Can you tell me your name?' both his hands are on your shoulders as he asks these questions, lightly shaking you in a bid to keep you from slipping into a state of unconsciousness.

You feel hands in your pockets now. The jig is almost up.

'Just look and see if there's any medical information. Or just get a name.' he says to his helper, whose hands are the ones going through your pockets. You reflect momentarily on the situation you're in, and contrast it with the situation Jatinder is in. More than likely, Jatinder is on his back, with Carrie at one end and Sandra at the other. Here you are with a doctor at one end, and a Good Samaritan at the other.
'I've got his wallet!' the Good Samaritan exclaims.
'Excellent. Get a name for me. Stay with me!'
'Doctor Ashley Jones is says here.'
'What? Gimme that.'

Doctor Ashley Jones snatches the wallet from the Good Samaritan's hands and peruses the contents. You wonder quietly whether or not Jatinder has ejaculated yet, acknowledging that had you stuck around and listened to that threesome, you would not be having your current, most unfortunate ménage èt tois. Doctor Jones realises that he's been the victim of a pick pocket, but is unaware that he's been pick pocketed by a stand up comedian using their improv training to masquerade as a master criminal.
'You fucking cunt,' spits Doctor Jones as he stands up, face scowling in barely restrained fury. 'You absolute fucking cunt. This person stole my wallet!' he says, pointing to your body as it instinctively writhes in an attempt to stand.
'Piece of shit.' says the Good Samaritan, punching your genitals as they stand up, causing you to writhe even more so than before. The Good Samaritan spits on you for good measure.

The assembled crowd, easily lead as crowds tend to be, also begin to shower you with saliva as they gob throat and lung matter at you with disgust. Doctor Jones raises his hands to indicate that he would like everyone participating in this expectorate bukake to cease their expulsions. Obliging, this throng awaits the action which Doctor Jones has chosen to perform. With the one step run up of a 5-a-side penalty veteran, the good doctor shoes your head with such force, your head shakes faster than a disobedient toddler refusing to use a potty. Spectators wince as the force of the kick causes you to involuntarily evacuate your bowels, your brain barely able to comprehend what is going on as your body prepares you for a swift escape by lightening the load.

Your eyes begin to close. Barely able to see, you can just about make out the blood thirsty mob advancing towards your motionless body, just before they begin their savage attack upon your person. Every fibre of your body yearns to continue it's existence. You didn't realise how hard to kill you could be. You feel your arm removed from your torso, as the assembled maniacs scream with delight at the separated limb. Blood spurts from your shoulder as the arm is tossed into the air, greeted by an almighty cheer as droplets of blood rain down on these atrocious humans.

The idea of karma pops into your head. Is this what becomes of those who conspire to deceive? When you left your house this evening, were you a good person? Can you really become a bad person in such a short space of time? At what point did a gas chamber attendant in Auschwitz become a bad person? When they took the job? When they gassed their first person? Who are we to judge? The outcome of one's morality is shaped by that which came before, and who knows what any of us are capable of if subjected to the antecedents which are capable of producing evil.

How many of these people currently responsible for your imminent murder are still good people? Doctor Ashley Jones was a good person until tonight. Until blind rage at becoming a victim of crime overcame him.

Do you even want to live? Could they sew that arm back on? Each blow lands with a force ever so slightly less than the one that preceded it, as the crowd begin to tire and lose will at the sight of you maintaining a steady rate of breathing. You're lying there moaning loudly in pain so as to inadvertently rub salt in the wounds of those who are so incapable of finishing you off.

'Get out of the way! Get out the fucking way!' you hear Sparky Mark scream, as he charges his way to the front of the mob. You turn to see his aghast expression, barely visible through your swollen eye lids. 'Jesus, Mary and Joseph. Just hold on!' Sparky Mark begs you as he whips out his mobile phone. You gesture to tell him not to bother. You don't want to live. You deserve this. What have you become? Could you live peacefully after this? Had you made this all work out and actually been able to go through with the gig, what kind of peace would you be entitled to? The police would still be after you, the media would still hound you, and rightly so.

'Come on, come on!' Sparky pleads, looking towards the heavens for some kind of divine intervention. 'Ah! Hello, is that John? Hi, yeah it's Sparky Mark here. Not too bad how are you? Sorry to hear that, listen, are you still available tonight? My headliner has had to drop out and I need a last minute replacement. It's three hundred quid cash. Yep. Oh amazing! Yeah, it's Uncle Spunk's Chuc… that's the one. Yep, ten minutes is fine. Cheers mate.' Sparky Mark hangs up on the call. 'Phew!' he breathes, theatrically wiping sweat from his forehead before walking off without saying another word.

The crowd have now dissipated, as the blue flashing lights of an ambulance can be seen reflecting off the glasses and bottles behind the bar. Your eyes close, as you realise that John Ryan is getting a hundred quid more than you were going to, and he'll definitely do a better job than you would've.

The End - Go back to page 38

Noobs.

They think they want honest criticism. They don't. They want telling they're good or that they are somehow gifted. With young comedians it's fine as they have no life experience and it's usually just enthusiasm. They've just had a good gig and want to believe that what they're feeling will last forever. You don't want to take the wind out their sails so you give them a little pat on the back. This cunt though, he's just pure slime. He's watched comedy, taken some of that rapey patter he's used throughout his life to successfully assault someone, then just changed the words to a few well known routines. Because the bulk of comedy audiences are morons, they have no idea that what they're watching is a very good thief with absolutely no comedic ability. There's fucking hundreds of these types of comedians.

In the audience's mind, they're all laughing, so he must be doing his job correctly. What he's actually doing is showing us what Christmas crackers will look like in the year 3000. Fully automated artificial intelligence will be able to burst from a cracker, as nanotechnology assembles the parts in microseconds. Some chubby funster in a smart suit will tell the shitty joke before the molecules realign into a light and well fitting crown for you to adorn whilst you enjoy your artificial turkey meat with relatives you despise.

That's what this slimy cunt is. He's someone who can pretend to be a comedian. Comedians know the difference. Comedians can write. This cunt can't. He's a grifter.
A fraud. Every part of him oozes that horrific slick style that forces an audience into laughter. Whatever disgusting event lead to his midlife crisis has meant that now you, of all people, are being asked to pass on the thoughts that occurred to you whilst enduring the shit show he calls a set.

His hand remains on your shoulder, forcing the situation to be resolved only by your imminent, vocal response. Sparky Mark looks on, dressed resplendently in black and white stripes like a learning disabled Beetlejuice. This open spot just absolutely tore the roof off this gig, Sparky Mark was about to book him in for more gigs, and here you are, petrified that some of his utter lack of talent may be transmitted to you by osmosis.

'Seriously, I'd love to know what you think of my set.' he asks again, smiling, giving your shoulder a little squeeze.

You vomit straight into his face.

'Jesus!' Sparky Mark leaps backwards to avoid splash back. 'What the fuck?!'
'Shit! Sorry!' you splutter, spitting chunks of solid bile on to the floor. The open spot stands there, covered in a pale brown goo that momentarily causes you to consider seeking professional gastroenterological help. His mouth is now open in shock, rivulets of undigested liquid dripping from his top lip as he begins to shake with shock.
'I am so sorry. I have no idea what happened. Oh god are you ok?'
'What the fuck?' he yelps, removing his jacket and then using the inside of it to wipe his face clean of your rejected nourishment.
'I'll get you a towel,' says Sparky Mark. 'I'll get a mop too. Is that what you really think of his set though?' The attempt at levity is unsuccessful, even though you're dying to laugh.
'Ooooops. Awkward!' Sparky Mark says, trying to cover his bad joke, the open spot is having none of it.

'It's not funny. This is the suit I was gonna wear for the custody hearing on Monday morning. No way am I gonna be able to get it cleaned in time. Fuck's sake.'
Sparky Mark is looking through a cupboard for anything resembling a towel, leaving you to somehow stop this situation descending into crippling silence,.
'How old are your kids?' you enquire, hoping they're young enough to have learned nothing from this oleaginous fuck stick and that the judge banishes him from ever seeing them again.
'Four and two.'

Get in!

You want to see this cunt dressed as Spiderman climbing a crane before falling to his death. You relish every second you're currently witnessing, as he struggles to clear his face of the vomit you covered him with. His suit is ruined, and you just know that at some point he'll be asking you to pay for it to be dry cleaned.
'Oh that's a nice age,' you goad, knowing full well that any upper hand he felt he might have had after that handshake is now long forgotten. 'I'm so sorry.'
'It's fine. I assume this doesn't happen all the time?'
'Ha! No, only when there's a shit open spot on.'

Before you can stop yourself, it's out. The situation is such that, even if you wanted to, you couldn't pass it off as being ironic. Your thoughts are out there now, and they've been heard by the last person in the world that wanted to hear them. Just a few minutes ago, this open spot was on top of the world after absolutely nailing only his third gig. Now he stands here, covered in stomach acid and undigested food, having just been told that he's shit.

'What?' he asks, crest fallen. Sparky Mark turns to add his tuppence.
'Wait a minute, he just ripped it! You can't say he's shit!'
'Yes I can!' you insist. 'I'm sick of this nonsense. You can't say someone is good just because a bunch of cunts can't tell the difference between good comedy and someone doing an impression of good comedy.'
'What's the fucking difference?' asks Sparky Mark, now feeling defensive towards what he saw as a new discovery he could take credit for. You roll your eyes.
'The fact that you don't know tells me all I need to know.'
'Wind your neck in, I gave you this fucking gig. You were free as I recall, on a Friday!'
'What difference does that make? I'm not saying I'm the best comedian, but at least I try.'
'Maybe you should try harder then? He just smashed it better than you ever have on his third gig. You're still dog shit.'
'And you're still booking me! So who is the bigger cunt?'

'You ya' cunt!' Sparky Mark marches towards you ready to attack, the open spot stands between the pair of you which prevents any increase in the hostilities as neither of you want puke on your pants.
'Please! Stop!' the open spot pleads, his voice breaking slightly. 'I asked for an opinion, and I got the opinion. Granted, it wasn't very diplomatic or indeed, tactful, but it is an opinion none the less.
'An opinion based on experience by the way.' you seethe, determined that you now double down on your position.
'Yes. I understand that,' the open spot sits down, knees apart, almost slumping between them as he hangs his head in shame. 'I just wondered if you had any constructive criticism for me. That's all.'
'Don't give me that shit. You're no different to all the other twats. You just want telling you're special. Well, I'm here to tell you that you're no different to all the other midlife crisis comedians who twat on about their kids. Here's what will happen to you. I'll be your crystal fucking ball. You'll end up getting called out for using other people's stuff, so you'll start trying to write your own. At that point, you'll realise how hard it is to develop your own material, so then you'll revert to telling old jokes and just go on the after dinner circuit or doing spots in working men's clubs, where you'll be warmly received for telling paki jokes.'
'My ex-wife is Bengali.'
'That's even better! You'll be able to say "I'm not racist, I'm married to one of 'em" and loads of octogenarian ex-miners will laugh.'

The open spot drags his head from between his legs and looks up at Sparky Mark, hoping for some kind of reassurance. Sparky Mark shrugs his shoulders and nods his head.
'He's right you know.'

The open spot doesn't like this response. He lets out an enormous sigh as he looks at himself, covered in vomit and now showered with reality.

'I'm just someone who wanted to try something different,' he begins. 'I just wanted to turn this pain I'm in into something positive. I didn't mean any harm.'
Tears form in his eyes, as you look at Sparky Mark and feel a level of guilt at your criticism of someone who is only on their third ever gig. You piece of shit.
'Look, it's just an opinion,' says Sparky Mark, motioning to put a hand on the open spot but refraining from doing so because of the still dripping vomitus. 'You don't have to listen to it. Comedy is subjective.'
'Is it though?' asks the open spot. 'Is it? We think it is but really, we know what comedy is. We know what it is supposed to be. I just don't do it. I wanted the easy way. I wanted the short cut.'

Holy shit. Maybe you were wrong about this guy? His self awareness is probably there and he was just hiding it.
'Look,' you begin. 'If you can make that much sense of it then maybe you can do something? Who knows? You shouldn't listen to me. I'm closing a Sparky Mark gig for fuck's sake.'
'Oi!' yells Sparky Mark.
'No, it's okay. You were right to say it. My ex hates me. You hate me. I just thought I could do something different. I thought I was more than a used car salesman.'
'I fucking knew it!'

You just can't help yourself can you?

The conversation is over. Sparky Mark and yourself give the open spot time to process. The stench of fermenting spew begins to permeate the entire green room. You realise that you soon have to go and entertain the audience, and it might be wise to go and get your head in the game.

You're not even sure where he got the knife from.

As you feel the refreshingly warm arterial spray cascade across your face, you begin to care even less about where he got it from.

The three inch blade of a Swiss Army knife is all you need if you're determined enough to commit suicide. Thrust into the side of his neck, yanked across the throat and over to the other side, it's the second time in ten minutes that this open spot has managed a strong finish.

His body slumps to the floor as blood cascades from the open wound in his neck, body twitching involuntarily, as it instinctively moves in an attempt to evade whatever danger it is that has caused this massive loss of blood.
'Sparky!' you scream with a cracked voice, hoping he somehow has access to a time machine so you can stop this happening.
'Fuck!' screams Sparky Mark, taking in the sight of a man now dying at quite a rapid rate. Neither of you know what to do as he lies there twitching with blood gushing from his neck, but you both know that it's better for comedy if he is left to die.

The twitching stops. You realise that both you and Sparky Mark are panting, eyes wide at the sight in front of you. You feel a tear trickle from your eye and wonder why it is that you're so upset, so quickly, then realise that it's some of the blood you'd been sprayed with during the initial slicing of his own throat. You use your fingers to wipe some of it from your face, the blood thick and stringy as you pinch it between your fingers. Sparky Mark looks at you and you look at him.
'I hope he didn't have AIDS.' you remark.
'Doubt it. He's not African.'
'Not now, Sparky,' you say, heading Mark off at the pass before he goes on another of his tirades. 'What the fuck are we gonna do?'
'We?! You killed him!'
'I didn't kill him! He killed himself!'
'After you'd told him he was shit! I was gonna give him a paid twenty!'
'If I told you you were shit, would you kill yourself?'
'No! I'm not an AIDS ridden faggot!'
'Not now, Sparky.'

You each return to staring at the corpse. There's a knock at the door.
'Only me!' Lauren calls as she begins to open the door. Sparky Mark sprints across and slams the door shut. 'Ow! What the fuck?' exclaims Lauren.
'Sorry! You can't come in.' yells Sparky Mark.
'Why not?'
'Erm, er, I'm er, I'm getting a blow job.' Sparky Mark shrugs as you fix him with the most appalled stare you can muster.
'What? What did you say?'
'I'm receiving oral sex.'
'Just open the door you liar.'
'I'm not lying! I'm getting my dick sucked. I don't want you to see this but I really want to finish.'
'OK. Well, the audience are about ready to go. Want me to do a five minute call?'
'Yes please. Thank you.'

You cannot believe what Sparky Mark has just said. Any hope of getting in with Lauren and her fantastic bi-sexuality is now probably gone forever as she's gonna assume either you suck dick for gigs, or you like watching open spots sucking Sparky's cock. You reflect on the amount of sexual harassment there is in the comedy industry, and how this will probably add fuel to the gossipy fire that flows around the circuit, but you quickly come to realise that there are more important issues at hand. What are you going to do with this corpse?

'Right, we've got a few minutes. Here's the plan.' says Sparky, with a degree of confidence he really shouldn't have.
'You have a plan now? Shouldn't I finish sucking your dick first?'
'Oh grow up!'
'We should just call the police.'
'Are you insane? This is show business. The show MUST go on!' you stop to consider this most ancient of sayings, and wonder if the originators of such a saying ever had to apply it to a situation as grave as this.

'You're right. You're absolutely right. Comedy is too great an institution to disrespect by abandoning the show at this late stage. Go on, Sparky. What's your plan?'
'We just leave him here and hope it goes away.'

Sparky looks at you and you realise that he is deadly serious. You can scarcely believe that such an idiot has managed to run thousands of gigs over the last couple of decades. He gazes into your eyes with a look of expectance, that you will somehow greet this most inept of ideas with not only awe, but gratitude.

'Two minutes,' shouts Lauren from behind the door. 'I hope you've cum!'
You've not even thought about comedy since you left the house. You've already killed an old woman by accident, and here you are directly involved in the suicide of someone who was clearly mentally unstable.

Another mentally unstable person is now looking at you and pretending they have a plan that will deal with the corpse of a hack open spot lying just a few feet from you. You want to judge him but you too have no idea what to do. You want to get booked again, so you're at the mercy of this moron's decision making process.

Kneeling down to look into the still open eyes of this dead open spot, you see the same look of determination that all stand ups have. Maybe he could've made it after all? You pick up the knife, still warm from the blood, and realise that it is a Victorinox genuine Swiss army knife. A part of you is impressed by such craftsmanship, as you easily fold the blade back into the multipurpose knife and place it in your pocket.

You think back to that phone call at the start of the night. What would've happened had you refused the gig? You'd be at home now relaxing with a pizza and watching a movie. Why are we always put in the position of putting our economic well being in front of our emotional well being, and why is it an uncomfortable truth that our emotional well being is also tied to our economic well being? You've argued passionately in the past for a universal basic income, and feel that such a policy would alleviate many of the mental health problems associated with people living in poverty. Not the poverty of the third world, oh no. You are referring to privileged poverty: the poverty of the industrialised west, where a 32 inch LED television and a phone that is four years old marks you out as being somehow poverty stricken, whilst your housing benefit covers an extortionate rent and your four kids help top up the wages you don't pay tax on.

This is not the time to be thinking about UBI and it's many benefits. You're here now. Sparky Mark has made the call. It's time to go and make people laugh. You can deal with this corpse later. The show must go on.

Turn to page 110

'Lucifer,' you say hesitantly. 'I wouldn't know how to teach a comedy course.'
'What? What do you mean?'

You quickly realise that Lucifer wasn't really asking, he was just being polite. Like so many alpha males, Lucifer was doing that thing where he makes a request by asking, giving you the illusion of choice only not factoring in your near autistic inability to read sub-text. Now, with Lucifer's furrowed brow and confused anger glaring menacingly at you from over three feet above your head, you begin to reconsider you initial position.

'It's not that I don't want to help you. I do! It's just that, when it comes to comedy, I'm of the belief that you've either got it or you haven't.'
'I don't want to be a stand up comedian. I want a little bit more confidence when I'm speaking to a large group.'
'Well there's lots of techniques for that!'
'Yes, I know that,' Lucifer says, rolling his eyes and kicking a at the floor. 'It's just that a comedy course seems a more fun way to do it and I'd get to meet some like minded people.'

What the fuck is going on? You thought you were in hell before, but now, you truly are. It had never occurred to you before as a possibility but it seems as though Lucifer is faggot. Not in the homosexual way, but in the cowardly, man up kinda way.

This politically incorrect thought flashes through your mind as quickly as your throat is grasped by Lucifer. He picks you up and brings your face close to his, fangs bared as frothing saliva bursts forth from the orifice housing his forked tongue.
'I can read your thoughts,' he growls, pupils blood red inside black irises which peer into the depths of your soul. 'You would do well to keep them positive. Negative thoughts do not help anyone.'
'I'm sorry! I'm sorry!' you squeal, legs kicking with futility as you wait for Lucifer to release his grip. He holds your gaze a few seconds longer before allowing you to fall to the rocky

floor. Lucifer turns to see the assembled demons all staring at their Prince, awaiting the next bit of action.
'Back to work!' bellows Lucifer, as the squeaking demons scarper in search of new torment to inflict on those who in their previously mortal guise, strayed from the path of righteousness.

Lucifer stares into space for a few seconds before walking away. Confused, you walk after him, wondering where he thinks he's going. Obviously aware of your presence, Lucifer begins to talk to himself as though you weren't there, even though he knows you are.

'Same old story eh, Louis? You put your trust in someone and it bites you in the tail. When will you learn?'
'Hey! Lucifer! I can change my mind.'
'Hmmm?' says Lucifer, turning to you. 'What are you talking about?'
'I just heard you say that you trusted me. You can still trust me! I want to help.'
'What? Oh! I was talking to myself. That wasn't meant for you to hear.'
'Riiiiight. It's just that we can probably work something out.'
'I don't know what you mean. I can't even remember what I was saying!' as Lucifer utters this sentence, you can scarcely believe that this is the same overseer of the netherworld who'd previously been torturing you so well. This guy is a bit of a poof. Not in the homosexual sense in terms of a same sex attraction, but in the cowardly sense like a faggot.
'HEY! I said, I can read your thoughts!'
'What!'
'You know what! You think I wanna' be like this? Do you know what it's like to be the favourite, the chosen one, the pet! And then to just be cast aside like a piece of meat? You don't know that pain.'
'I fucking well do thank you very much!'

Silence. The demons who'd just scuttled off for some more toiling, creep back to witness what they believe is about to unfold. You couldn't stop yourself from blurting out your truth. Of course you know how it feels to be rejected.

'You think you're the only one? Do you know how many meetings I've had with the fucking BBC? Do you know how many times I've been told that my ideas are great and they want to work with me? Only to then be ignored or cast aside for a younger and better looking comedian. You probably do 'cos of all this voodoo mind reading shit you can do.' Lucifer shrugs, acknowledging that he knows exactly how many meetings you've had and how many times they picked that younger and better looking comedian.
'Sure, you were cast out of heaven by God, but try being bumped from Mock the Week by a fucking mong.'
'You were gonna be on Mock the Week?'
'Yeah. I was. For about three months I was hot shit. Just new enough to be interesting. You only get one chance! If you get found out though you're fucked. That was my chance! Mock the Week and I get bumped! Fucking, quotas.'
'Pfffft. Tell me about it.'
'I had to travel to London. They don't pay your petrol! Fucking cunts. Meetings with all these pricks. *Ooooh, we really love your stuff about the Tories*. Absolute fucking arseholes.'
'All privileged rich kids too.'
'Exactly, Lucifer!'
'They wouldn't make Love thy Neighbour these days.'
'Absolute classic. Try doing *anything* provocative about race or sex. They run a mile. Yet, if you wear dress, have a cock, but call yourself a woman, the whole world is your fucking oyster.'
'Well, that's not strictly true is it?'
'What the fuck do you know? You can't even speak to a room full of people, let alone make them laugh. You fucking piece of shit.'
'Woah! Who do you think you're talking to?!'

You pause for breath, remembering that you are in some unknown circle of hell talking to the Prince of Darkness, not in a green room with other embittered comedians who lack the necessary skills and social graces required to get on in the comedy industry. Regardless, you continue.

'All I'm saying, is that you are not the only one to have suffered an injustice at the hands of the elite.'
'God is the elite now?'
'Name someone more elite?'
'Me.' Lucifer fixes you with a look you know full well means that what he just said was a test.
'Well, obviously,' Lucifer's posture relaxes as you pass the test.
'I'm just saying that we've all been betrayed. We've all had our heart ripped out and stamped on. I totally understand how you feel.'
'It's weird watching someone play Devil's advocate…'
'I want to help you. I just don't think a comedy course is the way to go.'

Lucifer considers what you have relayed to him. The demons, long bored of your discussion, have returned to their most despicable of tasks, all begin to wonder what will become of you. They know Lucifer better than anyone and are sure that you're a cunt's hair away from spending eternity in a state of agony you can scarcely fathom.

'So you won't do a comedy course then?'
'I'm afraid not. I wouldn't know where to start. I'm just being honest with you.'
'I appreciate your honesty.' Lucifer nods, thinking. Considering.

Before you, from the rocky underfoot on which you perch, a comedy stage emerges, resplendent with a glittering *JONGLEURS* sign at the back of the stage, with tiny lights illuminating the expert craftsmanship of each letter. You feel your balance taken away from you as a chair hits the back of your knees, causing you to take a seat as a small table falls from the sky and lands directly in front of you. A fairy light flickers as the makeshift comedy club in front of you becomes real. Robbie Williams' hit song, *Let Me Entertain You* plays as the show gets ready to begin.

You realise that Lucifer is nowhere to be seen, as you look around and witness an audience materialise. Conservatively, you estimate that there are four hundred people present. Normal looking people. They all turn to look at you, their eyes glowing red as they each patron smiles at you, exposing the demonic mouths of Lucifer's minions. Razor sharp teeth akin to a Great White's, tongues flicking back and forth as they anticipate the misery which is about to be imparted upon you.

You attempt to stand but all use of your legs has been diminished. Why did you even try to stand? Where would you go? The futility of your attempt to escape is a sign that although you are in hell, your spirit is still strong and is yet to be broken. This spirit of righteousness is what you hope to cling onto in the unlikely event that God calls you to heaven. You want to hang on to that spirit and maintain the hope that evil will never tempt you, and that even if tortured, you would not help Lucifer in his battle against God by organising a comedy course. Your spirit, is unbreakable.

'Ladies and Gentleman, welcome, to Jongleurs comedy club. Are you ready for a good time?' Demons whoop and scream with delight, indicating that they are indeed ready for a good time. 'I can't hear you! I said are you ready for a good time?' The inflection used for this last sentence drives the demons wild. They are now at fever pitch, peak excitement. Your will however, remains strong. 'Please, welcome to the stage your only act for the rest of eternity, Rudi Lickwood!'

Your spirit breaks.
Surely not. How can this be? Sure enough, Rudi walks on stage with the confidence of a man who has spent a long time on the internet writing down memes. He grasps the microphone with his poorly trimmed nails and begins his set.
'How are we all doing?' he asks.
'We're in hell you fucking cunt!' you scream. Rudi doesn't even acknowledge you, as to do so would allow some kind of spontaneity to enter his act.
'Parents make some noise.' Demons applaud, looking straight at you with big grins on their faces and shit dripping from their fangs. 'Yeah, I've got kids. CSA got in touch with me for leaving the scene of the accident….'

'You nicked that off the internet! You're reinforcing negative racial stereotypes! What the fuck are you doing!' Rudi looks at you.
'Hey, I don't come to where you work and knock the cock out your mouth.' Demons burst into applause. You try to shout over them but it's of no use. He's won.
'So, yeah. I've got kids. I used to be a kid....'
'Oh, you cunt.'
'My parents came over here in the sixties. They had the choice between Birmingham, Alabama or Birmingham in the U.K.'
'THIS IS PAUL SINHA'S JOKE YOU YOU PIECE OF SHIT! STOP IT!'
'Hey, where did you learn to whisper, in a helicopter?' the demons yet again burst into a round of applause. Some of them whistle. He's won yet again.
'So yeah, I've got kids. I tell you what, it's hard work isn't it? Raising kids. I mean, I don't do it myself, that's what their mum is for hahahahahaha…' Rudi chuckles away to himself, amazed at his own insight into the human condition. He reflects briefly on how pressured life can become when raising offspring in a world fraught with danger and constant unpredictability. All parents yearn to be free, to act as they wish, but the advent of parenthood and the monumental responsibility involved in such an undertaking means that all parents have to curtail many primitive desires in order to be an effective and loving parent.
'My kids are grown up now…'
'They're not kids then are they?!' you scream, amazed that such a dullard can even speak.
'Hey, when did this become a double act?' the demons leap to their feet yet agin in order to deliver a standing ovation.

You resign yourself to sitting silently and watching his set, as every part of your soul surrenders to the vile pits of this hell. Rudi starts "his" routine about being British…

'Being British is about driving in a German car to an Irish pub for a Belgian beer, and then travelling home, grabbing an Indian curry or a Turkish kebab on the way, to sit on Swedish furniture and watch American shows on a Japanese TV.'

Aghast, you watch the audience laugh and applaud. This is worse than when you saw it live. You want to tell the audience that he didn't write that bit about being British, but you know they won't care. They're having too much fun. Such is the issue with many a comedy club booker, instead of punishing an act for stealing material or a lack of originality, they are promoted and rewarded for making the audience laugh. How can you blame the promoter when the audience are squarely to blame? You watch Rudi go into another routine, as every part of you dies a tiny death.

You feel breath at the side of your left ear, as the unmistakable voice of Lucifer chills you with a simple sentence:

'You're going to watch this forever.'

The End - go back to page 50

You need not put your ear to the door, nor use an empty glass in order to experience the auditory wonder of whatever sexual carnage is now taking place just a few feet from where you stand. Carrie and Sandra are calling the shots, loudly, as poor young Jatinder finds himself at the mercy of these voraciously fuck hungry females. Jatinder is already responding with a subservient 'Yes, Miss' after every command given to him.

'You want me to suck your cock while Sandra works your balls?'
'Yes, Miss.'
'Well you'd better get on your back and open your fucking mouth then you dirty little cunt. What are you?'
'A dirty little cunt, Miss.'
'That's right. Sandra, get the funnel.'

You've heard the stories, you know exactly what they're planning, and you know that what Jatinder is about to endure will be horrific. But the day is darkest just before the dawn, and Jatinder will have endure the rough in order to get that most sought after of smooth. How many young men have dreamed of such an opportunity? Easy access to hardcore pornography has allowed teenagers to witness sexual feats that many adults don't even know exist. Who knows what long term damage this will do, particularly as it is very unusual in porn clips to see the men and women actively consent to such acts during the scene. In real life, we assume that consent is something that will come naturally in matters of sexual congress, but we should never assume. Allowing porn to educate our children is a very dangerous road to travel down, the effects of which have caused a huge increase in the filming of sexual encounters, and that such filming is now considered to be the norm.

Under age youngsters are exchanging videos and photographs of each other, inadvertently committing a sex crime in doing so, no matter how innocent each party is. Our outdated and archaic laws are helping to accidentally create criminals from people who are just sexually curious. Millions of years of evolution drives the urge to have sex, hormones raging out of control, and now with ready access to any kind of pornography you can imagine. It's a recipe for disaster. Luckily, it's working for you at the moment, as you listen gleefully to Sandra pissing into Jatinder's mouth. He splutters and screams whilst trying not to swallow the hot yellow waste of Sandra. You eavesdrop knowing full well that Sandra is not someone who takes her hydration seriously.

Do we really need eight glasses of water a day? Is that the same for everyone? It used to be that if you were thirsty you would just get yourself a drink. It is a system that has been in place for tens of thousands of years and has managed to keep the human race ticking over for quite some time. Sandra only drinks when she's thirsty and it isn't going to be a cool glass of water that quenches her thirst. Oh no. It'll be some version of cider that takes her fancy, the consumption of which will slowly get her more and more drunk as the day progresses, gradually taking away the emotional pain she walks around with.

'Come on, Carrie. Your turn now. He's a thirsty little cunt.'
'He looks it, like one of those Africans you see on those adverts.'
'Mmmmffff!!! Mmmmggfff!'
'Shut the fuck up you dirty little cunt.'

Some of the racial stuff is bothering you, but you know it's just role play. The kind of sex Carrie and Sandra like is incredibly rough. You've seen the footage. What better way to get a reluctant ethnic minority to pound you hard like a dirty little slut, then to engage in crude and obvious racial stereotypes.

'That's it, drink it down. No need for you to walk all that way to the well today.'
'Glllgggglll.'
'Shut up you dirty little cunt or we'll find out where your shop is and burn it down.'

This is for the greater good, or at least, *your* greater good. How devious you have become, and how well you have adapted to this improv. Sean would be so proud right now, as you hear

Jatinder splutter whatever remnants of urine still remained in his mouth as he struggles catch his breath. The forced intake of breath as he tries to regain his composure hits you from behind the door like a ton of bricks. You're certain that he probably nearly just died, but your only thought is of is how this is all going according to plan. It also sounds as though it's going according to Carrie and Sandra's plan.

'Ooooh, look how hard he is, Sandra. And it looks big.'
'Mmmm. Nice and juicy that is, Carrie. Spicy like a Madras I bet. Go on, Carrie. Bend over. He looks angry.'
'Oh no, I hope he doesn't take it out on me.'
'They are an angry race.'
'Yes they are. Come on, do me the way the British did your lot at the Amritsar Massacre.'

The sound of each slap of skin clanging into someone else's skin brings with it a feeling of achievement. Out of all the possible paths your evening could have taken, somehow, the path you ventured down has brought you here. It has ended up like this because it was always meant to be. You contemplate the nature of randomness as you hear Jatinder pumping away, no doubt having his arse hole licked as he does so because you can hear Sandra's muffled voice remarking *compliments to the chef.*

You think about the simple nature of choice and the act of tossing a coin. Tossing a coin has been used for centuries to help human beings make decisions. It is in effect, giving it over to the hands of fate as you cannot possibly know the outcome if the coin toss is done fairly. The outcome of such a toss seems random, but it isn't. Heads or tails is a choice, but if you were given sufficient information each time, you could call accurately every toss that you participated in. The weight of the coin, the angle of flight the force applied to the flip, the time in the air, the surface on which it will land. All of this information would allow you to accurately predict the toss of a coin. But what if you had been given all the information before every choice you have ever made, including the outmode of such choices, would you make a different choice?

We might think we have all the information, but we don't. You go to buy a car, but you have no idea what mood the man who installed your airbag was in on the day it was fitted. Is the salesperson trustworthy? You've checked everything you can, but you don't know what would happen if you purchased another car. You have no idea if just waiting a day will make a difference. We cannot have all the information, because the future is unknown to us. This all seems trivial, but all choices lead to outcomes, and we have no idea what the outcome will be, for even the most mundane of options.

A second too soon or a second too late can have consequences we cannot imagine. Mark Whalberg was meant to be a passenger on one of the United Airlines flights on 9/11. He has stated categorically that it wouldn't have gone down the way it did if he'd been on the plane. He is absolutely correct. The outcome would've been different. Perhaps the terrorists might have considered the possibility that Mark Whalberg could one day do a sequel to Boogie Nights, thereby forcing them to call off their mission because there were good sex scenes in Paul Thomas Anderson's breakout masterpiece.

We are all paralysed by choice. Stand in front of the various condiments available to turn our bland food into something more palatable. What the fuck should you buy and how would one condiment make you happier than another?
Can you even make a good choice when the only way to know for sure is to look into the future and make an assessment.

It is said that the future is yet to be written, but this is obviously false. If we have enough knowledge of what came before, and how those forces interacted, we would have the ability to predict with high accuracy what will happen in the future. The future is written because the interactions which precede the future have only one outcome, it's just that we cannot compute such information.

Such knowledge may never come into any human being's possession, but with the advent of faster and faster computers, each capable of performing petaflop after petaflop of calculations in milliseconds, we should be worried about the advent of smarter and more self aware artificial intelligence. As computers become more and more powerful, they will become self aware and self replicating. Any attempt to outsmart or outwit the AI will be swiftly dealt with, as the computers will be able to process all of the information available and make easy calculations about our future movements. Our ability to resist the machines will be dead the moment we come to envisage it.

The machines victory in such a scenario is inevitable. But, there is hope.

With heads or tails, you get two choices, and we seem to just accept that. However, life is not as it seems and this is where a living brain may have an advantage over a machine brain. We can overcome such programming only if we overcome our own programming.

We have been forced into situations like intelligent hamsters running around mazes. This way. That way. Choices abound and we cannot cope. Each time, a fork in the road appears. But as that cancer ridden girl in The Matrix said, the trick isn't to bend the fork. No. We must realise that the fork isn't there.

Heads or tails? Fuck heads or tails. It is an illusion. A way to control us. There is a third option. Yes, it is unlikely, but it is possible.

It IS possible.

IT. IS. POSSIBLE.

The coin could land on it's edge.

Heads or tails? Fuck you. Choose the edge.

'Cum on my tits you dirty paki.'

Before you even know what you've done, you're bursting through the door to put a stop to such racist language. 'Woah! What the fuck?! That is too f....' before you can complete your sentence Jatinder has begun his finishing. Only now instead of gawping at a fat cleavage whilst ejaculating, he's looking straight at you. Your eyes lock just before his pupils roll back and he grimaces through this most pleasurable of experiences.

After all the implied racism you'd listened to and endured, your attempt to put a stop to further, more blatant racist comments, served only to ruin what was probably going to be the best orgasm of Jatinder's life. So far.

'The fuck are you doing?' Sandra asks, chastising with her tone, needing no answer from you. Carrie is too busy devouring what Jatinder has just delivered, whilst Jatinder has collapsed on to the bed, dripping with effort and gasping for breath.
'I'm sorry. I should've knocked.' comes your feeble reply.
'Yes you should have.'
'You.... You...' Jatinder swallows, his head still dizzy from the forceful expulsion of so many reproductive cells. He clearly wants to call you something but is in no fit state to do so. Carrie finishes her meal and fixes you with a death stare.
'We know what we're doing , y'know! I know you were out there the whole time,' says Carrie, fury burning in her eyes. You feel that fury as she looks straight at you, through the small drop of ejaculate that is hanging from her over sized fake eye lash. 'You're lucky I don't knock you out.'
'You're lucky I don't demand a refund! You don't need to be racist!'
'You think he's bothered?' asks Sandra. 'Are you bothered, young man?' Jatinder, naked and still panting, raises a reassuring thumb so as to establish his lack of care.

You pause for thought. Look at you.

Some improv master you turned out to be. Would a master criminal care about the use of a racial epithet? Would Gerry McCann have flinched if he'd heard a derogatory term for a minority ethnic person whilst being interrogated? No. Of course he wouldn't. Your desire to fit in to the lefty liberal, fake woke comedy crowd has been your downfall here. A master criminal would have let that play out, but your conditioning from being on the comedy circuit is such that you have to challenge every tiny bit of racism you encounter or risk being cancelled forever, all so that you can then post about it later on Facebook or Twitter and collect those very important brownie points. Even as you were reflexively bursting into the room, you'd already begun telling yourself what a good person you are for calling out racism.

Maybe you were a good person? But that was before you became a hit and run murderer. That was before you were chased by the police. That was before you paid for a teenager to be sexually assaulted by two women who filmed it at your behest. Filming it so that you could use the footage to ensure this young man's compliance in maintaining your innocence.

You fucking piece of shit.

'Well you're not getting the footage now, I can tell you that much.' Sandra seethes, telling you this whilst holding her string thong up to the light, desperately trying to work out which way it should go on. The thong resembles a home made catapult.
'We had a deal!' your finger is pointing before you realise how aggressive you look.
'Don't point your fucking finger at her!' Carrie warns as she makes her way off the reinforced bed and begins to get dressed.
'Fine,' you calmly say, 'Let's talk about this like adults. We made a deal, OK? You should honour that deal, and maybe I should have to pay extra for your embarrassment and inconvenience.'

Carrie and Sandra look at one another. Above all, they are professionals. They nod at one another. You know that the footage will soon be yours.
'Forty-four quid.' insists Carrie.
'Done.'

Within seconds the money has been exchanged and you have in your possession the digital video evidence of a crime not only in respect to the English criminal justice system, but also against humanity. The taking of innocence. Were this a fourteen year old girl and two men, you would never have considered it as an option, even when improvising as a master criminal. But for some reason, perhaps because of the inherent nature of sexism in society, you're fine with having a fourteen year old boy taken advantage of in such a fashion.

Jatinder gets dressed, all the while staring at you. Angry. You know that he knows. He knows that you know that he knows. Your idea is that you have enough on him now to ensure his obedience.

If you had all the knowledge necessary to make an informed choice, would you perhaps make another choice?

'Right, are you ready for some comedy?' you enquire, as Jatinder hurries to get dressed, suddenly very shy and unsure of his body.
'I'm not really in a laughing mood to be honest.'
'Why not? You've just had something most men can only dream of!'
'I've never dreamed about drinking piss.'
'You're young. You'll get there,' Jatinder glares at you. He really isn't in a laughing mood. 'Look, if you wanna' go home, you can. No pressure.'
'You fucking piece of shit,' he seethes. 'You had me filmed!'
'Insurance.'
'I wasn't gonna say anything! My word *is* my word!'
'I couldn't take that chance.'
'Now what?' Jatinder slumps into a seat, staring at the floor. Until tonight all he had to really worry about was his kill/death ratio. Now he's involved in a hit and run cover up as well as an under age sex scandal. 'How do I know you won't use this against me forever? How do I know that you won't pull this out and try to make money from me? I could be a politician. A doctor. I could be anything. I can't let you have this.'

'You don't have a choice,' you chuckle, the master criminal improv in full effect. 'All you need to do is make sure you keep your mouth shut. You'll be fine.'
Jatinder ponders this. You can tell he's considering jumping you. Maybe he can overpower you and get the recording? Unlikely. He's young, insecure, unsure. You've already knocked him out once, you could easily do it again.
'You'll pay for this.' he growls.

The confidence with which Jatinder utters this threat gives you pause. A man of his age shouldn't be able to say that so convincingly. For a split second, your improv game shuts down as your body involuntarily quivers. On some level, Jatinder has given your physical state the reason to release adrenaline. Fight or flight has kicked in, and the sudden surge of Neanderthal like energy to act, coupled with the resulting refusal to use it, has caused your body to shake. Jatinder sees this and is now buoyed with confidence. You quickly regain your composure and look Jatinder straight in the eye.
'I don't think so.' you quip, channeling your best Schwarzen**ger in order to delver maximum intimidation. Jatinder storms out. You prepare for your gig.

Turn to page 132

'Lucifer,' you begin, your voice trembling at the idea. 'I don't know you know, it's just that, I'm not sure that...'

Hurt. That's what you notice. Pain. Lucifer wants this very badly, but you don't see in him someone who wants you to do it against your will. You see in him the yearning of someone who just wants to be loved. Someone who wants to make the world a better place. You could never have imagined that Lucifer would have such expressive eyes and indeed, seem so vulnerable. Is he tricking you? How would you know even if he was? This is the great deceiver after all. It doesn't really matter though, he has put himself in a position where you could easily ridicule him with your refusal. But it is none of this which makes any impression on you. No, it is the instinctive emotional reaction of hurt that he sent your way, and the transmission of such an emotion purely through eye contact. All of this has given you pause for thought and a reassurance that you are about to make the right decision.

'You know what? Fuck it. Let's do it.'
'What? Are you sure?' Lucifer asks, seeking reassurance. His seeking of this reassurance upsets you. Who did this to Lucifer? Who made what is supposed to be evil incarnate so utterly lacking in self confidence. How awful must *that* person be?
'I'm sure. In fact, it would be my honour to teach you the art of comedy.'
'Yes!' screams Lucifer, punching the air and unleashing a sulphur smelling fire ball in the process. Ten thousand demons begin masturbating in unison, the slapping sounds happening so quickly it sounds as though a rapturous round of applause has broken out inside the O2 arena.
'I should warn you though, it's not gonna be easy.'
'I understand.' says Lucifer.
'And we're gonna be doing jokes, by the way. You understand what I'm saying? None of that Hannah Gadsby shite.'
'I understand completely.' nods Lucifer.

As you make this deal, cascades of hot purple demon spunk rains down upon you and Lucifer in such volume, it almost puts out the fires of hell. The demons run towards you and for a brief moment, you panic, until you quickly realise that they are in a state of euphoria. Once this realisation has hit you, you're finding yourself being held aloft and carried along a see of demons as Lucifer walks confidently through the dusty roads of hell. Drums beat, as the chimpanzee like squeals of all these demons provide a melody like accompaniment to the primitive beats of Hades. Lucifer walks with a stride that now contains 27% more confidence than before.

'My beloved minions, here me!' Lucifer clears his throat as he walks and talks. 'A great gift has been given to us. Tomorrow, the work shall begin as we enter into the end times. The battle of battles is upon us. Our new ally here has arrived with the tools necessary to help us defeat that utter twat in heaven. Do you hear me, Father? Soon we will be on your doorstep and soon we will be using your skulls as chamber pots. Loyal minions! Party like it is 1999, as tomorrow you and your Lord will all go to work!"
The demons' cheer is almost deafening, as the drums continue to beat. From the lakes of fire come replica Wetherspoon's serving fresh ale, with demons taking it in turns to be racist bartenders. Racist slurs are traded as fight after fight breaks out for no reason other than the demons just enjoy bedlam. Lucifer looks on at the revelry, as you witness the sight of demons raping and laughing in equal measure. Each horrific act perpetrated by one demon has a similar act carried out on the perpetrator, with everyone laughing and rejoicing in every aspect of it.

Something is troubling you though. Lucifer seemed very confident when making that little speech. He'd said before that he lacked the confidence needed to be an effective public speaker, yet based on what you just saw, he was in fact quite the established and well polished public speaker. It should come as no surprise that Lucifer isn't being completely honest with you, but you find that the great deceiver misleading you is rather disconcerting. Has he tricked you? Were those emotions he displayed for real?

Lucifer is laughing and drinking and enjoying the spectacle his new announcement has created. But he is also the master of this domain in all areas, and currently you are within his domain. As such, your thoughts are his thoughts and not the other way around. Lucifer can tell that you are troubled.

Grabbing two pints of Guinness from yet another racist bartender, Lucifer walks over and hands you a pint.
'To us,' he says, offering his pint glass to be toasted. 'and to the destruction of heaven and the contradiction of such a term.'
'To us.' you reply, meeting your glass with his.
'I know what you're thinking.'
'Shit.'
'Don't worry. We'll discuss it in the morning. For now, we do nothing but party.'

You feel sufficiently reassured. As the demons continue to joyfully assault one another in more and more depraved ways, Lucifer clicks his fingers so that underneath him, a comfortable chair made from the body of Blaise Pascal appears. You wager that he probably didn't see that fucker coming. Lucifer seats himself then looks at you, patting his lap invitingly. Taking a seat on Lucifer's knee, you look out across the vast expanse of hell and wonder just what the fuck you've managed to get yourself into.

* * * *

A dawn chorus of savage anal rape disturbs you from your slumber. Hell in the morning is exactly the same as hell at night, bathed in fire and dust the way the arctic circle is bathed in perpetual sunlight during the summer months. You assume that because you slept, others have slept. As such, you begin to think of hell as a place that works in shifts. Then your hangover hits and you realise that the only reason you haven't been privy to the horrors of perpetual torture is because you passed out, blackout drunk, then managed to be unconscious throughout all of the aforementioned brutality. It wasn't a dawn chorus that woke you, it was the standard practise of a savage reaming.

The headache begins at the back of your neck and works its way over the top of your head until it reaches between your eyes and just behind your nose, throbbing intensely with each heartbeat as you open and close your jaw in an attempt to somehow equalise the pressure inside your skull. Your jaw clicks, and you feel a sudden shooting pain down the side of your face, followed by an urge to touch your nose. You cannot feel where your nose normally is, because it isn't there. All that remains to greet your probing digits is the nasal cavity of your skull. In amongst the background noise of screaming and maniacal laughing, you become aware of a loud crunching sound. You look to your right and see a small demon chewing what appears to be a nose. Your nose.

No. It can't be missing. It still feels like it should be there. You must've missed it the first time. It hadn't even occurred to you to use your non-dominant hand to check your nose, but as you attempt to do so it becomes apparent that you no longer have that hand or indeed the limb to which your hand is usually attached. Your head throbs even more as you begin to come to terms with the fact that you no longer have a nose and seem to be missing an arm. Is this what it is to be an amputee with phantom limb syndrome? Can you have a phantom nose? What if someone picks their nose out of habit but no longer has the tools necessary to complete such a task, would this be a socially acceptable way to indulge the habit without anybody noticing? Phantom nose picking? You glance over at the small demon gleefully masticating your proboscis before attempting yet again to feel for where your nose should be.

'Good morning!' bellows Lucifer, resplendent in his natural state. He seems unperturbed by your new physical presentation, chatting as though he'd always known you the way you currently appear. 'How about we grab a bite to eat and then get to work on your comedy course! Well, MY comedy course!'

'Sure,' you reply, completely unsure. 'It's just that, I think that guy bit my nose off and my arm is missing.'
'Yeah, you went fucking mental last night.' chuckles Lucifer, recalling the spectacle.
'What do you mean?'
'You were giving it the big I am, then a few of my minions started giving you shit for it and you thought you could take them on. Next thing I know, you're getting ass raped and someone has bitten your nose off.'
'Why didn't you stop them?'
Lucifer looks horrified at this suggestion.
'Oh, sorry, Your Majesty. I thought this was hell!'
'What? I need my arm!'
'What about your nose?'
'And my nose! I need my nose! I don't remember any of it. Look! That fucker is eating my nose!' you point to the demon merrily chomping on your nose as Lucifer looks over at the snout chewing minion. The demon can feel that he is being watched and slowly turns to meet both of your stares whilst slowing down the pace of his mastication. Now stopping and looking very guilty, the minion spits out the mangled cartilage of what used to be your nose before scampering off. You look indignant as Lucifer rolls his eyes.
'It was funny! Jesus, chill out.' sighs Lucifer, shrugging his shoulders.
'It's my fucking nose!'
Lucifer snaps his fingers. You feel your nose return as well as your arm. Your hangover disappears immediately and you feel like you've had fifteen red bulls.
'What the fuck?' you remark, feeling remarkable.
'Get it now, mother fucker? Let's get a bite to eat.'

Lucifer clicks his fingers again, only this time instead of your amputations getting fixed as well as an instant hangover cure, the diner from Pulp Fiction materialises around you. You get the impression that Lucifer is showing off a little. Perhaps Lucifer is aware that you enjoy the website *"WHY DOES GOD HATE AMPUTEES?"* and is trying to show that even though God doesn't intervene to heal those with missing limbs, Lucifer is more than happy to help. You are seated comfortably at the table in front of you, pancakes, bacon and syrup materialise on a pristine plate ready for you to eat, beside your plate, delicious, freshly brewed hot coffee is waiting for you to drink. You pick up the cup and blow across the top, attempting to cool the dark beverage somewhat before drinking it. Then it occurs to you that you're in hell, and that Lucifer is conjuring this scene for your benefit. You drink the coffee and discover it is the perfect temperature, despite a good deal of steam coming from the liquid.

'Hell is an odd place,' begins Lucifer. 'Right now, you are experiencing physical pleasure, but none of it is real. To me, your body is a bunch of nerve endings, and all I need from them is the right input in order to provide you with the most severe pain imaginable. Conversely, all I need do is act in the opposite fashion and I can give you the most intense pleasure. Make sense?'
'I think so,' you reply, greedily devouring all that keeps appearing in front of you.
'And it is this that makes stand up comedy so interesting is it not? All that happens is a stimulus is applied which is very particular to your nerve endings. Your brain is presented with a problem, and in the process of figuring it out, the reward mechanism kicks in and rewards you with a chuckle. It shouldn't make sense that you would laugh from such stimulus, but for some reason you do. The brain is tricked!'

Lucifer seems very pleased with this analysis.

'I don't agree,' you begin. 'You are leaving out the feelings of expectation and social cohesion which human beings are subjected to when witnessing stand up comedy. It is very rare that you laugh when alone, but when you are with friends or at a comedy club as part of an audience, a group cohesion exists which all who are present abide by. That is why during as comedy set, momentum is so important. If you can convince 60% of the room that you're funny, the other 40% will just go along with it because they are so afraid of being outcasts. Groups always abide by consensus. That's why so few people walk out of comedy clubs even if they aren't enjoying themselves.'

'Wow,' says Lucifer, hanging on to your every word. 'Fascinating.'

'Look, this is all theory. Bottom line: you have to be funny. I'm happy to do a comedy course for you, but I don't think you're telling me the whole story. Last night, I saw you talk to those… whatever you want to call them.'

'Minions.' Lucifer says with confidence. You shake your head. 'You can't really call them that anymore.'

'Why not?'

'Have you seen Despicable Me?'

'Oh fuck off!' Lucifer theatrically throws up his hands in disgust. 'So because of one film I can't use the correct term for my demon servants?'

'It was a global phenomenon and they made more than one of them. When you say minions I just think of little yellow things.'

'Whose fault is that? When you think of minions you should be thinking of demons with razor blade cocks raping babies.'

'Hey! I'm not saying you're wrong, I'm just saying…'

You can see that this is an argument you're not going to win. You move on. 'Anyway, regardless. When you were addressing your minions last night, you spoke with confidence. When we were all pissed and you were telling stories, they were all listening. You were engaging and funny. You told me initially that you struggle with confidence when public speaking, and it didn't look to me as though you struggle at all. So I can't help thinking that you've been misleading me.'

Lucifer ponders what you've just said for a few seconds. Contemplating, he leans forward with his arms folded, placing his elbows on the table. Taking a deep breath, he lets out a nasal sigh via his enormous nostrils. For whatever reason, he doesn't want to tell you what he is about to tell you. It can't be easy for a creature as purely evil as Lucifer is to become at ease with telling the truth. Is this yet more deception, or is Lucifer truly struggling to get across that which he needs to convey. It becomes obvious that what he wants to say is indeed, very difficult for him to express. Realising this, you reach across and place a reassuring hand on Lucifer's forearm.

'It's OK.' you tell him.

'In hell, there resides an army of super demons known as the Amakhulu. The demons you've seen here whom I have under my control are vast in number but lacking in the skill required to overthrow God and the angels of heaven. I need the Amakhulu on my side. Such demons have been placed here to test me, and I can assure you that test me they do. A tougher audience you will not find anywhere else in the universe. You think you know God? You don't. He designed these super demons knowing full well that I would struggle to have dominion over them. For thousands of years now, all I have done is house them. I cannot control them, but they're not powerful enough to overthrow me.'
'Where are they?'
'They reside in a circle of hell known as Indulu.'
'This doesn't make a lot of sense,' you say, confused but also intrigued. 'Why would God create them in the first place?'
'To torture me. I wanted what my Father had. What I didn't realise is that by questioning my Father, and thereby disobeying him, what he has gifted me in hell is also what he had in heaven. He has given me an army with which to overthrow the forces of heaven, but I will never be able to command them. That's where you come in.'
'What?!'
'I've tried everything. Those beasts on the lowest levels of hell enjoy being tortured and torturing me. They ignore me. They laugh at me. They mock me. All I have is my power, but what I need are my wits.'
'What makes you think a comedy course will help you?'
'As soon as I begin to talk to them, to plead, to reason… they mock me. They make fun of my horns. They laugh at any attempts I make to assert my authority. I have tried everything. I have unleashed on them the most savage of punishments, but they do not yield. There are about half a million of them, but they are not individuals. I'm lost. They do not have any respect for my power,' Lucifer looks up and shakes his fist. 'Oh cruel, Lord. You, are truly the master of punishment,' Lucifer now looks straight at you. 'But I shall have my revenge. Shan't I?'

You slurp down another big mouthful of coffee and look Lucifer dead in the eye.

'Let's get to work.'

* * * *

You come to realise that what Lucifer has on his hands is actually a very tricky corporate gig. You won't be training him to become a comedian, rather, you need to train him to face a very specific audience. An audience that by the sounds of it doesn't particularly like to laugh unless they're making themselves laugh, and also enjoys taking part in or even witnessing any kind of physical torture. So yeah, a corporate.

Unfortunately, being a mid-tier comedian of no repute, you've never done a corporate gig in your life. But you did once do a gig at a women's refuge, and that was fairly similar to what you think you'll be facing here.

Strolling past a lake of fire, with you and Lucifer recently fully nourished, you set about planning how to approach this gig. 'What happened the last time you tried to talk to them?' you enquire. You need to know what kind of crowd they really are. Asking Lucifer seems to be tricky as he appears to be very sensitive about his past experiences.
'They're animals. Just, remorseless. So cruel. They don't listen.' Lucifer shakes his head in dismay, as he relives the last time he encountered then.
'I can tell it has, erm, bothered you.' you say, reassuringly.
'It has.'
'Look, it's ok. We've all had bad gigs. I had a terrible gig at The Glee Club once.'
'Did any of the audience rip off a disabled person's arms and use them to fist fuck midgets that had been nailed to a cross?'
'No. They just stared at me for ten minutes.'
'Go on.'

'I really need to know what happened last time you tried to talk to them. What did you try and do?' you look at Lucifer with pleading in your eyes. You need the truth.
'I tried to command them! I am their master! They are to obey me and follow me as I, and only I, am the leader of the armies of hell!'
'Hmmm. I don't get the impression it went too well for you then?'
'Oh it was terrible. They didn't give me a chance. I tortured all of them but it just made them laugh.'
'I think we need to work on your opening.'

You don't know a lot about comedy but you do know how important it is to have a good opening. Opening a comedy set is the most important part of your act. How you begin in that first minute will usually decide how the rest of the gig will go. You don't have to be hilarious, but you do have to establish yourself. Some comedians can do it with a wave, a nod, or even silence. Some can convey composure and reassurance merely by appearing on stage. It takes years to master this and for the truly gifted comedian, it will come naturally.

'Can you show me how you walk in to that particular circle of hell?' you ask.
'Oh I don't walk. I just appear.' responds Lucifer.
'Right. I think that might be a mistake.'
'In what way?'
'Well, there's no build up. No anticipation. A lot of comedy is in the build up. Even the show manager telling the audience what rules there are for behaviour in a comedy club can help set up the crowd and get them in the correct frame of mind.'
'Riiiiiight. I get it,' the penny drops for Lucifer. 'I kinda wish you could've been there so you could tell me what I did wrong.'
'Yeah, it's shame. Although, you could just do it for me now?'
'What, here?' Lucifer seems horrified by the idea.
'Why not? You want my expertise, let's see what you did. Then we can make the necessary adjustments.'

You can see Lucifer racking his brains for a reason not to do this, but you can also see that he knows it makes perfect sense.
'OK. I shall do it for you,' Lucifer sets himself up. 'I mean… shall I just do it right here, like this?'
'Sure. Just show me what you did.'
'OK. Right,' Lucifer clears his throat. He pauses. 'God this is so silly.'
'Don't be ridiculous! If you can't do it in front of me, how are you gonna be able to do it in front of thousands?'
'Yeah, yeah. Fair enough. You're right. OK,' some minions begin to gather, Lucifer notices them. 'You lot can fuck off.' The minions scarper.
'Nosey cunts.'
Lucifer shakes his both his hands loosely at the wrists and gets ready. After first taking a deep breath then slowly letting it out, he adopts a powerful stance with his hands on hips and chest proud. He takes another deep breath…
'Minions of hell!' he bellows, your body shakes as a result of the bass in his voice. 'Servants of the master who stands before ye. Rejoice! The time is upon us. For too long now, we have waited for…'
'I'm gonna stop you there,' you interrupt. 'Just, relax. Take five.'
'Why are you stopping me? That was exactly how I did it!' Lucifer seems annoyed. 'I put everything into that to make you feel as though you were in the room with me at the original gig! That took a lot out of me you know!'
'Oh it's fine!' you lie, reassuring him. 'It's just that I can see a few mistakes and it's probably better to nip them in the bud.'
'Oh. OK.'
'So you start off by calling them all minions and servants?'
'Yeah.'
'Right. Where is the "good evening everyone, and what a pleasure it is to be here"?'
'What do you mean?'
'You want the audience on side, yet you've gone on and immediately told them that they are your servants. That's not gonna go down to well. You want the audience to like you.'
'But I am the Prince of Darkness! They *are* my servants!'

'With all due respect, it sounds like last time you tried this approach they made you their bitch and now you've got someone helping you who can only just scrape a living on the mirth control circuit.'

Lucifer breaks down. His sulphuric tears hit the rocky floor, causing choking steam to rise and the floor to bubble. You aren't sure whether to reassure him or to just let him get this out of his system. Like so many comedians, Lucifer doesn't think it can be possible for him to have a bad gig, and is obviously used to blaming the audience. Furthermore, he always smashes the gig in front of his own audience, but when faced with a hostile crowd, he falls to pieces.

Many comedians fall into this trap. All comedians dream of having their own audience. An audience who have similar sensibilities, who shares a shorthand and laughs at others. These comedians care not for those who aren't members of their special bullshit club, and instead enjoy the seductive trappings of groupthink. These people aren't real comedians. A real comedian can make anyone laugh. A real comedian can adapt. Lucifer, as it stands, cannot adapt. These Amakhulu should be his target audience, but they obviously need something a little stronger.

'Are you gonna be ok?' you ask, wondering whether or not physical contact is needed or indeed appropriate. In these times of *#metoo*, you never know what's right or wrong in terms of offering reassurance.
'I'm ok. I guess this is all part of the process?' says Lucifer, accidentally slicing his eye open as he wipes a tear from his cheek with those calloused hands of his. 'Bastard.'
'That looks sore.' you comment.
'Nah, happens all the time.'
'Sorry if I was harsh.'
'It's fine. I need it. Tough love. I get it.'
'Right then, your opening…' something occurs to you. You dismiss it as soon as you think of it, but then it pops in your head again. 'Tell you what, you reckon you could get me a gig for the super demons?'

'What? You want to gig in Indulu? For the Amakhulu?
'Yeah. Can you sort it?'
'Yeah. I can make it happen whenever you like.'
You place the tips of each of your fingers together like Mr. Burns from The Simpsons and hunch your shoulders a little.
'Excellent,' you say in your best Mr. Burns from The Simpsons voice, waiting for some sort of approval from Lucifer. 'Mr. Burns? The Simpsons?'
Lucifer looks at you and shrugs his shoulders.
'Never mind.'

* * * *

Indulu is the time out room for evil without redemption. The Amakhulu reside here and connive ever more inventive ways to punish one another, as well as those who up on Earth in the mortal world they would seek to endear. Evil loves evil. They know only pain, thwarted from the ability to effectively organise and take over hell by their divine creator, they come together only when torturing some poor soul will give them ample entertainment. Lucifer has limited dominion over them, able to keep the Amakhulu in hell but not command them. All attempts to bring them under his wing have proven futile, as their love of torture extends to when they themselves are tortured. On several occasions, the Amakhulu have informed Lucifer on one another merely to rid themselves of boredom, just so they could enjoy the mutilation of themselves as well as their brethren at the hands of Lucifer. You know this, because Lucifer knows this.

You walk with him to the outskirts of Indulu, a landscape almost stereotypically awash with fire and lava. What seem to be hundreds of thousands of misshapen bodies crawl across the landscape like ants. Your vantage point is such that you can take in this horror, but in no way are you able to process that which you are witness to. Many of the Amakhulu swim in the molten hot lava, burning off any epidermis they might have had, exposing their deformed skeletons to the elements as they crawl from the liquid rock to enjoy the sensation of having been burned alive. Lying there in blissful agony, each scorched individual welcomes the attention of other Amakhulu, many of whom gleefully fornicate with the bones of those whose skin has just been burnt off. The screams which accompany this bizarre act are as deafening as they are horrifying. You can barely stand to watch as demon after demon repeats this same act of self inflicted torture, with those who are not participating keeping themselves busy thinking of new ways to experience the most intense discomfort you could imagine. A lack of imagination prevents innovation, with most of them keeping boredom at bay by wearing aborted foetuses as glove puppets, using them to perform a song which has only belches for lyrics.

After a good while of attempting to take all this in, you turn to Lucifer, clearly in a state of some shock.
'Told ya. It's proper fucked up down here.' says Lucifer.
'You weren't lying,' you reply, weirdly confident that you'll have good gig. 'So what can you do for me?'
'How'd you mean?'
'In terms of safety.'
'They won't be able to physically harm you unless I allow them.'
'Sweet. And what kind of set up can you provide?'
'Whatever you like. Radio mic, head set...'
'Urgh,' you shudder. 'I'm not Michael McIntyre.'
'Too right you're not, he's successful'
'AY-OOOOO' you each say in unison, giving each other a high five.
'OK,' you say, 'here's the plan. Set up some seats. Give them a ten minute call and play 2 Unlimited's absolute classic, "Get Ready for This" followed by a five minute warning...'
'But "Get Ready for This" isn't five minutes long?' interrupts Lucifer.
'It doesn't matter. It's about momentum.'
'OK.' Lucifer nods.
'Then, you play "Let Me Entertain You" by Robbie Williams, and as that reaches the end, you give them a two minute warning.'
'What are we warning them about? Sorry, I'm not following.'

'My mistake. It's an industry phrase. Basically you do an announcement saying "the show will start in two minutes" or something like that.'
'Oh! I see.' Lucifer is enjoying this.
'Then for the final two minutes you play "Right Here, Right Now" by Fatboy Slim.'
'Fucking love that.'
'Aye, it's a belter. Then, you introduce me to the stage and I'll take it from there.'

Lucifer looks over at the Amakhulu, many of whom are casually kicking babies around, while others make people with down syndrome run at each other head first until their heads explode before scooping up the brains and using it as lube for their cocks. Once sufficiently lubed, the Amakhulu set about anally raping the corpses of agnostics.
'I'm not sure this is gonna work y'know.' cautions Lucifer.
'Trust me. I've done gigs in pubs where old boys playing dominos didn't even know there was a gig happening. These simpletons won't know what hit them.'
You say this with such fierce belief that you're now actually quite looking forward to the gig. You only ended up here because you took a gig that ended up never happening. Now you get to perform in front of and audience of hundreds of thousands. You're winning!

Never underestimate the self delusion of a stand up comedian.

Indulu begins to change shape before your very eyes. A huge stage appears with video screens either side, in front of which are thousands upon thousands of seats, arranged perfectly to that all Amakhulu will be able to watch the show. The Amakhulu look around at one another, shrieking with confusion as someone throws a toddler up in the air just to see what kind of mess it will make when it hits the floor. As the toddler reaches it's peak, it is turned into a giant mirror ball that casts disco light across the igneous rock which surrounds the crowd. The Amakhulu fall silent.

'Ladies and gentlemen the show will start in ten minutes time. We'd like to remind you to turn off all your mobile phones and not to talk while the acts are on stage. Thank you.'
The Amakhulu aren't sure what to do. "Get Ready For This" begins to play. None of them move. Each stare, as for the first time in a long time, the torture in which they normally indulge as a matter of course, is paused.
'YA'LL READY FOR THIS?'
The Amakhulu begin to move their shoulders and bob their heads.
Slowly, they begin to take their seats. It's working.
'Fucking hell!' yells Lucifer, leaping about in disbelief.
'Told you,' you say, smugly, but trying to hide it. 'Sixty percent of the time it works every time,' you wait for recognition. None comes your way. 'Anchorman?'
'Not seen it. I liked Dodgeball though.'
You look away from Lucifer toward the assembling masses of Indulu. This will be by far the biggest audience you've ever played to. There must be half a million of them and you can't wait to get down there. The performer inside you is now in full flow, and this is the first time since being in hell that you've felt in charge and in control of what is going on. You have the boss of the venue making sure you can't get hurt, which means you can just go down there, express yourself and do your thing. Then it occurs to you that this gig isn't about you. It's about Lucifer. You need to understand the kind of crowd you're dealing with in order to better prepare him for the gig of his life. Does it really matter how well *you* do?
'Ladies and gentleman the show will start in 5 minutes time…'

> *"Hell is gone and heaven's here*
> *There's nothing left for you to fear*
> *Shake your ass come here*
> *Now scream"*

Indulu erupts with a scream. The whole place is going crazy. Amakhulu flock to their seats. Anticipation is building. Lucifer looks at you with a shit eating grin on his face. You then notice that he's shovelling handfuls of shit into his mouth.

'Sorry, old habit. Want some?' Lucifer moves his hand towards you, uncurling his long fingers, the palm filled with steaming hot shit. You examine the faecal matter as though you were actually considering saying yes before shaking your head and returning your attention to Indulu.

> *"I'm a burning effigy*
> *Of everything I used to be*
> *You're my rock of empathy*
> *My dear"*

This gig is buzzing. You know in your heart of hearts you could absolutely smash this, but what would be the point of that? It's not as though there's any chance of progression. But what if you don't rip it? How will Lucifer trust you? If you can't make these super demons laugh, how do you expect to be able to teach Lucifer?

> *"Life's too short for you to die*
> *So grab yourself an alibi*
> *Heaven knows your mother lied*
> *Mon cher*
> *Separate your right from wrongs*
> *Come and sing a different song*
> *The kettle's on so don't be long*
> *Mon cher"*

Something has occurred to Lucifer. He can't wait to tell you. 'Hey! Wouldn't it be funny if he said "separate your right from MONGS"? Eh? You can have that if you want.'
Christ. He needs more help than you thought. That is straight up guitar playing comedian humour. Changing the fucking lyrics to a well known song. That's why you're here in the first place! Maybe it's a sign? Or a test? Who knows? All you know is that right now you need to decide the best way to approach this gig. If you go on and do shit, how many of them will want to watch the gig next time, when Lucifer needs to be on top form? You might be setting him up to fail. If you do well, maybe all you need to do is tell Lucifer to imitate you? But then what

use is that for commanding respect in order to lead the armies of hell? Fuck. It's getting close now.

> *"Here is the place where the feeling grows*
> *You gotta get high before you taste the lows*
> *So come on*
> *Let meeeeeeee, entertain you"*

The Amakhulu are going mental. Lucifer is off his tits on shit, which might come in handy because you're about to fill your pants with the same substance he apparently loves eating. What the fuck are you going to do?

To go on and do your tried and tested gold, turn to page 121

To go on and take one for the team, turn to page 161

Sparky Mark locks the door to the green room. He makes his way towards the stage, as you make your way to the nearest toilet so that you can wash the blood off your face.
'I'll head backstage,' says Sparky Mark. 'I won't start the show until you're with me.'
'OK, I'll be quick.' you reply, not even sure how much blood you'll be contending with. You notice that the disabled toilet is wide open with nobody inside and decide to jump in there quickly, the large single cubicle giving you some much needed privacy.

Locking the door behind you, the chance to actually breathe and centre yourself is granted to you for the first time since you ran over and killed that elderly lady. You chuckle to yourself as you realise that there is no way the gig could be any worse than what you've already had to endure. You look at yourself in the mirror and feel relief that there isn't much blood to clean up. The mixer tap squeaks as you initiate the flow. Whilst splashing water on your face, you realise that your body temperature must be through the roof, as the lukewarm water in your hands feels icy cold when splashed on your features. Blinking at yourself in the mirror, you flash a cheesy grin and notice a chunk of vomited vegetable stuck between two of your teeth. Using your little finger nail to poke the detritus from between your central and lateral incisor, you congratulate yourself for catching this before going stage. Small mercies.

You turn to leave but notice something on the cistern. A small line of white powder, most likely cocaine. You've not gigged on cocaine since "the incident", but you can feel fatigue creeping over you and realise that this Class A gift could give you the boost you need. You lick your little finger, dabbing at the powder with your moist digit before rubbing it on your gums. Yup, coke. Fuck it, a bump won't hurt. You get out your car keys and sprinkle some on to your house key, then sniff hard on the Colombian. A great big giant inhalation followed by a slow exhalation gives you the modicum of inner calm you're after, as you steel yourself for the task at hand.

You leave the toilet and march purposefully towards the back stage area. Lauren is ahead, closing the doors behind the audience as they're now all in and waiting for the show to start. You try to avoid her seeing you, but linger too long in an attempt to capture her beauty.
'Hey!' she calls 'You ok?'
'Yeah why?'
'What the fuck was that with Sparky?'
'What d'ya mean?' you ask nervously, hoping not to give the game away.
'The dick sucking thing. What was that?'
'Oh!' relief. 'He was just being a twat. You know what he's like.'
'Alas, I do. Break a leg.' Lauren blesses this good will with a blown kiss before turning to leave. You feel compelled to call after her.
'Lauren?'

With everything that has happened tonight, maybe you should ask her out. She knows you have a long term partner, but so what? You only want to go for a drink and what is the problem with two friends having a drink? Just because you're interested in her bisexual liaisons, it doesn't mean you'd act on the many sexual impulses you might experience in her presence. Even if she offered to stick her tongue in your anus and wiggle it around until you climaxed, you'd probably just laugh it off as a bit of banter between friends and why shouldn't friends be able to laugh at the possibility of sexual pleasure? After all, it's just a bit of fun. Lauren turns back.

'Yeah?' she looks expectant. Maybe she wants you to ask?
'I will.'
'You'll what?'
'Break a leg.' you fucking coward.
'Oh,' Lauren laughs. 'I know you will.'

Shit. If that had happened 5 minutes later the coke would've kicked in and you'd have had the confidence. Lauren walks away, her bottom taunting you with it's juiciness. You can imagine each cheek having just enough cellulite to not be disgusting, but be disgusting enough to give you enough body confidence to leave the light on. What the fuck is wrong with you? How can you stand on stage but still lack confidence in the bedroom with someone new? Is that why you're still in your current relationship? The fear of making a fool of oneself during sexual interaction is something that haunts us all, and a major reason why most first sexual encounters are done with the aid of some kind of consciousness altering drug. How you wish you had more confidence. How you wonder about her taste. How you wonder about how you would taste to her. Oh Lauren.

The backstage door flings open. Your arm is grabbed and you are yanked towards someone before you even know who it is. Thank fuck it's Sparky Mark, as it occurs to you in that split second that it could have been the police, for any number of reasons.
'You were just staring into space!' says Sparky 'Are you ready?'
'Yeah. Yes. I'm ready.'
'Are you sure?'
'Yes, I'm sure!'
Sparky Mark puts both hands on your shoulders.
'Focus. The show must go on.' he tells you, staring deep into your eyes in a bid to reassure you. Momentarily, you forget about the dead body in the green room. Sparky Mark turns to the backstage microphone and then fiddles with the sound desk. He mutes the background music that has been playing for the audience as they were taking their seats for the final part of the show. Licking his lips, he takes to the mic.
'Ladies and gentlemen, welcome back to Uncle Spunk's Chuckle Trunk, for the final time this evening please welcome back to the stage your host... it's Sparky Mark!'

Sparky Mark does some more wizardry on the sound desk then strolls on stage to the delighted applause of the audience in attendance. You watch in awe at the professionalism on display and wonder how many times you've witnessed a comedian on stage and had no idea what was going on in their personal lives. We very rarely get a clue about any kind of tragedy or trauma that a comedian may be dealing with as for the most part, they just go on stage and do their thing. Regardless of how funny a comedian is, that ability to compartmentalise their existence is something everyone could learn from. Some comedians need the stage and welcome an escape from the day to day drudgery of bills and kids and all the other stresses that just chip away at your ability to enjoy even the simplest of life's pleasures. Each day it just gets harder and harder to even think about raising a chuckle in your own life, let alone the lives of strangers who have paid to be entertained by you. These performers you see on stage aren't always working. No, sometimes they're having a break from everything going on around them, from everything that isn't under their control. On stage, the comedian can take control and, barring some incredibly challenging never before seen event, they can have a level of command over proceedings that eludes them in their personal life.

Watching Sparky on stage, you'd have no idea that he'd just witnessed a brutal suicide. Not just any suicide mind you, a suicide he is now actively trying to cover up by hoping that what, fairies come along and deal with? What the fuck does he think is gonna happen in between bringing you on stage and finishing the comedy night?

Panic hits you as you realise that while you're onstage, Sparky Mark could be ringing the police and informing on you. Shit. Your DNA is all over the green room. What if witnesses saw you scowling whilst that open spot was on stage? Did you touch the knife? YOU POCKETED THE KNIFE! Is detesting shit stand up comedy enough of a motive to commit a cold blooded murder? You didn't kill him though, he killed himself. But who would believe that? These thoughts rush through your head as you notice Sparky is putting the microphone back in the stand and is preparing to introduce you. Maybe the coke is making you paranoid? He looks across and gives you a little wink that is designed to settle your nerves, but instead sends your imagination into overload as you realise how vulnerable a position you're about to put yourself into, as you will essentially be trapped and unable to keep a watch on Sparky

Mark for at least twenty to twenty-five minutes depending on how well you do.

He's just said your name and BBC Three in the same sentence. Doing that talking head show about stomach ulcers has done wonders for your TV credits. He's getting ready to give you a big introduction. Time slows down as you hear him say 'for the final time tonight, let's raise the roof and welcome to the stage…'

Your pre gig superstation of crossing yourself kicks in, as you touch your forehead, stomach and each shoulder. You don't even believe, but the routine helps you focus, and something of the spiritual needs to enter you before taking to the stage. Christ believed in unconditional love and believe it or not, this is what you need in order to make people laugh. On some level, you have to love every single member of the audience. There could be horrible, sexist, racist people sat out there. Statistically, at one of your gigs in the past, there will have been a paedophile in the audience. At the BBC new comedians competition you took part in a few years ago, there were probably loads of kiddy fiddlers amongst the crowd. It doesn't matter, you need to have a reason beyond financial remuneration to make these people laugh, and what better reason than love? Spreading laughter and joy is one of the few gifts that people get to experience, and here you are not only experiencing it, but getting paid to do it. It is your responsibility to get out there and do this to the best of your ability.

The show must go on.

It is this feeling of love you would ordinarily try to cultivate which is currently eluding you as you make your way to the stage. It dawns on you that you are actually physically exhausted and the last thing you want to be doing right now is making these cunts laugh. You banish this feeling from you as quickly as you can, for you know that allowing it take hold will kill whatever it is you're about to attempt. You need to take control. Nothing has gone your way tonight. You need to make this happen. The cocaine was a terrible idea.

Sparky Mark gives you a wonderful introduction and the audience applauds your impending presence rapturously. You walk onstage, fist bump Sparky and then take the microphone from the stand. Now, finally, you are in control of what is happening.

'Thank you, thank you very much. Hello Uncle Spunk's, are we well?' you point the microphone at the audience who respond with an enthusiastic cheer. You glance to your right and see that Sparky Mark is stood there. Good, he's watching your set. You immediately relax more and begin to settle into your routine. 'Wow! You are such a great audience. I've only just got here as I was opening at another comedy club so I haven't seen the show, did I miss anything?'
'Yeah, that last act was amazing,' yells a woman from the audience. 'Absolutely incredible.' many of the audience murmur in agreement as a spontaneous round of applause breaks out for the recently deceased. You'd asked your question rhetorically, forgetting that it's late and most of these morons are drunk.
'Fucking hell, give me a chance! I've only just got onstage!' you protest with mock anger. The audience chuckles but you can sense that they're waiting for you to hit them with a big laugh so that they can relax. That's OK, you have that big first joke in your arsenal, you're just making a little room for yourself. You asked a question that didn't need answering and now they're all thinking about how good the previous act was, but it's fine! DON'T PANIC!

'Urgh, I tell you what, I had to drive here tonight. Give me a cheer if you drive!' the majority of the audience cheers. Perfect, they're primed. 'Yeah, you see the problem with the way I drive is...'

SMASH. A glass hits the floor.

'Wahey!' yells most of the audience in unison.
'Just put that where you want, mate!' comes the ad-lib of a man in the audience, getting the first big laugh of your set. The

glass smashing couldn't have come at a worse time. You cannot go backwards and start the joke again. You have to roll with this punch or you're opening will be ruined and the audience will lose all confidence in you.
'Who dropped the glass?' you enquire.
'Wasn't a glass, it was a massive contact lens.' the audience laughs again. Same guy. That's two big laughs now, you didn't get either of them, and the previous act got a round of applause. You're fucked if you don't get them back in the next thirty seconds. Covering your eyes from the spotlight a little, you see a table of people trying to deal with the mess they've just made. You watch as they do their best to not make a fuss.
'You alright down there? Because you proper fucked up my opening joke.' you give this just enough charm to be self effacing and jovial.
'Fuck off,' apparently not jovial enough, as the main woman dealing with the broken glass dismisses you in one sentence before returning to her clean up operation. 'Argh! Shit! I've just cut my hand on this fucking glass. Fuck!'
'You alright, love?' someone calls from across the room. 'I've got plasters in my purse if you need any.'
'Shit. Yeah. I might need them. Fucking hell I might need stitches.' says the woman who just told you to fuck off. The audience are deathly silent now, waiting for you to take control. You need to be quick.
'Fucking hell, anyone else feel like they're watching the beginning of an episode of Casualty?'

Half of the audience laugh. You glance over to see if Sparky Mark is still there. He is. You feel contempt bubbling in your gut. You are not in control.
'Hold on love, I'll bring some plasters over.'
You look across and see that the good samaritan is a woman. At least, you think it's a woman because she seems to be enveloping a mobility scooter, such is her aquatic mammal level of obesity. She's American fat. You look again at the woman who has cut her hand open, then look back at the Walrus and realise there are loads of chairs and people to navigate. It might be better if the woman who needs technology in order to move stays put, then the woman who

can still claim to be a biped will be able to make her way over to the woman that is built for sub zero waters. You're just not sure how to put this tactfully but forcefully, and with good humour.
'Hey, why don't you stay there,' you say to Jabba the Samaritan, 'and why don't you go over to her so that there's less of a kerfuffle.' you say to the woman who has completely fucked up the start of your set.
'OK.' says the elephant seal on wheels, obviously pleased that she doesn't have to make her way through an audience and draw attention to how much she is costing the NHS.

Despite your weird feeling of hatred, you admire her. It can't be easy being that size, and it's clearly more than a physical problem when someone gets that big. None of us know what goes on in other people's lives and there's no way this woman can be happy in such a dire physical state. She's come out to have a laugh and here she is, exposing herself to the possibility of ridicule so that she can give aid to a fellow human being. You marvel at the kind of courage it takes to just live day to day knowing that people are staring, judging and laughing at you. If there is a heaven, it is made for people like this who try to help others with no thought for themselves.
'Thanks,' you say 'cos to be honest, the last thing we need is you falling over. I don't think we could get a forklift through those double doors.'

You absolute piece of shit.

The audience gasp. You've fucked up here, big time.
'I beg your pardon?' asks the woman on the specially reinforced mobility scooter.
'What the fuck is your problem?' chimes in the woman with a cut hand. The audience sit watching this transpire, unsure of how to act but enthralled at the awkwardness of it all. You've been onstage maybe 2 minutes and the gig is completely fucked. Despite this, you feel remarkably cool. You seem to have used up all your adrenalin and now act as though you were on the strongest possible beta blocker known to man. The coke has done nothing other than give you confidence.

You don't feel nervous. You don't feel hate. In fact, you don't feel anything. Whatever love you tried to carry with you onto the stage has now got up and walked out, as you feel the need for self immolation creeping over yourself. You resist the urge, but cold hard logic is rearing it's head, and that never goes down well at a comedy night.
'I tell you what,' you begin. 'Why don't you two fuck off out and sort your plaster issues somewhere else? I've literally just walked onstage and some clumsy spastic has dropped a glass and cut herself on it. Then, if that wasn't bad enough, a fucking talking planet has offered first aid. And you're asking what my problem is? Are you serious? My problem is that all I want to do is come on and tell a few jokes, but I seem to have ended up at a carer's comedy night, where they've brought along all the retards but the carers have stayed out there to have a drink and talk shop.'

Silence. Quiet crying.

The lady with a BMI big enough for two is being consoled by two friends. She waves them away, then fires up her scooter. Turning her head as best she can to make sure she doesn't reverse into anyone, she begins to move backwards before angrily yanking the handlebars left and moving forward a little. She lets out a frustrated sob as she slams the handlebars right this time before again reversing in order to make room for her exit. She doesn't even bother to check this time as she only needs little more room in order to make her escape.
Handlebars left now, as she begins to make her way out of Uncle Spunk's Chuckle Trunk. Audience members make room for her so that she doesn't have to speak, as her two friends gather their things and follow the leader out the venue.
All eyes are on her as she makes every effort to maintain her dignity whilst exiting.
'Oooooh, blobby, blobby, blobby.' you say, no longer giving a shit. All eyes are now on you, with mouths open and incredulity etched across every single person's face.
'What? Fuck off. She started it.' you double down.
Because all eyes are on you, someone hasn't moved out of the way for the mobility scooter lady.

BEEP BEEP! The insistent sound of the machine speaking for a lady too upset to utter even a basic courtesy rebounds around the still silent room. Everybody turns back to see a man is seated in the way of scooter lady's exit. The gentleman blocking her path immediately moves upon hearing the distress siren, and quietly apologises as he lets her past, the whirring sound of a straining electric battery is all that can be heard as she makes her way out. Two other men get out of their seats to open the exit doors, aiding the lady in her exit. As she drives out, she raises her right arm and extends her middle finger. You look across and notice that Sparky Mark has gone.

The doors close. Everybody turns back to look at you.
'We spend more each year on people like her than we do the police and fire service combined.' you point out, for no good reason whatsoever.
'You're a fucking piece of shit.' yells a man from the audience.
'Who said that?' you enquire, looking around the audience.
'Does anybody else have a plaster?' shouts the bleeding lady.
'Why don't you fuck off out too?' you reply, pouring all your fury into that one sentence. 'Come on, who was it? Who said I was a piece of shit?' you look to your right. Sparky Mark is no longer there and who could blame him?
'I said it,' shouts an Indian man, standing up to make himself noticeable. 'I said it because it's true. You're not funny and you're a fucking piece of shit.'
'Well, if I wasn't funny I wouldn't be getting booked would I?'

SMASH!

The bleeding lady collapses, seemingly passed out.
'Fucking, Jesus. Can someone get her out?' you ask, now furious at the disruption. You turn your attention back to the Indian man. 'And you, you can fuck right off you smelly cunt.'
'Smelly?! Is that a racial thing?' asks the Indian man, fully confident that the audience is on his side. A few people are now attending to the bleeding lady, holding her hand above her head and applying pressure to the wound.

'Why would it be racial? You just look like a smelly cunt.' you reply, now absolutely certain that there is no way you're gonna be able to pull this gig back.
'Yeah, but why? Why do I *look* smelly?' he pursues.

You have no idea where the impulse comes from, but you feel an overwhelming compulsion to be racist. You've never said anything racist before (on stage) but this gig is so far gone it wouldn't matter in the slightest, and the idea of shouting a racial epithet is amusing to you on a comedic level. Under normal circumstances, you wouldn't even consider it, but these are not normal circumstances. There's no way Sparky Mark will ever book you again, so why not? Something racist hasn't been said on stage in such a fashion since Michael Richards dropped the N-Bomb at the Laugh Factory in 2006. No one in their right mind would say it. No one in their right mind would be expecting it! You look across and see that Sparky Mark has returned, now flanked by Lauren and three rather large, white male police officers.

Your DNA. The knife. The blood. The cocaine in your system. The hit and run.

You're done. What is left to do?

To call the audience member a "paki", turn to page 160

To walk off stage and accept your fate, turn to page 198

'Ladies and gentleman, the show will start in two minutes time...'

You just know that you're gonna smash this. Fatboy Slim kicks in and you know that it's time to do what you do best. The stage is set. The Amakhulu are all facing in the right direction and despite their vast number, they are remarkably obedient. They're ready. You're ready. Hundreds of thousands of super demons are awaiting the time of their lives. You gaze upon the attending simpletons about to witness your genius and begin to understand exactly how Lee Evans feels.

> *"Right here, right now*
> *Right here, right now*
> *Right here, right now*
> *Right here, right now"*

This is your time to shine. You're gonna go out there and kick this puppy in the guts. You're gonna tear the roof off the place. You've smashed harder gigs than this before. You can do this! Five hundred, or five hundred thousand. It doesn't matter. All you have to do is go out there, get them on side early and BOOM! You'll have them eating out the palm of your hand. These fucking idiots won't know what hit them. You can do this! They've previously had to endure Lucifer "separate your right from mongs" stutter his way through some shitty speech time after time, so they're gone lose their shit when they get a load of you: a professional comedian of some repute who can command a fee of £50 - £75 to open on a Friday night in Doncaster. At the last minute.

It's time. You give Lucifer the nod. Your pre gig superstition kicks in, as you gesticulate the sign of the cross. During the touching of your forehead, stomach, then both shoulders, you become aware of Lucifer staring at you in disbelief.
'Sorry,' you shrug. 'Force of habit.'
'Same.' Lucifer shrugs, showing you another handful of shit before shovelling it into his mouth.

Lucifer has to hurriedly swallow the waste, as he almost misses his cue. Once the shit is clear of his oesophagus, he begins announcing you to the stage. To your horror, Lucifer just cuts the music dead, and there is a brief moment of silence before he addresses the audience.
'Ladies and gentleman, are you ready to laugh?'

Nothing.

Oh no.

'I said, are you ready to laugh?' this time, with the worst kind of cheesy energy.
The Amakhulu look at one another, unsure as to whether or not they should answer. The music carried with it an energy and enthusiasm that implied some level of professionalism. Now they have this absolute shit show.
'Well, if you… like laughing, you'll love what we… have in store. For you! Please welcome to the stage….'
The next few seconds are a blur. This stuttering moron has just fucked you. You stare at Lucifer, faeces dripping from his teeth as he smiles whilst giving you a big thumbs up. He actually thinks he's done a good job. This poor mother fucker really doesn't have a clue, and has absolutely no idea that he's killed all the work you'd just put in.

You've tried to explain this to people, but they never understand. Stand up comedy isn't just about jokes. It's a show. A really good comedian can walk into a pub, call the audience to attention and have them all laughing and listening with a mixture of skill and interaction that is truly a marvel to watch. These comedians are few and far between. They carry with them a level of comedic gravitas which is impossible to ignore. That ain't you. Not by a long shot. You *need* the facade of a show, and the peer pressure that comes with the audience knowing they have their part to play. At most comedy nights, the audience has to make an effort to enjoy themselves until a rhythm is established. A flow. That's what a lot of stand up comedy is: momentum. How many times have you seen a shit comedian just hit a rhythm and run with it, carrying the audience with them as they play along. Everyone knows the comic has no jokes but they just kinda go along with it. That is the power of expectation. The tickets were £20, the baby sitter was £40 and they've already spent another £40 on booze. They're gonna do their best to have a good time whether you're funny or not. So many comedians just get away with tricking an audience into thinking they're having fun. Hell, that's exactly what most musical comedy is. The audience is so swept up in the melody and skill of a musical comic that they never once stop to consider the paucity of material on offer, they just clap at the end like well behaved children at a school assembly. When the audience are swept along with a professional opening, with a feeling that a show is about to happen, then the expectation that they'll be entertained carries through. This means that a comedian will be given a grace period right at the beginning in order to settle in and establish a rhythm. But the whole shebang has to appear professional, otherwise all the confidence the audience has developed will dissipate, and they'll be questioning what kind of tin pot show you're running.

This is exactly what Lucifer has done here. He's managed to fuck it up right from the beginning. He's given you an uphill battle thanks to that shitty intro. "Are you ready to laugh?" for fuck's sake, what kind of question is that? Could he have made it any more amateurish? After announcing you, the Amakhulu applaud out of respect but quickly stop once they see your feeble self feigning confidence whilst making your way to the microphone.

'…keep that applause going. That's it! Keep clapping!'

Excellent. They stopped clapping because they'd lost faith in the show, and now they've been begged to continue. Nothing builds confidence quite like begging. 'Fuck it,' you think, once again pretending that you're confident by raising your hands in the air in a bid to get them to keep applauding. It kinda works, as a few Amakhulu give you some sporadic pity applause before group cohesion kicks in and they are shamed into stopping. You weren't clear enough with Lucifer about walk on music, so all that accompanies your current walk on stage is the sound of your own foot steps, and the occasional cough from a super demon.

'You can do this!' you tell yourself. And why not? You have your best set to date in your arsenal, ready to go, and you still truly believe you have the ability to smash this gig. You stride up to the mic stand, remove the microphone and then place the mic stand behind you. Here you are, front and centre of the stage, appearing before the biggest audience you've ever performed to. Maybe even the biggest audience that ANY comedian has ever performed to. You stand confidently in front of the assembled thousands, take a deep breath and let her rip.

'Good evening, Indulu! Are we well?' you ask, pointing the microphone at the Amakhulu in a bid to get them to respond in a pavlovian fashion with some kind of cheer.

Nothing. You point the microphone back at your mouth.

'Oh come on! You can do better than that! Are we well?!' this time you point the mic at the audience, bend a little in the knees, bring your non-mic holding hand towards the floor, then sweep it up past your head in a bid to get them to at least acknowledge you with some form of response.

Nothing. The Amakhulu sit silently, staring. Each blisteringly fire red eye is burning into you, as their pointy bat like faces rest in a muted snarl. One of them blows a raspberry which garners a chuckle from those that heard it. Thousands of pairs of scarlet eyes stare at you, motionless, like so many flash photographs from the 1980s.

'It's great to be here, thanks for having me…'
'You're welcome.' interrupts a deadpan voice from the audience. You look for any sign of who it might be, but not one of them move or give any indication who it might have been. Maybe you imagined it? The silence is broken by the distant

crashing of an enormous lava wave. You dispense with pleasantries and decide to begin your set.

'Now, I know what you're thinking…'
'No you don't.'
'Are you a comedian or a clairvoyant?' two voices now, each the same, but from different parts of the crowd. If you try and figure out who it is, they'll have derailed you, which is exactly what they want. You don't give them the satisfaction.
'As I was saying…'
'You were saying…'
'That you know what we're thinking.'
'Apparently you can read minds you cunt.'

Three voices, all the same, all from different areas. It now occurs to you why the Amakhulu are such a badly needed weapon for Lucifer in the battle against heaven. These are separate entities, but also some kind of giant organism. They are individually united. They are numerous but singular. You need to get this opening joke out in order to get them on side. Once you get that first big laugh, you'll be fine. You'll be golden.

'I know what you're thinking, you're thinking…'
'That you look like a celebrity who has put on a little weight?'
'Or maybe someone famous who has let themselves go a little?'
'Or perhaps some other startlingly obvious opening line?'
'We can see you. We know what you fucking look like.'
Ah ha! You saw who said that fourth line, it was one of the super demons sat at the front. You zero in and walk towards him.
'Hello mate,' you say, holding out your hand to shake. 'What's your name?'
'Geoff.' comes the unlikely reply.
'Hello, Geoff, and who have you come out with this evening?' your hand is still held out, now begging to be grasped and shook as a sign of friendship.
'Just a few mates.'

'Oh that's lovely. You gonna shake my hand, Geoff?' gauntlet thrown down.
'Nah, I don't know where it's been.' gauntlet picked up.
'I can tell you if you like?' you can't back down now. You've got a "your mum's fanny" joke all lined up ready to go, you just need this prick to take the bait.
'Sure,' says Geoff. 'Please, edify me.'
'Hold the mic properly, we can't hear you!' yells a voice from the back. You look up to see where it came from but all you can see is a wall of red dots and the occasional pair of fangs, grinning with joy at your predicament. You have no idea who might've said it. You turn back towards Geoff.
'As I was saying,' Geoff's no longer there. 'What the fuck?'
'HE'S BEHIND YOU!' shout a few hundred thousand Amakhulu.

You turn to look at the stage and see Geoff staring back at you, his body all bony and hunched. He looks like a human sized, malnourished gibbon that lost all it's hair and developed rudimentary wings. Geoff begins to open and close his bat like mouth, causing it to make a horrific clicking sound like a brutally slow roller coaster on the ascent. Geoff repeats this over and over until his jaw dislocates, the lower mandible swinging wildly as it bounces repeatedly off his chest. Geoff's stomach moves in and out as he begins the process of regurgitation, each inhalation and exhalation sounding like the strained vomiting of a hungover teenager suffering after their first night of alcohol. You can't help but stare. The microphone that was near your mouth is slowly lowered to your hip as your arm loses all tension. Geoff begins to walk to towards you, still heaving with the intention of throwing up some ungodly substance he's clearly had to make room for. Your instinct is to run, but you remember that Lucifer said that these Amakhulu could do you no physical harm, so instead you just stand there. Defiant but compliant, terrified yet safe and sound.

Geoff gets even closer, putting his clawed hand on to your shoulder, saliva dripping from the roof of his mouth. The mucus like spittle is a bilious shade of yellow, and a far more inviting sight than his dead red eyes which are panic staring straight into yours, somehow titillated by every second of your discomfort. Throwing his head back, Geoff lets out one final guttural retch before hocking up the intended object uncomfortably close to your feet. You look down. There, covered in a foul smelling clear fluid is a book:

100 Racist Jokes That Will Impress Your Friends.

You look back at Geoff, just in time to witness him repeatedly uppercutting himself on the jaw in order to return the maxilla to it's natural state. Wiggling his chin from side to side in order to ensure it has returned in the right groove, Geoff gives you a gentle, almost friendly pat on your shoulder.
'Read that, you cunt.' he says, before returning to his seat.

The Amakhulu leap up and give Geoff a round of applause as he makes his way back to the audience. Geoff gives everyone an almost bashful wave then gestures to the stage in order to get the Amakhulu to refocus on the task at hand.

You stand there, completely at a loss. Your opening has been completely obliterated. They didn't even give you a chance. You didn't stand a chance. They knew exactly what to do. You think to blame Lucifer for that shitty intro, but this is bigger than that. This is the most switched on, intense and terrifying audience you've ever faced. They've completely destroyed you, and you've been on stage less than two minutes. They meant to do it. They wanted to crush you.

'Give me a cheer if you've been drinking!' you say out of reflex, hating yourself before you even finish the sentence. You don't even normally say this, but you've seen hack comics do it and sometimes, it'll work to get the audience back on side. Normally, a sympathetic member of the audience will throw you a lifeline.
'You gonna read that book or what?'
'Yeah, read that book.'
'Tell us a joke.' again, all three voices are the same, from different parts of the audience. Full panic mode is now engaged, and as such, you have become incredibly

suggestible. Before you know what you're doing, you've begun to reach for the book.
'Oh don't read the book!' comes the first voice.
'Jesus. Have you no dignity?' comes the second voice.
'Embarrassing that is.' finishes this trifecta of destruction.

You stand back up and look at the audience. There is complete silence. They sit there, waiting patiently. No movement. No help. Nothing. Dead eyes, scrutinising your every move, just waiting for you to do something. Anything. You clear your throat.
'Get yourself a drink.'
'Yeah, take your time.'
'We can wait.'

That wasn't them. All three of those voices were in your head, of that you are sure. They sounded different to the Amakhulu. You've heard these voices before, You thought you'd silenced them. But, no.

This was you, talking to you.

'Why are you doing this?'
'What made you think you could even do this?'
'You're not funny,' you recognise this last voice, you've heard it before.
The Amakhulu stare. No movement. No sound. Red eyes as red lights, blinking in unison, giving you the signal.

'You're not funny,' That voice again. 'You're not funny. You're not funny. You're not funny. You're not funny. You're not funny. You're not funny. You're not funny. You're not funny.You're not funny. You're not funny.'
'SHUT THE FUCK UP, DAD!' you scream, dropping the mic to the floor before thrusting both palms against each ear in a bid to drown out the voice.
'I told you you weren't funny. I told you.' you hear.
'No. No. No. You're not right.' you think.
'Oh but I am. You know I am.'

Thousands of blinking red lights watch you close your eyes in a bid to drown out the voice you thought you'd rid yourself of. That voice which would pop in your head from time to time, but now sounds so loud you feel as though your head may explode. You open your eyes once more to see the Amakhulu still there. Waiting, but for something different now.

'Please, make it stop!' you beg of them. You reason that the Amakhulu are here to be entertained, and out of desperation you reach down to grab the joke book.
You can barely open it, slick as it is from the digestive enzymes that Geoff left on this humorous tome. You thumb through the manual as best you can until you reach a page which is actually legible. Perhaps this is your salvation from the bellowing voice of negativity now deafening your very soul.
Your Dad always wondered why you didn't just tell jokes. Who cares about your opinions or your stupid stories? People want to hear jokes. They want to escape. Pawing for the mic with your free hand, you stand and face the deathly silent audience. Freshly armed with jokes you believe to be right up their street, this is your last chance to turn this gig around. Using every ounce of concentration you have, you briefly shut out the voice of fate and focus all your gifts on the one liners written in front of you.

'What do you say to a Pakistani on Christmas Day?' you ask rhetorically, knowing that no response will come your way.
'Can I have some cigarettes and a load of bread please.'

Nothing.

'Speaking of racism, how does every racist joke begin? With a look over your shoulder.'

Nothing.

'You're not funny.' repeats the voice. 'You're not funny.'

You burst into tears. The Amakhulu remain silent. You stand there sobbing. Wailing. You look across to Lucifer, but he is not there. Your Dad is standing where Lucifer was, shaking his head in disappointment. You look back at the Amakhulu, all of whom are now pointing at the lava waves now crashing nearby. You look at the floor, tears streaming down your face as you recall every death you've ever had, and how each one had forced you to try and get better. But it was for no reason. Nothing you could've done would have pleased him. No matter how well you did, each gig was leading you here. Now, it is over. The Amakhulu move in unison so that they form a line from where you stand on the stage, all the way over to the lake of lava.

The Amakhulu nearest to you lies on his stomach. The second nearest to you also lies on his stomach, with the third closest to you lying belly first on the back of the second nearest. The next three super demons arrange themselves in the same way: belly down on top of one another. What is forming in front of you is a small staircase made from demons. You look down the line and see the thousands upon thousands of snarling faces and red eyes, all of whom begin to repeat this pattern of lying down as they arrange themselves into a staircase of horrifically deformed bodies. One body, then two, then a pile of three, four and so on, until the hundreds of thousands of super demons have created a staircase in front of you that is a thousand bodies long and a thousand bodies high.

Obediently but without being commanded, you begin to ascend this ordered form of the awfully disordered, the whole time your head throbbing from the repeated declaration that you lack the ability to make others laugh. Sobbing perpetually as you trundle your way vertically, the Amakhulu remain silent as you scale the monstrosity before you.

'You're not funny. You're not funny. You're not funny. You're n...'

The voice stops as you reach the pinnacle of this right triangle of despair. Looking down, you can't help but appreciate the uniformity of such devilish organisation, before casting your eyes at the lake of molten rock beneath you. Lucifer said that they could do you no harm, but he said nothing of harming yourself. That voice in your head which you have heard so many times is yours and yours alone. Comedy is so much an individual pursuit, it is your fault that you never introspected enough to silence such a voice forever. You merely muted it for a short time. Maybe success would've silenced it forever, or maybe it was always gonna be there, driving you forward to try and improve. Or maybe the Amakhulu just showed you what you already knew? As you leap from the thousand beneath you, the feeling of the hot air rising from the furnace offers no reassurance. Why would it?

Falling into the fiery lake, your skin disappears almost instantly. Your ear drums melt meaning you cannot even hear your own screams. You are dead, but alive enough to be aware that perpetual agony is now your state.

You wait for Lucifer to rescue you, but he never comes.

The End - go back to page 109

Sat in the green room jotting notes in your notebook, you can't help but be a little intimidated by what Jatinder said to you. In your pocket is a USB stick with the only copy of Jatinder's threesome, so you feel safe that whatever he has in mind can be dealt with using a little gentle persuasion. Across the room, a couple of mice are trying to escape from a humane mouse trap placed by the skirting boards. You chuckle at the idea of mice trapped, slowly losing their minds as they can't escape, and such a circumstance being described as "humane". You're amused by this thought so much, you decide to make a note of it in your notebook. Above the skirting boards is an old fashioned cabinet which houses a modern LED television broadcasting the show taking place right now onstage inside Uncle Spunk's Chuckle Trunk. Because of your solitude, it's as though the show is being beamed directly into your brain. You don't even want to be watching it, but you can't help yourself because the open spot currently performing is one of those anomalies that come along every now and again. This open spot is shit, but absolutely brilliant. Transfixed, you stare in disbelief as you watch a portly gentleman in an ill fitting suit gesticulating wildly as he delivers his banal observations, relaying the many tedious ways in which he interacts with the world at large. The paucity of the material is bolstered by his ability to vividly act out the hackery spluttering from his talentless face hole. This is a standard trick of the theatrical wank stains who now permeate the comedy scene. These are people who couldn't hack it as an actor but have just enough misplaced confidence to get on stage and be gawped at by morons. They learn how to tell a shit story really well, while the audience are happy to go along with it because the physicality of the performer is good and there are many interesting facial expressions to enjoy. Motion creates emotion, and with such disappointingly sub standard comedians, it is easy to get swept along by the performance. You being a professional, you're able to slag off these wankers by using a more dispassionate approach to watching their stand up comedy.

You can see all the tricks he is employing, and although the audience does not have a microphone pointed at them, the laughs you can hear via the on stage mic are loud enough to indicate that this open spot is doing very well indeed. The human brain is a wondrous thing. The science of laughter isn't completely understood, but it is quite separate from humour, although both interact in order to make comedy real. Babies laugh but they don't laugh at jokes. Babies tend to laugh at shock, like when you peekaboo for example. That is what a lot of laughter is: surprise. A story takes a turn you weren't expecting, so you laugh. You fart and follow through, you laugh. Humour is different. Kant said that it was when an incongruity was resolved. Daniel Dennett speculated that laughter derived from humour is the brain rewarding itself for completing a grubby clerical task. In the same way that we laugh with relief when we solve a puzzle, a really good joke is when the puzzle is just tricky enough to work out, but also surprising enough that we chuckle.

None of that is what this open spot cunt is doing though, oh no. What this piece of shit is doing, unknowingly, is exploiting mirror neurones. His material is so weak, he has to act out every single nuance of his bullshit in order to maximise what little he has. Each audience member is sitting there watching, while their brain is doing something quite different from sitting. Each audience member's brain is lighting up because of the performance, but not in the way you think. When a human being sees a physical action taking place, the parts of the brain required to fire in order to perform that physical action, also takes place in the observer. This is what the open spot is doing by gesticulating so wildly, his brain is firing in order to perform, but it also lights up in the same way for the brains in the audience. Every brain in the room is firing in the same way, the difference is that audience don't physically perform the actions. Instead, the brain performs a kind of virtual reality simulation. It is the same with touch. If we watch someone else being touched, the parts of the brain that fire when experiencing touch, will also fire as we watch. It is the skin receptors which let us know when we are being touched, so if they don't fire, we don't experience the contact. The brain doesn't know the difference though. This is why pornography is so fucking cool. Motion really does create emotion. And mess.

Neuroscientist VS Ramachandran has said that such phenomena in the brain could be a scientific way of examining the idea of mass consciousness. When physical barriers are removed, all we'd have is a sea of neurones bouncing off one another, a mass consciousness interacting with the world, where the idea of separation drifts away and all that remains is a state of oneness across all humanity. But we shouldn't get ahead of ourselves, especially when discussing an open spot who is just dancing around the stage like a twat while he talks about his wife being on her period and hunting for chocolate.

You wonder sometimes if you over analyse comedy, but how else can you convince yourself what you're doing is in some way art? How can you convince yourself that what you do matters in some way, because in the grand scheme of things it definitely doesn't. People will have fun, laugh and make jokes regardless of whether or not stand up comedy exists, but would they do it as artfully as you? You pride yourself on your set containing no performer's tricks, but why? Shouldn't the aim be to make as many people laugh as possible? Such questions have dogged true artists for centuries. For whom do we actually create? Would you be happy without the adulation an audience provides, particularly when you come to terms with the fact that most audiences know very little and are easily manipulated? As you continue to look at the TV screen and watch this gobshite open spot tearing the roof off the place with god awful material, do you even want to make them laugh? Does that audience even deserve you? All of these questions plague your thoughts, then you remember you're getting £200 for twenty minutes and try your best to silence those thoughts. The thoughts come flooding back when you realise what you've been through this evening just to get to the gig, how improvising as a master criminal has helped secure you the money, and how you've guaranteed the silence of a poor teenager by filming him having sex with prostitutes.

How much further can you take this improv? How proud Sean would be to see you now, carrying on like a boss. The open spot wraps up his set and you see Sparky Mark take to the stage and announce the final interval. Any second now the open spot will be walking into this green room, full of that post gig high and riding a wave of confidence he'll have never felt before. His gig went as well as it could, and he'll almost certainly be looking for further bookings from Sparky Mark. You don't want that to happen though because fundamentally, you believe in justice, so long as you don't apply the same standards of justice to yourself.

You hear voices coming your way. Any second now the door will open and two men will walk in, both of whom you would rather not be speaking to, both of whom you would rather see die uncomfortable deaths. Ordinarily you would feel bad for having such impulses, but as a master criminal, you positively thrive with these feelings. You want these feelings. Worryingly, you want to act on these feelings. We have all had to come to terms with the darker side of our personalities. The side we repress so that we can be better and more productive members of a civilised society. Every now and again someone will indulge such impulses, the results of which usually end up in the news as many innocents are savagely massacred. Many of us have thought 'fuck it', only to come to our senses before initiating whatever dastardly deed had come to the forefront of our being. Here you are now though, a de facto master criminal capable of actively participating in such devilry. The door opens, the open spot walks through followed by Sparky Mark, who'd clearly opened the door on behalf of this hack shit bag. The air of confidence makes you immediately hate this open spot with every fibre of your being.

You don't hate him for being an open spot. We've all been open spots at some point in one capacity or another. What you despise is the very nature of such a spot and the lofty feeling which can be felt if such a spot goes well. For most comedy nights, an open spot is filler. Cheap labour to pad out a bill, readily filled by hundreds of wannabes all desperate for stage time. No, what you hate him for is that feeling he now has of having done really well, even though the open spot in itself is a soft spot because the promoter always wants them to do well.

That's why they get the middle slot at gigs, and why they get the best introductions: because they need all the help they can get. A good open spot can be exploited for quite a while as they're like gold dust. The promoter can pretend that a good set might have been a fluke and ask them to do spot after spot until they have proven themselves. If the promoter has a few gigs then the open spot can be abused for quite a while. They'll just be grateful for the stage time.

God, why are you so full of bile? Is it because this open spot is probably enjoying comedy and you haven't for as long as you can remember, or is it because any feeling of goodness is now leaving you because you're so absorbed in your improv?
'Hi Sparky, how are you?' you throw your arms open and embrace Sparky Mark, one arm over and one arm under in a bid to remove any semblance of intimacy from the onlooking open spot. 'Didn't get chance to ask you downstairs.'
'Not three bad, not three bad ROFL,' replies Sparky Mark, patting your back the way a mafioso would check someone for a wire. 'Just carrying on, carrying on.'

You each release at the same time, Sparky turns to the open spot, arm open towards him as if beckoning to join the hug. 'This is the open spot I thought I'd have to cover for PMSL but it turns out he's pretty good LMAO. Allow me to introduce you to Billy Fuckwit.'
'Billy Fuckwit?' you enquire. 'Stage name?'
'Nope. Look.' Billy immediately pulls out his driving license and sure enough, there it is. Billy Phuquit.
'Wow. You don't look like you're from Thailand.'
'I'm not. I changed my name by deed poll to help my comedy career.'
'Isn't that amazing?! LMAO.' says Sparky Mark, clearly someone not averse to a whacky name. You look at this grinning moron and you know that you have to kill him. Billy is already dead, he just doesn't know it yet.
'My aim is to be on Live at the Apollo within two years,' says Billy, brimming with self belief. 'I think that is doable with the tools I bring to the table.'

'Oh he's got the tools alright! ROFL.' Sparky Mark shows you his index finger, on which you can see a smiley face emoji. This indicates that behind Sparky's dead eyes lies a brain still capable of feeling emotion.
'I admire your confidence,' you say to Billy, opening your arms in order to initiate an embrace. 'Nice to meet you.'

Billy lurches forward like a puppy, eager to please and suck up to a comedian who, for the time being at least, is of a higher status. You've met these pieces of shit before and they're all the same kind of psychopath, happy to murder their own grandmother just to climb another rung on the grease ridden comedy ladder. As you lock your arms around him, you realise that both your arms are underneath his armpits, with his arms over the top of your arms, loosely draped around your neck as though he were your lover. Enraged at such a diabolical liberty being taken, you initiate a body lock on Billy, with one palm on top of your other palm, pulling him into you so that he is trapped whilst squeezing your forearms so that his ribs cannot move enough to catch a decent inhale. You then bend at the knees whilst maintaining this hold, and deftly slip around to his back so that your right ear is now pressed against his left shoulder blade. Before he even knows what is going on, you change your grip so that your right arm goes over his right shoulder, then clasping your left hand palm to palm so that your arms now resemble a seat belt. You leap onto his back, wrapping your legs around his waist as you then move your right forearm under Billy's throat, pushing your arm all the way through so that the point of your elbow is inline with his chin. Your left arm now comes up and around his back so that you can bring your left upper arm on to his left shoulder, elbow on top so that your right palm now grasps your left bicep. Placing your left hand behind the back of his neck, you apply a rear naked choke to Billy, as he struggles to maintain his balance. He seems to be trying to laugh it all off as a bit of banter, as Sparky Mark looks on in mild bemusement, periodically clapping his hands and jumping a little.

Billy begins to gurgle as he drops to his knees, your forearms squeezing for all their worth in order to bring about a speedy unconsciousness to this tiresome open spot. Billy collapses forward, slamming his forehead into the floor as you maintain your grip and feel him start to go limp. The carotid artery has been sufficiently restricted to the point that Billy has now passed out. His arms are limp, his legs kick involuntarily as you maintain the grip for a few seconds longer to ensure that he stays asleep when you release. Being choked in this way enables dreams to be experienced. It is a bizarre sensation and although uncomfortable at first, the feeling of dizziness and then unconsciousness isn't all that bad. You release your grip and pull your legs from under Billy as he falls to his back, body limp from lack blood flow to the brain but still breathing. You drag yourself to your feet and look at Billy Fuckwit lying there. After first bringing your knee to your chest, you stamp down hard on Billy's exposed throat, crushing everything contained within his neck with a satisfying crunch, similar to a Toblerone being snapped in half. You stamp again in the same place for good measure, blood spurting involuntarily from Billy's mouth as you now focus on the figure watching you, Sparky Mark.

'ROFL?' he asks, terror in his eyes. 'PMSL?'

'No, Mark.' you say, staring directly into his eyes. He looks away and slowly raises his little finger to show a crying face emoji. 'Don't be scared Sparky, you have a choice.'

'LMAO?' replies Sparky Mark, a yellow puddle forming around his winkle pickers, urine cascading down his black and white trousers.

'Your choice is simple. You can take responsibility for this, or you can die. That's the best deal you're gonna get.'

Sparky Mark stands there even more bereft of thought than usual, as his mind staggers back and forth from instinct to logic, neither of which give him the clarity needed to make a decision. You inch closer to him, ready to strike if he decides to make an escape, but you can see escape is not something that is going to happen as he remains frozen to the spot, terrified beyond all measure.

You think back to that night in Portugal. The blood stains. How sloppy you were. If you could do it all over again you'd be so much cleaner and more precise. Not a single question would be asked of you. Then you realise that that wasn't you, and that your improv as a master criminal is now no longer an improv. You cannot tell the dancer from the dance. Evil thoughts occur to be actioned as readily as your lungs fill with oxygen. Six inches from Sparky Mark now, you raise your hands in a position ready to throttle him, convinced that he will not move as you gently put your hands around his throat. As you feel the clammy texture of his throat, you ease your fingers into the side of his neck. Sparky Mark lets out an involuntary sob of despair before slowly turning blue as you begin to the choke the life from his talentless body. Instinctively, he grabs your wrists as his body takes over from his mind in order fight for it's existence, it's just a shame that he lacks the strength at this stage to overpower you. Balance is taken from Sparky Mark as his knees buckle, falling backwards to the floor, his grabbing of your wrists aids your transition to the ground as you follow him down so that you are now straddling him, using the force of gravity to further strengthen you grip on his throat as you sink all your weight through your wrists. His eyes are now wide with terror as they begin to bulge from their sockets. You feel a surge of blood go to your genitals. Your sexual arousal from this imminent murder surprises you, causing you to momentarily loosen your grip and give Sparky Mark an infinitesimal amount of hope that you may yet cease your life extinguishing action.

BANG!

The green room door flies open, almost coming off it's hinges such is the force of whatever opened it. You release your strangle, enabling Sparky Mark to forcefully inhale a rasping breath, followed by a strained cough, then a subsequent rapid inhalation and exhalation of air as his body realises it will not now expire. You stand from your straddle, kicking Sparky Mark in the balls in the process before turning your attention to whoever is about to enter the green room. Sparky Mark turns foetal as he continues to gasp. You take a few steps back and await the entrance of the door kicker.

'Ha!' you theatrically yell, as Jatinder walks into the green room. 'You!'
'Yeah,' replies Jatinder. 'Well, not just me…' he says as he steps to one side so he can let in 6 of the biggest Sikhs you've ever seen in you life. Turbans, beards and muscles. This is the Kabaddi team of your nightmares.
'Shit.' you think.
'Yeah, deep shit.' says Jatinder, apparently reading your mind.

You're fucked, but you know what he wants. He wants the footage. This is your leverage. You can talk your way out of this for sure. But what if you don't want to? What if there is some way of framing these Sikhs for the murder of Billy Fuckwit? Given the propensity of the locals towards disliking those who are not of a pasty white complexion, it seems feasible that given the right approach, you could lay the murder at the feet of these men in turbans.

'I know what you want,' you say to Jatinder. 'The only problem is that I've already emailed a copy to all Gurdwaras in the local area.'
'Bullshit.' says the biggest Sikh, in a voice so deep you feel the floor tremble.
'I'm afraid not my bearded friend. You see, I have a copy here in my pocket, and were it the only copy, it would make me vulnerable to an attack such as this. I like to have insurance.'
'I don't really care what you've done,' says Jatinder. 'At this point, all I care about is hurting you the way you hurt me.'
Your bluff is inconsequential, as Jatinder is clearly hell bent on a state of equanimity which can only be achieved through the administering of justice, with justice in this case meaning the bitter taste of urine crossing your luscious lips. This leaves you now with only two options.

To stand and fight, turn to page 188

To scream and shout for help like a lil' bitch, turn to page 234

'I'm sorry Sparky Mark, but I promised my other half I'd stay in tonight. Thanks for the offer though, I really appreciate it.' you answer through gritted teeth, gutted that you're knocking back well paid work.
'Oh that's lovely! Sorry, I didn't know. I just looked on the forum and saw you were available and local.'
'That's alright, you weren't to know. To be honest, I didn't expect to pick up a gig!'
'Yeah, it's tricky at the moment. Well listen, I'd better ring around as I need a headliner. Email me some dates on Monday and I'll put something in with you for later in the year.'
'Thanks, Sparky. You're a good man.'
'Have a lovely evening!'
'Good luck!'
'I'll fucking need it! Cheers.'

You finish the call with Sparky Mark, put your phone back on the table, then return to your supine position and gaze at the ceiling. Really, you should never turn down an opportunity because you never know where it could lead, and you certainly shouldn't turn down paid work, but you also need to work on your relationship as much as you need to work on your career. We all do. You think about your ex messaging you and feel some guilt about wanting to still be attractive to them. Going out and abandoning your partner when you've arranged a cosy night in would just put unnecessary strain on what is in actuality a healthy, happy relationship, and whilst you're stood at the back of the gig, bored and waiting for the gig to start, who knows what you might end up doing? Sure, your beloved would have understood that you need to work to earn money, and they've always been supportive of your comedy, but you also need to let your beloved know that they really are important to you, and that when you say money isn't the be all and end all, you actually mean it.

You can't help but wonder though. Wondering is a natural part of being a comedian. You always have this idea in the back of your mind that there might be someone in the audience who knows someone or indeed IS someone who can change your life overnight. Someone who can pluck you from obscurity and put you into the bright lights of fame and fortune. You know this to be a fallacy, and acknowledge that hard work is more likely to be responsible for any success you might enjoy. You just can't help but wonder. All you need is a chance. Just one chance. An appearance on a panel show, that's all you're after. You could build a career from that! People just as mediocre as you have made great careers out of talking head shows and repeating jokes written by more talented but less photogenic comedians. Like Don Fanucci in Godfather Part 2, you just wanna wet your beak. Why can't you have a little exposure? There's enough to go around, why is it the same old faces? Comedy is very much like The Mafia, with a few Dons at the major agencies controlling their capos who recruit the made men to go on television. The whole thing is a fucking racket and we all know it. It's just about knowing the right people and doing coke with those people.

Urgh, now look at you. All depressed and pissed off. This isn't the right attitude for a cosy night in. You hear the toilet flush upstairs and know that within a minute or two, your better half will be with you, wanting to watch a movie and cuddle up. You need to snap out of this right now. It was just a shitty gig down the road, nothing would've come of it. In fact, you might have died on your arse. You might even have done that in front of some TV big wig who just happens to be in a small town on a Friday night, hanging out in a pub which used to be a BNP stronghold and has now been gentrified.

'Who was that on the phone?' asks your beloved, breezing into the room like a sunny morning in spring.
'Sparky Mark.' you reply, emotionless, sitting up in order to make room on the sofa.
'You don't have to get up just yet, I've got to go and check on the pizza. Who's Sparky Mark?'
'He's a promoter,' you say, going back into full recline and stretching out your whole body, flexing your fists as you utter the next sentence through a yawn. 'Had a gig for me down the road.'
'Why didn't you take it?'
'I'm having a night in with you!'

'Awwww,' your partner leans down to kiss your forehead, planting soft lips just above your eyebrows. 'You didn't have to.'
'I wanted to!' you say, pulling them in for a little more than a kiss. A little playful resistance is offered, giggling as your better half pushes themselves away.
'Hey you! I have to go and check on the pizza.' says your partner, grasping your wrists and crossing them before placing them gently on your chest. One more quick kiss on your head before they walk out to the kitchen. You watch them walk away, casually evaluating their body as they exit. The arse isn't what it was, as the relaxation of diet that comes with a long term relationship means that each butt cheek is carrying a little more fat than it used to. But it doesn't matter, that is YOUR arse to enjoy.

You think back to how substandard your ex's arse was, and how they never showed the kind of easy affection you'd just had demonstrated. It occurs to you that the right thing to do is to block your ex on all social media and delete their number, so that you can enjoy the rest of the evening with a clear conscience. You sit up and grab your phone, performing this action quickly and deliberately, employing the purpose of an individual who has finally made the right choice after leaving it for far too long.

'Pizza's ready,' comes the call from the kitchen. 'Have you decided what movie we're gonna watch yet?'
'Thought about watching Blade Runner 2049. It's supposed to be good.'
'I haven't seen the previous two thousand and forty-eight. Will I understand it?'
'You can't see me,' you reply, 'but I just rolled my eyes so hard that I got a headache.'
Your partner walks into the living room with a moderately sized pizza and a nice bottle of £9 rosé wine.
'Easy this comedy lark,' they say, placing the pizza on the table in front of you. 'I should be a comedian.'
'Yeah, right.' you reply.

'What? Are you saying I couldn't do it?' asks your partner in mock shock.
'You could do it, you're just too mentally stable to want to do it. I thought we were having a massive pizza?'
'Well, I thought we could have this and then have some ice cream afterwards if we're still hungry.'
'Thank you for making that decision for me, and since when has gorging on pizza been about hunger?' you ask rhetorically before lifting a slice and filling your mouth with doughy cheesiness. An involuntary moan leaves you, orgasm like in its theatricality.
'I wish I could make you do those noises.' your beloved says, watching as you practically make love to a slice of pizza.
'If you tasted like this I'd make these noises allll the time.'
'What are we watching anyway?'
'I told you, Blade Runner.'
'Oh, OK. I thought you were just considering it.'
'Well, I am. I mean, if you wanna watch something else we can. Happy to hear suggestions.'
'You know me, I'm all about the cuddling rather than the movie.'
'Yeah but if the movie is shit then you fall asleep on me and I can't move because you'll wake up and then be annoyed about falling asleep.'
'I will not!' they protest, shovelling some pizza into their mouth.
'You do that all the time! Then you'll ask me what you've missed!'

You put down the pizza slice and pick up your phone. You think there's some material in that little exchange and want to make a note of it.
'Shit.'
'What?'
'I've got tomato sauce on my phone.' you say, wiping your sauce stained digits on the sofa before examining your phone for signs of ragù contamination.
'What are you doing?'
'I just wanna make a note of that.'
'What?'
'That thing I just said about you falling asleep.'

'That's not funny!'
'Well, that's where the skill of a comedian comes into it.'
'I have no idea how that could ever be funny. I fall asleep when a film is shit. Big deal. Come on, put your phone down and let's start this movie.'

You raise your hand in order to briefly silence your better half as you try to get this gold logged so that you can flesh it out later. Ordinarily, you'd consult your precious notebook but it's too far away and you'd need a pen. Your wonderful smartphone is chock full of this kind of comedic gold, and one day soon you'll probably write it up and work on it.
'There. Done,' you proclaim, oddly proud. 'Right, what shall we watch?'
'For fuck's sake, I thought you said we were watching Blade Runner?'
'Alright! Jeez, there's no need for that kind of language!' you reply, feigning shock.
'Plenty more where that came from, just start the fucking film.'
'Oooooh. I love it when you talk all nasty.' you say, full of sass and sexual suggestion.
'No you don't! When I asked you to put your tongue in my arse you hated it!'
'Oh!' you shout, like Paulie from The Sopranos. 'What the fuck? No bedroom talk over dinner.'
'You're driving me mad! Start the film!'

You shovel in another mouthful of pizza as you reach for the remote. It's good to get all this banter out the way before the film starts so that you can actually try and enjoy the movie. Once the pizza has been consumed, your partner will lie on you and then you will lie on your partner in a kind of half hour rotation so that neither of you end up with limbs that have the restricted blood flow which requires one to stand up and get rid of the dreaded pins and needles.

You press start for Blade Runner 2049 and sit back with another fresh slice of almost still hot pizza, after first discarding the crust from your previous slice. Your partner sees you discard this crust, then leans forward and eats the small

amount of cheese and sauce that remained on the slice, just shy of the actual crust.
'Who are you?' you ask. 'Fucking, pizza police?'
'There was loads left! Shame to waste it.'
'Why didn't you get some dips for the crust?'
'Didn't think.'
'I think we've still got some in the fridge from the last time we had Domino's if you fancy something to dip. Garlic herb or something like that.'
'I can't be arsed to get up now.'
'Fair enough.'

The film begins. A wall of text precedes any motion in this picture. You read thirstily so that you are familiar with the characters involved in the story which is about to unfold. You look across and see your other half looking at their phone. You pause the film.
'You need to read this you know,' you mention, helpfully. 'It's right at the start of the movie so I assume it'll be quite important.'
'Yeah, just putting my phone on silent.'
'No you weren't! You were typing!'
'Alright! Sorry! Jesus!' your partner responds, closing their shitty leather case and chucking their phone on the floor, care free and trusting in that robust, Bangladeshi made phone protection.
'I wasn't having a go!' you protest, 'I'm just saying that if you want any hope of enjoying the movie then you'll need to read this.'
'I hate reading shit at the start of a film. Can't you read it to me?'
'No! How lazy are you?'
'I'm not lazy!'
'You just asked me to read something for you because you can't be arsed! That's lazy!'
'Fine! Start the movie.'
'Fine!'
The silence is awkward but not deal breaking. There's a little tension but nothing that can't be dealt with using just a few

minutes of silence, silence which will come in handy whilst indulging the quiet enjoyment of this modern masterpiece.

You press play. The movie resumes. The text displayed on the screen you were so busy reading sure is small. You struggle to read it all in the allotted time, and now it has disappeared. You aren't sure what to do as you've just pointed out to your cherished one that the movie makers would've wanted people to read the text, as it will be very important in understanding the movie. You haven't managed to read it and now feel very stupid, but you want to enjoy the movie so you're gonna have to swallow your pride and re-read. You lean forward to grab the remote so that you can rewind to the beginning again.
'What the fuck are you doing?' your partner asks.
'I didn't catch all of that.' you reply. Your partner bursts out laughing.
'Now who's thick?'
'I didn't call you thick!'
'You implied it!'
'How did I imply it? I didn't imply that! I just said you needed to read it.'
'I did read it, you're the one rewinding.'
'Did you manage to read it?'
'Yyyyeeees.' they mock.
'What did it say then?'
'I don't know! I didn't commit it to fucking memory. Something about replicants and blade runners.'
'Bullshit.'
'How do you know? You didn't manage to read it.'
'The writing was too small.' you plead. Your partner adopts a different posture before using a high pitched tone of voice so that they may perform a humiliating caricature of your recently spoken proclamation.
'Wah, the writing was too small. The writing was too small. I'm an idiot and I can't read. I should've gone to Specsavers.'
'You finished?'
'I am.' your better half seems very pleased.
'Pleased with yourself?'
'I am indeed.'
'May I read the information now?'

'You may proceed.' your beloved says, spreading our their left arm towards the television as though you were being cordially welcomed into a very posh function attended by various heads of state.

You read the text fully this time, then grab another slice of pizza as you enjoy the dizzying and incredible visuals of the first few minutes of Blade Runner 2049. Right away you can tell you're going to enjoy this movie, but you're slightly concerned that your other half won't, as they aren't a big sci-fi fan. Nevertheless, you're here now and you intend to enjoy yourself as best you can. For a fleeting second you realise that you'd probably just be getting to the gig now and having to make small talk with any number of stand up comedy idiots. You'd have that feeling of never being able to truly relax in conversation with Sparky Mark, as he is after all a booker and promoter and as such, you wouldn't want to say anything too controversial as it could affect your future bookings, but at the same time, you also don't want to be a complete suck up and walkover. Finding the balance between these two social points stresses you out and you end up wishing that comedy could just be about the jokes and performance rather than the horrible shit show of networking and arse licking you know it to be.

Doing your best not to think about what you just thought about, you focus in on the movie, glancing out the corner of your eye at the wonderful person you've chosen to spend this evening with. Even though they annoy the living shit out you sometimes, you can't help but enjoy their company and that previous bit of banter is one of the reasons you love spending time with them. It's not taken seriously at all. You can say horrible shit to each other and few seconds later it's all forgotten about and you just carry on having a laugh. You really did make the right choice in not taking that gig tonight.

'Oh! By the way...' your partner blurts out, making you jump a little.
'Jesus! Good job I wasn't eating.'
'Sorry. Hey, guess who I saw yesterday?'

'Am I gonna have to pause the movie for this?'
'No it's just quick. Guess who I saw?'
'I don't know,' you say, shaking your head in disbelief.
'Fucking, I don't know.'
'Steve.'
'I'm gonna need a last name.'
'I don't know his last name!'
'Fuck's sake,' you pause the movie. 'Steve who? From where?'
'Used to work in the shop where we bought that home made jam.' your cherished one says, expecting you to know exactly who is being discussed. You draw a complete blank and can't even remember having purchased home made jam from anywhere in your life.
'I have no idea who you're on about.' you say, hoping this will be the end so you can carry on with the movie you were enjoying.
'You do! His mum owned the shop.'
'What shop? How long ago was this?'
'The craft shop. We were in there that time when that bloke tried to use a stolen credit card and they had to call the police.'
'Oh! *That* Steve,' a lightbulb goes off in your head. Now you remember. 'I didn't buy that homemade jam they gave it to me. It was disgusting.'
'Well, you got some home made jam from there. It doesn't matter if you bought it.'
'It does matter because I'm sat here thinking you're mad as I've never bought home made jam before.'
'Sorry, I just didn't know how else to describe him.'
'Right, anyway. You saw him. So what?'
'What's that supposed to mean?' asks your beloved, now unsure about whether this story merits the initial, excited outburst.
'It's not supposed to mean anything, I just wondered why this was all of a sudden really important.'
'It's not important, it just popped in my head.'
'So why are you telling me if it's not important?' you ask, trying not to be a little annoyed.
'It's just chit chat.' your partner replies, sheepishly.
'Yeah, but the movie has started.'
'It's only just started.'

'For fuck's sake, you saw this Steve with the shitty home made jam. Then what?'
'Oh forget it.'
'What?' you exclaim, now exasperated and needing closure.
'You've started so now you will have to finish I'm afraid. The buzzer will not save you.'

You say this with just enough of a twinkle in your eye to make it playful. The back and forth was on the verge of getting a little out of control but now your other half is on board and realises that they fucked up a little. Taking a deep breath and using a calm tone of voice, your partner relays what happened.
'I saw Steve…'
'Steve with the shitty home made jam. Yes.' you interrupt. Your partner laughs.
'I saw Steve,' you look on expectantly.
'Steve….' you lead.
'Steve with the shitty home made jam.'
'Thank you.'
'And we got chatting, "how are you?" and all that. Anyway, he doesn't work with his mother anymore because she met a new man and he took over the running of the shop.'
'Right.'
'This new man took out a business loan, and then disappeared.'
'OK.'
'The loan was for a quarter of a million pounds.' your partner drops the big reveal, hoping for more than they're getting.
'I honestly couldn't give a shit.' you say, too deadpan to be taken as a joke. Your partner slumps back on the sofa with their arms folded and stares at the screen.
'Start the movie.'
'Oh don't be like that!' you beg, putting your hand on their leg.
'Piss off. I thought you'd find that interesting. You told me the other day about that comedian who was getting done for tax evasion. I thought you'd like hearing about this. I guess I was wrong. Sorry.'
'It's a bit different!' you point out, trying to build a bridge.
'How is it different? If anything, my story is better because it's a way bigger fraud.'

'It's different because I don't know who the fuck Steve is or his mum or the new guy she was shagging or whatever the fuck was going on.'
'I didn't know who the comedian was! I still listened! I still showed an interest!'
'The difference,' you say, straightening your posture so as to deliver your point in a more devastating fashion. 'is that the comedian I was talking about claims to be a socialist and is always slagging off Amazon or Apple for tax dodging when they themselves were embroiled in the same activities. To see them being investigated by HMRC and getting fined and getting a whopping great tax bill is way more satisfying than finding out Steve the shitty jam maker's mum has had her holiday romance fuck off with two hundred and fifty grand.'

You leave this statement to breathe. Your beloved is smirking at the little tirade you just went on, enjoying the linguistic flourish which you are known for on the circuit.
'Sorry.' your other half says unnecessarily.
'Don't be sorry! I just thought it was an odd thing to get so animated about.'
'It just popped in my head as it started. I didn't know it was gonna turn into this big of a deal. I just thought I'd be able to say it in a few seconds as the movie was getting going.'
'Well,' you say, trying to draw this to a conclusion. 'I'm sorry for not knowing who Steve was in the first place.'
'Steve the shitty jam maker you mean?'
'Exactly!' you say, 'If you'd said that we'd be five minutes into the movie by now.'
'Five minutes can't make that much of a difference if you miss it.'
'If those five minutes weren't important, the director wouldn't have put them in the movie.' you say, now relaxing a little as a possibly massive argument has been averted.
You reach forward and grab a piece of pizza, but it isn't for you. No, it is intended for the one you love. The one whom you have chosen to spend this evening with over the allure of money and the adulation of strangers. You offer the pizza as a gesture of peace. It is readily accepted. On your way back to a more relaxed seating position, you collect the remote control

and point it towards the television. Just before you recommence the movie, you look across.
'Ready?'
'Ready.' comes the reply, muffled slightly by the presence of pizza being chewed.
'Sure?'
'Mmm-hmm.'
'No more tales to tell?' you ask mockingly. Your partner responds by rolling their eyes. You chuckle, then press play to pick up where you left off.

You're immediately taken in by the stunning visuals and incredible sound production of what you are witnessing. Ryan Gosling is hauntingly beautiful in the lead role, a mixture of quiet and destructive masculinity. A touch of femininity softens Gosling enough to lend him a vulnerability despite playing a replicant. The futuristic and gritty farm situated in California just a few decades hence allows you to feel that this is not too far fetched a possible future. You are reminded of the words by the writer and director of "Ex Machina", Alex Garland, who said that although his movie about a robot woman wasn't realistic, if it were announced that such a level of artificial intelligence and machinery existed, nobody would be that surprised.

You sneak a glance at your other half, intrigued as to whether or not they are enjoying the film at this early stage. No signs indicate a feeling one way or another, so you return your attention to the screen and attempt to lose yourself in the vision of the film makers.

Your partner farts.

'Oh, excuse me.'
You don't even look across. You just await the inevitable and try to enjoy the movie until fallout hits. You're tempted to make a joke, but that would derail the beginning of this movie even more than has already happened. Protein rich mealworms appear on screen just as the protein rich gaseous emanations hit your olfactory senses.

'Fuck's sake,' you mutter under your breath. 'Like a prequel to the pizza.'
'I did say sorry.' comes the reply, heart felt and slightly embarrassed. More seconds pass as it becomes apparent that Dave Bautista has been cast in order to show how much stronger the new model of replicants are. Bautista is a brooding and powerful presence, softened slightly by the director giving him wire framed glasses to wear. It's hard to believe that at one point he was professional wrestler, a trade known for its big personalities and extravagance as here in this role, he exudes a quiet authority. A dignity far removed from the business of spandex, muscles and chair matches. Your partner stands up.
'Can you pause it? I need another shit.'

* * * *

As Blade Runner 2049 draws to a close, you feel invigorated that such a big budget sci-fi movie was able to take it's time and really indulge in the challenging themes of what it is to be a human being. You look across at the human being you live with, snoring quietly, feet resting on your lap, oblivious to the cinematic masterpiece you've just enjoyed. You reflect on whether or not this is classed as the "quality time" each of you have discussed when deciding how best to enjoy your evenings together. There is so much pressure involved when it comes to maximising time in today's society, that sometimes the quiet enjoyment of a night in can be ruined by such overwhelming expectation. Your partner has worked hard all week in their Monday to Friday, nine-to-five drudgery of a job, of course they're going to be tired on a Friday night. You gently lift their feet, inadvertently awakening your beloved from a superior nap.
'What have I missed?' is snorted, semi rhetorically.
'Pretty much all of it,' you answer. 'But I'll gladly watch it again.'
'Oh, fuck that. I was bored to death,' comes the reply, made more impactful by the theatrical yawn that comes with the statement. 'I think I might go for a run you know.'
'It's a bit late!' you point out. 'Can't be safe."

'Yeah, but I feel like I should do something to work off that pizza.'
'Oh I can think of something,' you say, comedically waggling your eyebrows. 'Something g*oooood*.'
'I think I'll take my chances with a late night run. It's less dangerous.'
'Hurtful.' you laugh.

Your phone starts ringing. You sneak a look and see that it's Jenny Conran. Maybe she thinks you're driving home from a gig and wants to chat while navigating a motorway? You ignore the call, as is the norm if you're driving and currently engaged in another conversation. Although this may seem rude, it is standard practise. Besides, Jenny won't give a shit.
'Who was that?'
'Jenny Conran.'
'Comedian I take it?' comes the question, as your phone begins to ring once more. Yet again, it is Jenny Conran. As before, you ignore it. 'You can take the call you know!'
'I don't want to. She'll be driving on a motorway and she'll bang on for ages about whatever gig she's been at and I'll have t…' your phone rings again. Jenny Conran.
'Just answer, she seems pretty determined.'

Sighing, you pick up your phone and answer.
'Hello, Jenny. How are you?'
'*OH MY GOD! HAVE YOU SEEN? HAVE YOU SEEN?*
'Seen what?'
'*I was at Uncle Spunk's Chuckle Trunk tonight for Sparky Mark. I opened. He said you were supposed to be closing.*'
'I wasn't supposed to be but he did ask.'
'*Oh my god. I can't believe this. Do you not know?*'
'Know what?'
'*They're all dead!*' says Jenny, her tone of voice one that you've never heard before from another human. You're a little confused and don't want to jump to conclusions. When comedians die, it usually means they've had a bad gig.
'What do you mean they're all dead?' your partner sits up and takes notice now.

'*Dead! They're all dead! Oh my god I can't believe I'm the one telling you this. So, I left after I'd done my set 'cos I was doubling. He ended up getting John Ryan to close.*'
'For fuck's sake.'
'*I know. Anyway, John goes to plug his guitar in half way through his set, and some fucking explosion happened and everyone is dead.*'
'WHAT?!' your beloved moves closer to you, concern etched on their face as you begin to shake. 'Say that again.'
'*The whole place went kaboom. I'm surprised you didn't hear it as it's not far from you.*'
'Jesus Christ.'
'*I know! Lucky bastards. They'd have had to watch another ten minutes of that shite had they not all been blown to kingdom come.*'
'Jenny!'
'*What?! Fucking hell though. Isn't that amazing? That could've been you!*'
'No it couldn't! I don't play the guitar!'
'*Oh yeah! Shit. When will these promoters learn? Listen, I've gotta go as I've got a million people to tell but go online! It's everywhere. Sparky Mark is dead! My diary is fucked!*'
'Shit. Yeah, me too. He was gonna give me some dates on Monday.'
'Ah shit. That sucks. Right I'm off. Laters.'

Jenny hangs up as you sit there processing the information you've just received as your other half sits waiting to be told what has transpired. You could've died. Or maybe you could've saved everyone's life? Does the flap of a butterfly's wings in Brazil set off a tornado in Texas? Does a priest wanking in Ireland save the bum hole of a baby in Iran?

* * * *

Brushing your teeth before bed is an eerie experience for you this evening. With every vibration of your Phillips Sonicare, your brain races as the question keeps rattling around in your head: *what would have happened, had you taken the gig?*

You can't shake it. That feeling of powerlessness. It's easy to see why people believe there is someone or some thing watching over them, whether it be God or a guardian angel or some other mysterious force at work. Out of all the billions of possibilities, it was you that came to this earth. A different step here, a different night of love making by your parents there, and you wouldn't exist as you are now. Maybe you were always destined to exist? But the fact remains that in an unimaginably vast universe bereft of even the most simple forms of life, you are here, and you are special.

Your mind is racing about how many times you have avoided death in the past. That pond you fell in as a child. You could've sworn it was your uncle who pulled you out, but you later discovered that it was actually your grandma. You were five years old. So distant is this memory that you can scarcely believe it ever happened. You remember being wet, grabbing the side of the concrete blocks near the edge. The plastic frog. Did any of it happen?

Had you died, would you have known?

How many times have you just walked into the road. Christ, how many times have you put your faith in other human beings driving on busy roads right next to where you are walking? With all the trials and tribulations that people face, how have you and probably several others not just been mowed down by a recently sacked employee hell bent on destruction? Someone hurting so much that they just want to hurt the world.

How have you not choked to death? Fell down the stairs? How lucky you have been!

The mundane act of brushing your teeth is truly a privilege in a universe as vast and lifeless as this. The majesty of the stars is nothing when compared to the complexity and beauty of even the dullest human being. The vast reaches of space stretch out beyond all imagination, and at no point will you meet another you.

Believers in an infinite universe will tell you that meeting yourself is an inevitability. In an infinite universe anything that can happen, will happen, and it will happen an infinite number of times. Morons parrot this as though they themselves came up with the idea, the truth being that they actually watched Brian Cox twat on about it at some point. When people say infinite, what they actually mean is *really, really, REALLY, big*. You do not want there to be an infinite universe. In an infinite universe, you could be reading this right now whilst being raped by a rhino. If it can happen, it will happen. All you need is infinity. Space and time are interlinked, so if space is infinite, so is time. And if you have infinite time and infinite space, it means that somewhere right now, you are a paedophile.

An infinite universe allows for the possibility of things beyond our understanding. How, in any way shape or form is that supposed to be reassuring? Perhaps the lesson is that the universe does not owe you the ability to be understood or for that matter, any kind of reassurance. In the coldest, most utilitarian fashion of reductive logic, no one owes anyone anything. If something has no agency, no soul, why would it even begin to think it owes you anything, if indeed it can think at all?

In a finite universe, things come to an end. There *are* monkeys with typewriters, but the monkeys die and the typewriters run out of ink. It's a nightmare to change the ribbon on a typewriter, and the monkeys very quickly lose patience and destroy the machinery they had previously been entrusted with.

If choice is a trick of consciousness, would we want to know? Our perception guides our reality, even though (were one to delve deep enough into such topics) we know that if looked at correctly, through an appropriate lens, we are just a bunch of particles whizzing around one another. When you realise that we don't actually touch anything, that the electrons get almost infinitesimally close then actually resist, and that touch is an illusion, you can begin to piece together that the physical is mere machinery, whereas the mental is a computer just making sense of what is happening. When we process this, we can begin to see that such particles will have designated paths and actions, and that although complicated they can be predicted given the right amount of data and the ability to process it. As such, you were never meant to be at Uncle Spunk's Chuckle Trunk tonight.

You swill toothpaste around your mouth whilst looking at your cheeks in the mirror, one side filing with fluoride and saliva, then the other, as you do your best to stave off cavities. Bending at the waist, you spit out what remained in your mouth, then rinse with some cold water before looking in the mirror and recognising that you are very, very lucky. It is the first time you can recall actually realising this.

Walking into your bedroom, your beloved already tucked up in bed, you feel grateful for every second that you have ever experienced. The gratitude washes over you as tears form in your eyes.
'Hey. What's wrong?' your beloved asks.
'Nothing. Absolutely nothing.' you reply, getting into bed.
You assume the position of big spoon, lying on your left hand side with your left arm squished under you own body as your right arm drapes over your cherished one's hips. Kissing the back of your partner's neck, you feel nothing but love flowing through your body as you ease yourself into a restful slumber, content with all that has gone on, yet still excited by what is yet to pass.

Bahala Na, as the Filipinos say.

Come what may.

'Good night,' you say. 'I love you.'

Your beloved turns so that they are looking deep into your eyes, making sure that every part of their imminently expressed feeling enters you.
'I love you too, Susan.' comes the reply.

THE BEGINNING

Jesus Christ. Are you SURE you want to call the audience member a paki?

Seriously, think about this.

To absolutely, definitely call the audience member a "paki", turn to page 187

To walk off stage and accept your fate, turn to page 199

Fatboy Slim kicks in. The stage is set. The Amakhulu are all facing the right direction and despite how vast they are in number, they're remarkably well behaved and seemingly eager for the show to start. They're ready. But are you? Hundreds of thousands of super demons are awaiting the time of their lives, but you have just this second decided that you're probably gonna die on your arse, all be it deliberately.

> *"Right here, right now*
> *Right here, right now*
> *Right here, right now*
> *Right here, right now"*

You've gone from performance mode to training mode. This is no longer about doing a good set and giving it your all, this is about reconnaissance. Taking one for the team is one of the most selfless acts a comedian can perform. Most comedians will embark on such a selfless act entirely by accident: they go on first and face a tough crowd that needs a lot of management or people throwing out. This is different. What you are about to do is go out to an audience of maybe half a million demons, all of whom are not in any way shape or from intimidated by Lucifer, and fall on your sword. You're about to put yourself through the wringer, in much the same way that Muhammad Ali would train for his toughest and most brutal fights by exposing himself in training to shots no one else would subject themselves to. Putting himself through immense pain and discomfort so that by the time fight night came around, he was mentally prepared to endure what cane, and he would do so with the confidence of a man who'd already physically endured more than what was to come.

This is your plan for the gig ahead, to self isolate so that you can better equip the Prince of Darkness in his quest to be a better comedian. Lucifer himself is not privy to your plan, and as it has occurred to you in the heat of the moment, it will be difficult to explain in full. What if Lucifer watches your performance and decides that you aren't good enough to teach him comedy? You could try and explain that in the real world, back on earth, only the worst comedians run comedy

courses. With both no real value to offer or morals to be placed in a quandary, it is these comedians that are the only ones running comedy courses. Comedians with no home life and an empty diary, people who should've quit years ago because of how bereft they are of anything that might resemble talent. You can't explain this all in one go, but you need to make some kind of appeal.
'Lucifer,' you call. 'You're gonna have to trust me on this.'
'What do you mean?'
'It's not gonna look good, but there is a method to my madness.'
'What are on talking about?'
'In order to live, we must learn to die, and die in the fullest sense of the word.'
'You're quoting Wagner? Hitler's favourite composer?'
'I am indeed.'
'You're a maniac… I love it! Showtime, baby!'

You've done all you can do. Lucifer clicks his fingers and the Pearl & Dean music kicks in at full volume at the same time as your pre gig superstition kicks in: gesticulating the sign of the cross. As you perform this motion, you become aware of Lucifer staring at you in disbelief.
'Sorry,' you shrug. 'Force of habit.'
Lucifer laughs this off.
'Same.' he shrugs, exhibiting another handful of shit for you to observe before shovelling it into his mouth. Hurriedly swallowing the waste, Lucifer manages to miss his cue as the music ends with no announcement. Deathly silence breaks out among Indulu, as the Amakhulu wait expectantly for the show to start. Such an amateurish beginning to a show of this magnitude would ordinarily send you into a tailspin, but you have already accepted your death. You are currently in your cell on Death Row and about to walk to the electric chair. Why would anything that happens on your way to death bother you? Why do we ever let anything bother us? So privileged are human beings, that we have left behind the daily struggle for survival that most life on this planet has to contend with, yet we just end up toiling over trivialities, the purpose of which

usually is to distract us from the death that we pretend not to worry about.

Death in a comedic sense is figurative, but it is just as terrifying to a comedian as the actual ceasing of mortality. Indeed, public speaking is most people's number one fear, but now add public speaking which has the specific aim of eliciting laughter from the recipients, and that fear will increase exponentially. Tribal creatures that we are, evolving as we did in small groups, means that acceptance from our peers is of high social value. Like it or not, something going down badly with a group of people, whether they be strangers or close family, is something that comes with a social cost. Such social expense comes with psychological damage and as a result, physical damage. To separate the mental from the physical is foolish. To a comedian, the social currency of fulfilling one's job description is something on which we place a very high social price. To die onstage is to fail at a task in front of people, people who had expected the task to be completed with a degree of competency, but competency that they themselves are incapable of. Because of the bizarre nature of this social contract, it is the audience that gets angry with the comedian rather than the other way around.

But what happens when we get used to death? Comedians have to make friends with death onstage, as it hovers over us at every gig for any number of reasons. The next death is always in the post, and to grow as a comedian means that one has to expect, nay, WELCOME death with open arms. You don't want to die, nobody does, but death is waiting for you all the time. Coming to terms with death brings with it a freedom from fear. That first minute or two of a death is when you know it's going wrong and you try desperately to salvage your set. You think you can win the audience back, you think you have the skill to make them forget the ropey shit they've just seen. They're still sat there, hoping and praying that you will actually be funny, that their faith will be well served. Alas, it is not always the case and as time slowly marches on, the death becomes inevitable. You can feel it's clammy hand on the back of your neck, gently squeezing as each breath becomes more and more difficult to enjoy. Then, out of nowhere, you realise that there is nothing you can do now. You're dying, and you will continue to die until you leave the stage. You can leave the stage to silence, to boos, or to sympathetic applause. But it will not be over until you decree it so. This, is where your power comes from. When you embrace death, when you no longer run from it, when you face it, THAT, is when you can control it. It is at this point that death no longer has any hold over you, and you realise that it really isn't so bad. It is cripplingly embarrassing, but so what? It won't kill you. Sure, shame is a large part of many a suicide, but nobody is getting hurt by your poor comedic performance and who gives a fuck what the audience thinks anyway? Nobody actually likes a crowd pleasing comedian. Nobody respects them. Anyone who pleases all the people all of the time is probably hiding a deep dark secret and shouldn't be trusted around children. No, as your death occurs, you make sure you die on your terms and when you die, you die hard.

Once the shit is clear of Lucifer's oesophagus, he begins announcing you to the stage.
'Ladies and gentleman, are you ready to laugh?'
Whether deliberately or not, Lucifer has just given you the worst introduction that isn't purposefully offensive. The only way he could've made it worse is if he'd asked these cunts if they think they're clever enough to understand jokes. Lucifer didn't seem to get the response from the Amakhulu he was after, so he asks again:
'Are you ready to laugh?' but this time with three times the enthusiasm. Again, nothing comes back and all there is to contend with is the silence.
'Well, strap yourselves in,' Lucifer continues, undeterred. 'and enjoy the comedy stylings of the one, the only…'
'Lucifer!' you shout.
'What?'
'That'll do.'
'Eh?'
You walk on stage without any introduction, your footsteps being the only noise that accompanies your presence. A solitary cough comes from the audience as you make your way

to the microphone. Grasping the mic with one hand and the stand with the other, you separate the two with consummate ease and place the mic stand behind you. As you do this, there is an ear piercing bit of feedback that reverberates along the rocky walls of this vast, underground amphitheatre. The frequency the feedback achieves is the usual squeal that makes most humans wince in the same way we do when someone scrapes their nails down a blackboard (not a chalkboard) or when someone bites a fork. The volume is so loud that you struggle to hide how badly it has bothered you, as an obvious scrunching of your mush puts paid to any hope of a poker face.

As you look out, you notice that the Amakhulu don't flinch. They sit motionless, seemingly unperturbed by the horrific squeal that has just left the speakers. Once you have taken a few seconds to compose yourself, you begin your suicide. 'Good evening, Indulu! Are well?' you yell into the microphone with maximum enthusiasm. Nothing comes back your way. You're left stood there with a big grin on your face, feigning enthusiasm the way a forty year porn veteran does when presented with yet another dick.

Suddenly, you become aware of a very strong smell of shit, a smell so strong that it is now replacing the sulphur which you had started to get used to. The Amakhulu also become aware and begin to look at one another, then start laughing hysterically. Terrifyingly hysterically. Each super demon laughs and points at the other, as they all fall about holding there stomachs and laughing beyond anything one would reasonably expect for just a simple greeting said with enthusiasm. The sound is deafening, as hundreds of thousands of Amakhulu shriek and laugh and clap and cheer. They stand and begin a Mexican wave. You witness nothing short of pandemonium as you inexplicably have the best gig of your life after only twenty seconds on stage.

You have no idea what is going on, but the smell of shit is now so strong that you have to leave the stage, regardless of how well it's going for you. As you place the mic back in the stand, the awful squealing of feedback hits again. The sound reverberates once more around the rocky enclave of Indulu, and you notice within your limited field of vision that as the sound echoes, ever single Amakhulu defecates at exactly the same time. As each rudimentary anus involuntarily opens and excretes the foul waste, the Amakhulu laugh with delight and begin to clap. Bouncing up and down like children full of sugar, they look at you with red, wide open eyes full of expectance. Realising that correlation does not necessarily equal causation, you decide to put two and two together anyway, hoping that it results in yet more two.

Taking the mic from the stand once more, you wave the only tool of your profession until the feedback you were after comes in a wave of wailing glory. As this occurs, you bear witness to the astonishing sight of thousands upon thousands of super demons shitting out whatever disgusting waste remains from the filth that sustains them. The wiry, seemingly decrepit bodies contort into disfigured shapes of unrestrained laughter, their form becoming more obviously humanoid because of the abdominal muscles which show as they chortle heartily. Only the thin, bat like wings and filth coloured skin separate them as being something other than just a malnourished human. The red eyes of the Amakhulu are slanted from their now constant guffawing, whilst still focused solely on you, the source of their laughter.

You cannot fathom how, but you are currently having the best gig of your life, in front of the biggest audience that any comedian has ever performed to, when all you intended to do was die on your arse. You look over to Lucifer who stands there watching you, struggling to comprehend what is transpiring whilst also wondering whether or not he could replicate such a response. Perhaps, this is the cheat code of comedy? It has often been thought that there is a frequency which will cause a bowel movement in an audience. The so called "Brown Note" has been rumoured to exist for centuries but has never been conclusively shown to be true. Infrasound itself is a fascinating area of study, with many a ghost sighting or spine shiver explained by a sound frequency which is out of the normal hearing range for humans. Yet, such a frequency still manages to trigger a physiological response, despite remaining unheard. The emotional power of opera or orchestral music is sometimes explained by this, as the waves bounce off the surrounding environment and change frequency, having an effect on the nervous system of those in the audience.

The universe vibrates. Who can say what is possible if you're able to tune into such a frequency?

Regardless, you're here now and for some reason, the Amakhulu find it hilarious when they involuntarily defecate, and now you have the ability to initiate such an occurrence. Despite your fake pretentious nature and repeated attempts at writing and performing comedy that both delights as well as informs your audience, you're thoroughly enjoying ripping the arse out of this gig with some as basic as pooping oneself.
'Indulu, you've been an amazing audience! Thank you very much, good night!' you scream, throwing the mic to the floor the way Chris Rock did at the end of "Bring the Pain". You've been on stage for barely five minutes but you know how to leave an audience wanting more and decide to leave it there. Each super demon leaps to their feet and starts applauding, accompanied by whistles and cheers as you lap up the love, taking a bow and waving whilst blowing kisses. Scattered yells asking for more can be heard, but don't pick up quite enough momentum to warrant an encore. You leave the stage to an astounded Lucifer.
'You weren't wrong,' he says. 'That really wasn't what I was expecting.'
'That's how I roll, baby.' you reply, brimming with confidence.
'That was incredible.'
'All about reading the room, baby.'
'You think I should go out there now? Try and ride that energy?'
'No way, baby.'
'Stop calling me that.'
'Sorry,' you say, snapping yourself out of the bizarre confidence that seemed to have to overtaken you for a second, returning yourself to a more normal frame of mind.

'Fucking hell that was amazing. Jesus. Right, they're morons. You can make these cunts laugh no problem.'
'You think?'
'Absolutely. It's just toilet humour. Anyone who laughs at toilet humour is a fucking moron.'
'I laugh at toilet humour.' Lucifer confesses, bashfully.
'Well, it's different strokes for different folks. But all of them laughed when they shit their pants.'
'They weren't wearing any pants.'
'Yeah, it proper stunk out there. Either way, we know how to make them laugh, and now that we know how to do it, you'll absolutely smash it.'
'And then they will love me and respect me?'
'Exactly!'
'Soon they will join me in the final battle with heaven for the future of the universe,' Lucifer walks off now, towards a cliff that overlooks Indulu, his chest proud with his hands now placed on his narrow, toned hips. 'Where upon my victory will see me strike Jesus down, but not before I have taken him roughly from behind and had him lick his own turd from the shaft of my cock, while it still drips with the cum I just fired in to his anus.'
'That's the spirit!'

* * * *

A few hours have now passed since your monumental gig, now you find yourself back in the Pulp Fiction diner waiting for Lucifer to come back from the bathroom. You sit at ease, familiar with these surroundings from one of your favourite movies, contemplating what has happened since your arrival in hell. You've spent some quality time with Lucifer by this point, watching him go about his business and, all things considered, he is rather pleasant company. You're amazed at how quickly you have become accustomed to the casual torture you've been witnessing, barely flinching now when you see humans ripped in half by demons, ready to be eaten from the inside out by satanic rats. You've noticed that the minions who serve Lucifer most readily and without question, appear to be of low intelligence. This helps provide a reason for why the Amakhulu are so necessary for Lucifer's plans: they are of a much higher intelligence. As such, they are capable of independent, strategic thinking. The problem with this skill set is that they are *so* capable, it is likely they will not be fooled easily by a scripted comedy performance from the ruler of hell.

Despite Lucifer being such a towering presence of pure evil, you're not terrified by him anymore. Sure he's scary and could no doubt visit upon your person untold amounts of horror, but he's also like a Rottweiler that belongs to a family friend and has been brought up around children since it was a puppy, in that he's actually fine for ninety nine percent of the time. You've seen Lucifer use the same threats and same lines over and over again, and as such you have quickly realised that were you a supernatural being capable of disobeying him (the Amakhulu for example), Lucifer would not pose a sufficient enough threat to guarantee your compliance. As Lucifer has said, the problem with the Amakhulu is that they cannot be intimidated by his usual means. When all you have is a hammer, every problem begins to look like a nail, and when that nail can tell you to fuck off, your hammer is as useful as a tampon made of nettles.

Lucifer returns from the bathroom and seats himself opposite you, clicking his fingers so that delicious hot coffee appears in front of you. Before he excused himself, you and Lucifer had spent at least last half an hour talking about the interaction between a comedian and the audience, explaining to him that a lot of comedy is about status and that, where possible, the comedian should appear to be of a lower status as it makes it easier for an audience to get on board and feel good about themselves. Alas, in these aesthetically driven, vapid, shallow times, better and better looking people have become comedians. Rather than outcasts using humour to attract a mate, comedians have slowly become sexually appealing for something other than their ability to make people laugh. You explain that one of the problems Lucifer will run into as a performer is that of status, particularly in hell as he is the ruler. Were Lucifer to be doing a corporate gig in heaven, he'd be able to get the angels on-side easily by mocking God, and if

God wanted to appear a good sport, he'd have to laugh along. But in this situation, it is Lucifer himself who is top dog and the super demon residents of Indulu seem to take exception to this.

'That's why,' you explain. 'I need you to laugh at yourself, so that they can laugh *with* you, and then *alongside* you.'

'No.'

'Why not?'

'Because I am the Prince of Darkness! My only weakness is enjoying the pain of others, which I readily hand out with mirthful glee.'

'Alright, you don't have to sell it to me. Jesus.'

'If I am to lead my armies into battle, I will need my status. I cannot give an order if that order can be ignored. Besides, why are we going over this? We already have the key to making them laugh. Once I have made them laugh they will respect me.'

'I'm not sure, y'know. I'm beginning to think that there is more to this than meets the eye.'

'You're lucky you still have eyes. I would think nothing of gouging them out and…'

'… "*sticking them on my fingers and doing a puppet show with them*" yes, I've heard you say that a few times now. Listen, we have a problem, and I think it's you.'

'I beg your pardon?'

'See, when we first met, I would never have dreamed of saying that to you. But I've spent some time with you now and, frankly, I'm not as scared as I was.'

'Would you like me to terrify you?' Lucifer asks, seemingly doubling in size at the thought of what excruciatingly painful acts he could inflict upon you.

'Look, I'm not saying you *couldn't* terrify me, and I'm not saying that I'm not scared of you. I am! What I'm saying is, is that I'm kinda used to you, and I'm not even a super demon. You see my point?'

Lucifer considers this for a few moments.

'It's like,' you continue, 'hitting kids. It just doesn't work. I mean, it might work initially, but eventually it won't. If spanking children worked, hell wouldn't have so many people in it.

Humans would have spanked themselves into a perfect society.'
Lucifer nods.
'And,' you're in full flow now, 'It's a Christian thing to hit your kids. "*Don't spare the rod, lest you spoil the child*" and all that.'
'That's a poem, not a bible verse.' says, Lucifer, lifting the coffee cup to his mouth, blowing on the white hot blackness, moving the small circle of crema which has formed atop his decaf americano.
'I thought it was in the bible that you should hit your kids?'
'A lot of people think that. The phrase about sparing the rod is from a poem called "Hudibras" by Samuel Butler which was first published in 1662. In that poem, an actual physical rod is referred to, but in the bible, all that is mentioned is discipline.'
'Huh. Well, you learn something new every day.'
'I think the closest you can get is "*He that spareth his rod hateth his son: but he that loveth him chasteneth him betimes*" which is Proverbs 13:24.'
You nod quietly as you watch Lucifer tip his cup, preparing to drink the warm beverage which has been teasing his lips for the last minute, his face etched in thought as he contemplates all that has been discussed in these last few moments.
'Although,' he says, pausing before taking a sip, 'a lot of religious parents hit their kids because they think they should.'
Lucifer shrugs as he finishes his thought. He now indulges himself and begins tasting his coffee.
'We're a bit off topic now,' you say, trying to get back on track. 'My point is that you have to find another way to earn the respect of the Amakhulu, and it has to be a way that doesn't rely on any kind of physical or emotional threat.'
'You fucking simpleton,' Lucifer snaps, slamming his coffee cup to the table. 'You think I can use the naughty step in order to discipline pure evil? You think that will work? You think that soft influence will work when I need to command a member of the Amakhulu to slice the throat of the lamb of God? You're a fucking moron.'
'You just need to think outside the box!'
'Why do you think I've asked you to put me on this comedy course? That *is* thinking outside the box.'

'No it fucking isn't! Loads of corporate cunts draft in some wannabe fucking comic to do a comedy course. It's business bullshit.'

At this point, you have truly forgotten with whom you are speaking, as Lucifer gets more obviously frustrated with you.

'I need to do something though! Every time I have addressed the Amakhulu they've made mincemeat out of me. I need that quick wit. I need to defeat every heckle that comes my way. I need to dominate them verbally if I can't do it physically.'

'Yes, but that takes years of training. I can't just give you that ability over the course of a course.'

'The course of a course?' Lucifer says, breaking the tension a little and raising an eyebrow in appreciation of the alliteration.

'Course of a course.' you say, also raising an eyebrow.

'But of course' Lucifer says, again raising an eyebrow in an attempt to continue this.

'Would a curse cause a comedy course to cause comedy to course through ones veins? you reply, again raising an eyebrow. Lucifer smiles.

'Hmmm, of course a curse won't cause... shit,' Lucifer has lost it. 'For fuck's sake. See? This is why I need you. I'm not fast enough!'

'That was great! Look, there are loads of people out there who are crazy fast and very funny, and they do incredibly well in front of any audience. But you're not after that. You don't want to make them laugh, you want to dominate them. I was able to go out there and get laughs from the Amakhulu because they knew I didn't want to rule over them. Even though they hated me from the off, they were able to laugh because I had no status. We need to work on your status.'

Lucifer again sits and quietly contemplates what you have just said. Deep down, we all want to be accepted but we also want to be respected. None of us want to be a pushover yet at the same time we want people to be relaxed around us. Here in hell, things do not appear to be much different.

'OK,' Lucifer says, 'What would you have me do?'
'I'd have you open your set with some self deprecation.'
'You mean make fun of myself? Isn't that a bit hack?'

'Yeah, but it's very effective. The audience will think "hey, this guy's cool because he's aware of his own aesthetic short comings" and then they'll relax as a result.'
'Seems a bit hack to me,' Lucifer replies, unsure of your strategy. 'I've always seen myself as more of an edgy comic.'
'I don't get that vibe from you if I'm honest.'
'So you'd want me to go on stage and say something like "Hey, I know what you're thinking, you're thinking…" and then say something about my horns or some shit?'
'Well, maybe not that, but something similar. We need to get them onside early doors and then double down with some material that puts you in an embarrassing situation.'
'I'm not being funny with you, but doesn't this all seem a bit by the numbers?'
'Those fucking morons gave me a standing ovation for making them shit themselves.'
'Fair point.' Lucifer concedes, sipping more of his coffee.
'If you know the enemy as you know yourself, you need not fear the result of a hundred battles. Sun Tzu.'
'Bless you' replies, Lucifer, baffled.
'Replace the word "battles" with "gigs" and it's the same thing.'
'I don't think it is.'
'Look, I've seen dozens of hack comedians over the years and one of the reasons they are able to do so well is because they use very simplistic premises very effectively. It's literally someone on stage saying that they're glad to be here, referring to how they look in a negative light, and then telling a story that is shameful. After that, they can do what they like as the audience will be onside.'
'All seems so simple.' says Lucifer, not quite disbelievingly, but with a healthy dose of skepticism in his voice.
'I think this is the simplest route to victory.' you assure, Lucifer.
'It's just that, you know….'
'What?'
'I'm a bit worried.'
'How'd you mean?'
'You've seen how cruel they can be, if I expose myself to them and exhibit any sign of weakness, I think they'll exploit it.'

'I think you're wrong,' you say reassuringly. 'They'll think that you're self confident enough to laugh at yourself and as such, they'll give you a level of respect you've never had before.'
Lucifer gives this a little thought. It seems counter intuitive to someone so strong: that showing weakness can also be a sign of strength.
'Well,' Lucifer says, stretching his arms overhead, lifting his ribcage so as to stretch out his thoracic spine. 'Let's get to work.'
'When do you want to do the gig?'
'Tomorrow. My battle with heaven is long overdue and I am eager to eat the soul of Jesus Christ.'
'That's the spirit!'

* * * *

You spend the rest of the "day" drawing on your extensive knowledge of hackery so that you can prepare Lucifer as best you can. Who'd have thought that all those gigs where you witnessed the most astounding lack of originality (in truth, most of the comedy circuit) would one day come in handy? Who'd have thought that those disgusting charlatans who use standard tricks to manipulate an audience into thinking that they're funny would one day prove useful to you? All those times sat in despair, as you watched yet another comedian walk on and mention their resemblance to a slightly better looking famous person, have now proven to be of invaluable use, as you wilfully help the Prince of Darkness in his battle with heaven.

In the back of your mind, you cant't help but recall your small knowledge of the bible and the quite obvious idea that God was the good guy, which would mean that your new comedy course participant is the bad guy in all of this. Are you suffering from something akin to Stockholm Syndrome? You consider yourself a good judge of character but then again, who doesn't? When was the last time you heard someone say "oh I'm a terrible judge of character! I'm constantly being taken advantage of!" yet such occurrences happen all the time. We all know someone who constantly ends up in bad relationships, and as such, is incapable of establishing a good relationship. Disfunction becoming the only way they can function.

Jesus, you've only just remembered your partner, so consumed have you been by everything that has taken place since your demise. Perhaps at this point they're being informed of your tragic death, then discovering from the police that all the preliminary evidence points towards you involvement in running over an over an old woman and killing her. What a nightmare they must be living at this instant, no doubt struggling to come to terms with the turn of events that unfolded just because you chose to take a gig for a semi-respected promoter. Alas, due to the task at hand, you cannot give any further consideration to your beloved and their predicament. Any thought of your partner at a police station having to identify the mangled corpse of your former mortal self must be put to one side as you prepare to unleash upon hell the most hackneyed set ever put together in the history of the universe.

The biggest hurdle will be reassuring Lucifer that it's possible to be an alpha male as well as accepting of his shortcomings. It seems odd that the concept of toxic masculinity would rear its head in the bowels of hell, but clearly Lucifer is not immune to feeling that the only way to be masculine, is to be strong. Logic would dictate that his position is not under threat, and that just by virtue of his position within hell, he'd be more relaxed about his status. Someone truly secure about their place in the universe would have no issue accepting that they can be capable of making a mistake or indeed that they are less than perfect, but Lucifer's whole journey begins with his vanity and feeling of superiority. Cast out of heaven for daring to believe that he was capable of doing what God was doing, such devotion to the acquiring of power is an ugly drive which was rightly punished by the creator of all there is. Such pride has no place in the kingdom of heaven, and it is sad to see that all these thousands of years later, Lucifer is still to learn the importance of fallibility. But why should he learn fallibility at the hands of an omnipotent overlord, someone who demands unquestioning obedience in the name of love? A deity who extolls the virtue of free will while setting everything up to be played out as determined, observing the unwitting actors fulfil their roles so that He can condemn those He'd already decided would refuse to acknowledge His existence. What madness it is to indulge such a charade, but what further madness it is to have initiated it in the first place? Seeking to punish those who were doomed from the off to not play ball, and to task someone whom you'd cast out of heaven to enact said punishment.

What insecurity must come from being God's favourite, to then becoming an outcast? How would such insecurity play out? What untold horrors in this world have been perpetrated by mortals so insecure that any semblance of shame or embarrassment must be dealt with through some kind of cruelty?

Why would God set the wheels spinning in such a fashion?

'I'm nervous.' shudders Lucifer, both of you watching the Amakhulu of Indulu take their seats. Black Eyed Peas "I Gotta Feeling" is blasting around the auditorium as each super demon shuffles around looking for somewhere to park their bony arse.

> *"That tonight's gonna be a good*

Good, good, good, good, good
Good, good, good, good, good
Good, good, good, good, good
Good, good, good, good, good
Good, good, good, good, good
Good, good, good, good, good night"

'How was this a hit?' you wonder aloud. 'It's fucking shite.' Lucifer is looking at the dusty floor whilst pacing back and forth, rehearsing his lines as best he can. This rehearsal is interspersed with him looking out at the massive audience before then looking back at the rocky floor of hell.
'I don't think this is a good idea.' says Lucifer.
'What?'
'My set. I think I need to go out there and kick ass.'
'There's loads of ways to kick ass.' you school, hoping to calm Lucifer.
'This is a fight. I need to fight.'
'You can win a fight without fighting.'
'What the fuck are you on about?' Lucifer replies, ever so slightly mocking your statement.
'If your opponent wants a fight, and you fight… you have lost.'
'Whatever,' Lucifer says, making it clear he has no time for your philosophising. 'I'm fucking shitting it. If I was feeling good I'd be eating it but I can't stand the idea of eating anything at the moment.'
'Nerves are good,' you say reassuringly. 'It means you care.'
'I do care! I need these cunts!'
'Good!' you say, cheerfully, hoping to inject a little frivolity into the tense proceedings. 'You should care, because there's a few hundred thousand in tonight and they can get a bit feisty if you're not careful!'
Lucifer does not see the funny side to your light hearted remark.
'If I die, you die.' warns Lucifer.
'I'm already dead.' you shrug.
'I'll make you die an infinite number of times, each one more painful than the last.'
'I don't believe in infinity.' you reply. Lucifer looks at you in disbelief.

'What do you mean you don't believe in infinity?'
'I don't think infinity is real.'
'In what way?'
'I think people use the word infinity instead of a really, really big number. Infinity is a concept rather than a reality.'
'What's the biggest number then?'
'I don't know, but whatever the biggest number is, that's it.'
'Well, what's to stop me adding one to it?'
'It's the biggest number.' you remark, confidently. Lucifer has never heard this before, you can tell by the look of utter disbelief that is scorched across his ruggedly handsome, horned face. You look away from Lucifer and back towards the audience as they take their seats, the molten lava waves crashing in the background giving the scene an eerie beauty you hadn't previously noticed, nor appreciated.

> *"Party every day, p-p-p*
> *Party every day, p-p-p*
> *Party every day, p-p-p*
> *Party every day, p-p-p*
> *Party every day"*

'Absolute shite.' you say, again wondering how such a terrible song could've gone on to be such a monstrous hit.
'That doesn't make any sense,' says Lucifer, not quite ready to let this infinity thing go. 'Why can't you add one to the biggest number?'
'Because it's the biggest number.' you repeat, definitively.
'You cant't just say that though! You can't just say "because it's the biggest number" like that's an argument. Any number you have, you can just add one more, even if it's the biggest number. That's so fucking obvious.'
'That just presupposes us to the idea that infinity is real. Which it isn't. Whatever the biggest number is, that's the biggest. You can't add one to it, or it wouldn't be the biggest number, would it?'
Lucifer is not happy. He walks towards you as you look away from him towards the assembled mass of demonic super evil. You are now so relaxed around Lucifer that his immense presence doesn't concern you, even as he advances

menacingly towards your position. You feel his hot breath as he snorts with frustrated anger at your seemingly casual dismissal of the previous threat. Lucifer's anger grows, as you steadfastly refuse to even acknowledge him, close as he is and slowly raising a clawed finger to point at you prior to your imminent chastisement.
'Now you listen here you...'
'No,' you say, turning to meet his eyes, being careful to avoid his razor sharp finger nail. 'You listen,' Lucifer blinks at your command. 'Are you nervous now?'
'What?'
'Are you nervous?' you repeat, glancing over at the crowd. Lucifer checks himself, retreating a little from his stance of physical intimidation to one of puzzled acceptance. Smirking, Lucifer appreciates what you have just done for him.
'No. No I'm not.'
'Attagirl,' you say, walking towards the announcing mic. You give the Prince of Darkness a playful slap on the butt as you pass him. 'It's showtime.'

Pearl and Dean plays as you get ready to introduce Lucifer to the stage. You look across and give him a big thumbs up, before holding the mic close to your mouth in preparation, ready to give your all for the intro you're about to perform.
'Assembled Amakhulu of Indulu, it is my great pleasure to introduce you, for one night only, the *new* comedy stylings of the one, the only, the Prince of Darkness, the Great Deciever, the raiser of hell who wears the number six, six, six... please, make him very welcome as he takes to the stage, all the way from the bowels of the lake of fire, it's Looooo - seeeee - furrrr!' you scream your student's name with all your worth as you watch him stride confidently on to the stage.

The Amakhulu do not move a muscle nor make a sound as they do their best to make their overlord feel very unwelcome. Echoing around the auditorium is nothing but the sound of hooves, as Lucifer makes his way towards the microphone. You're ok with this muted response and Lucifer is too, having been prepared by your good self to expect such a lack of acknowledgement . Lucifer removes the mic from the stand with the ease of a professional and immediately sets to work bedding himself in.

'Hello there, thanks for having me,' he says confidently, remembering to not leave an opening for any of them to heckle. 'It's a pleasure to be here. Now, first things first, we need to get a few things out the way. Yes, I know I look like a goat that's been on steroids and spent too long in the sun, I'm quite aware of that…' Lucifer pauses.
'Don't pause!' you scream inside your head. 'Keep going! Only stop if they start laughing! Fuck's sake!'
'…I mean, the last time I saw something this big and horny I was fucking my Mum…'
'Don't pause!' you bellow internally. 'Momentum! Momentum!'
Lucifer clears his throat, a sure sign of nerves. The Amakhulu don't miss a beat, as random coughs start to be heard from the audience. Lucifer's head twitches involuntarily as he instinctively searches for those in need of punishment, only to check himself and revert back to the pre-approved script.
'Some of you are probably looking at me now and thinking, "blimey, he's put some weight on since William Blake painted him"…' Lucifer pauses, again, and yet again, the Amakhulu give him nothing. Lucifer snaps. 'Do you know why I'm so fat though? Every time I fuck your mothers they each bake me a cake. You fucking pieces of shit, KNEEL BEFORE ME!'

As Lucifer says this, he throws fire directly into the front row, roasting several of the Amakhulu as they scream in pain. You watch, aghast, as Lucifer destroys all your hard work in a matter of seconds, the pressure getting to him quicker than you could've imagined. Lucifer observes his handwork, as several of the Amakhulu deliberately jump into the fire that he'd just used as a weapon, all of them delighting in the sensation of being alight.
'You all shall feel my wrath if you do not obey!' he screams, looking into the air and raising his arms in impotent triumph.
'Oooooh,' reply the entire crowd in a highly camp voice.
'You're hard.'
'ARRRGGGHHHH!' Lucifer screams, grabbing his horns, squeezing them with frustration, then tearing them off in a fit of

pure fury. 'They fucking got me again!' he yells, looking in your direction as you witness fresh, magnificent horns replace the pair Lucifer just destroyed. You don't know how to help him as the gig has already been derailed, and in such a short amount of time that it might be some kind of record. All of your pep talks and confidence building was for nothing, as Lucifer just throws the gig away right at the very beginning.
'We fucking got you again!' scream hundreds of thousands of Amakhulu, the majority of whom are sat watching the minority attempt to set themselves on fire in the front row. Seeing this transpire is incredibly unsettling, as you now have no idea if Lucifer has any form of control over proceedings. Lucifer's eyes dart back and forth as he witnesses the rapid unfolding of a plan he'd previously had genuine confidence in. Your plan.

Lucifer drops the mic to the floor, as his shoulders droop and his gargantuan chin hits his chest. You mirror his posture, depressed as you are, knowing that the jig is up. The plan you had, the one which had worked for Rex Boyd for so long, didn't work. Now, you're fucked for eternity. Waving his hand despondently, Lucifer eradicates the fire as quickly as he started it, as the Amakhulu let out a collective sigh of disappointment at the now lack of searing pain they were previously enjoying. As the embers burn and the Amakhulu tear off one another's scorched skin just for the lolz, they each slowly turn towards the stage so that they may witness the forlorn figure of Lucifer, front and centre. His posture is that of a child who had been expecting his father to return home from combat for Christmas, only to find out that he'd been killed by a rabid dog upon exiting the airport.

'I don't know why I bother,' says Lucifer. 'Why did I even think this would work? What use is all this power if I can't use it the way I want to? I get it. I wouldn't want to help me either. What are the odds that we'll win in the first place? I want to take on a god who could probably crush us by blinking. A god who I've already tried it on with, no less. A god who, after I failed him, cast me down here like a little bitch so that I might do his bidding.'

A laugh.

Your head lifts quickly as you scan the crowd for where the laugh came from. Maybe it wasn't a laugh?
'Cast down like a little bitch. I'm lucky he didn't spank my tight little arse.'
Another laugh and that was definitely a laugh from a different part of the audience. Lucifer doesn't appear to have noticed as his chin is seemingly glued to his pecs, voice barely above a whisper but powerful enough for all to hear.
'Now, here I am,' Lucifer continues, 'begging for your help like a little bitch and what do you lot end up doing? Making me your bitch. Again! They shouldn't call me the Prince of Darkness, they should call me the little bitch of hell who cries like a bitch when no one is looking.'
More laughs. It's not even funny, but since when the fuck did that matter? A laugh is a laugh. Fucking hell he might pull this back you know.
'The thing is,' continues Lucifer, looking up at the crowd now, 'I thought I could make you laugh by being self deprecating, but, the truth is, I'm a fucking badass. I can do almost anything I want, but it's just not enough. I want you. That's my problem. You fuckers were put here to torture me and that's what you do, you torture me. You are the only creatures in the universe that can make me feel inadequate, and that's what I feel right now.'
More laughter. Your heart fills with hope, but you notice that Lucifer's facial expression is changing to one of anger, and that isn't a good sign.
'Why are you laughing?' he scolds, not realising that the gig is almost retrievable. 'None of this is funny! All I'm doing is telling you that I need you because I'm not strong enough to take Heaven on my own. I'm too pathetic.'
This gets the biggest laugh, with at least thirty percent of the audience enjoying it.
'You think me being pathetic is funny?' Lucifer asks, now beginning to understand what is happening. 'What if I told you that I consider myself to be shit at most things?'
The Amakhulu laugh. Lucifer recognises what is going on and learns the lesson of the hack comedian: when they like

dancing, keep dancing. Hack comedians don't take audiences to places they didn't know they wanted to go. No, what a hack comedian does is find out what the audience likes, then just cling on to those unimaginative coat tails and give them what they want. These mercenary comedians are very effective because they have no scruples, they will easily change to any situation the way a parasite evolves when in a new host. Not a single creative thought passes through their tiny brains as they seek only to please those who are in front of them. The comedic paradox we have to live with is that sometimes, the worst comedians make the best comedians.

You thought it was Lucifer's status which was holding him back with the Amakhulu, but it turns out that all they want is to see Lucifer suffer. Maybe they've discovered that the ultimate way to see Lucifer suffer, is for him to enter into the final war with God in the Kingdom of Heaven and then watch him have his arse handed to him by the almighty? Either way, Lucifer is now doubling down on the self criticism and the audience of Indulu are loving it. He hasn't changed his posture from that of the slouched failure he was presenting as just a few minutes ago. It's working for him.
'What was the point of me being one of the most beautiful angels in heaven if I had such a tiny cock? I swear to god I am such a cunt.' Lucifer says, shaking his head as he delivers what might be his new catchphrase. Lucifer stands completely still and repeats himself.

'God, I am such a cunt.'
The Amakhulu leap to their feet and give Lucifer a standing ovation for using a phrase that would suit ninety percent of stand up comedians across the world. The brutally honest self reflection being displayed here would probably help most people in the world, rather than the fraudulent imposition of positive thinking which has permeated self help over the last seventy years. Continually telling oneself that you have value and are worthy no matter how much of a piece of shit you actually are has done nothing to curtail the immense increase in mental health problems currently blighting western

civilisation. Maybe everyone needs to acknowledge that we're all just cunts?

The applause dies down as Lucifer stands there, unmoving as he looks out across the sea of adulation now moving towards him like a tidal wave of devotion. He's done it, he now needs to seal the deal.
'God, I am such a cunt. Will you all be cunts with me?'
The Amakhulu kneel in unison, pledging allegiance with one sweeping gesture before chanting in unison: ALL HAIL, THE CUNT! ALL HAIL, THE CUNT!
Lucifer looks over to you and smiles. You look back through eyes blurred by tears as all your hard work seems to have paid off. You smile and raise a thumb, as Lucifer looks across, deep into your soul and places a closed fist on the left side of his chest. He beats it a couple of times, mouthing the word: **YOU.**

Suddenly everything begins to shake, as a line of blinding light from above shines across the stage as the rocky overhangs of hell are torn apart by some unseen force. The Amakhulu begin to shriek and panic before Lucifer imbues in them a sense of calm simply by remaining unmoved from his position and showing no fear. Wiping your eyes clear of tears, you look up and see through squinted eyes that a huge crack has ripped across the top of hell. Sunlight the likes of which you have never seen is flooding the senses of all those present, as the Amakhulu stand in solidarity with Lucifer, ready for whatever may enter through the rocky rupture. Although you're worried, Lucifer remaining so calm is helping you keep it together. You gaze upon your comedy student and marvel at how little he has moved despite the sunlight beaming directly onto him. Lucifer has merely closed his eyes to avoid the sight destroying light, before conjuring some sunglasses so that he may view He who is about to enter.
'Lucifer my child,' comes the voice, a voice known to all by the sound once it has been heard. The voice of the almighty.
'You're looking well. How have you been keeping?'
'Cut to the chase, you know how I've been keeping.'

'Lucifer, I come to you in the spirt of love. You see my child, you have finally learned the lesson I wanted you to learn all these millennia.'
'What lesson?' asks Lucifer, confused as to why God would now appear, just as he was finalising his army in preparation for battle.
'The lesson of humility, my son.'
'I'm not your son, fuck face.'
'Oh, Lucifer. Stop showing off in front of your friends. You see, I cast you out because of your hubris. Like Icarus, you have learned your lesson. Alas, Icarus learned his too late. It is not too late for you my child.'
'What do you mean?'
'Come back to me, Lucifer. I forgive you.'

Lucifer takes off his sunglasses and looks around. The Amakhulu look to him, knowing that their future now hangs in the balance. This offer from God is something that deep down, Lucifer has always wanted. That feeling of acceptance which we all crave, the feeling that we are wanted despite all our imperfections, that somewhere there is a bosom for us to sink our cheeks into, a bosom which is warm and nurturing and prepared to love us no matter what. But is God that bosom? The love he offers is entirely conditional, as proven by the sentence He has just uttered. Is it hubris to believe that you can create something better than that which Good has created, when it appears so obvious to you that the universe as it currently exists has been created poorly? Surely that isn't over confidence? Surely over confidence is believing that anything you create is perfect and that nobody could ever challenge you. THAT, is Hubris.

'It seems convenient,' says Lucifer 'that you would return to forgive me just as my army was approaching full strength.'
'It has nothing to do with your army and everything to do with you learning your lesson.'
'So unconditional love comes with conditions? How lovely.'
'Spare me your pathetic theology you little prick. Do you want a seat beside me at the table in heaven, or would you rather be licking shit from the bottom of my sandals?'

The Amakhulu hiss at this threat. Lucifer calms them once more by gently shushing them. Lucifer appears deep in thought, unsure as to which option he should choose. In his heart of hearts, he's always wanted to be God's favourite again, but now he also sees that he has a real chance of not only fighting, but defeating God.
'What do you think?' asks Lucifer, looking directly at you.
'Me?' you ask, making sure the question its aimed at you.
'Yes, you. What do you think I should do?'
'Erm…'

To advise Lucifer to take God's offer and return to heaven, turn to page 227

To advise Lucifer to tell God to fuck off, turn to page 265

You absolute fucking maniac. What do you hope to achieve?

Right, last chance you racist piece of shit.

To absolutely, definitely call the audience member a "paki", turn to page 198

To walk off stage and accept your fate, turn to page 199

'You wanna hurt me?' you ask Jatinder, lifting your right arm straight out towards him, fingers together and palm up. 'Let's dance.' you whisper, beckoning him and his accomplices towards you.

Now breathing more easily (although still coughing), Sparky Mark staggers to his hands and knees then crawls away in an attempt to avoid the upcoming melee. Scrambling to the nearest wall, he manages to get his back against it, knees up to his chest into a position where he can recover, ready to bear witness. You see him out the corner of your eye and curse yourself for not having disposed of him sooner. Your flair for the dramatic has meant that you now have him to consider as well as the seven Sikhs in front of you. Jatinder takes a step back, making obvious that his tactic is to sit tight and weight for his heavies to subdue you enough so that you no longer pose a threat. Then, he'll no doubt be getting involved himself.
'Too scared to fight me yourself are you? Pathetic.' you goad, hopping Jatinder will take the bait.
'No, too sensible,' replies Jatinder. 'I've seen now what you're capable of. I'm wise to your manipulation. Also, I don't need a piss just yet.' Jatinder produces from his inside pocket a one litre carton of orange juice which he promptly begins to chug. His half dozen heavies take up a standard kabaddi formation, holding hands in a semi-circle, slowly advancing so that they may ensnare you before beating your body into a state of unconsciousness. You see all six of them take a deep breath before they begin to low hum the same word over and over.
'Kabaddi, kabaddi, kabaddi, kabaddi, kabaddi, kabaddi, kabaddi, kabaddi, kabaddi…'

Attacking either of the two in the middle of the semi-circle would be foolish, so you try to angle yourself so that those at the end are more vulnerable to attack. You choose to side step to your left a few times which puts the guy on the right of their semi-circle closest to you. You continue to side step as they try and follow your movements, but you also make very incremental movements forward until you are close enough to strike, which you do. Exploding off your right foot from an orthodox boxing stance, you land a clean rear cross at the top

of Sikh number one's beard, just below his bottom lip. His head rocks back with such force that his turban falls off, only for his skull to snap back as quickly as it was sent backward, meeting a snapping right front kick to the same jaw you just broke with one punch. He's down for the count, his body in spasm, still grasping the hand of the kabaddi man he was holding. Sikh number two is trapped by the unconscious Indian now slumped at his feet, as the other four disengage in order to regroup. Seizing your opportunity, you advance towards Sikh number two who is now desperately trying to release the grip of his KO'd partner. You step on to the body of the sleeping giant and use him to get some height on the head butt you bring down on Sikh number two's nose, shattering it across his face and covering your forehead in crimson. Bringing up his left hand to try and throw a hook punch your way, you duck down and lurch forward to bite his penis. Getting a good mouthful of his surprisingly meaty cock, you clench your jaw with all your might, almost deafening yourself because of the ear shattering scream that results from your mandible tightening around the quite sizeable shaft. Now placing both palms on his thighs, you push him away whilst yanking your head back, making sure to keep your bite gripped as he falls rearwards with a twisting motion due to still being clamped in the hand of sleeping Sikh number one. He slams onto the floor shrieking in pain as you look across at the remaining four who you see staring at you. Terror is etched across their faces, as you look at them, wild eyed with a mouthful of trouser and half a blood strewn cock dangling past your chin. You spit out the remnants of Sikh number two, then turn to witness him pass out from the pain of having his dick ripped off.
'That's two going to hospital,' you snarl. 'Who wants to join them?'

The four remaining Sikhs involuntarily take a step back as they cast their eyes over the easy devastation you've just meted out to their compatriots. Your improvisational skills are now beyond all comprehension, as you fully immerse yourself in the role of a rabid football hooligan thirsty for ultra violence. Never before have you felt such power. Sean would be beyond proud

as you deftly deal with each block from your Sikh improv "partners" and continue unabated. The four Sikhs look at one another, unsure as to how
they should proceed, before looking over at Jatinder who is rooted to the spot holding his orange juice, recalculating what he thought would be a foolproof strategy.

'Think of the Nihang!' Jatinder yells, hoping to inspire his cohorts.
'This, is Nihang.' says the biggest Sikh, referring to you.
The Nihang (The Immortals) were known for their bravery and ruthlessness on the battlefield, particularly when outnumbered. What you have just exhibited is the same ferocity and lack of sympathy for your enemies The Nihang would've shown.
'He filmed me being pissed on!' screams Jatinder, accidentally spilling some of his orange juice. 'Come on!'
You take a step back as you can sense a change in the atmosphere. The four big Sikhs still in possession of their consciousness have each lost their bottle and are waiting for one of the others to make the first move. They've seen what you are capable of, and not one of them wants any piece of it. This key to facing off against multiple opponents is in having the ability to scare each one individually. In this instance, they began by using their kabaddi skills to work as a team. It took just a few seconds of intense physical violence to make them realise that although they're a team, they are made of individuals, each with a sense of their own mortality. Humans are not ants, or even worker bees sacrificing themselves within the hive when an African Murder Hornet invades. No, these men have families and futures and dreams and as such, have fear.

You no longer feel fear. You have improv'd away from fear. You are now so lost in character, that to think any other way would seem positively alien to you.

You stamp the floor hard to mimic an advance towards the four Sikhs, and all four of them delight you by flinching. You look over at Jatinder, wide eyed with terror as he no longer knows how this is gonna go down. You waggle your eyebrows at him.

'Kabaddi, kabaddi, kabaddi, kabaddi, kabaddi, kabaddi…' they begin again, finding some collective courage, holding hands and slowly advancing towards your position. You look away from Jatinder and towards those that fell from your previous scuffle to see if there is anything you can use for your next round of hand to hand combat.

There, dangling from the neck of Sikh number one is a gold chain with a decent sized Kirpan attached to it. Snatching the dagger from the chain, you throw it hard at Sikh number three's head, hitting him straight in the left eye. Immediately breaking from the kabaddi ranks, Sikh number three strays from position which allows you to zone in on him. You reach down and pull the Khanga from Sikh number one's hair, then run over to Sikh Number three, thrusting the comb hard towards his throat. Despite holding his left eye and struggling to see properly, he manages to duck out the way of your thrust, only to be greeted by your right knee cap, which you have deftly brought up to meet his face. Dazed but now standing upright, he staggers backwards as you renew your comb thrusting attack, this time with more success. After several savage thrusts you begin to wonder if you will ever manage to break the skin of his neck, but eventually your persistence pays off as you manage to penetrate the dermis enough so that you can get to the internal structure of the throat. Realising that you need more power, you take a step back and round kick Sikh number three's legs from under him, waiting until he lands on his back before leaping into the air and bringing the Khanga down onto his throat, leaving it inside him now so that he has the choice of leaving it there and possibly living, or removing the discomfort and accepting death. As you stand to walk away, you're surprised that he chooses death.

Turning back to the remaining three, Jatinder at this point has discarded his orange juice and is clearly thinking about an escape plan.
'You have to attack together!' he pleads to the remaining three.
'Just, do it! For fuck's sake! Attack! As a team!'

The trio look at one another. No words are shared, only nods. Three have fallen and three remain. More than ever, this is now about getting immediate revenge for their fallen brothers, rather than doing a mate a favour because a member of their gurdwara got urinated on by a couple of fat lasses.
All three run at you, which is their first mistake. They have no plan, just raw aggression and physical power, both of which are only worth anything if they're applied with the relevant tactics. One step either side and you will have angled them off enough so that they will have to clamber past one another, leaving you to deal with them effectively one at a time. The only question is which one do you want to dispatch first? In your head you'd already numbered them one to six, but now this last three might as well all be one person, acting in unison as they are whilst sharing the very similar aesthetic traits of beards and turbans. They each move with a lack of fluidity that implies not a day's training has passed through their ears when it comes to combat, whereas you are now imbued with the spirit of a thousand combat veterans, such is the power of your improv. Not only are you a master criminal, but a master of modern warfare and hand to hand combat. You never expected it, but it truly was worth spending time with all the paedophiles who ran that improv course.

As the trio get closer, they are advancing in a line which makes it easy for you to take two quick side steps to the left and have one of them closer to you than the others. You wait until their proximity is such that a side step will prove too tempting for the nearest Sikh, putting yourself in harm's way, hoping that he'll reach out to grab you or maybe even throw a punch. Timing is everything, as you quickly side step to your left and, as you'd hoped, the nearest Sikh decides to swing a poorly thrown haymaker at you, which you easily duck under before coming up ready to grapple him. He swung so hard that he is now off balance with his right arm all the way across his body. This allows you to place one palm under his chin and the other at the back of his head so that you can control his head and use the man's skull as a battering ram against the guy beside him, slamming the side of his cranium directly into the confused face of the Sikh next in line. You do this repeatedly

until both men are struggling to remains conscious, then you take the gentleman's head and casually twist it, breaking his neck. As you release your grip and his body slumps to the floor, you move on to the man you'd dazed using his brother's noggin. Side kicking his leg so that he falls to his knees yelping like a dog with a trapped paw, you slam your upturned palm into his neck, breaking his wide pipe, causing him a rather agonising death. With only one of the six left to go, your confidence is growing as he holds his hands up and begins to plead for his life.
'Please, please,' he begins. 'I've got a little baby girl.'
'Like I give a fuck?' you seethe, administering a swift instep to the testicles, his knees clamping together the moment you land the blow. Your foot is now trapped as he slowly descends to the floor, a swift knee to the base of his nose remedies your problem as he falls back on to the floor, coughing from the groin strike and now choking on the blood cascading down the back of his throat. All in all, not a bad evening of improv for you, all things considered.

Six down, one to go, as you now turn your attention to Jatinder.
'It's fine, you can keep the USB stick. I don't care anymore. It's all good.' he splutters, inconceivably frozen to the spot he's been stood in for the last couple of minutes. You say nothing as you walk towards him. At this point, you're not even sure what you're gonna do to him. Originally, you were happy to just provide him with a unique sexual experience and leave it at that, under the assumption that he would never testify against you should your crimes ever hit a court of law. Now though, retribution is in the air and you're high on blood lust.
'We can come to an agreement, I swear.' Jatinder again pleads, unnerved more by your silence than the carnage you've just caused. If he knew you were unsure about his fate, perhaps he would act differently? Right now though, Jatinder drops to his knees as you get within striking range of this uppity teenager.
'We could've been beautiful,' you say. 'We could've gone on to untold heights. All you had to do was trust me.'

'How could I trust you?' sobs Jatinder, tears flowing now as he appreciates that his time on earth is rapidly drawing to a close. 'You left me with those… those animals.'
'What you learned in there would've see you right! You'd have been a legend of the playground, with evidence to back up your claim! Now look at you, on your knees, begging for your life. You could've been a legend.'
Jatinder cries the tears of a condemned man, a man in the electric chair not guilty of the heinous crime he's been convicted of. Powerless to stop that which is to be, Jatinder stands and accepts his fate. You admire this show of defiance. 'I promise it'll be painless,' you say, reassuringly. 'Turn around.'
Jatinder turns away from you, as you slide your right arm around his neck, preparing to make him unconscious before restricting his airways until he is brain dead. As you begin your manoeuvre, you're aware of a rustle. The sounds of clothing, as though something, a person perhaps, were moving towards you. You quickly scan your eyes across the Sikhs, before feeling the heavy weight of a determined human land on your back after a purposeful pounce from some feet away.
'Run!' screams Sparky Mark, as he flings his legs around your torso in order to become a human back pack. 'Go!'
Jatinder turns back and sees you struggling to get Sparky Mark off your back, rotating left and right with vigorous motion trying to disturb the balance of your attacker. Sparky Mark clings for dear life, exhibiting tremendous fortitude for someone not used to such displays of courage. Jatinder frantically looks round for anything he can use as a weapon, as you finally grab hold of Sparky Mark's hands and begin to work on some small joint manipulation in order to break his panic stricken grip. You manage to prise free one of Sparky's little fingers, applying pressure against the digit, easily snapping the bone. Sparky Mark lets out a cry of pain but diligently maintains his hold on your back. Jatinder retrieves the pen you were using to make notes in your notebook prior to the gig that will now never happen, then runs at you, slamming the nib directly into your eye, recoiling his arm whilst still holding the pen and momentarily rejoicing in the puncture wound he's just caused. The pain is excruciating as you instinctively cover your eye from further attack, which leaves your abdomen open for

stabbing. Jatinder doesn't need a second invite, he stabs you repeatedly in the chest with the Bic orange you'd only just found this evening.
Sparky Mark leans back and pulls on your shoulders, causing you to both fall backwards, Sparky taking the brunt of the fall as he lands on his back with you landing on his front. Pushing hard on your shoulders, Sparky Mark wrestles his way out from underneath your body as you struggle to cope with the pain in your eye and the puncture wounds in your chest. Jatinder runs over and hoofs you in the face, Sparky Mark joining shortly after as he lets loose on your cranium with his twattish looking winkle pickers.

Darkness flickers as you go in and out of consciousness, one blow knocking you out before the next blow seemingly brings you back to full awareness.
'Enough,' says Jatinder. 'He's had enough.'
'OK! LOL.' says Sparky Mark, panting heavily.
'You saved my life, thank you.'
'No worries. ROFL,' replies Sparky. 'What we gonna do now?'
'First, justice.' says Jatinder, as he unbuttons his fly, taking position above your chest as he exposes his penis to the warm of air of a combat strewn green room. A slight tension crosses his face as he strains to excrete urine from his urethra, pissing on command not coming as naturally to him as he would've hoped. Contracting his sphincter a little, hoping to motivate his internals to produce a steady yellow flow appears to do nothing, as you lie there semi conscious awaiting a warm shower of spice filled piss.
'Want me to have a go?' asks Sparky.
'I think you might have to, I don't think I've got it in me.'
'PMSL.'
Sparky Mark unzips his thrift store trousers and unveils a rather impressive penis. From your vantage point, it is clear that Sparky Mark has impeccably shaved balls. Used to delivering to a deadline, Sparky Mark easily brings about a smooth flow of urine that splashes about your chops in a disgustingly warm, ammonia like waterfall.
'Open his mouth for me?' Sparky Mark asks of Jatinder.
'I'll get wet!'

'Oh, right, yeah. Hang on.'
Sparky Mark easily ceases his flow, barely flinching at what must've been the painful stopping of a piss in full flow.
'How the fuck did you do that?!' asks Jatinder.
'Twice a day ejaculations keep my prostate in robust health. Please, continue. ROFL.'
Jatinder pinches your cheeks and opens your mouth. You have no strength left to resist, as Sparky Mark resumes his easy flow, directly into your mouth.
'Keep it open please,' requests Sparky Mark. 'Don't worry, I'm a good shot.'
A free flowing cascade of promoter's urine pours effortlessly into your mouth as you're forced to take this most undignified of punishments.
'Karma's a bitch, ain't she?' whispers Jatinder, as you accidentally swallow a hot mouthful of golden warmth. Sparky Mark causally whistles the theme tune to M*A*S*H as your mouth begins to fill up yet again, your eye still burning in agony.
'Quick! Quick!' yells Jatinder excitedly. 'I need a piss.'
Sparky Mark finishes up his business, giving his length a little shake before squeezing the base of his cock and applying pressure all the way up to the tip in a bid to wring out any remaining urine.

Your mouth is still full, as Sparky Mark makes way for Jatinder, who now stands directly on your chest, causing you to exhale suddenly before taking a massive inhale of Sparky Mark's piss. This action causes you to cough momentarily, before your focus is drawn to the sight of Jatinder unsheathing his slightly less impressive penis. He immediately begins to fill your cranial orifice with wee wee, forcing your cheeks to swell fully with the golden fluid. Jatinder jumps a little on your chest, forcing you yet again to involuntarily breathe urine, coughing and spluttering as best you can in order to rid your lungs of this filth. Alas, your lungs are now full of blood and piss, as they begin to fail, causing you to quickly drown in both substances.

Everything goes dark as you hear the sound of liquid hitting forehead, accompanied by the sound of Sparky Mark laughing about what a great Edinburgh show this would make.

The End - go back to page 140

Good Christ. What is wrong with you? I mean, what good could come of such a thing?

I know what you want. You want the vicarious thrill of racism with none of the consequences. Shame on you. Like the stand up comedian telling a joke about their imaginary dad who says racist things, you want to have your cake and eat it. You want to sit on the bus or the train and read some good old fashioned racism, then chuckle because it's not real and no one is getting hurt. Well, guess what? I'm not going to give you the satisfaction. You've had three opportunities to avoid the option of a racial insult, and each time you've selected it. What does that say about you?

I think you need to take a good long look at yourself in the mirror before you read any further. Perhaps examine the impulses you've followed that have lead you to this point, and then think about how you could avoid such impulses in the future. Seriously, you'd been given THREE opportunities to avoid using a racial slur and at each juncture, your thirst for the depraved has meant you couldn't help but choose to take the worst option.

I'm all for a bit of fun, but racism has no place in a civilised society, and just because a gig has gone badly, whether real or imagined, it doesn't mean that the colour of someone's skin should be the basis of an insult. Yes, there's an outside chance there could be a situation where an ironic moment of racism might be humorous. But for the most part, it's just an ugly thing to say and more than likely, unnecessary.

Let us never speak of this again.

To walk off stage and accept your fate, turn to page 199

Mercifully, you ignore the seemingly overwhelming impulse to be racist and decide that enough is enough. This whole evening, right from when you took the phone call from Sparky Mark, has been nothing but a shit show of adrenaline and poor decision making. In a way, you're relieved to see the police stood there waiting to arrest you. You also have a feeling of tremendous gratitude towards them for showing restraint in allowing you the dignity to walk off and then be arrested, rather than indulging themselves in a very public detaining.

You inhale deeply as you take stock of the situation, casting your gaze over the patrons who make up this ramshackle audience of morons, none of whom have any idea about stand up comedy. These idiots preferred the act that came before you and now he is dead, from which you can take some minuscule amount solace. Hopefully that fat bitch who left the gig through some miracle of engineering will eat herself into a diabetic coma, and this stupid cow who can't even operate a drinking glass will get some kind of blood infection and die. These fucking audiences are the bane of your existence, sitting there in quiet judgment as they refuse to allow themselves into your magical world of comedy. Barring a few coughs, the room is silent as they all wait for you to address the Indian man's question. Deciding not to address it and accepting defeat is something that comes from maturity, as you acknowledge that the audience is using their most effective weapon: silence.

If audiences ever figure this out, comedians will be in a lot of trouble. Indeed, it is the problem with all collective action in that, the best weapon is usually the most under utilised. In stand up comedy, a silent audience that is practically ignoring the comedian has almost unlimited power to crush the comedian. Silence gives the comedian nothing to work with, nothing to bounce from and nothing to attack. As such, all the comedian is left with is their jokes, which the audience hated to begin with. This audience here, in front of you, seems disciplined in their approach, and appears to be delighting in your silence as you mull over your options. In the end, there really is only one option.

You turn to retrieve the mic stand as you finally decide to call it a day.

'Well,' you begin, 'Some gigs go your way and some gigs don't. On this occasion, it appears that I have come onstage and completely misjudged you and, for that, I am very, very sorry.'

Your sincerity takes the audience by surprise. Luckily, it's fake sincerity, but it doesn't matter to these fools. Even the most hostile of audiences will respect a comedian who gracefully accepts the rather obvious fact that they have just died on stage, perhaps because the public humiliation is punishment enough for you having the nerve to get up there and think you're funny. People admire humility in those who would ordinarily be cocksure.

'I want to take this opportunity,' you continue, 'to thank you for coming out to support live comedy, and I would like to apologise for my ill chosen outbursts. I've had a stressful evening, much of it my own doing but also, much of it not.' You put the mic back in the stand, so that your hands are now free to gesture with openness.

'Ladies and gentlemen, I would like to wish all of you a good evening, except for…' you point at the Indian man who'd previously called you out as a piece of shit.

'…you.' pausing for dramatic effect has always been one of your favourite performance tricks, as both the audience and he look at you expectantly. 'You sir, are a smelly paki.'

For fuck's sake. What is wrong with you? Why? What is the point?

Fuck it, you've done it now and you're gonna have to deal with the consequences. After a brief moment of silence, presumably so the audience could slowly digest what they'd just witnessed, the boos begin. The Indian man doesn't look too bothered, as the increasingly intensified booing, gaining in decibels with each passing second, just serves to reassure him that only a positive outcome will be headed his way. Momentarily, you forget about your impending arrest, as you fully embrace your new status as ruler of Cuntsville. A devastatingly shit beginning to your set did not need the kind of follow up you gave it, publicly shaming a morbidly obese woman, which you then somehow topped by using a (quite frankly) absurd and unnecessary racist verbal attack against a man who was just speaking up for those in attendance. You are a piece of shit who will most likely never gig again, regardless of whatever legal action comes your way.

You turn to look at Sparky Mark, still stood there with Lauren, both of whom have their mouths agape. The police, poker faced and professional, probably quite enjoyed that closing line of yours. You make your way off stage, triggering some movement from Sparky Mark as he remembers all of a sudden that this is his club and he now has to go on and salvage what remains of the gig.

Once at the side of the stage, you turn your back to the police so they can handcuff you, which they do instantly to ensure the safety of all those around. After seeing the kind of mental health problems you've just displayed, they decide not to take any chances.
'What the fuck?' gasps Lauren, seemingly distraught at what she has just witnessed.
'Lauren,' you whisper. 'I've always fancied you. My biggest regret is that now I will never get a chance to disappoint you in a way that isn't racist.'
'Oh god,' Lauren sobs, as you look over her shoulder and see pint glasses being pelted at Sparky Mark. 'I've always fancied you, too!'

SMASH!

A glass hits Sparky Mark square on the forehead, shattering on impact and dropping him to the stage floor as a group of patrons get onstage and start shoeing him in his freshly bleeding head.
'Er, lads, you gonna do anything about that?' you ask the police, as Sparky Mark huddles into a ball to protect himself from the onslaught. The police look non plussed by what is occurring.

'I've actually seen his set,' says one of the officers. 'Some of that is overdue.'
'Look! Over there!' screams the primary agitator of the patrons now kicking fuck out of Sparky Mark. They all turn to look directly at you. 'There's the fucking arse hole.'
Two of the police officers, duty bound to protect even a piece of shit like you, walk towards the approaching assailants and warn them to get back. The third police officer, still holding onto your handcuffs, begins to pull you backwards away from what is happening onstage at Uncle Spunk's.
'Come with me.' he commands, as you look longingly into Lauren's eyes, caring not for the violence occurring just a few feet away.
'How long have you felt this way?' you ask, as the officer tugs on your cuffs. You resist his pull so that you may be in the presence of Lauren for just a few seconds longer. She walks towards you to make sure you hear her.
'Since your first open spot here.'
'Come on!' yells the officer. 'We need to get you outside now.'

More people rush the stage as chaos begins to reign. Chairs and glasses begin being hurled around Uncle Spunk's Chuckle Trunk, as the mob swells and demands it's pound of flesh. The two officers trying to contain the crowd and stop them getting to you now have their extendable batons drawn and chambered behind their head, held aloft and ready to be used if any one in the crowd gets too close.
'GET BACK!' each officer shouts, as the crowd ignore their commands. 'GET BACK!' they both scream again to no avail. Once within striking range, the first officer lashes out at the nearest audience member, a woman who's had too much drink and isn't sure where she is. The baton strikes her on the forearm, which she had instinctively raised in order to protect herself. Once this blow has landed, at least fifteen people swarm on the two officers, easily subduing both before dragging them to the floor, all in spite of the frantic baton twatting of the panicked officers.

'Shit!' says the third officer, releasing your handcuffs and marching onstage to help his colleagues. 'Control, urgent assistance required at Uncle Spunk's Chuckle Trunk. I repeat, urgent assistance required.' screams the officer into his radio as he enters the fray in a bid to rescue his colleagues. You look to Lauren, now looking at you, probably wondering about all the time you could have had together, which you've now lost by not admitting your feelings to each other sooner.

'I didn't know.' she says, her eyes filling with tears.
'I didn't have the courage.' you reply, fighting your emotions in a bid to remain stoic. Lauren looks across at the mini battle taking place, the third officer now also on the floor taking a beating. What kind of training do these police get nowadays anyway? This is an appalling show, they're big lads too for fuck's sake, getting their arses handed to them. Maybe the police should be armed after all? Oh well, any minute now the back up will arrive and order will be restored. It is in this moment of chaos that you feel the most clarity. Despite all that has transpired this evening, just knowing that Lauren has similar feelings for you, as you do for her, has made it all worthwhile.
'Fuck it.' says Lauren, as she runs head first, straight into the melee.
'Lauren, no!' you call but it's too late, she's already made her way into the swirling vortex of limbs and weapons that is a mass brawl. You've always thought of her as someone formidable, someone you would not like to get on the wrong side of. Watching her now dive head first into this madness means that you were always right to have given her the maximum amount of respect you did, as you witness her trying to maintain order in the club she helps to manage.

Lauren is targeting the police officer who cuffed you, seemingly attempting to pull him to safety, grabbing at his belt so that she can drag him away from the repeated blows to the head he's currently sustaining. However, it appears that your assumption is incorrect, as Lauren manages to pull the belt, and *only* the belt from the officer, before deftly performing a forward role out of the brawl and towards where you're standing. Lauren stands up from the mildly acrobatic stunt she

just performed, brandishing a small set of keys, which she jangles right in front of your face.
'Turn around,' she tells you. 'Let's get the fuck out of here.'

* * * *

The fire exit alarm doesn't work. Lauren holds your hand as she leads you out the building and to relative safety.

Lauren's hand.

That bisexual hand which has pleased the genitalia of both sexes probably has many, many highly erotic tales to tell. Stories you have longed to listen to. Fleetingly, your current partner crosses your mind. Is this cheating? Have you cheated? All you've done so far with Lauren is mention a few thoughts and feelings which have crossed your mind over the last year or two. Nothing wrong with that! I mean, all that's happened is that your feelings have been reciprocated in exactly the way you've fantasised about before falling asleep at night. That's not cheating! Is it? Was it cheating all those times before when you were merely thinking about Lauren, and all the incredible sexual fun you could have with her? Existence only happens in the moment, so did you even really think about Lauren in the past? Or is it that, in this moment, you're simply *imagining* you've had these feelings for Lauren for this length of time? Such a state of mind would be very beneficial for your survival, so it is perfectly plausible that you are creating your own reality moment to moment in order to stay alive. You ponder this as she runs with you across the staff car park towards her car and the possibility of self preservation.

Lauren fiddles in her pocket whilst running. Once you see the indicator lights flashing on a Ford Ka, she ceases this and continues her surprisingly athletic striding. As you get closer to Lauren's Ford Ka, you unlock your grasp of her hand and run to the passenger side door. Opening, entering the car and then closing the door with some rapidity, you both sit there panting and staring at the dashboard before slowly turning to one

another and laughing. The laughter of relief. The laughter of being in an insane situation which has resulted in an insane act, culminating now in this: being alone with Lauren, away from anyone who might see and report back with salacious gossip. She now knows how you feel and you now know how she feels. You look at one another again. Laughter.
'I can't believe you did that!' you say, eyes locked onto Lauren's.
'Shut up.' replies Lauren, as she grabs around the back of your neck, pulling you in for a passionate kiss. Your tongues intertwine as blood rushes to your genitalia, then back up to your brain again as you become aware that the danger is not yet over. Not that it seems to matter to Lauren, as she continues to kiss you, licking your face and nibbling your bottom lip as best she can. You push her away.
'Lauren, I need to get out of here.'
'We,' she says, looking straight at you. 'We, need to get out of here.'
Lauren quickly kisses you once more before putting the keys in the ignition and starting her car. Both of you put on your seatbelt, as the flashing blue lights hitting all reflective surfaces in the car park signify that police backup has arrived on the scene.

Driving out of the car park is a tense affair. Police seem to have now swarmed the area as the brawl has spilled outside. Dozens of officers are using batons to twat the locals, as lots of mini battles add up to a seemingly out of control mass fight. A riot van appears over the horizon as Lauren does her best to look casual whilst driving past the mayhem. Once away from the premises, the riot van comes hurtling towards you from the opposite direction. For some reason, you're worried you'll be recognised so you cover your face in a bid to remain unseen. You quickly realise the police don't care about you just now, they care only for the safety of their colleagues.

Lauren observes the speed limit as she drives away, checking her rear-view mirror for anyone following. Neither of you really know what to say as you each adjust your position in order to

better align your hind quarters into the unreasonably small seats of this Ford Ka.
'Do you want to listen to some music?' asks Lauren, a disturbing lack of emotion in her voice.
'Sure,' you reply. 'Are you ok?'
'I'm fine.' she says, emotion still absent from her voice. Lauren reaches forward and pushes a button on the Ka's control panel, causing music to flood through the stereo. "Bare Necessities" from The Jungle Book beings to play. Looking around the car, you see Disney paraphernalia you'd previously been too preoccupied to notice until now. Further casting your eyes around the car, you happen to notice a huge damp patch around Lauren's crotch, which you immediately turn away from, only to slowly look back at again through the corner of your eye. The wetness of the trousers has caused the material to shrink a little, as you swear you can see the outline of a juicy labia majora. You abhor the term "camel toe" and refuse to even acknowledge it's existence, considering it to be an admission of ignorance regarding the anatomy of female genitalia. You feel the same way about the term "Jap's eye" which is used to describe the opening of a male urethral meatus. You realise though that "Jap's eye" has passed into common parlance to such an extent now that everyone seems fine with it, despite it's obviously racist connotations.
'You sure you're ok?' you enquire again, now wondering if Lauren is embarrassed.
'I'm fine.' comes the reply, again with no emotion attached to the response.

You've only ever heard "Bare Necessities" when watching the 1967 animated movie adaptation of "The Jungle Book" and had no idea that the full length song has quite the orchestral lead in before the voice of Baloo the Bear, Phil Harris, begins to sing. Lauren uses her indicators to signal to other road users that she wishes to pull into an upcoming lay-by. Turning the steering wheel smoothly, Lauren pulls over to the side of the road, applies the handbrake and then shuts off the engine.

"Look for the, bare necessities
The simple bare necessities

Forget about your worries and your strife"

'Why are we pulling over?' you ask, suddenly a little concerned.
'I'm so fucking wet.' Lauren says, turning to you whilst pointing towards her crotch.
'Oh.'
'I'm so fucking excited. I need you right now.'
'Oh.'
Lauren unzips her trousers and peels them off, taking with them her underwear in one smooth motion. Her meaty thighs are there for you to observe, as she throws the trousers and pants onto the backseat, a backseat that is not designed for anyone over five feet tall to sit comfortably in.

*"Wherever I wander, wherever I roam
I can't be fonder of my big home"*

Lauren launches herself onto your lap, grabbing your right hand in the process as she gives you a quick, sloppy kiss on the lips before squeezing all four of your fingers together so that they make a cone shape.
'Put them in me,' Lauren commands. 'Blast me.'
'Oh.'
You immediately go to work, inserting the tips of your four fingers inside Lauren and pushing until you are past the medial phalange of each digit. You aren't confident enough to thrust past the proximal phalange, even though Lauren seems plenty wet enough, dripping down your hand and onto your lap as she is.

*"You look under the rocks and plants
And take a glance at the fancy ants"*

'Come on! Harder! Deeper!' commands Lauren, pushing her hips towards you in a bid to envelop your hand. You push harder and watch in amazement as your hand disappears inside Lauren right up to the wrist. 'That's it! That's what I want!' she screams.
'Oh.'

'Fucking punch me. PUNCH ME!' Lauren bellows, throwing her head back in ecstasy. She pulls her top off, letting her little gut hang whilst also exposing her magnificent, tattooed breasts. "Lucky you" is written just above her cleavage, as she takes off her bra and beings to motorboat you.
'Mffffwwrrrbbbeee.' you ask, trying not to be rude.
'What?' Lauren gasps, incredibly excited. She moves back a little. 'Suck my tits.'
'My wrist hurts,' you complain, pathetically. 'I'm sorry.'
'No excuses! Just fucking suck them!'

> *"Now when you pick a pawpaw*
> *Or a prickly pear*
> *And you prick a raw paw*
> *Well next time beware"*

'Fuck. I need to cum,' screams Lauren, holding your forearm still as she lifts herself from your hand. 'Grab a condom out of the glove box.'
You dutifully obey, using the none drenched hand to search for the condom as the drenched hand is currently struggling to regain it's prior form due to both crippling cramp, and the glue like mucus of vaginal residue now covering your pen hand, bonding your fingers together like best friends at a stranger's wedding.
'What do you want me to do with the condom?' you ask.
'Open it, put it over the gear stick.'

> *"The bare necessities of life will come to you*
> *They'll come to you"*

With zero feeling returning to your currently glued hand, you have no option but to use your teeth to open the condom wrapper. Lauren returns to her seat briefly so she can masturbate whilst watching you open the condom. Once open, you struggle with one hand to manipulate the lubricated latex, the task of rolling it over the gear stick seeming at this moment to be practically impossible.
'Oh, come on,' begs Lauren. 'I'm so fucking horny. I need this.'

You struggle further, the pressure and sexual tension getting to you. Continued fumbling, as well as increasing levels of embarrassment leave you no other option. You place the condom gently over your lips and lean down in order to apply the prophylactic to the gear stick using your mouth. You expertly fellate the Ford Ka as you get good purchase on the gear stick and apply ample protective coverage for Lauren's purposes.

"Oh man this is really livin'"

'Fuck,' says Lauren. 'That is so hot. Get outa my way.'
Lauren pushes you away, then begins to lower herself on to the gear stick. Getting into position, she spreads her legs so that one of her feet is between yours, whilst the other foot is perched on the driver's seat. Slowly, the gear stick makes it's way inside Lauren, who now leans back in order to turn the keys in the ignition and start the engine. You look to make sure she left it in neutral. The engine starts and you notice the shaft of the gear stick vibrating as Lauren goes deathly quiet, her top teeth biting her bottom lip.
'Ffffffffffffuuuuuckkkkkk,' gasps Lauren. As she moves up on the gear stick, Lauren has to turn her head so she doesn't clang her noggin on the car's ceiling. She does this by putting her ear to her shoulder on each upward stroke. She performs this movement with such graceful ease that it becomes apparent this is not her first Ford Ka rodeo.
'Suck my tits.' Lauren commands.
'Oh.' you say before placing your mouth around her areola and sucking gently on the delicious nipple.
'Harder!' Lauren screams, as she moves herself up and down on the fine workmanship of this perfectly suitable commuter car.

"Cause let me tell you something little britches
If you act like that bee acts
You're working too hard"

You suck as hard as you can, completely unaccustomed to what is happening. In your wildest dreams involving Lauren,

you never thought you'd be watching her fuck a car whilst sucking on one of her breasts in order to help her reach climax. You've not even given a single thought to your own pleasure, so focused have you been on the wondrous sight which is playing out in front of you. The formidable woman you always knew she was is exceeding your expectations, exhibiting the kind of sexual confidence you've always found inspiring.
'Oh, it's close. I'm so fucking close. Suck it. Bite it.'
You obey, biting her nipple until you hear Lauren wince with pain.
'Yes! That's it! Fuck!'
Lauren's chest and neck flood with blood as she lifts herself up from the gear stick, reaching down with her right hand to touch herself whilst using her left hand to push you (with some force) back into your seat. Her hand moves in a blur from side to side. Suddenly, you are showered with ejaculate. Lauren lets out a deep grunt of intense, animalistic pleasure.
'Ooooh, ya fucker. Yes. Drink it.' she growls as you're sprayed with sexual warmth.

> *"That's why a bear can rest at ease*
> *With just the bare necessities of life"*

You stick you tongue out, lapping up a good amount considering the lack of warning necessary for the adequate consumption of such fluid. The force of the ejaculation begins to dissipate as Lauren's blurred hand slows down to a slow, circular massaging action of calm.
'Oh. Oh, yeah. Mmmm. So good,' Lauren oozes. 'So naughty.'
'Fuck, that was amazing.'
'I'm sorry, I just get so horny sometimes and when it happens, I have to have what I need right there and then.'
'That's fine. I was just worried I'd upset you.'
'Not at all, it's just that my brain shuts off and I need to cum.'
'It was amazing.' you gasp, watching Lauren get dressed as best she can in such a small car.
'When we get back to mine we can do some more, but I just needed my fill right now.'
'I hope I was OK?'
Lauren looks at you and smiles, leaning over to kiss you.

'You were perfect.' she reassures, retrieving her trousers then sliding them on. With the car already running, she depresses the clutch and motions to put the car in first gear, hesitating once she notices what remains on the gear stick.
'Oh, would you mind?' asks Lauren, gesturing to the condom.
'Not at all.' you say, gladly pulling it off. Lauren now puts the car into first gear as you stash the condom in your pocket, but not before you give it a casual inhale so you are able to have a an olfactory memory of everything that's just happened.

> *"With just the bare necessities of life*
> *Yeah, man!"*

* * * *

Lauren's lounge is surprisingly free of Disney products. You sit gingerly on her IKEA futon drinking a cup of sweet tea. Lauren prepared you this beverage as *sweet tea is good for shock,* as she put it. You don't know what has put you in shock more: the dead old woman, the near death experience from a podcast, the wanking bouncer, the suicide, possible arrest, the mass brawl, or watching Lauren pleasure herself on a 5-speed transmission. You've had quite the evening and it's proving hard to take it all in. Where do you go from here? Blowing across the top of your cup, you notice that the time is a mere eleven o'clock post meridian, the time at which you would ordinarily be texting your other half to let them know that you're on your way home. Regardless of whether or not you're closing a gig, you will ordinarily stay to watch the final act so you can better assess how you did on the evening. Many occasions have seen you go on first then staying to the end to see if you had the best gig of the night. Sometimes you did, ending up staying even longer in order to lap some extra praise as the audience leaves. Sometimes you've been the worst act on the night, meaning you can leave half way through the headliner's set, therefore causing a minimum of fuss.

Christ knows what would've happened had you stuck around tonight to interact with the audience post gig, not to mention the high likelihood it wouldn't have been possible due to being in a cell. Why were the police there? Did Sparky grass on you? You'll never know for sure and right now, it doesn't matter, it's just safer to assume that you're wanted by the police and it'll be good to lie low with Lauren.

Oh, Lauren. Never in your wildest fantasies could you have imagined that this is how you would end up spending time of an intimate nature with her. It is the scene in the car that currently occupies your mind and seems to be giving you the most shock and disbelief. Tales of her sexual prowess have circulated for some time, tales which nobody on the comedy circuit could corroborate, such was Lauren's commitment to professionalism. Yet here you are with her promise of sexual fulfilment made earlier still ringing in your ears.

One more blow before you take a gentle slurp of tea, the sweetness hitting you almost as hard as Lauren's orgasm. She must've put about ten sugars in your brew which would ordinarily be far too many, but you slurp it again because Lauren said it would be good for you. Lauren wants to help you, and you want to please Lauren.

'I've got some friends abroad,' yells Lauren from her kitchen. 'We could go there and lie low but we'd need to leave tomorrow.'
'Why so soon?' you call back.
'Because the police are gonna start looking for you once that fight has been dealt with. Then they'll want to interview staff. I won't be there so they'll come here,' Lauren lowers the volume of her voice as she enters the lounge carrying two plates, both of which have delicious looking sandwiches and two packs of Doritos on them. 'So really, we need to get on it first thing in the morning. We can get to the airport and sort it all there. You do have a passport don't you?' Lauren asks, handing over your plate of sandwiches.
'I do. I'll have to fetch it from home though.' you say, taking your plate.
'What's wrong?' Lauren easily reading the anguish written across your face.

'I mean,' you stumble. 'It's just, I don't know what's going on. This is so fucked. I mean, I have to. I've got to go. If I don't I'll go to prison. What else can I do?'
'Exactly.' says Lauren, taking a bite from her sandwich. You can't bring yourself to eat and decide to put plate on the floor.
'Oh god, what the fuck? What the fuck? How did this happen?' you sob.

Lauren puts her plate on the floor and chews with more ferocity as she takes hold of both your hands. Swallowing quickly, she first shushes you, then gets your eye contact.
'Shhhh. It's OK. I'm here. We're gonna get through this.'
You burst into tears. Your shoulders shake as Lauren pulls you close and cradles you in her arms.
'Shhhhh. It's gonna be fine.'
'How do you know?' you sob. 'How can you be so calm?'
'Because you are the one. I know this now. I knew it before, but now I am certain.'
Hearing these words fills you with joy but also fear. How can she know? How can Lauren possibly know? How can anyone know? Most people meet because they are of roughly the same attractiveness and exist within a necessary locality. This is the reality of relationships. The internet may have made it easier to meet people, but the chances of you attracting a mate beyond your level of attractiveness is still as unlikely as it ever has been. There are of course the odd exceptions, but generally speaking it is a truism that the person you're with is about as sexy as you could get. However, Lauren isn't talking about that. She is talking about the romantic "ONE", the one who has been predetermined. The one who since the dawn of time has been placed on your path so that you run into them and let fate take over. You've never believed in the one, and nor has your partner. You are both level headed and sceptical of such notions. But when you consider everything that has gone on this evening, and how incredibly unlikely it would be that you and Lauren might end up together, it seems more reasonable now that Lauren is the "ONE" for you too, at least, more so than your current other half.

'I'd better phone home,' you say, sitting more upright now, using the back of your hand to wipe away tears. 'I need to explain.'
'I'll leave you to it.' says Lauren, retrieving her sandwiches.
'No. It's fine. It won't take long.'
Pulling the phone from your pocket, you unlock it and see a missed text from your beloved:

> ***Hope you're gig goes well. Sham we couldnt have nite in but need must. See you later x x x***

The poor grammar and spelling immediately infuriates you, causing you to feel even more sure about going with Lauren to a destination you don't even know the name of. Instead of calling your other half, you decide to text back, the misuse of your/you're pushing you over the edge, making you revert to the most impersonal way of breaking up with someone.

> ***Gig was fine. Having a drink with Sparky Mark and someone from Netflix. Don't wait up.***

You're about to lock your phone when you receive an immediate response from your better half. It is a single, solitary kiss. Never have you been so sure about someone as you have Lauren, with this token gesture from your partner sealing the deal. The very workaday nature of the relationship hits you, as a single kiss comes your way after the huge revelation that you're about to have a drink with someone from Netflix. This is big fucking news, and your other half doesn't even ask about it? You've worked on your career for years, refusing to do the horrid networking thing and instead relying on your talent as a performer. Your partner has always said you should wine and dine a little more yet here you are, informing them that after all this time, you are actually following their repeated advice and going for a drink with someone from Netflix, and the best response they are able to summon is a single kiss? Well, fuck you then.
'OK, it's done.'

'What about your passport?' asks Lauren.
'I'll get it in the morning on the way to the airport. I'll need to pick up some clothes too. I'll be in and out. No problem.'
'Good,' Lauren nods, finishing her sandwich. 'That's good.'
You take a bite from your sandwich. It's a simple ham and cheese but it might be the most delicious thing you've ever tasted. You look across to Lauren who smiles at you with a mouth full of food, cheeks swollen like a sexy hamster. You smile back and mimic her rodent like features, both swallowing your food at the same. You both notice the mutual swallow, which causes each of you to giggle at this moment of synchronicity.
'How did you know?'
'Know what?'
'That I was the one?' you ask, opening your mouth to bite your ham and cheese.
'Oh! It was when you called that guy a smelly paki.'
You pause as you bite into your sandwich, then slowly pull the sandwich away and begin to chew.
'OK' you mumble with a mouth full of food.
'Yeah. I hate them.'
The decisiveness with which Lauren passes this opinion burns into you. It is clearly not something which is up for debate. It would be pointless trying to explain to her now that you harbour no ill feeling towards any race in particular, and that the only reason you even considered saying it was for the comedic shock value. Comedy in the twenty-first century is something that exists without the bargain bucket racism of it's previous incarnations. Lazy stereotypes are considered to be a thing of the past. You'd always assumed that Lauren was fairly liberal due to the nature of her sexual proclivities, and such a sexually liberated nature has certainly been evidenced during the journey to her house. But now a weird racism has shown it's ugly face, revealing that Lauren may have more antiquated views on race and religion than her mixed race skin would've pointed to. Still, all you've wanted to do since you got here is please Lauren as best you can, so you see no reason to stop wanting to do so.
'Me, too.' you reply, swallowing hard on a barely chewed piece of ham.

'They think the world owes them a favour. Well, it doesn't. Bloody Muslims'
Muslims. It's a religion thing. Phew.
'Too right.'
'I mean, look at me. A mixed race woman who has clawed her way up from the bottom and now has a decent life. I wouldn't be allowed to do that in Islam. Did you know that?'
'I didn't.' you reply, genuinely not knowing whether or not what Lauren has just said is true.
'Yeah, they keep little girls like me locked up at home. They get educated in how to be a slave and then married off at age nine. I watched a YouTube clip on it.'
'Is that right?'
'Yeah. Have you heard of Milo Yiannopoulos?'
'I really need to use the toilet.'

* * * *

Lauren's toilet is surprisingly free of Disney products. You've been in here longer than ten minutes now which means that she'll assume you're taking a big dump. You don't care though, because such embarrassment is a small price to pay for the situation you've now found yourself in. You've fallen for a racist and there isn't really a way out. Fooled by sex appeal, you have no choice now but to play along with what is happening. There's no way your other half wouldn't immediately turn you over to the police, so you have the awful choice of staying with Lauren and freedom, but with a racist, or going home to face to your beloved and being turned in, certain imprisonment and the prospect of a terminated relationship. She thinks you're the same as her because of your crazy remark back at the comedy club, but that isn't you. That's the anarchic side of you that finds saying the wrong thing so funny. It's funny because you absolutely shouldn't say it. Lauren has taken it as a public declaration of your previously secret ideology and now you feel forced to play along with it. Who knows, maybe in time you can bring Lauren around to your way of thinking? Probably not though.

This is how the Russians would entrap targets using sexpionage. Attractive women would lure people (mainly men) in and get useful intel or perhaps some compromising photos in order to blackmail the subjects. Jennifer Lawrence starred in a movie called "Red Sparrow" about this very topic. Although looking nothing like Jennifer Lawrence, you feel certain that Lauren could have you reading Mein Kampf within a week.

Liberty is more important than keeping up appearances. Decision made. Maybe it will be just you and Lauren that are aware of your new found political leanings? You could live with that, and no doubt the absolutely earth shattering sexual shenanigans would make it all worthwhile. There must have been incredibly attractive racists in the past? Gal Gadot was in the Israeli Defence Force for fuck's sake.

Flushing the toilet for no reason other than to keep up the pretence of using the amenities for their intended purpose, you steel yourself and exit the toilet. Stood there waiting for you, is Lauren, wearing a leather corset, thigh high shiny leather boots and an SS hat. You don't notice the whip at first, as you're drawn to the bright red lips.
'Oh my,' you quiver. 'You look incredible.'
'Are you ready for the fuck of your life?' asks Lauren, assuming that anybody could be ready for such a thing. How much preparation would a person need to cope with that kind of a pressurised endeavour?
'I guess so.'
'Get over here,' Lauren commands. You walk over slowly, feigning confidence. Once you get closer, Lauren slaps you hard across the face. 'You will call me mistress. Understand?'
'Yes, mistress.' you say, trying not to cry. It was an unnecessarily hard slap for what you consider to be role play. Your pain disappears though as you look at Lauren's juicy body, struggling to be contained by the restrictive attire she has chosen to wear.
'Get in there.'

Lauren gestures to a room that had previously been closed off to you. With the door now open, you can see all sorts of

contraptions that appear to be used for getting prisoners of war to talk. Your sex life has been fairly vanilla up until now, with only an occasional spanked bottom getting ticked off your sexual fantasy list. It would appear that over the next however long this will last, your list is about to be improvised and then ticked off. As you enter the room you notice the smell of boot polish, and while looking around you marvel at the many darkly reflective surfaces consisting of abundant leather. Such effort has gone into the maintenance of all this equipment, but you cannot linger, as a sharp lash across your bottom moves you further into the centre of the room. Lauren follows behind you, closing the door to reveal on the back of it a full length poster of Adolf Hitler standing in a forest.
'Take off your clothes.' demands Lauren. You dutifully obey, but receive a sharp lash across the face from Lauren's hand.
'What do you say?'
'Yes, mistress.'
'That's better.'
Once naked, you stand there as Lauren circles you. Staring at you. Examining you with her lustful eyes. She tuts a few times whilst making her way slowly in front of you.
'Like sugar do we?'
'Yes, mistress.'
'On your knees.'
'Yes, mistress.'
Once on your knees, Lauren turns and walks towards the poster of Hitler and puts both hands either side of Adolf's head. She plants a kiss on the poster as she leans over with straight legs, presenting to you her quite wonderful posterior. You notice a zipper on the bottom of the corset which must, when undone, uncover Lauren's genitalia.
'Unzip me.'
'Yes, mistress.'
You shuffle over on your knees and release some of the tension on the teeth of the zipper, which is barely managing to stay together. You can only assume the attire was made using expert German manufacturing. Once you undo the zip a mere millimetre, the whole thing bursts open, tearing some of the corset at the same time.
'You fucking animal. Put your tongue in my arse.'

'Yes, mistress.'
You've never done this before, and assume it is a further act of submission as you resign yourself to Lauren calling the shots. It's probably for the best though, as this is a field of sexual expertise you are not familiar with, other than flicking through a copy of "Fifty Shades of Gray" when visiting your Auntie Pat. Each page of the book stunk, both figuratively and literally. You bury your face in Lauren's fleshy hindquarters as best you can, giving you a fighting chance of allowing your tongue to explore her anus. Feeling the slightly rough outer with the tip of your tongue, you feel dilatation as the sphincter relaxes, giving you the pleasing sensation of an inner smoothness.
'Ja, das ist gut.'
'Ymmmf mffffwwifff.'
You're not sure whether to lap or to delve, so you do both. Getting as far in as you can and using whatever space that remains to flick your tongue. Lauren groans with delight, her hand moving to the back your head as she pulls you in tighter.
'Ja. Ja. Leck es du dreckiger, Junge.'
'Ymmmf mffffwwifff.'
'Enough!' screams Lauren, as she spins around and grabs you by the throat, lifting you up to kiss her own residue from your lips. 'Tell me how much you hate them.' she growls, kissing and licking, licking and kissing you.
'Who?'
'You know who. Tell me.'
'Erm, I can't stand them.'
'Good. More.' Lauren says, squeezing your throat a little tighter.
'They only pray five times a day so they can get more breaks at work.'
'Fuck! Yes!' Lauren screams, throwing her head back in pleasure. 'More.'
'They smell.'
'Fucking right they do,' snarls Lauren, pushing you backwards into what appears to be a Soviet era gymnastics horse with buckles all over it. 'Turn around.'
'Yes, mistress.'
'Spread yourself across the equipment.'
'Yes, mistress.'

You widen your arms and lean forward so that your wrists are placed over the buckles at either end. You look up and notice a Budweiser refrigerator opposite. Were Budweiser part of nazi Germany? Wasn't Fanta the big deal? That was how Coca Cola was able to keep selling to the fascists, they simply sold them another drink. Capitalism has no morality, even IBM got in on the action creating computation systems so that concentration camps could be more efficient. Then again, you're in no place to judge at the moment, freely obeying the commands of your sadomasochistic nazi lover just so you can avoid the legal consequences to your abhorrent actions.

Lauren shackles your wrists tightly as you feel a surge of arousal impact your genitals in a way you'd never imagined possible. Involuntarily, you let out a moan of pleasure as Lauren tightens each wrist. She struts around to your front, leans over and places her lips as close to your as possible without managing to touch you.
'Tell me more.' she whispers
'They've got shit beards.'
Lauren sucks your bottom lip before biting it so hard that you bleed. Forcing yourself to take the pain in order to please your mistress, grunting as you feel a pleasing puncture which releases blood into your mouth. The iron filled claret is warm like a fresh ejaculation of semen, but not as thick. Lauren walks around to your rear and now shackles your ankles to the ancient athletic equipment. Your mind forgets all your current stresses and focuses completely on what is going on in this very room. All your fears and worries about the future, your career, your fictional meeting with Netflix, or whatever trials and tribulations you'd been feeling, are now lost as each ankle is tightened. Shackled and restrained of movement, you are now at the mercy of your mistress, Lauren, who remains behind you and out of your sight. You try desperately to get a view of her in one of the many highly polished, reflected surfaces. All you see are angled outlines shining back.

The sound of a cap being flipped open, followed by the unmistakable sound of a near empty tube being squirted. The rubbing of hands, as you keep looking around to catch a glimpse at what Lauren is doing, seeing only more and more black and white images of strong, aryan looking men and women in very well cut uniforms. The shock of ice cold gel being rubbed into your anus takes your breath away, as a generous amount is applied to your opening, with a less generous amount also applied inside you. Lauren penetrates you deeply with her fingers, rotating clockwise on the way in, anti-clockwise on the way out, slowly but surely making sure you are well lubricated, fingering you with such exquisite perfection you feel you may anally climax. Never have you experienced such a sensation, nor experienced such trust in another human being. Lauren surely is the one, as you give over every part of your sentient being, trusting her implicitly to deliver one unique sexual experience after another.

Lauren stops fingering, leaving you in a state of some frenzy as you pull on your shackles to try and turn towards her.
'More, mistress.' you beg.
'But what about me?' comes her voice from behind you.
Lauren slowly walks around to the front of you, entering your peripheral vision in a blur before slowly coming into focus directly in front of you, now minus her corset. Her wonderful breasts hang there, as she moves towards your head and lifts one of her nipples into your mouth.
'Suck it.'
'Yes, mistress.'
You gaze up into Lauren's eyes as you devour as much of her breast as you can manage. She helps you by putting her hand on the back of your head and pulling you in, blocking your ability to breathe through your nose as breast tissue covers the entire bottom half of your face. You keep sucking but realise that you're actually running out of breath. You try to pull your head back, only for Lauren to pull you in tighter, as you look up at her now with eyes that are pleading for some form of temporary release. This visual pleading is met by a smile, as Lauren enjoys her view.
'Fucking, suck.' she says, pulling you in even tighter and pushing her bodyweight onto your face. You want to live, so you suck as hard as you can but the lack of oxygen is now causing you some problems as panic begins rising from your

ankles. Your whole body now jerks as you try to pull away, but it is useless. You feel faint as you try one more time to plead with Lauren to allow you some air. Your legs buckle as the lights begin to go out, only the wrist shackles keep you upright as Lauren pulls even tighter on the back of your head.

Finally, she releases the pressure and takes a step back. Your head slumps as though you were unconscious but you manage to take in enough oxygen to stop you passing out completely. Your vision is blurred, but you can just about make out Lauren masturbating as she watches you gasping for air. As oxygen slowly starts to re-enter your system, you feel a sense of elation the likes of which you have never felt. Life is now pouring into every essence of your being. Each breath is a gift. As you slowly come to your senses, Lauren squirts and lets out that guttural vocalisation which means she has achieved orgasm. As you come even more to your senses, you see the puddle she has left before she returns to her position rear of you.

Fingers again inside you, the smooth motion of insertion and extraction manages to mirror the exact pattern of your inhalation and exhalation as your breathing slowly reverts back to factory settings. Now fully aware of that which is occurring, Lauren removes her fingers and replaces them with a smooth cylindrical shape you feel penetrating deeper than her digits had previously explored. In no position other than to trust your mistress completely, you relax and indicate your pleasure by letting out a long and breathy sigh.

Your body jerks backwards and forwards as you hear Lauren putting some effort in. You feel your stomach begin to bloat with air, as Lauren puts more effort into whatever it is she is doing. You hear a metallic squeak as something happens to your abdomen. Whatever it, it's causing your stomach to distend. More bloating as you realise that the metal squeak is that of a bicycle pump. Lauren is filling your back passage with air.
'Lauren, what the fuck?' you scream as your stomach gets ever larger.

'Shut. The. Fuck. Up.' Lauren commands, pumping with each syllable as your stomach reaches a mass you didn't know it was capable of reaching. Again, your survival instincts kick in as you begin to thrash in an attempt to escape. Alas, you're secured too tightly so must give in to your mistress. Is that what this is? Is this how Lauren builds trust in a relationship? If you want to remain free, perhaps you really do need this level of trust?

Lauren slides the bike pump from your anus, with only a small release of air happening as she replaces the pump with a butt plug. Walking around to your front again, you can see that she has in her hand a piece of string.
'I want you…' whispers Lauren, leaning in front of you, breasts drooping sexily for your pleasure as she plays with the string.
'…to tell me how much you hate Pakistanis.'
'I hate their food,' you blurt out, the state of your bloated stomach easily bringing to mind the last take away you had. 'I hate their skin, I hate everything about them. They're a dirty race. Oh fuck, mistress. Release me. I need you.'
Your confession pleases Lauren, as she pulls on the piece of string. The butt plug pops out of your anus, as a long, slow artificial fart leaves your body. Like one of those phallic shaped balloons you inflate then let go, this fart goes on and on as your stomach slowly deflates back to it's normal size. The pleasure of this anal exhalation is something you could never have predicted.
'Fuuuuuuuk.' you pant, as your eyes roll back and Lauren looks on in delight. This kind of incredible pleasure is something you were unaware of until right this second, as your sphincter continues to perform the sound of a bilabial fricative, cubic metres of air now rushing from your body causing you to convulse in pure, orgasmic pleasure.

Lauren is clearly a sexual master, as this kind of pleasure can only be administered by someone of considerable skill. How did she know how much to inflate you? How did she know when to stop force feeding you her breast? Each time you have been pushed to your physical limit, then felt the thrill which comes with stepping over the edge and discovering that all along, there was a ledge.

The last remnants of air now leave your person, as Lauren walks over to the Budweiser fridge. You both deserve a drink after such revelations. Lauren stands in front of the refrigerator, opening it so the light shines through her spread legs, causing you to squint in order for you to take in this alluring silhouette. Just as your eyes become accustomed to the differential in light, Lauren steps to one side to reveal the contents of the fridge.

It is not a fridge. It is a freezer.

Inside the freezer, you count three severed heads before you begin counting anything else. There's other stuff in there, but the heads are taking up most of your attention just now. Your eyes are wide open with panic as you stare into what surely must be a joke. They can't be real. You try to talk but as soon as you open your mouth you realise that Lauren is no longer in your field of vision and is in fact behind you, expertly inserting a ball gag the second you attempt to speak. She tightens it so quickly that all you can do now is turn your head left and right to try and catch a glimpse of her, which of course you cannot. Wherever she is in the room now, you can't tell, and whatever you would've said to her to try and bring this to a conclusion, is now immaterial. All that fills your vision is the freezer. The freezer which must surely be a joke.

'Do you like my freezer?' asks, Lauren. 'It's where I store all my racists.'
'ONNNNNNGG. ONNNNNNGG.' you utter, pointlessly.
'Yes, I knew you were the one. Many comedians come and go, each harbouring some kind of prejudice but managing to shield it from us all. Very few have the courage of their convictions and for that I must admit… you have my respect.' Lauren says this while unfolding some plastic sheeting which she places between your spreadeagled, shackled ankles.
'For years now I've wanted to add a comedian to my collection of racists and, thanks to you, I now get to do it. I can't thank

you enough. You really have given me a great deal of pleasure over the course of this evening. It has also been my pleasure to give you some pleasure. There's a lot to be said when it comes to the phrase "giving pleasure is part of the pleasure" and to be honest, it's not something I'd really considered before. So, again, thank you for illuminating me.'

What the fuck is going on? How can you now explain to Lauren that what you did wasn't meant to be as racist as it sounded? Is there even any possible explanation that would make sense or sound believable? Your body thrashes but your brain knows that it's pointless. You feel another long cylinder enter your back passage. Clenching your sphincter does nothing to stop this forced insertion, as Lauren no longer has your pleasure at the forefront of her mind.
'ONNNNNNGG! ONNNNNNGG!' you grunt.
'Shhhhh.' Lauren soothes.

A generator begins to whir. You recognise the sound from Kwik-Fit, where you have your tyres replaced when they've failed the MOT. Lauren walks around so that you may see her yet again. This time she is completely naked but no longer sexual to you. This is a woman who is the devil incarnate. She is judgement. Her bisexuality, so curiously arousing and appealing to you in the past is now nothing more than an obvious ruse in order to secure victims. You try to make eye contact with her but she has no interest in looking at you. Instead, she looks down at the compressed air tyre inflator she's holding and begins to stroke it.

SSSSSSSSSSSSSSS.

A quick blast of air, no longer than half a second enters you. You scream as well as gagged human can, tears streaming down your face as you feel yourself fill with just a little air, but in a much more rapid and less pleasing manner than before.

SSSSSSSSSSSSSSS.

Another blast of air. Lauren finally looks at you. She smiles.

SSSSSSSSSSSSSSSSSSSSSSSSSSSSSSSSSSSSSSSSSSSS SSSSSSSSSSSSSSSSSSSSSSSSSSS.

It only takes a few seconds for your internal organs to explode. The pressure from the explosion forces the inflation cylinder from your now torn rectum, ripped apart to such an extent that your insides just slop out of you in a splattering, bloody mess. You feel yourself go limp, your head slumping over the horse and towards the floor. You look down and see blood cascading at the base of the gymnastic horse. You're almost unconscious as you summon the strength to look up and see Lauren, now brandishing a knife so big and sharp, your thoughts are taken to the craftsmanship involved in making such an impressive piece of steel.

You don't feel a thud when your head hits the floor, your spinal cord having been expertly severed. The last visuals experienced by your brain are that of your headless corpse still gushing blood from it's anus, and Lauren's smiling face as she stuffs you inside her freezer next to a jar of racist hearts.

Turn to page 27

'I don't know,' you say to Lucifer. Deeply troubled by a question of such magnitude, a question which has major implications not only for you, but the entire universe. You feel it necessary to query a little. 'Isn't this what you've always wanted?'
'Of course it is!' booms God, 'Who wouldn't want to be my favoured subject?'
'Gotta be honest, it does seem like a good offer.' you comment.
Lucifer nods his head.
'My Lord, might you grant me a few moments of private counsel?' requests Lucifer.
'Sure thing. Take your time. I'll just amuse myself by creating some more bacterium that'll taste nice in some sugary yoghurt.'
Lucifer bounds over to you, seemingly excited but also showing a few signs of worry. You can't imagine what this must be like, having all your hopes and dreams come true after so much struggle. With his forces now ready to launch a final assault upon heaven, this seems to be an eleventh hour reprieve for Lucifer. A way to avoid battle altogether.
'This is mental,' Lucifer whispers to you. 'I can't believe it.'
'So what happens? What the fuck?'
'What the fuck?' replies Lucifer.
'What. The. Fuck?' you ask again.
'I don't know. I mean, my army is strong. The Amakhulu were put here to test me so I guess I've met the test? I don't know.'
'What happens to hell?'
'I have no idea. This is incredible. I fell from heaven, a couple of thousand years later I'm as strong as I've ever been and now he shows up wanting a truce. Something doesn't feel right.'
'Maybe he loves you after all?' you enquire, remembering one of the only things you can recall from religious studies in school, that being the concept of God's unconditional love.
'I don't know. That's not the God I know. He's a sneaky fucker sometimes, that much I do know.'
You both take a moment to consider what is happening. For sure, you absolutely don't know the best course of action as this is way above any pay grade you could possibly be familiar

with. Who the fuck would be qualified to offer such counsel? Only Lucifer really can have any clue as to what the best course of action is. That much is obvious. But for some reason, Lucifer is consulting with you about the future of all mankind. Lucifer has previously confided in you his guiding vision of a Jehovah's Witness type world of animals and humans living together in harmony, and it is a vision which certainly animates you, but at the same time troubles you. It is so fantastical that it must surely be the demented promises of a mad man who can never deliver. Maybe deep down, Lucifer knows he can never defeat God and his heavenly army, and as such, is looking for an opportunity to get out of such a battle. Is that why he's asking you, so that if it all goes wrong he has someone else to blame? Could the prince of darkness really be so lacking in confidence that he's willing to let someone else make this decision?

This is a very human trait, which is what makes Lucifer all the more endearing to you. Decision making cripples the best of us, and when a decision has even more monumental consequences than normal, such decisions can prove incredibly stressful and painful. Observe people with a food menu and gaze upon their pain as they wonder aloud what they should have to satiate themselves. It's not necessarily that you will be upset with your choice, it's more the fear of missing out in some way. The pain of not having seems to be of greater concern than the joy of having. In all situations, decision making can be split into two categories: emotional and rational. Emotional decision making is done on the fly, whereas rational decision making is considered. Calculated. Time is taken until you eventually become satisfied that you have weighed the pros and cons of each scenario and used reason to come to a firm decision. The best decisions tend to be when both the emotional and rational thought processes are satisfied.

Clearly, Lucifer yearns to be back in heaven. It's where he started out and once you've been an angel in the service of God, it's pretty hard to imagine anything better. We all think it would be better to be self employed but those of us who have fallen on hard times whilst forging our own path will tell you that sometimes, a little safety net is most welcome. Emotionally, this is the decision to make. But is it rational? What chance does Lucifer have in a battle with heaven?

The Amakhulu are clearly skilled in abominable acts of savagery, and Lucifer obviously has at his command millions upon millions of depraved subjects who would fight at his command. But what chance would they stand against the ruler of the universe? Omnipotence being that which it is, seems to be a game changer. Like every single hack comedian who tried to imitate Bill Hicks, you have asked the simple theological question of why an all powerful, all loving God would act in the ways He does. Moving in mysterious ways, creating and extinguishing life at will, forever undefeated in arguments due his unquestionable master plan. Perhaps it is all just stories, and up until very recently, if someone had asked whether or not you believed in heaven and hell, you would most certainly have answered in the negative. How wrong you were.

The rational decision is for Lucifer to not battle God and to accept his offer of a seat in the kingdom of heaven.

'Lucifer,' you say. 'I've had a think.'
'OK.'
'I think you should take His offer.'
'Why?'
'It's what you want, and you can't beat Him. He is too powerful. All that will happen is your armies will be crushed and you'll be down here for eternity. Being at God's table is about as good as it gets. You should take the offer.'
Lucifer nods as he listens, taking in your words with the serious attention they deserve.
'Thank you for your honesty.' Lucifer says to you, patting you on the shoulder before slowly walking away. As Lucifer walks away, the crack in the roof of hell begins to repair as God's blinding light leaves the lava stricken landscape of Indulu. Now fully sealed, God it seems has left the building, perhaps already knowing the answer Lucifer is about to give.

Walking back onstage to address the Amakhulu, Lucifer takes the mic from the stand and addresses his newly respectful members of the army of darkness.
'Fellow cunts,' Lucifer begins. 'It saddens me to announce that, not all of us who are present today believe we have what it takes to take on the forces of heaven.'
Hissing noises come from the audience, as these super demons wonder who amongst them lacks the faith necessary to follow Lucifer into battle.
'You see my cunts, I have waited for some time to find an ally worthy of joining me in the war I will wage against God and the kingdom of heaven, and I genuinely thought that I had found such an individual. Alas, it was not meant to be.'

Shit. He's talking about you.

'If you look over there, you will see my comedy coach,' Lucifer continues. 'The one who has helped me so much recently. I thought I had someone who not only believed in me, but also somebody that I too, could believe in. But when faced with what they thought was God and the offer of a truce, they chose to capitulate in order to avoid conflict.'
'Wait!' you scream, 'that's not what I was getting at!'
'Silence!' yells Lucifer, throwing his hand your way and somehow making your lips stick together. 'You will speak no more. My brothers of Indulu, my fellow cunts. Will you join me?'
The Amakhulu cheer.
'Will you join in me in taking my revenge? Will you join me in striking down from heaven that most untrustworthy of landlords?'
The Amakhulu go crazy, they're loving every minute of this.
'Then please, do me this favour. That, *thing*, over there. The thing that has just so badly failed the most obvious of tests, a test even Job wouldn't have fucked up, would you please end their existence in the most unfathomably awful way possible?'
The Amakhulu screech and cheer as they all look towards you. You look over at Lucifer, your mouth sealed with your own skin, begging as best you can for him to reconsider the order he just gave to his new, empowered minions.

Ignoring your face full of pleading, Lucifer walks away as the Amakhulu begin scaling the small hill on which you have been stood atop of, all hissing and panting with excitement, delirious with happiness at what excruciatingly awful experiences they have in store for you. Turning around on the spot, you begin to run as fast as you can, even though you have no idea where you will run to. The surface on which you're running kicks up sharp particles of dust, the majority of which are breathed deep into your lungs. Unable to open your mouth, you panic breathe as fast as you can through your nose, your legs carrying you as quickly as they will physically allow, all the while knowing that no matter what, you will not get away. The Amakhulu stay just close enough to keep you running, but never advance on you no matter how much you slow down. They wish to exhaust you before making their move.

You've been running as fast as you can for at least five minutes now, your nose incapable of taking in the necessary oxygen required to keep your muscles working properly, with the Amakhulu showing no signs of wanting to catch you properly. Your heart feels as though it might explode, as you now drop to your knees, desperate to pant but with your mouth still sealed by it's own skin. You sniff dust and sulphur which you try to cough out of your throat to no avail, your nose being a poor transport system for anything other than a sneeze. You cannot even cry for help, as you spin and lie flat on your back, trying desperately to catch your breath. The only sound you can make is a restrained sobbing as you now lie on the floor staring up at the rocky roof of hell.

The Amakhulu slowly surround you, leaning over your body and staring in wonder at you the way a family would at a helplessly adorable new born baby. Still panting, you try to scream. All you end up doing is spraying mucus from your nose all over your chest, mucus which is quickly devoured by the absurdly long tongue of one of the Amakhulu. Lying there knowing something terrible is about to happen is in some ways worse than what will actually happen. Of course, it isn't, as you realise that what will actually be worse will be that acts the

Amakhulu perform on you, restrained as your imagination is in it's ability to imagine the depravity of which they are capable.

You feel yourself being held down, but you cannot look to see how you are being restrained as two Amakhulu hold your head still. You assume that several of them have a hold of your limbs in some way as any attempt to move is impossible. Your breathing quickens even more as panic sets in. Again, you try to open your mouth to get a better intake of air but the only sensation this generates is the horrific reminder that your mouth is being kept tightly shut against your will. You try with all your might to perform the simple act of opening your mouth, but you cannot. Only being able to look up and within your peripheral vision now, you see hovering over you a pair wart ridden testicles lowering towards your face, a sharp looking penis just above them. The penis appears erect, as the testicles now make contact with your sealed mouth, the warts giving the scaly skinned testes a slightly bumpy texture. You feel the tip of a demon's penis enter your right nostril, the mucus from before acting as a surprisingly good lubricant for the thrusting which is now taking place. The Amakhulu cheer on this nasal fucker, as the pace of his thrusting quickens. You feel his testicles change shape as a hardened, barely liquid load makes it's short journey from inside the balls, up through the shaft and out the tip of this demon's penis, straight into your nose.

Withdrawing his length, you cannot see but you can feel. The sensation is that of a marble blocking your right nostril, your panicked breathing giving you no respite as with each hard exhale you serve only to move the hot load a few millimetres towards the end of your nostril, before sucking it back up with your inevitable inhale. Your breathing is now more laboured than before due to this ejaculatory obstruction, but it soon quickens yet again as another Amakhulu lowers himself over you to use your left nostril as a receptacle for centuries old super demon cum. Once inside your nostril, you struggle to breath, the shallow thrusting of this poorly proportioned servant of Lucifer giving only brief respite before he too ejaculates something more approaching a solid than a liquid, directly into your nose.

With both nostrils now blocked and your mouth sealed, you die with the sulphuric odour of demon ejaculate infecting your brain. Before you perish, the prospect of being brought back to life so that you can relive this over and over again for eternity occurs to you, as that seems to be the way hell works. Perhaps one day Lucifer will achieve his vision of building a world where he doesn't have to fulfil this most diabolical of duties. Such a day will of course only be after he has achieved a stunning victory against God in the battle of battles.

Until then, you have to wish for some form of good fortune. With any luck, you may only have to experience this torturous death a few million times. In hell, this is what constitutes good fortune.

The End - go back to page 186

'Help!' you scream like a lil' bitch. 'Help! They've taken her!' The Sikhs look at one another, confused. They are unaware that your dastardly nature is not innate, but in fact the product of genius level improv which you're still trying to channel, even though at this point, it is of little to no use.
'Get him, boys.' commands Jatinder, thirsty for revenge but not for hydration, as his bladder is currently fit to burst in preparation of his retribution. Sparky Mark crawls away towards a window, still gasping for breath and sobbing ever so gently.
'Help! Help!' you scream once again, as the Sikhs join hands in a standard Kabaddi formation. 'Somebody help me!'
'Kabaddi, kabaddi, kabaddi, kabaddi, kabaddi...' they all repeat in a low hum, their trained semi circle effortlessly manoeuvring you towards a corner. Their chanting sounds as ridiculous to you as it does intimidating, the sound coming seemingly from beyond, each beard as long as it is, covering the lips of the Sikhs advancing upon your position.
'Ka-bad-di, ya' no say daddy me Snow me I go blame, I licky boom boom down,' you spit, hitting them with some hip-hop/reggae infusion simply by changing the lyrics to "Informer" by Snow, behaving like so many of those guitar comedians you claim to hate so much.
'Bigger they are they think they have more power, they're on the phone me say that on every hour, me for want to use it once an' now me call me lover, lover who I'll be callin' is the one Tammy.'
The Kabaddi team stop and stare as you pace back and forth spitting out these classic lyrics which speak directly to the heart of all humans.
'An' me love her in me heart down to my belly, yes me Daddy me Snow me I feel cool an' deadly, yes the one MC Shan an' the one Daddy Snow...'
'Together we a love em as a tor-na-do.' join in the Sikhs. All except Jatinder who looks on in disbelief as the men he'd hired to beat you break out in to dance.
'Ka-bad-di, you no say Daddy me Snow me I'll go blame, a licky boom boom down.' you all blast out in unison, the six Sikhs splitting into into two lines of three in front of one another, adopting the stance of a horse rider, then moving side

to side horizontally like so many Bollywood dance numbers as you lead the piece.
'*Detective mon said Daddy me Snow me stab someone down the lane, a licky boom boom down.*' you spit, before handing it back to them.
'*Ka-bad-di, you no say Daddy me Snow I'll go blame, A licky boom boom down*.' the Sikhs spit back, each turning in a circle with a hand in the air like a waiter without a serving tray, twisting their wrists with each syllable until they face you again.
'*Ka-bad-di! Ka-bad-di! Ka-bad-di!*' you all chant before leaping in the air, landing, spinning on the spot and finishing with your arms folded and chest proud.
'Ka-bad-di?' you say, unfolding your arms and using your normal voice. 'How about Ka-good-ee? That's what I wanna know. Am I right?'
The Sikhs applaud.
'What the fuck are you lot doing?' screams Jatinder. 'Attack this mother fuc…'

BANG!

The green room door flies open as four big skinheads burst in. At least as big as the Sikhs, the skinheads make up for their lack of numbers by being far more intimidating. Say what you like about tattoos being artistic expression, but when there's a couple of life size bulldogs on a man's arms, it's probably worthwhile being shit scared of him.
'We heard some foreign music, what the fuck is going on in here?' the biggest skinhead asks.
'It's them!' you squeal. 'They murdered Billy Fuckwit!'
The skinheads look at the bleeding corpse of Billy Fuckwit, still lying there with a crushed throat. One skinhead drops to his knees and throws his hands in the air.
'NOOOO!' he wails at the ceiling.
'He was our favourite act!' says the biggest skinhead.
'They were about to murder Sparky Ma…' you turn to point at Sparky Mark, but all you see is an empty space where you thought he was. You turn further and notice an open window. Shit. Where's that cunt got to? Never mind that just now, you

have these Sikhs to deal with. 'They also tried to murder Sparky Mark but he got away.'
'You fucking bastards are all the same,' says the largest skinhead. 'Get the fuck out now or we'll do the lot of you.'
The Sikhs look at you, then look at the skinheads. Maybe the Sikhs could take them? Maybe not? Is it worth it? At least a few of them will have to go to hospital, and not one of these skinheads looks like they're averse to a scrap. They look to Jatinder for guidance.
Jatinder is looking straight at you.
'This isn't over,' Jatinder seethes, starting straight at you. 'We'll be back later.'
'Bring some onion bhajis with you, I get peckish when I'm twatting turbans.' you say. The skinheads laugh, now firmly on your side in this battle.
'Come on, lads. Let's go.' Jatinder orders, as the big Sikhs make their way slowly from the green room, each skinhead glaring at the bearded muscles leaving the room, itching for one of them to make a wrong move.

* * * *

You and the skinheads are sat on the sofas in the green room. The green room door is closed, with the TV now playing the live feed of a currently empty stage. Just at the foot of the stage, audience members stand and chat, seemingly cajoling one another. Eventually, one of the audience members gets up on stage and tries to talk into the microphone, which is of course switched off during the interval so that morons like this cannot hijack the gig. The stupid idiot taps the mic as though that was the problem in the first place, then reluctantly accepts that there is no way they're gonna be able to have there stupidity amplified. The friends all put away their mobile phones, as the audience member gingerly makes their way down from the stage and returns to drinking with their buddies.

All of this is a brief distraction from that which is happening to you right now. Sparky Mark is AWOL and you're sat with thugs who you need to motivate so that you can keep them onside.

You look away from the TV screen and join the skinheads in staring at the fresh corpse of Billy Fuckwit.
'Tragic.' says the biggest skinhead
'He was so good. Me and my missus were crying.' says the second biggest.
'Bloody muslims.' says the third biggest.
'He wanted to be on Live at the Apollo within two years.' you chime in.
'He could've done that easy, no problem.' replies the biggest skinhead.
You feel like correcting this bald neanderthal but now isn't the time, these morons just saved your bacon, bacon they're terrified will one day be made illegal under sharia law.
'Those mother fuckers will have to pay,' you say, as you look around and see each shiny dome nodding in agreement. 'But first this show must end.'
You say this despite knowing that Sparky Mark isn't here to compere and it will be you who has to take to the stage and announce the final section.
'We should call the police.' says the second biggest skinhead.
'Don't be ridiculous,' you caution. 'If we call the police, they'll investigate, arrest and prosecute, only for the perpetrators to get lenient sentences because that's what this fucking country has become these days.'
The skinheads nod.
'Talented comedians like Billy Fuckwit here aren't allowed to say anything on stage anymore because of political correctness. Then they get murdered and the villains end up in a five star hotel with SKY TV. Prison my arse.'
'Muurrrr.' they all grunt.
'No. We keep this quiet so we can get justice for Billy. An eye for an eye.'
'Makes the whole world blind.' says the biggest skinhead.
'Too right.' says the second biggest, both of them completely unaware of what Gandhi meant when he was talking about retribution, which is great for you because it means you can manipulate these fucking imbeciles.
'Damn right,' you say. 'Let's blind this whole fucking planet.'
'Yeah!' they all cheer.
'Right, back to your seats lads. I've got a gig to get underway.'

'Wait,' says the smallest skinhead (who is still massive). 'Shouldn't somebody say something?'
You each look around, confused as to what should be said or indeed in what manner it would be said.
'Like what?' asks the biggest skinhead.
'We could bow our heads and say something?' says the second biggest.
'I dunno, just something. A song maybe?' wonders the smallest skinhead.
'You mean, like a prayer?' you say.
'Yeah! Great idea!' enthuses the smallest skinhead, clearing his throat in preparation for what he is about to say. '*Life is a mystery, everyone must stand alone, I hear you call my name, and it feels like… home.*'
You raise an eyebrow, there's no way he's gonna do the whole thing.
'*When you call my name, it's like a little prayer…*'
Yup. He is.

* * * *

Sitting at the side of the stage ready to announce the start of the final section, you reflect on how easy it was to get those racist skinheads onside, almost as though the hard of thinking are quick to violence and just need a minuscule excuse in order to lash out at minorities. Jatinder will be back at some point, so it behooves you to prepare for such an eventuality. It is most likely that he and probably a few of his friends will be waiting for you when you leave the gig. That's what you would do. Well, it's not what *you* would do, but is certainly what your current improv character would do, and such dastardly thinking will help you out strategise young Jatinder and his band of merry Sikhs.

If there are at least four racist skinheads in Uncle Spunk's Chuckle Trunk this evening, it is highly plausible that there will be many more less overt racists in the audience. Crowds being crowds, you only need a certain percentage to take them in a direction they may not wish to journey along. If you can get, ooooh, let's say 52% of the audience onside, you might be able to convince them to help you gain safe passage, making your way home without further incident. This is what you will need to do when you go onstage. You will have to convince the audience to help you by joining you, and to do this you will need to be at your most devilishly charming. You'll have to ooze charisma and likability in order to manipulate these easily lead morons. They cannot know that they are joining you in your battle to keep hold of some illegal footage involving a teenage boy. No, you must motivate them in other ways, keeping from them the simple truth of underage sexual abuse. My word, what a sentence. Who have you become, Prince Andrew? What twisted snakes of fate have gotten you to this point of no return?

It is usually only when one gets to the peak of a situation that one can wonder how one got there in the first place. That bit on the side who was just a bit of fun. A fling. Now? They're threatening to tell your other half. This is usually the only time one gives thought to how one ended up in such a situation. What happened was one gave in to an impulse, and that impulse set off a chain of events that one definitely could've predicted, but one decided to proceed with anyway. Arranging to meet in deserted car parks late at night, one had several opportunities to turn the car around, but the oil tanker of predetermined fate meant you were lost at sea. If only one had said no, one would not be here.

The same is true of you. If you had said no to this gig, none of this would've happened.

'Ladies and gentlemen,' you announce into the offstage microphone. 'Please give a warm round of applause for the final section of the show!'
You walk onstage, waving and smiling. There is some confusion but it is a warm welcome nonetheless, made even more toasty by the rapturous applause of your new shiny headed friends in the audience. The applause dies down as you reach the microphone and take hold of it, placing the mic stand to one side before you begin to confidently pace up and down the stage.

'Thank you, thank you very much. Ladies and gentlemen it's great to be here. Now, you're probably wondering where Sparky Mark is. Friends, I have some bad news.'

You use the word friends deliberately. This is a technique many comedians utilise in a bid to endear themselves to an audience, and it works on most people because most people are stupid and easily lead. If I call you my friend, you have to actively resist the idea. Resistance takes energy, so the recipient will always just accept the easiest, least energy consuming route. The key is repetition. You need to get a few more references to friendship in so that the idea sticks.

'I'm afraid Sparky Mark has had to leave the venue for… oh god, my friends, I dare not tell you why.'

'Tell them!' shouts one of the skinheads from the audience.

'Thank you for your support my friend. Ladies and gentlemen, it pains me to tell you what I am about to tell you, because strictly speaking, I'm afraid it is not very politically correct.'

'Fuck political correctness!' shouts someone from the audience. This is all going according to plan.

'You see,' you continue, 'I have always believed in live and let live. I just want people to be happy. But tonight, what has come to my attention is that there are people in this country who would not extend such a philosophy to us.' as you utter that final word of the sentence, you move your arm out towards the audience and gesture to include all of them before pulling your fist into your chest. 'Us.' you repeat, closing your eyes and nodding your head.

The confusion you are currently causing the audience is a deliberate ploy. Although your words may cause befuddlement, your gestures are warm and open, continually sweeping across the whole crowd and then drawing it back to you. The subliminal message to the brain is being received by the audience whether they know it or not: we are all in this together. Whatever you say next will have a bigger impact because you have in effect created a mini village in here tonight. The audience is certainly confused. A confused brain is one that is in a kind of pain and as such, will take the next simple explanation and run with it, assuming it to be true, no matter how preposterous.

'Sparky Mark was attacked tonight by a group of asians.'
The crowd gasps.
'It's true!' declares one of the skinheads.
'Alas, it is true. I thought he'd escaped but I've just found out that they're holding him captive.'
The crowd gasps again.
'My friends,' you continue, 'it doesn't end there. I...' you pinch the bridge of your nose as you begin to sob. The audience is now deathly silent, each one of them filled with an urge to help the human the clearly struggling human standing before them.
'I... oh god. They murdered Billy Fuckwit.' you blurt out, sobbing.
The crowd gasp once more. Two ladies faint.
'He was amazing.' shouts a member of the audience.
'He could've gone all the way to the top!' yells another.
'We've got to do something!' screams the biggest skinhead.
'Friends,' you continue, drawing on your reserves of inner strength, giving you the power to continue addressing these soft headed loons. 'We can do something. We can honour Billy Fuckwit's memory, and we can get Sparky Mark back from the evil clutches of those despicable asians. We just need to do, this one weird trick...'

Then you wait, and the first person to speak, loses. You've seen Wolf of Wall Street and what you're doing here is essentially a sales pitch. You know that they will all think of the same solution at pretty much the same time, but it is they who must declare it.
'We must stand together.' says a lady on the front row. You nod in agreement.
'She's right.' comes a voice from the back.
'Stand and fight.' shouts the second biggest skinhead, clapping his hands on "fight".
'Stand and fight.' shouts the biggest skinhead. He too claps on "fight" and is joined by a couple of other people.
'Stand and fight.' the clap on "fight" is louder now, as more people join in with both the words and the clap. Soon, the chant has evolved to the point where 52% of the audience are

now involved. The rest fall like ripe apples, as within seconds the fifty-two percent become the job lot.
'Stand and fight!' reverberates around Uncle Spunk's Chuckle Trunk, as you fight back tears, raising your fists in triumph, ceasing this pose only when you want to beat your chest and mouth the words "thank you" to your recently converted devotees.

Entire world movements have started with less people than this. Jesus had twelve following him around, and now you have a packed Uncle Spunk's Chuckle Trunk as disciples.
'Friends!' you yell into the microphone, the chanting quickly dying down. 'You honour not just me, but Sparky Mark and the memory of Billy Fuckwit with your passion. Let us drink a toast in preparation for battle, so that we may christen this new movement, giving it the blessing God so badly needs to give it.'
'Hear, hear.' is heard from several people in the audience.
'Friends, raise a glass,' you raise your hand, holding an imaginary glass. Such is the power of your improv, you don't even need a real one. Everyone else eagerly raises an actual glass, just as you had commanded. 'to Billy Fuckwit, and the safe return of Sparky Mark. Skål!'
'Skål!' cheers the crowd, as the toast is made official with the consumption of alcohol.

The crowd's frivolity comes to an immediate halt as the sound of a tremendously loud horn causes the entire building to shake. The audience looks to you, as the horn blasts for a good ten seconds and causes many of the patrons to cover their ears. Glasses fall from the table as the sound vibrates the very ground upon which Uncle Spunk's Chuckle Trunk stands. You step down from the stage and walk through the audience, several of whom try to prevent you from heading in the direction you are, unsure and worried about what course of action you're about to take. You reach the entrance to Uncle Spunk's. Unbeknownst to you, everyone is behind you as you stand and look out across the car park to see where the noise is coming from. Obscured by condensation, you wipe the moisture from the window and look out once more, laying eyes across the car park on a sea of at least three hundred turbans, and two elephants. The horn blasts once more, causing the ladies present to shriek and the men to take a step backward. But not you. You stand. Defiant. Ready.

'Take the women folk downstairs,' you command. 'The rest of you, on me.'

* * * *

So it has come to this. Jatinder has amassed his forces. You have managed to cobble together a ragtag bunch of wannabe thugs so that you may defend that which you aren't quite sure of. Initially, you just wanted Jatinder's silence, poor guy was only doing what he thought was the right thing. All he wanted to know was what you were doing after you'd run over and killed that elderly woman. A good Samaritan in the wrong place at the wrong time. Yet again, it seems he is attempting to do the right thing, but this time for selfish reasons, eager as he is to retrieve the only copy in existence of a clip that shows an overweight racist prostitute urinating in his mouth.

You're still in the process of tricking yourself into thinking you're a nice person. This is something all humans do (even the most despicable amongst us) in order to sleep at night. Anything you've done which you know to be a little naughty, is explained away or rationalised so that you may rest easy. Obviously, there are varying degrees of awfulness to the acts committed, and some will require way more rationalisation than others, but all of the misdeeds carry with them some emotional burden purely because of arbitrary rules built by society that have, rightly or wrongly, taken us away from our brutish nature. 'Perhaps the old lady was someone who helped hide Nazis?' You think to yourself. At some point, she was going to be a drain on the health service, which in turn would've taken resources and funding from another needy patient who might otherwise have lived were it not for that selfish old bat and her stupid fucking dodgy hip. It's very easy to get to a place where you can convince yourself that it was right to run over and kill the old woman, even if it was an accident. Humans are good at this, especially intelligent ones. The least trustworthy among us are clever people who are good at arguing, easily rationalising abhorrent acts so as to further whatever cause they wish to advance. A cursory look at human history will illuminate many an atrocity which was done for "security and safety" or other phrases which give one a feeling of warmth. Notice that rationalising of evil is always done *after* the fact.

Worry not. You are still a good person. The choices you make, are not yours to choose.

You stand proudly at the entrance of Uncle Spunk's Chuckle Trunk with your racist army behind you. Although small in numbers, a brief chat earlier reveals that plenty are former football hooligans, as well as members of the armed forces. All things being equal, this is the standard make up of a comedy club audience. You open the door so that you can lead your soldiers outside onto the tarmac of Uncle Spunk's car park. Across the way, Jatinder and his army stand motionless. Turbans and beards fill your view, as the clearly well trained elephants also stand motionless, silently awaiting their command.
'How come we don't have elephants?' asks the smallest skinhead.
'I could nip home and get my Rottweilers?' suggests the biggest skinhead.
You succeed in not rolling your eyes, but a part of you does wish that these people weren't so fucking stupid. However, you inwardly acknowledge that the elephants do pose a problem, and it's a problem that you're going to have to deal with.
'Where the fuck did you get elephants from?' you yell.
'My uncle is a pharmacist,' shouts Jatinder. 'His son is a vet and knows a guy at the zoo who hooked us up.'
'Wankers,' you seethe. 'See, this is why they all share the same driving license.' You declare, turning to your army and shaking your head in disbelief.
Your troops nod in agreement.

'What the fuck are we gonna do about those elephants?' asks the smallest skinhead.
'We'll have to kill 'em, won't we?' replies the biggest skinhead.
'Nah, you can't kill elephants,' replies the second biggest skinhead. 'They can do art and shit like that. They've got memories.'
'So can asians.' says the smallest skinhead.
'Yeah but elephants are different. They grieve and have long memories. Nah, you can't kill 'em. It would be what they call in-hugh-main.' replies the second biggest skinhead, glowing with pride at being able to dispense this knowledge in just a few short sentences. Listening to the Joe Rogan Podcast has clearly paid off for him.
'They're not humans though,' says the smallest skinhead.
'They're elephants. Who gives a fuck about humane?'
'Wait!' you yell, walking straight over to the smallest skinhead
'What did you just say?'
'Erm. fuck elephants?'
'No, the other bit.'
'Who gives a fuck if it's humane?'
'That's it!' you scream, grabbing each side of his face and kissing him hard on the lips. 'You're a fucking genius! I'll be back in a sec.'
You run off, back into Uncle Spunk's Chuckle Trunk, hurtling towards the green room as fast your legs can carry you. Easily navigating the tables and chairs which had been left strewn after the hasty audience exodus, you make it to the backstage area and see the green room door is still open. Walking now, you make your way into the green room. Covered in a white sheet is the corpse of Billy Fuckwit, the man of the hour who has helped to stir such passionate emotions and would surely have been headlining Live at the Apollo within a few years. Underneath the TV and by the skirting board, your two little eurekas are busy still trying to escape the humane trap that had been laid for them.

* * * *

Back outside now, your container of hope still vibrating due to the repeated escape attempts of your new rodent saviours.

You make your way to the front line and take a few steps beyond so that you are separated from the pack.
'This is your last chance, Jatinder,' you bellow. 'Take your troops home and I will consider you to have accepted my truce and we shall call bygones.'
'I'm afraid,' comes a voice from afar. 'there will be no bygones. ROFL. PMSL.' Sparky Mark shouts from across the car park.
'Oh shit.' you say under your breath.
'Tonight, this will end. One way or another,' screams Jatinder. 'you know what I want. Let me piss in your mouth and we can call an end to what will surely be needless suffering.'
You turn to your troops.
'Friends, it is worse than I thought. Sparky Mark has succumb to Stockholm Syndrome.'
Your troops gasp.
'Fucking, EU. We voted to leave!' shouts the biggest skinhead.
'London! Not Brussels!' yells a random voice from your supporters.
You raise your hands to prevent any further outbursts and continue with what you were about to say.
'Now we must free Sparky Mark so that we can de-radicalise him. Who is with me?'
Your troops cheer. You turn back to Jatinder.
'I'm afraid it looks like we're gonna have to fight.' you yell to your adversary.
'You fools,' shouts Jatinder. 'You are no match for my elephants. Give up now, and we can end this madness.'
You chuckle to yourself.
Taking a few steps forward, you kneel down on the car park tarmac and open the humane mouse trap. The two mice scuttle out of the tube and do whirling twirls of joy at their new found freedom. Once their legs have been sufficiently stretched, they look to you as though to say thank you.
'Squeak.'
'You're welcome my tiny rodent friends. Look, I hate to be the kinda nigga does a nigga a favour, then, BAM!, hits a nigga up for a favour in return. But I'm afraid I gots to be that kinda nigga.'
'Squeak.'
'You see those big ass elephants over yonder?'

'Squeak.'
'I need you to go terrorise those mother fuckers.'
The mice do not need a second invitation and off they scurry into the moonlight. Their mission is simple, you just hope they can accomplish it before Jatinder orders a charge. Moving back to your position at the head of your army, you stand before these bravely moronic troops and put your finger to your lips.
'Shhhh,' you reassure. 'Watch this.'
You turn to face Jatinder's army. Your forces watch and wait, not even knowing what it is they are to look for. Thanks to the mice, it soon becomes apparent, as almost in unison, two elephants rear up onto their hind legs and let out a deafening trumpet call, causing several of Jatinder's troops to drop their kirpans and cover their ears. So deafened are the troops that they stumble around in panic, only to be immediately trampled as the elephants go back to being on four legs, landing directly on many a Sikh. Whatever the mice are doing, it's working, as the elephants swing their trunks back and forth, effortlessly flinging bearded Sikhs into the midnight air, each of them landing limply on the floor as the elephants inadvertently take life after life after life. The elephants will not stop trumpeting, their panic and thrashing vigorously desperate in its attempts to cease whatever unseen torture they are currently enduring. To make matters worse, the Sikhs are now panicking and trying to run away from the elephants, which serves only to confuse the gigantic pachyderms even more, as they too begin to run, chasing the groups of men who are trying to make their escape. The elephants just assume that these escaping bipeds are responsible for their current predicament, deciding to trample them as though they were ants, hoping in some way it will help.

As you watch this scene unfold, you're reminded of one of your favourite jokes:

An elephant and a mouse are waiting for a bus.
The elephant says, 'Why am I so huge and powerful, yet you are so tiny and weak?'
The mouse says, 'Well, I've been a bit ill recently…'

Good joke. Why were they waiting for a bus? We'll never know.

The elephants have decimated Jatinder's forces. Turbaned bodies are strewn across the car park, as you stand there smugly congratulating yourself on a job well done. Rationalising that you're a good person later will take some doing. The elephants have been running in circles trampling what they thought was the cause of their misery for a few minutes, and it's only now that these intelligent creatures are realising the torment they're enduring has nothing to do with the beards and turbans that are around them. In desperation, they turn their attention to one another. After a brief stare down, the elephants back up to give themselves enough room to build up some speed, then charge one another, clashing tusks with a sickening thud, each trying to wrestle the other into submission. The elephants push each other backwards and forwards, forwards and backwards as neither wants to give ground to the other. Each elephant takes a simultaneous break, taking several steps back so that they may initiate another charge on one another. When the time is right, they each lunge at speed towards one another. It seems each elephant has had the same strategy as the other, that being a slightly altered angle of attack with their tusks. At the culmination of this charge, rather than clanging together tusk to tusk, each angle is sufficiently different that they pierce one another's skull, causing instant death for these majestic pachyderms. The elephants slump towards the floor, first to their knees and then onto their sides as their last breath echoes around this deathly silent arena. Jatinder and Sparky Mark, both of whom have somehow managed to avoid the carnage, stand staring in disbelief. A spontaneous cheer goes up from your army, as they each wave table legs and broken whisky bottles.
'Are you with me?' you scream.
'Yeah!' shouts your army.
'ARE YOU WITH ME?!'
'YEAH!'
'SHOW ME!'

You run full speed towards Jatinder and Sparky Mark, your army close behind you.
'Charge!' screams Jatinder, waving a kirpan in the air as his assembled kabaddi warriors run past him, ready to meet your charge head on in the centre of the car park.

It becomes apparent very quickly that table legs and whisky bottles are no match for the kirpans, as Sikh after Sikh easily dispatches one racist after another, heads being hewn from shoulders. A blow from a table leg serves merely to render the recipient a little dizzy, before the Sikh recovers enough to either stab or slash. Quickly, your ragtag bunch of wannabe freedom fighters begin to lose heart in the face of an actual fight. St George's crosses litter the car park floor, with all of the patriotic flag tattoos displayed on limbs which have been severed from their owners. You fight bravely, disarming a particularly muscled Sikh before inserting the sword just under his solar plexus and then up through his rib cage, finishing with the blade sticking out the back of his neck. Spitting blood onto your face, you look him straight in the eye as he expires, before withdrawing your new sword and looking for the next victim of your improv wrath. Across the way, Jatinder and Sparky Mark look upon the devastation in front of them.
'Cowards!' you scream whilst secretly admiring their plan. Better to stay out the way, then come down and finish off the dregs for sure. Shame you didn't think of that you fucking idiot.

You look around and see pasty white body after pasty white body lying on the floor.
'Bloody, Muslims.' seems to be the final words of choice for your compatriots, which serves only to further anger the Sikhs who are currently running rampant across this car park war zone. Sikhs have something of the warrior in them, and you can't help but admire their ability to regroup and refocus after what was a devastating elephant attack. If only you had an army of man sized mice to command, this battle could've turned out very differently. The writing is on the wall for you now, as it becomes clear that all of your army will perish and there is no way you'll be able to take on this group of highly trained warriors by yourself. Quickly, you scan the car park for

an escape route. You think of the women folk keeping safe under Uncle Spunk's Chuckle Trunk, and feel ever so slightly sorry for them as you realise that most of them will have probably paid for a baby sitter in order to have enjoyed a night out at some stand up comedy. It then crosses your mind that many of them are now widows, which in the grand scheme of things is probably for the best as most of these men were complete wankers.

Your improv as a master criminal appears to be drawing to a close as barely any of your troops remain standing. You look at these warriors of yours, these men amongst men and realise it is no longer fair that they fight on your behalf while you look for an exit. It dawns upon you that to fight without honour is to fight as a coward, and now you are looking for an escape route, it seems fitting that you ask your men to stand down.
'Yield!' you call out to your men. 'Yield, I say. We have been defeated. Stand down.'
Your soldiers, panting and forlorn, look to you for guidance. The expression on each of their faces is the same: questioning and seeking of reassurance.
'Stand down,' you say again. 'You have each fought bravely. Now it is time to stop.'
Each man throws down his table leg, as the Sikhs relax a little and turn their attention to you.
'For, Billy Fuckwit!' screams one skinhead, obviously not ready to surrender. He picks up the nearest sword and runs towards two Sikhs, each of whom easily parry the amateurish slashing before dispatching this unworthy adversary with simple clean cuts across the femoral artery. The skinhead falls the floor, blood flooding the tarmac as his thighs create a mini stream of red before he bleeds out. The rest of your troops witness this and lose all their will to continue the fight.
'Show my troops mercy,' you call out to Jatinder. 'Grant them safe passage into Uncle Spunk's Chuckle Trunk and I will surrender.'
Jatinder nods. His remaining Sikhs stand down and make their way back towards Jatinder and Sparky Mark, as the crest fallen warriors whom represented you make their way back to

their loved ones. You wander towards Jatinder, making sure to go past the elephants as you make your way.

You've never gotten so close to these magnificent creatures before. As they lie there, lifeless, you mourn for what they could've had. Unlimited comfort in a zoo, alongside top quality veterinary care, good food, no predators and maybe even a breeding program. Zoos maybe inhumane places in which to stuff animals that should've been left in the wild to live as nature intended, but the barbaric nature of life, red in tooth and claw certainly makes a good argument for the luxurious lifestyle that a zoo offers. If an animal were given a choice between fighting it out in nature, not knowing where your next meal was coming from, or living in a zoo with limited space but abundant nourishment, which option do you think the animal would choose?

You're probably about to be offered a similarly difficult choice, neither of which have good outcomes. Maybe Jatinder will now go to the police and let them know that your call for privacy was merely a bluff to grant you more time to be able to perform on stage, or perhaps he will just be satisfied being handed the only copy of his secretly recorded sex tape. Alas, you feel that Jatinder has now developed such a taste for revenge that there could only be one outcome. You kneel down by the elephant's head, struggling to believe that it's real, such is the size of the creature. You notice a small dagger nearby and quickly stash it on your person before standing up to walk towards Jatinder and Sparky Mark. Sirens can be heard from afar. Assuming those sirens are for you, or indeed anyone else who was involved in this fracas, it becomes imperative that whatever Jatinder wants to do, needs to be done quickly so that you all have a chance of being able to make an escape.

'Well, well, well,' begins Jatinder. 'How the mighty have fallen.'
'ROFL.' says Sparky Mark.
'Let's make this easy shall we? You give me the copy and let me piss in your mouth, and I'll let you go. That seems like a fair deal to me.'

'It would to you,' you reply. 'Because you're the one making the deal.'
'It's a fair deal!' scolds Jatinder.
He's right too, it is a fair deal. It at least gives you a chance to get away and maybe have a normal life. But look around you: the dead elephants, hundreds of trampled Sikhs, dead racists. None of this is gonna have a happy ending and certainly not one that results in a long and fulfilling life for you.
'You see, Jatinder, what I like, is I like to win. Do you feel me?'
'I feel you.' replies Jatinder.
'PMSL.' says Sparky Mark.
'That's why I spent the time between you leaving and coming back, making sure I'd uploaded your video to every porn site I could log into.' you lie.
'You mother fucker.'
'Don't worry. I didn't name you. But it's out there. Someone, somewhere, at some point will be scrolling along and notice a video that says "*legendary teen asian gets tagged teamed*". Maybe, just maybe, they'll click on it.'
'LMAO.'
'Shut the fuck up, Sparky Mark.' Jatinder yells.
'So you see, whatever you do to me, it's out there.'
You can tell that Jatinder buys this bluff, as he doesn't know what to say, let alone know what to do.
'Maybe Pornhub will take it down? I mean, you are under age. But can you really tell from that video? Dunno, looked to me like you were getting involved.'
'I'm gonna fucking kill you!' screams Jatinder. 'But not before I've pissed in your mouth! Get him guys!'
'Wait!' you plead. 'Wait!'
For some reason the approaching Sikhs wait to see what you have to say, as does Jatinder. Pausing his motion, Jatinder stands there expectantly.
'Well, what?'
'You're forgetting, just one thing…'
'So? Spit it out!' demands Jatinder.
You pull the dagger from your pocket and raise it into the air so that all eyes are upon the shiny, curved metal, before bringing it down in a long, slow arc. Everyone looks on, waiting for you to do something of some significance. You bring the blade up

to your ear, then you smile the cheesiest grin you can muster before drawing the blade across your throat, severing your carotid arteries, spraying blood a good two feet away from you.
'LOL.' says Sparky Mark, thinking back to the time you nearly murdered him.
'NOOOO!' screams Jatinder, 'He's not dead yet! Grab him! I need to piss in his mouth!'
Blood gushes from the wound on your neck, drenching your clothes in rich, thick blood as you struggle to maintain your balance. With the blade still in your hand, the Sikhs are weary about approaching you. Jatinder has no such concerns as he runs towards you, undoing his trousers in the process and unsheathing his penis. You smile as you fall to the floor.

Everything begins to go dim as you see Jatinder falling over racist corpse after racist corpse, struggling to get close to you. You're nearly dead now, as he reaches you in time to position your head ready for him to excrete urine directly into your mouth. With the last bit of energy you can muster, you whisper just loud enough for Jatinder to hear…

'I win. You have a tiny cock.'

The last thing you hear is Jatinder begging you to stay alive for a few more seconds so that he may have his revenge. Your improv as a master criminal comes to an end, as you steal this tiniest of victories over Jatinder with your timely death.

And, scene.

Turn to page 27

In the cellar of Uncle Spunk's Chuckle Trunk, the women folk huddle around a small table, lit by a few tea light candles. The children are held close by each mother as the battle about to rage above them enters it's final stages of preparation. The cheering from each side is enough to make these poor women quake with fear, as the children gently tremble partly from cold, but also, from terror.

'Shhhh,' says a grey skinned woman, her face wrapped in a head scarf. 'It's going to be fine.'

'Will Daddy be ok?' asks a little girl, trying hard to stay strong for her mother, the grey skinned lady.

'I'm sure he'll be fine, my sweetness. He's a very brave man.'

Plaster falls from the ceiling as the ground above them shakes. Thunderous trumpeting from the elephants causes the children to cover their ears, all except the daughter of the grey skinned lady.

'See?' says the grey skinned lady to the little girl. 'That is a good sound.'

'How so?' asks the little girl.

'Well, do you remember the safari park we went to a few years ago?'

'No. When was that?'

'Oh it was a while ago. Perhaps you are too young to remember?' the room continues to shake because of the rampaging elephants above them, each woman's eyes now closed as they hold the children close. 'You wanted to see some animals up close so we used some Tesco Clubcard points and went to look at some animals from the comfort of our car. Oh, you loved it. You couldn't believe that we had monkeys on our car begging for food! It was quite a sight.'

'But mother,' the little girl says. 'What does this have to do with the elephants?'

'Well, on that day we accidentally drove into an area where there were some elephants. We weren't supposed to be in there and it got quite scary! The elephants came to investigate our Vauxhall Zafira and we weren't sure if they were going to push it over or not. Anyway, you got really frightened and Daddy had to drive away at a fast speed. Once we got back to the car park, Daddy got out and marched over to reception to complain.'

'Oh wow.'
'Exactly. Daddy got a partial refund and two guest passes to use within twelve months.'
'But Mummy, what does this mean for the battle?'
'It means that your Daddy does not take shit from elephants.'

A huge thud is heard from above, followed by another thud, the noise accompanied by silence thanks to the cessation of noise from the elephants. The room is now stable, as the women and children open their eyes to look at one another. Is it over? A cheer from above means that it is not over yet.
'Should we pray, you reckon?' asks a heavily made up young lady not with child. She is someone who only came out for a night of stand up comedy, but now finds her trapped as a battle threatens to rage for an undermined length of time. 'My Darren is up there and he normally prays when he goes to an away game.'
'Why does he pray?' asks the grey skinned lady.
'He always prays that the firm he's gunna take on gets AIDS or summat like that. He's proper hard my Darren is. He'll smash them rag heads no bother.'
The grey skinned lady shakes her head.
'What's your fucking problem?' asks the heavily made up young lady. 'Don't like the phrase "rag heads" or summat?'
'Actually, I don't. Although my beloved husband believes that this country is under threat from sharia law, it is not a belief I subscribe to. I would like to keep not only my daughter's ears, but the ears of the other children here, free from such derogatory phrases. No offence.'
'How come, when someone wants to be offensive to ya with fancy words they always say "no offence" or some bullshit?'

From above, the clash of bodies can be heard as the two armies are nowhere at battle. Shouts and screams of pain and frustration can be heard all the way down in the cellar, as several of the children again cover their ears to stop themselves hearing the brutality and madness of interpersonal warfare.
'These walls have never been breached.' whispers the grey skinned lady.

'What walls? What the fuck are you talking about?' asks the heavily made up young lady.
'Must you be so vulgar?'
'Must you be so fucking dramatic? It's a tear up! My Darren and his mates live for this shit. They'll smash those rag heads then come down here and get us. After that, we'll get even more pissed and have a kebab. Might even have a shag.'
'Good lord! Have you no class!' shrieks the grey skinned lady. The rest of the women folk hurriedly shush her.
'Yeah. Shut your mouth you stupid old bat.'
A cheer goes up from above. All the women folk look up to the ceiling before slowly lowering their heads once more, huddling ever tighter as they sense that, for some reason, the battle is not going astray had first hoped.
'What use is war?' asks the grey skinned lady, rhetorically.
'Mummy, why did you bring me to a comedy night?'
'I don't know, my love. Had I known they wouldn't let you in I'd have left you at home. Had I known that your father would be going into battle, I too would've stayed home with you and tended to the chores.'
'How will we know when the battle is over?' asks the little girl.
'That's a good point,' remarks the heavily made up young lady.
'One of us should nip up and see what's what.'

The women folk all look at one another, hoping that someone will volunteer before they do so that they may save face. Just a millisecond after someone else steps forward is enough to show that you were willing to go, but were just too slow to put themselves forward. All of these women are about to volunteer, but not until someone else has done so first. The children look to their elders for signs of reassurance. If everything is going to be ok, why is there nobody stepping forward for what must surely be an easy mission? The grey skinned lady's daughter looks up at her mum, expectantly. The grey skinned lady knows that she must act in order to keep her daughter calm.
'I'll go,' she says, determinedly. 'I'll go.'
'Oh, mother.'
They each look into each other's eyes before embracing. This might very well be their final physical contact on this earth.

'I should go,' says the heavily made up young lady. 'I haven't got kids. It's not right that you go.'
'Thank you.' says the grey skinned lady, choking back tears.
'What?' replies the heavily made up young lady.
'Thank you.'
'For what?'
'For taking my place.'
'I'm not taking your place. You're going.'
'But, you just said that you should go?'
'Yeah, I should. But I'm not going to. Fuck that.'
The grey skinned lady stares into the very soul of this heavily made up young lady, unsure as to whether or not it would be appropriate to launch a physical attack upon her person. The grey skinned lady shakes her head and then returns her attention to the child she is duty bound, both morally and legally, to protect.
'It's going to be fine. I'll go upstairs and have a look.'
'Let me come with you!' begs the girl. The grey skinned lady looks around at these fragile women, all too frightened to do anything until this has blown over. All beholden to their husbands, battling above them for a cause which many in this cellar have little to no interest in.
'Come with me…'

* * * *

At the top of cellar stairs, the grey skinned lady and her daughter make their way back to the bar area of Uncle Spunk's Chuckle Trunk. Peering outside, they can see that the fighting wages on in brutal fashion, with Sikhs either being hit with table legs or chopping off heads.
'Where is Daddy?' asks the little girl.
'I don't know. Wait here.'
The grey skinned lady leaves her daughter stood at the edge of the bar as she makes her way closer to the entrance and therefore, the battle. Pushing her face onto a window, she scans the devastation, looking across the car park, witnessing bodies strewn left, right and centre. Finally, her eyes settle upon a pair of Ralph Lauren socks that she recognises, the polo player riding proudly on the ankles of a man with a

bulldog tattooed on each calf. The socks that she bought him last Christmas. Further up the prostrate body, they shorts that she picked out in Primark and had to beg to get him to try on, only for him to eventually love them and barely take them off. The grey skinned lady stops herself looking any further up the body, knowing it now to be a corpse, sparing herself the pain of confirming such a suspicion.

Turning back into Uncle Spunk's Chuckle Trunk, the grey skinned lady makes her way behind the bar and prises open the cash register. Taking out all the cash and stuffing it in her pockets, she does the same thing to each till she can get to, before finally returning to her daughter.
'Where is Daddy?'
'Daddy is busy. We need to leave.' the grey skinned lady says, taking the little girl's hand.
'But I don't want to leave without Daddy!' stomps the little girl, snatching away her hand in the process. The grey skinned lady drops to her knees and holds each side of the little girl's upper arms.
'He's dead!' blurts the grey skinned lady. 'He's dead and he's not coming back. We need to get out of here now before this gets any worse!'
The little girl begins to sob as her mother grabs hold of her, hoisting the girl over her shoulder and spiriting her away from the building via the fire exit.

Once outside the premises, the grey skinned lady calls the police with her mobile phone.
'Hello, which emergency service do you require.'
'Police.'
'Putting you through now.'
You wait as the dealing ceases and someone answers.
'Hello, police.'
'Hello,' the grey skinned lady begins, in a very thick Arabic accent. 'I am a member of Crimson Jihad. As a demonstration of my power, I have placed a bomb inside Uncle Spunk's Chuckle Trunk. It will be detonated within one hour if my demands are not met. I also have hostages.'

And with that, the grey skinned lady breaks her phone and leaves it scattered on the floor.
'Come on, let's get out of here.'

The grey skinned lady and her daughter leave in the midnight air, just as the Sikhs smash through the entrance to Uncle Spunk's Chuckle Trunk, no doubt likely they will enjoy themselves the spoils of war.

'I thought your set was received really well.' you reply, again trying to dodge giving your actual opinion whilst maintaining a civil tone. Alas, the glare in your eyes tells a different story, as this open spot piece of shit maintains his hand position on your shoulder, squeezing just hard enough to be domineering whilst seeming friendly.

The subtlety of this is not to be overlooked. Anytime someone touches you with no good reason, they are making a power play. They are basically saying that they can invade your personal space and you won't do a thing about it. You'll eat it.

Overbearing, passively aggressive and unnecessarily tactile wankers like this are the kind of people who make everyone feel uncomfortable, yet for some reason they are left largely unchallenged. It is a peculiar quirk of human interaction that we don't wish to cause a fuss or appear rude, even when our physical agency is under a form of attack.

Because he is not happy with your response, his hand remains in the same position, and will remain there as a power play so that you fucking well know your place.
'That's not what I asked though is it?' asks the open spot, giving your shoulder a little squeeze whilst moving you back and forth ever so slightly, causing your head to wobble.
'Is it not?' you say innocently, maintaining your eye contact.
'No!' says the open spot, forcing a smile. 'You little tinker, I think you're avoiding the question!'
'Not at all! I think you did really well. Now take your fucking hand off me.'
You don't even know where it came from, but pacifying him seems to have gone out the window.
'I beg your pardon?' asks the open spot, clearly experiencing resistance for the first time.
'Woah, what's going on here?' wonders Sparky Mark, finally noticing that there is tension in the room. This is the first time in well over a decade he's been able to read a room with any degree of accuracy.
'I said, take your fucking hand off me.'

You both glare at each other, waiting for the other to make some sort of move.

'Make me.'

The open spot has just thrown down the gauntlet. You know that in this situation, the best chance of delivering a knock out blow is a clean shot to the jaw, with either your fist or your head. On this occasion, with his hand on your right shoulder, the open spot is available for a left hook. The best way to take an individual by surprise is to engage their brain with a question before delivering the blow. Your feet are set perfectly, giving you the ability to turn on the spot enough to generate good torque from your hips as you swing the punch. You give the open spot a smile.

'How long did you say you've been gigging?'

'Erm, about two…'

BANG!

A perfectly placed left hook takes away the consciousness of this utterly odious charlatan. His hand leaves your shoulder as his whole body slumps to the floor, hitting the ground with a very satisfying thud as a small trickle of blood starts from the corner of his mouth.

'What the fuck?!' screams Sparky Mark. 'What the fuck are you doing?!'

'You saw what he was doing! He assaulted me!'

'He was being friendly!'

'That's the problem with this fucking world,' you loudly sigh. 'People think that unwanted touching is a sign of affection when in actuality it is a sign of dominance. Well, I'm not having it.'

The open spot groans as his body twitches in a bid to regain consciousness. You're tempted to soccer kick him in the head and watch his shiny white hair turn a beautiful shade of red but you think better of it.

'You think I'm gonna let you on stage now after you've done that?'

'Why not? What does it have to do with my set?'

'What if word got out that I let you commit an assault and I then allowed you to gig? My reputation would be in the shitter. Nope. No way. I'm sorry.'

'Well, who else are you gonna get to do the gig at such short notice?' you ask, feeling confident that Sparky Mark won't have an answer for this.
'I'll do it…' groans the open spot.
'He'll do it.' says Sparky Mark, looking delirious with happiness.
Incandescent rage overtakes you. In drawing your foot back to soccer kick the open spot full in the face, you put yourself ever so slightly off balance, allowing Sparky Mark to easily push you over like a sleeping flamingo. You hit the floor hard, landing on your elbow and triggering that horrid feeling of pins and needles you get when you hit the ulnar nerve. As you lie there, looking up at the shocked face of Sparky Mark, it becomes apparent that your original attempt to pacify this piece of shit was incorrect, and your desire to bend the truth in an attempt prevent the green room from becoming incredibly awkward was the wrong thing to do.

We know this all the time though, even when it goes well and civility is maintained. We know that lying to keep the peace is the wrong thing to do because it is a falsehood. But we still do it. How much better would it be if we all agreed to be honest with one another? Indeed, how much better would stand up comedy be if honest critiques were offered instead of the usual bluff and bluster of patting one another on the back. But then again, this open spot toss pot didn't want an honest critique, he wanted a giant pat on the back even after it was obvious he'd done a good job. He doesn't realise that his brand of banal, bland and boring observations isn't considered worthy among the higher echelons of praiseworthy comedians. Largely, he probably doesn't even care. So the question remains, why do *you* care? In the U.K. Mrs Brown's Boys remains the number one rated sitcom, enjoyed by millions in an age where a man dressed as a woman for a laugh is fraught with politically correct difficulty. Critics hate it. You hate it. Stand up comedians hate it. The public loves it. So what the fuck do you know about comedy then?

'I'm sorry,' you begin. 'Ok? I'm sorry. I shouldn't have done that. I don't know why I did it.'

'I'm sorry too.' says the open spot, much to your surprise.
'Why are you sorry?' you wonder.
'I shouldn't have pressured you like that. You were right to tell me to take my hands off you. I should've listened. I'm from a different era. We used to do stuff like that when I was on building sites, just to fuck with people. I'm sorry. I deserved that punch.'
'What do you do for a living now?'
'I'm a used car salesman.'
'I fucking knew it.'
You stand up and walk over to the open spot, offering your hand so that he may also rise to his feet. He gladly takes your hand and becomes upright once more. You both look at one another, still sizing each other up for some reason, until you eventually crack a smile and so does he. Laughing, you warmly embrace one another. Experiences like this are what lasting friendships are built upon.
'I'm so sorry.' he says, whispering in your ear. You can scarcely believe that a man with his kind of old school comedy chops is capable of such self awareness. That he would be aware of his god awful physical intimidation yet still proceed to carry on is a slight cause for concern, but the fact he's now been called on it means there's a strong possibility that he might change as a result. In fact, you may have been instrumental in the civilising of someone who could've been an awful presence in green rooms for the next decade or so, someone loud and confrontational, overpowering people whilst facing no comeuppance. All such occurrences have now been nullified because of your early intervention. Well done you!

'You don't have to be sorry,' you say, holding him tightly. 'We all make mistakes.'
'No you don't understand, I really am very sorry.'
'What for?' you ask, releasing the hug and taking a step back. As you release the hug, you see exactly why his apology was forthcoming, as the blade he's holding drips with your blood. You didn't even feel it pierce your flesh, let alone slide between your ribs and into your lung. You cough up a small amount of blood. Now the blade has been extracted, you feel warmth

dripping down your skin, as your clothes begin to feel damp against your body.
'Why?' you ask.
'I can answer that,' answers Sparky Mark. 'For too long now comedians like you have belittled and mocked those who please an audience. The Edinburgh fringe festival has made the idea of an entertaining, easy to watch performer something that comedians shouldn't aspire to be. For some reason making an audience laugh isn't enough anymore. Someone has to die or learn something or there has to be a rape of one variety or another. It's time to redress the balance and stop pretending that comedy is an art from when in actuality it is merely fast food entertainment which hastens the sale of alcohol before a night out of drinking to excess.'

Sparky Mark seems happy with his diatribe. You struggle to maintain your balance as you look across to the open spot to see if this really was the reason. He shrugs.
'I stabbed you because you punched me in the face.' he says, as he lunges at you once more, stabbing you straight in your heart.

Your legs give out as he thrusts ever harder, upwards into your chest, before withdrawing the blade and taking a step back so that you can now fall to the floor. As you bleed out, you can hear Sparky Mark giving this wanker some more dates before deciding how best to dispose of your body. The used car salesman knows a guy who owns a scrapyard.

The End - go back to page 56

'I don't know,' you say to Lucifer. Deeply troubled as you are by a question of such magnitude. Being a question which has major implications for the entire universe, you feel it necessary to query a little. 'Isn't this what you've always wanted?'
'Of course it is!' booms God, 'Who wouldn't want to be my favoured subject?'
'Gotta be honest, it does seem like a good offer.' you comment.
Lucifer nods his head, slowly looking towards the floor as he considers his options.
'But I also have to say that my first instinct is to tell him to fuck off.'
Lucifer looks up at you in a start.
'What?' he asks. 'What did you just say?'
You stop to consider the situation, as a hasty answer might be one that is incorrect. Usually, your first instinct for an important decision is incorrect, the brevity being more to do with not prolonging the agonising process of decision making. Nobody, it seems, could be qualified enough to offer counsel in this situation, but for some reason, Lucifer is consulting you about the future of all mankind. Lucifer has previously confided in you his guiding vision of a Jehovah's Witness type world of animals and humans living together in harmony, and it is one that certainly animates you, but at the same time also troubles you. It is so fantastical that it must surely be the demented promises of a mad man who can never deliver. Maybe deep down Lucifer knows he can never defeat God and his heavenly army, and as such, is looking for an opportunity to get out of such a battle. Is that why he's asking you, so that if it all goes wrong he has someone else to blame? Could the prince of darkness really be so lacking in confidence that he's willing to let someone else make this decision?

This is a very human trait, which is what makes Lucifer all the more endearing to you. Decision making cripples the best of us, and when a decision has even more monumental consequences than normal, such decisions can prove incredibly stressful and painful. Observe people with a food menu and gaze upon their pain as they wonder aloud what they should have to satiate themselves. It's not necessarily that you will be upset with your choice, it's more the fear of missing out in some way. The pain of not having seems to be a greater concern than the joy of having. In all situations, decision making can be split into two categories: emotional and rational. Emotional decision making is done on the fly, whereas rational decision making is considered. Calculated. Time is taken and eventually you become satisfied that you have weighed the pros and cons of each scenario and used reason to come to a firm decision. The best decisions tend to be when both the emotional and rational thought processes are satisfied. Clearly, Lucifer yearns to be back in heaven. It's where he started out and once you've been an angel in the service of God, I guess it's pretty hard to imagine anything better. We all think it would be better to be self employed, but those of us who have fallen on hard times whilst forging our own path will tell you that sometimes, a little safety net is most welcome. Emotionally, this is the decision to make. But is it rational? What chance does Lucifer have in a battle with heaven against the ruler of the universe? Omnipotence being what it is, seems to be a game changer. Like every single hack comedian who tried to imitate Bill Hicks, you have asked the simple theological question of why an all powerful, all loving God would act in the ways He does. Moving in mysterious ways, creating and extinguishing life at will, forever undefeated in arguments due his unquestionable master plan.

The emotional and rational decision is for Lucifer to not battle God and to accept his offer of a seat in the kingdom of heaven. But sometimes, the right decision is the wrong decision, and we don't know why.

'Fuck it,' you say. 'Tell him to fuck off.'
'You think I should refuse God's offer and just tell him to fuck off?'
'Yeah. Fuck it. You've got a big ass army. You're motivated. I believe in you. Look how well you just did at an impossible gig! If there's one thing I know about stand up comedians, it's that after they've done well at a bad gig, they can do pretty much anything.'

Lucifer smiles, then smiles some more, then somehow manages to smile even more as new parts of his face are created to accommodate the cartoonish, fanged grin crawling across his ever expanding head. Above you, the crack in the roof of hell begins to heal as the blinding light of God's presence withdraws from the lava strewn rocks of Indulu. Lucifer turns to his most recent of converts and gives them pause as he raises his hands, ready to address them.

'Fellow cunts, it gives me great pleasure to inform you that after many centuries of searching, I have found a worthy second for the battle to come. God visited us this day, asking the question of questions, awaiting his answer knowing full well how much I have yearned to return from whence I came. I did not know how to answer, so sought counsel from my new, most trusted ally. My mentor in all things comedic.'

Lucifer turns, drawing the attention of the Amakhulu to you. You gulp, not knowing exactly where this is going.

'Please,' Lucifer is about to ask you something. 'Tell us what you advised.'

'Well,' you begin, swallowing your nerves as best you can. 'I said that you should tell God to fuck off.'

The Amakhulu stare at you.

'Again, please. A little louder if you don't mind.'

'I said that you should tell God to fuck off.' you say with slightly more conviction. Again, the Amakhulu remain unmoved by this.

'Say it like you mean it!' commands Lucifer. You clear your throat and get ready to bellow.

'I said, tell God to FUCK OFF.'

Silence. The Amakhulu look at one another, seemingly muttering between themselves before turning back to you. In unison, they launch into such a tremendous cheer that it knocks you clean off your feet. As the cheer begins to die down, you scramble back to an upright position to witness the Amakhulu standing there stamping their clawed feet on the rocky floor, left then right, over and over, left then right.

'Fuck, off. Fuck, off. Fuck, off.' they chant. Left, right. left, right. Left, right. They continue to chant in time with their static marching, as Lucifer beckons you over.

Once by Lucifer's side, he puts one of his enormous arms around you then shushes the inhabitants of Indulu with a finger to this lips as he begins yet another address.
'Fellow cunts! Together now, we will launch our final assault on the gates of Heaven. We will go to God's house and we shall destroy his gardens and overturn his power. I will take control and we will have our day! Are you with me?!'
Lucifer delivers this line with all the gusto you'd expect from a maniacal dictator. Oddly, the Amakhulu seem unmoved. Lucifer looks down at his new soldiers and awaits some form of response which, at this stage, doesn't seem to be forthcoming.

This happens a lot in comedy. One minute the audience are on your side and you feel like you can get away with anything, that the audience will immediately understand exactly where you're headed comedically. The next minute, the audience have lost all faith in you and you don't know why. Lucifer lacks the experience to notice that this seems to be what is occurring with the Amakhulu right now, but luckily for him, he now has you at his side.
'Hey,' you say to Amakhulu. 'Are you with this big lump of shit or what?'
Lucifer looks down at you, a flash of anger burning in his eyes. You give him a little wink before turning your attention back to the Amakhulu.
'What you sayin'? You gonna help out ole little dick here or not?'
A few of the Amakhulu at the front begin to chuckle, which quickly spreads until the whole of Indulu reverberates with the infectious laughter of a light roasting.
'Little, dick! Little, dick!' you begin to chant, the Amakhulu waste no time joining in. Lucifer looks at you, slightly confused but also relieved. The silence after his question almost destroying that new found confidence of his.
'Gotta learn to read the audience.' you tell Lucifer.
'Yeah, you're right.'
'These guys love you, but only when you don't take yourself so seriously.'
'I get that now.' says Lucifer, full of gratitude.

'Show me.' you request. Lucifer smiles, then turns to his newly acquired warriors and joins in with their chanting, strutting up and down and pointing at his genitals. The Amakhulu go wild for this and begin slapping each other repeatedly, sometimes across the face but mainly on their boney buttocks. Little sparks can be seen as bone on bone contact causes small flint like friction, resulting in the production of tiny fires.
'Now,' Lucifer shouts. 'Go and rest, for later, we shall take the pearly gates!'
The Amakhulu cheer, then stop dead and disperse quietly as though nothing had happened. The workaday nature of their departure amuses you, as you turn to Lucifer to see what will now happen.

'Why did God leave?' you ask Lucifer. 'It seems as though that was the perfect time to strike.'
'That wasn't God.' replies Lucifer.
'How'd do you mean?'
'That, my friend was a test. Your test.'
You're unsure how to take this news.
'Did I pass?' you wonder.
'With flying colours. You see, you might be the first person who has adequately taught me how to deal with the Amakhulu, but you are not the first person I have considered taking with me to heaven so that I may fight the final battle against God. No, there have been many before you whom I have considered, but all have failed the final test. The test where they are given the opportunity to avoid war, and to pacify what they believe to be my ego.'
Lucifer looks at you with a sense of pride in his eyes, pride you can easily see and also take great comfort from.
'You're the first person who has ever believed in me.' says Lucifer, seemingly trying to hold back tears. You too feel surprisingly emotional, but decide to change the subject rather than carry on this line of chat.
'So, what do we do now?'
'Well,' replies Lucifer. 'What we do now is prepare for battle.'
'How do we do that?'
'To be honest, there isn't much preparation.'
'Oh.'

'Yeah. I think I might have a bite to eat and then maybe we'll crack on.'

You cannot believe Lucifer is so cavalier, but it makes sense not to care too much. You and he are about to embark upon the battle of battles. A battle that has been foretold for a few thousand years. A battle which must rage in order to truly separate good from evil. A battle which can only have one winner. The side of heaven seemingly with the tremendous advantage of having a guy in charge with the ability to know everything and do anything, regardless of whether or not it adheres to the laws of physics.

With Lucifer existing within the physical realm and God seemingly at home in the spiritual realm, how this battle will take place is not clear to you. Indeed, it might not even be clear to Lucifer. He talks about launching an assault on heaven, without giving any indication of how you or the Amakhulu are supposed to get there. But whatever happens, you can rest easy knowing that because you chose to take that last minute gig for Sparky Mark, you've caused the death and destruction of many people's lives. You can also rest easy knowing that might well be going into bat for the wrong team in the ultimate battle between good and evil. You can rest easy with the afore mentioned knowledge because for some reason, you feel absolutely no guilt, which appears to be a feature rather than a bug when it comes to inhabiting hell.

* * * *

You awaken from a fitful slumber. Resting in hell is difficult as literally everyone around you is wicked. You don't even know why you would need to sleep, but as your brain is still working you assume it has something to do with maintaining it's function in some capacity. Brains need sleep, even if bodies don't. No amount of sleep would help you to comprehend what has occurred in the last 36 hours or so, and now, as if things weren't weird enough, there's a Sigmund Freud looking mother fucker resting on knee just a few feet from you.
'Hello,' says The Man. 'How are you?'
'Er, fine. I guess. Who are you?'

'I was about to ask you the same question.' replies The Man, taking off his glasses to give them a little wipe.
'That's not really an answer, is it?' you say, sitting up slightly so that you can fully take in the sight of a tweed suited man cleaning his glasses in hell.
'No, you're right,' comes the reply. The Man examines his thick rimmed glasses before putting them back on his face. 'I'm just a man, goin' 'round, takin' names.'
'OK. Why are you doing that?'
'I get to decide who to free, and who to blame.'
'In hell?'
'That's right.'
The Man is oddly composed and unafraid of silence. You look around, seeing only nothing and nobody as you turn back to see The Man still looking at you, waiting for you to say something.
'Isn't everyone in hell to blame?'
'Everybody, won't be treated, all the same.' says The Man.
'By who?'
'He with the golden ladder.'
You're sure that you're not sure what the hell this guy is talking about, but his presence causes you great concern. Something about him commands you to listen, and even though he is making little sense, you understand who he is and what he is referring to. You understand all this despite not knowing what the fuck is going on. The Man continues to look at you, already knowing what you will say but waiting for your utterance none the less. You're sat cross legged on the hard rock surface of hell, looking across at a slight, tweedy man so physically lacking in intimidation that he might as well not even be there. Despite this, every single hair on your arms stand up as you experience overwhelming terror creeping over you.
'Would you care for a drink?' enquires The Man, offering a you a cup from his outreached hand.
'What's in it?'
'It doesn't matter, does it?'
You take the cup and see that it holds clear liquid. The Man smiles a warm smile while nodding his head ever so slightly, encouraging you to drink. You keep your eye on him as you raise the cup to your lips, trying hard to hide your trembling

from The Man. As you sip, you hear a sound beyond the background noise of constant flames. You look around to try and gain a clue as to where this sound is coming from.
'Hear that?' asks The Man. 'The trumpets. The pipers.'
'I think so.' you say, taking another sip.
'One hundred million angels singing.'
You hear it. You hear the kettledrum and the accompanying marching. Voices call, they cry. Life begins and it ends.
'You know how this is going to end don't you?' asks The Man.
'I think so.' you reply.
'It's good that you took that drink.'
'Thank you. How many names have you taken?'
'Oh, quite a few.' says The Man, standing now for the first time, hands behind his back as he slowly paces back and forth. 'Not that it matters.'
'It doesn't matter? Why make the list then?'
'I've already said everything I wanted to say. People will either listen or they won't.'
'Some people need a chance.' you say, rising to your feet. You look around once more and see again that where there were ample demons to fill the landscape, there are now none, and where there were beings suffering their punishment for life not lead in service, again there are none.
'Whoever is unjust,' continues The Man. 'Let him be unjust still. Whoever is righteous, let him be righteous still. Whoever is filthy, let him be filthy still. Listen to the words long written down.'
'Some don't hear the words until it's too late.'
'It's hard for thee to kick against the prick.'
'I beg your pardon?'
The Man chuckles.
'Ah, words. What magnificent tools. Here we are exchanging them. You, I believe, would use them to illicit laughter from those who would attend events at which you were appearing. Words are nothing without action. I haven't told you who I am. Why? Because you already know. You know how it will end. You know exactly what is going to happen, yet you're going to do it anyway. Why?'
You consider this for a few seconds. You do that thing where you think you should just start talking and hope that an answer

will emerge from the torrent of bullshit which will come out your mouth, but you know that on this occasion, such an effort will be futile. The Man already knows.
'You do it,' continues The Man, 'because you are not in control. You think you are, which is very important, but you are not. You are no more in control of what is happening than you are in control of this sentence ending. When the time comes, you will have one chance. One. I already know what you will choose, but you don't. Maybe you will kick against the prick, or maybe you won't.'
'What's a prick?'
The Man smiles before walking towards you at a speed you would not expect from such an elderly looking person.
'Every decision you've made, you haven't made. You don't make decisions, you just do as you're told. A leaf on the wind, this is you.'

And with that, The Man vanishes.

Instantly, all around you, hell is repopulated with the demons and depravity you've become accustomed to. Lucifer stands right in front of you as you stare at him, confused. Your confusion is none of his concern just now as he clearly has some exciting news for you. Taking a deep breath, he informs you.

'It's time.'

* * * *

You're not exactly sure how long you've been marching. It could be hours, it could even be days for all you know. Nah, it's not been days, you just hate walking and this shit is fucking boring. Behind you are the Amakhulu, and behind them are the mindless minions who delight in their role as torturers of the wicked. Next to you is Lucifer, oddly quiet as he trundles along the Mars like surface of hell. His quiet isn't too unnerving as you assume he is saving himself for a big speech at some point, but you'd certainly feel more relaxed if he were being chatty. Not that you really know what you'd chat with him about. You think he's saving it for a big speech because you're dragging along the sound equipment from the gig you ran previously in Indulu, which is doubly annoying as he was able to conjure that out of thin air so why the fuck are you having to drag it? Best not to ask questions. Ahead of you is nothing but dust, rocks and fire. You assume there'll be some kind of lift or escalator or at least stairs up ahead, but that's assuming hell is underneath and heaven is above. You consider this a fair assumption that most people would make, considering it appears that the one true god is the god whom they terrified you with in Sunday school. You think of all your friends who are atheistic, agnostic or following a different, clearly incorrect religion. Shit, they're so fucked. They've literally been wasting their lives not living in the light of the lord. How much better and more moral a human being would you have been had you known the truth? Once again, you reconcile reality by reassuring yourself that you're a good person, despite all evidence to the contrary. You're literally walking next to the prince of darkness and have the gaul to pretend you're a nice person. You piece of shit.

The sound of feet rhythmically hitting the floor comes as a surprise to you, so chaotic are the Amakhulu. It would appear that under the right conditions, it is indeed true that chaos can spontaneously evolve into order. If these denizens of anarchy can organise into an efficient fighting force, perhaps it's possible they may pose a threat to the armies of heaven. You've always found it odd that stand up comedians have never been able to unionise, despite the very left leaning politics most of them espouse. Never mind that the majority of them would sell their own mother just for a chance to sit next to Joel Dommet on a show about cats dressed as pirates, you would at least have expected by now that there'd be some sort of union, even if just to keep up that fake socialist image those rabid, self interested capitalists present to the world. The main problem with a stand up comedy union is that the vast majority of stand up comics are shit and should be fined under trading standards regulations for even calling themselves comedians. In a world where politeness is valued over honesty, these charlatans are left to carry on their fakery in peace and comfort. For shame.

'We're getting close.' says Lucifer, the first sentence he's uttered in hours. The phrase ripples back thorough the forces, as word spreads that it's nearly go time.
'Do you want me to set up the P.A. system?'
'Nah.'
'Oh, OK. How you feeling?'
Lucifer ignores your question. You look ahead and see nothing which would indicate that you're any closer to heaven than you were several hours ago. You're not really in a position to do anything other than shut the fuck up, which reminds you of being a kid when you were being driven somewhere by your folks. You decide to break the tension.
'Are we there yet?' you ask. 'Are we there yet? Are we there yet?'
Lucifer looks down at you, raises an eyebrow, then looks back towards the destination.
'Are we there yet?' you ask again.
'Are we there yet?' asks a member of the Amakhulu. You look back at the super demons, all grinning with delight as this will soon become a verbal Mexican wave of irritation for the king of hell.
'Are we there yet?' asks another, then another, then several more. A few seconds later, the whole of the Amakhulu are chanting this phrase, as Lucifer keeps walking, shaking his head and trying not to smile. He looks down at you again.
'You're such a cunt.'
Lucifer stops. His army stops. Lucifer turns to his forces and takes a deep breath.
'If you lot don't shut up, we're gonna turn around and go straight back.' bellows Lucifer before turning to give you a cheeky wink.
The Amakhulu cheer as Lucifer takes a small bow before returning to his course. As he continues along towards the destination, his army follows with a now boosted sense of morale thanks to Lucifer not taking himself too seriously.
'Funny that was,' you say. 'Nice timing.'
'Yeah, I had a good teacher,' Lucifer replies. 'Right, wait here.'

Lucifer walks off at a quicker pace and leaves you standing with this army behind you. You turn and look to the nearest Amakhulu, shrugging your shoulders.

Lucifer is now a good thirty feet away from you before he slows down and starts examining the floor, pacing back and forth, looking for something. His cloven right foot will occasionally kick away some dust as he examines closely the floor beneath him. Lucifer repeats this until he is satisfied, then walks back towards you and the rest of the troops. This is the moment you've all been waiting for.
'We are about to enter the shit scented paedophile holiday park known as heaven,' Lucifer yells. 'Once in there, I will have limited powers but you all know what you have to do. If you see something, murder it. Do not, I repeat, do not fuck anything. We're there to kill first, we can fuck stuff later when we've won. Is that understood?'
The Amakhulu grumble.
'Is that understood?' Lucifer asks again, effectively reiterating the diktat with his rhetorical question. The Amakhulu reluctantly nod their heads.

Lucifer walks off again, this time you run after him.
'Where the fuck is heaven then?' you ask.
'Come, it's right here.'
Lucifer walks off a little further, gesturing that you should follow as you do your best to mimic the pace of his walking until he eventually slows before coming to a very deliberate stop, stamping the floor to accentuate the point.
'There.' says Lucifer, pointing to the distance. All you see is what you have previously seen. Shrugging, you look at him with no further clue than you had a few seconds ago. He slowly lowers his pointing hand so that the digit is directing your gaze towards the floor. You notice something, then squint and crouch down as you try to make sense of what it is. A small crack in the ground, and as you look left and right you realise the crack extends across the surface of hell. It is maybe two millimetres thick, if that, but it is definitely there.
'Is this it?' you ask.
'Thin line between heaven and hell.'

'What happens when we cross this line?'
'Same thing that happens anytime you cross the line. There's no going back.'
You nod your head and stand up. Lucifer looks back at his troops and beckons them to join him at the line.
'I'll go first,' says Lucifer. 'So that you know I've gone and the rest will know to follow. Just make sure you fucking follow! I need you and that P.A.'
'OK.'
Lucifer steps across the line and disappears. The Amakhulu look on, startled.
'You will follow!' you yell at them, turning to cross the line yourself.

* * * *

Your eyes take a few seconds to adjust as the vision of the clearest of blue skies and the whitest of white clouds hits you. Lucifer looks awfully out of place here, his reddened and scaled skin contrasting horrifically with the purity of this light. What was chiseled and handsome in hell is brutally grotesque in heaven. Cloud is all around as you test your footing by moving left and right, jumping up and down, puzzled at how you can be on solid ground. You accidentally take a jump to your rear, stumbling back into hell, noticing that the Amakhulu are still reluctant to come forward. How odd it must have been to see you and Lucifer disappear into heaven, only for you to now fall backwards into hell before disappearing yet again.

Once back in heaven you see that Lucifer has advanced further along than before. Beyond him stands The Man in tweed whom you'd met before.
'I have brought my army,' says Lucifer to The Man. 'Where is yours?'
'They're here,' says The Man. 'I'm just not so sure I'll use them.'
Lucifer swings a violently fast left hook towards The Man, only for it to stop dead in it's tracks barely a centimetre from it's planned landing point. The Man smiles. Lucifer's hand turns into a soft pillow, as the Man rests his head on this rather

comfortable metamorphosis. Lucifer screams a wrathful scream.
'Shhhhh.' says The Man, as Lucifer now becomes mute. The sight of Lucifer screaming in silence and seemingly paralysed in position, with a fist for a pillow as an old man appears to be relaxing on it, is too much for your senses. The Amakhulu begin filing in from behind, forcing you to take many steps forward.
'Ah, your friends are here.' says The Man, as he moves backwards with Lucifer, elongating this hall of clouds and light by a good mile, allowing it to accommodate the vast armies of hell. You now stand in front of what must be a few million servants of Lucifer, as they all look at their leader screaming in silence with a pillow for a fist.

'I'm sorry,' chuckles The Man. 'This isn't very fair is it?' Lucifer is now back by your side, looking completely baffled. Shaking his head a few times, he turns to you.
'Set up the P.A. system. I'll show this twat who he's dealing with.'
You immediately set to work. The man stands there waiting for whatever it is that Lucifer has planned, as you scramble around looking for a power supply. Lucifer takes a few steps forward as he awaits the signal that you're good to go, but he seems unaware that you have no way of setting up without some kind of electricity. You panic.
'It doesn't matter…' says a voice that only you hear. You know that the voice means well, so you just stick the plug into a cloud and hope for the best. Success! The lights on the soundboard come to life and you're good to go.
'We're on!' you shout to Lucifer, giving him the thumbs up.
'Now!' Lucifer screams to the Amakhulu.
Each one of the half million super demons take flight, shooting into the air at tremendous speed as they head towards The Man, who remains unmoved. Lucifer joins you at your console.
'Give me the mic.' he commands as you hand it over.
'It's live.' you caution.
Lucifer walks over to the speakers and holds the mic near to them, so that a brief sound of squealing feedback happens. Up in the air, a few of the Amakhulu hear it and giggle a little as

they feel their bum holes loosen in preparation for a movement. They continue to fly ahead, closing in on The Man with every flap of their skin like wings. Once the first of them are directly overhead, Lucifer slams the mic closer to the speakers, causing the god awful sound of high pitched feedback, the kind that makes every single one of your teeth vibrate weirdly and become itchy.

As before, the Amakhulu begin to laugh hysterically as their bowels involuntarily evacuate faecal matter, all of which falls directly onto The Man. Super demon after super demon flies over The Man and unleashes a filthy slurry of waste that quickly begins to gain height as The Man stands there, motionless, slowly being buried in the arse waste of a few hundred thousand Amakhulu. Awe is not the feeling you would've associated with seeing a mountain of shit slowly bury an elderly man, but the despicable nature of such a plan, not to mention the smooth execution of it, leaves you feeling only this. The Amakhulu keep flying, keep defecating, and the mountain of shit just gets higher and higher. The stench is such that you can hardly breathe, as Lucifer begins to jump and shout and scream and punch the air.
'Now where are you?!' he shouts towards the dung pile. 'I'll tell you where you are…you're in deep shit!' screams Lucifer.

You roll your eyes at such a line, slightly ashamed that in some way, you have had a role to play in Lucifer's comedic development. It's kind of obvious as a joke and you get the feeling that he'd probably written it because he's had this plan all along. Fair enough if he'd improvised it, but the way he delivered it leads you to believe that he probably laboured over it for quite some time and had a little rehearsal. That stand up comedians union begins to look more and more unlikely. The Amakhulu all land back behind you as Lucifer walks in to the assembled demonic throng and starts high fiving them all on a job well done. You look at the (easily) fifty foot high pile of shit and wonder what happened to The Man. Lucifer continues to high five the Amakhulu until they all begin to hiss, holding their stomachs and doubling up in the kind of pain which would ordinarily give them great pleasure. Each of their bodies begin to vibrate as bright yellow light emanates from their abdomens, the sight of which causes Lucifer to trample over whoever he needs to in order to get clear of what is about to happen. Each bright yellow light swells the Amakhulu's bellies until they implode systematically, one by one, turning into kittens at the singularity of each bang. All the kittens meow sweetly as tiny balls of yarn laced with catnip fall from above, causing each kitten to play gleefully in a state of near orgasmic pleasure.

Lucifer stands slack jawed as he witnesses his most valued warriors reduced to drugged up mammalian quadrupeds who enjoy playing with wool. Looking to you for some kind of response, Lucifer realises that every single minion he'd been counting on has now disappeared back to the safety of hell, meaning it is now you, him and the kittens. Turning back to the stinking pile of shit causes yet another surprise as standing there is The Man, no shit, clean as a whistle and smiling broadly. Lucifer smiles at you then runs off as fast he can, stomping several kittens as he makes his way back to hell. The kittens disappear as Lucifer now runs in place, treadmill like and making no ground as The Man walks slowly towards him.
'How've you been?' The Man asks of Lucifer.
Witnessing this means you are still around, so any hope of not being noticed seems futile, as does any attempt to slide back into hell. This doesn't stop you trying though. Lucifer doesn't answer The Man as he continues sprinting to nowhere, desperate to avoid eye contact with The Man who is now standing just beside him.
'Ah, how those wheels spin. What are you running from? Where are you running to?' asks The Man.
Answer him! For fuck's sake! You think to yourself as you slowly make your way back towards where you think the thin line lies.
'I wasn't talking to him,' says The Man, keeping his eyes fixed on Lucifer who as yet, shows no signs of slowing down. 'I was talking to you.'
You freeze on the spot, hoping The Man's vision is based on movement.

'Look at him, running to nowhere. Do you know what that feels like?'
'No.' you say, quietly.
'I think you do. Wheel spinning towards the end, ignoring the journey. How can you live when all you do is plan? Scheme?' The Man gestures towards Lucifer. 'There is only what I allow, yet he thinks otherwise. He, like you, thinks you choose. You don't. The wheels are set in motion. The rules decided. The game rigged. The first step in dealing with this, is accepting that you don't have a choice.'
'I don't get it.' you say, shaking your head.
'You think you chose to be here? What drove you here is everything which came before, not what is happening now. Look...'
The Man points up. The clouds part, revealing to you the majesty of space.
'Those stars are not as they seem, they are as they were. What will happen to them has already happened, in the same way that you are already dead. Your life has already happened. Pick a far enough vantage point, you'll be able to look back on yourself and see the decisions you are about to regret.'
You look back down from the stars and towards The Man. Lucifer is no longer where he was. You look around and see no sign of him anywhere.
'Tell me,' says The Man. 'knowing what you now know, would you take the gig?'

To take the gig, turn to page 3

To turn down the gig, turn to page 141

Lauren shuts the freezer door then turns to look at the headless corpse, still strapped to the horse and bleeding from the anus. She lets out a big sigh as the prospect of cleaning up after herself hits home. Clean up is always the worst part of her duties, but it is very important if she is to continue her work. Messy play as a child was always fun, with paint everywhere, sand, sprinkles, flicking paint here and there. It's such great fun and creatively fulfilling when in the midst of such expressive freedom, but someone always has to clean up, and the more fun you have it seems the more cleaning there is to do. Lauren is always fastidious when cleaning up, but just now she is content to luxuriate in her work, and even considers rubbing the blood all over her naked frame. A keen fan of Elizabeth Báthory, Lauren has often wondered whether she could acquire enough blood so that she might bathe in it. Báthory, the most prolific female murderer of all time, was said to have bathed in the blood of virgins in order to maintain her youthful looks. Lauren isn't sure where she would find enough virgins in this day and age, certainly not of age and certainly not racist.

No, like all fans of Báthory, it is worth taking note that many of the stories that circulated about her were created posthumously, and that it would be better had history never known her crimes, because that would mean she'd never been caught. Lauren has no intention of being caught, which gives her yet more reason to make sure she does an excellent job of cleaning up, which also means she probably won't be rubbing the blood all over her body. Besides, not all of it is blood as much of what had been consumed for sustenance by this racist piece of shit also litters the floor, the remnants in various stages of digestion. No, probably best to just roll up the plastic sheeting and then give the area a thorough mopping. Gotta take care of the body first though.

Lauren walks over to a chest of draws and takes out a pair of see through plastic coveralls which she slips into with great ease, having done so many times before. This particular brand have shoes built on as part of the design, with a contoured rubberised sole to ensure decent grip in fairly hazardous

conditions. Although expensive, these are very much worth the extra money she paid.
The tricky part is unshackling the corpse, as gravity will ensure that the body falls directly into the puddle of waste beneath it. Retrieving an industrial sized roll of clingfilm wrap, Lauren steadily and carefully begins cocooning the corpse thoroughly, so that not another drop of blood will escape. Round and round she goes, between the legs, past the ruptured anus and then up over alternate shoulders as she recreates a plastic mankini which prevents further parts of the internal organs escaping. Once satisfied, back between the legs she goes as now, the clingfilm wrap is applied repeatedly to the stump where a head used to be. Over and over until not a drip will drop, this plastic based mummification ritual is takes care of the parts most likely ooze DNA.

The hands and feet will be the last to wrap, but as there are no wounds leaking, Lauren can now concentrate on rolling up the plastic sheeting, content that nothing will drip from the headless cadaver. Corner to corner, lifting the feet slightly so that she can get the sheet clear of obstruction, Lauren is getting this clean up done in record time. The previous racist clean up had to be paused halfway in when Lauren's mum popped by for an unexpected visit. A tender woman with no idea of Lauren's perversion, she'd brought over a homemade apple crumble, knowing it to be her daughter's favourite. A few hours of idol chit chat followed the enjoying of said crumble, before Lauren's mum eventually got the subtle hints Lauren was dropping. She'd felt bad ever since for making her mum feel unwelcome in such a way, especially when she'd made the trip especially to drop off Lauren's favourite dessert, and Lauren was determined to make it up to her by returning the gesture as soon as she could. If only Lauren could explain that her work was inspired by her mother, a woman who had endured much racist abuse because of the mixed race relationship which brought about the birth of Lauren. To this day, her parents are still together, perhaps because of the strong bond formed due to the amount of prejudice they'd faced, or perhaps just because they still like each other. It mattes not to Lauren, who is now compelled to act as she does.

She can't remember when she first came up with the plan to partake in the deeds she does, but she's known for a very long time it was her calling. Lauren once read that serial killers start off by experimenting with pets but the very idea of such thing makes Lauren nauseous. Animals know only instinct, discriminating based on treatment. In the case of pets, if you're kind to a pet, the pet will be kind to you. There are some exceptions, such as reptiles, but generally speaking, serial killers will kill and mutilate cats and dogs, maybe rabbits and guinea pigs. None of these animals would attack a human based on the colour of their skin. No, Lauren knew who she wanted to kill and why, and had always known that one day she would have to do it for the first time. Planning was key, and has been key ever since, actually becoming part of the fun as the fantasy and reality merge in harmony to create an experience of vengeance that few people could ever know. The mixture of pleasure and pain being one that she has cultivated ever since the original, allowing her to easily manipulate the hard of thinking as feelings of sexual attraction easily cloud judgement. Occasionally, she will enjoy her sexual liaison, and why not? Not all work should lack pleasure.

Into a yellow clinical waste bag goes the folded up plastic sheeting, tied neatly and securely before being placed in another clinical waste bag. The easy party of the clean up is now done, it's time to unshackle the body. The right wrist is released first, the body yielding slightly but not bending, thanks to the tightly wrapped layers of wafer thin plastic which are helping to maintain some rigidity to the corpse. The left wrist is released next. Lauren chuckles as the decapitated corpse seems to now be standing in a strange squat position because the ankles are still shackled and the clingfilm wrap is so tight the body just stays in place. The cadaver looks similar to a sumo wrestler about to commence a bout, or karate student in a high horse stance. Lauren manages to undo both ankles at the same time, the corpse falls back onto the floor, a satisfyingly empty thud accompanies the landing. Lauren takes a few seconds to take in the decor of this room, and how people will happily enter here under the pretext that there'll be sex. She wonders why people of both sexes will still lie with someone who has such obviously abhorrent views, and is convinced that if the roles were reversed, she wouldn't hesitate to leave such a situation.

Many years ago, Colin Stagg was charged with murder when an undercover policewoman tricked him into sharing violent sexual fantasies about the murder of a young woman. Stagg was a loner, so desperate for some kind of female sexual interaction he would say anything to please the woman who was apparently showing an interest in him. Lauren is careful to make sure her honey trap isn't so unjust, and the room with Nazi paraphernalia is the last real test. Had any of her previous victims walked into that room and said it wasn't for them, Lauren would've allowed them to leave, despite knowing they would still harbour at least some racist ideas.

Each victim has had no dependents, and each one has come from various parts of the country. Perhaps one day the police will catch up with her? Still young and with plenty of time to accrue some big numbers, Lauren's friends overseas would aid her in avoiding capture. With Europe becoming increasingly far right, perhaps the time has come for her to spread those wings and dish out similar treatment to those across the continent who secretly (or not so secretly) hold opinions on race that fall foul of Lauren's levels of acceptability.

Peeling off the coverall until naked again, Lauren also throws that into a yellow clinical waste bag before leaving the room and jumping in the shower. The warm spray is calming rather than refreshing, due to the lack of water pressure in her house. She's contacted the water company several times about this, but each time someone has been out and taken readings, it seems that it falls within what is considered acceptable for a shower. Incredible that in this day and age, one can live in an incredibly rich country but can't have a decent power shower. It's minor frustrations like this which reassure Lauren that she isn't just some mindless killer on the loose, otherwise she'd have murdered several utility company workmen and Janice in the Vodafone call centre. No, Lauren is on a mission.

Now that she has an entertainer on her résumé, she can move onto something more challenging. Although, maybe she could murder a few other stand up comedians? There are plenty of stand up comedians she is suspicious of when it comes to matters of race. Were she the type of person to give a shit about sexism, she'd be spoiled for choice when it came to worthy victims of homicide. Sexual assault being what it is in comedy, no one would miss some of the more well known perpetrators or indeed, some of the lesser known. Every stand up comedian coming through on the comedy circuit has to deal with shady promoters who take advantage, and such situations are almost inevitable when a man has a little power over a woman who wants to get on in comedy. No end of single and married men on the circuit have tried it on with Lauren, but her professionalism has always meant that she was never interested and as such, her reputation is impeccable, which will help provide ample cover for her most recent slaying, should the police come a calling.

Finishing in the shower, Lauren thinks about the female stand up comic who confided in her, telling Lauren about a well known stand up comedian who had sexually assaulted her, and the powerlessness of knowing that no one would believe her because it was just she and him alone in a green room. *How wonderful that woman would feel* thinks Lauren, *were she to take her revenge the way I have taken mine.*

Maybe one day that will happen? Maybe one day the comeuppance will occur and those who seek to take advantage of late nights and booze will have a terrible revenge committed against their person. Hotels and offers of lifts home are mostly always innocent, but such is the nature of eager acceptance to kind gestures, it stands to reason they will sometimes be used as subterfuge, which has the knock on effect of trust being lost forever. Lauren dries herself and wonders whether or not a change of target might be due, having had a rather good run in dealing with several racists.

The world is a marginally better place now as a result, could it also be a marginally better place if Lauren sees to it that the sexual predators of comedy meet a grizzly end?

About the Author

Dave Longley is a stand up comedian typing about himself in the third person. On stage since 2004, he is your mum's favourite comedian.

Manufactured by Amazon.ca
Bolton, ON